Saved by a Dark Billionaire

By Rae Knight

Dedication

I dedicate this book to my husband, who inspired some aspects of the character Lucas, as well as my lovely readers. To my biggest supporters: Missie, Frances, Sammi and Kate. You guys have made a lot of my writing dreams come true, so thank you for your support. You are amazing!

And a big thank you to Christin Louth for creating this beautiful book cover. I don't think you know how much your support and love means to me. Thank you for sticking with me through this journey.

Trigger Warnings

This book has mentions of physical and emotional abuse. There is mention of a past suicide attempt and a past rape. If these are topics you cannot tolerate, this may not be the book for you. This book is about overcoming these things and still finding love in the end.

Chapter 1

Olive's P.O.V.

"Fuck, don't stop." I moaned as he continued his deep thrusts inside me. Until I gripped the bed sheets beside me, finding my release over his enormous shaft. His mouth continued to suck at my breast as he forced me to ride out the ecstasy he caused. A few thrusts later and he followed closely behind, spurting his seed deep inside me.

His tousled blonde hair fell across his face, partially obscuring his serious brown eyes. Tattoos adorned his arms and the side of his neck, adding to his intimidating aura. I couldn't help but find him incredibly attractive, yet I couldn't understand why he had agreed to this encounter with me.

One-night stands were never my thing. I had remained a virgin throughout high school, only losing it six months ago to my now ex-boyfriend, Julius. The memory of catching him in the act with my friend and roommate, Clover, still haunted me. The sound of their bodies colliding and Clover's moans filled my mind. A painful melody. What hurt the most was the smile Clover gave me when she saw me, as Julius finished inside her. When Julius noticed me standing there, he froze.

He chased after me, begging for forgiveness, claiming it was a mistake and that I was the only one who truly mattered to him. But I couldn't forgive infidelity. With tears streaming down my face, I sought refuge with my best friend Hailey. Her family owned a luxurious penthouse in Manhattan, and she graciously offered me a place to stay.

It was Hailey who dragged me to the nightclub where I

encountered this captivating man tonight. Through a mix of luck and liquid courage, I found myself in his room. But now that the act was over, I was left wondering what to do next.

I had no experience in this realm. What were the rules? Did people cuddle afterward? As he excused himself to the bathroom, I hurriedly gathered my clothes, overwhelmed by the urge to flee before he returned. I didn't want to face the potential humiliation of being asked to leave. I recognized this feeling for what it was—an attempt to avoid any misinterpretation of the situation. We both got what we needed, and now it was time for me to make my leave. The door creaked open, and I hastily pulled my shirt down as he emerged from the bathroom.

"Leaving already?" he asked, leaning against the doorframe with his arms and legs crossed. His intense gaze made me feel like I was melting into a puddle on his floor. We had just shared an intense two-hour encounter, leaving my legs feeling like jelly, yet I had never felt more alive. He knew exactly how to pleasure me, bringing me to heights I had never experienced before. With Julius, it had always been rushed, leaving me unsatisfied more often than not. Lucas was different. He was skilled, knowing exactly where to touch.

"Yeah, I have an early class tomorrow morning. I need to get back so I can get some sleep before then," I lied, unsure of what I was doing.

"Stay here. I'll give you a ride in the morning," he offered, but I shook my head.

"No, it's fine. I'll just call an Uber. Thanks for... everything," I said, my voice tinged with awkwardness as I reached for the doorknob. But before I could turn it, he grabbed my hand, pulling me back towards him. I stumbled into his solid chest, feeling the strength of his muscles enveloping me.

"Don't I at least get to know the name of the woman who screamed my name for the past few hours?" he asked, his hand gently tilting my chin up to meet his gaze.

"Why do you need to know? Names weren't part of the

game, Lucas," I replied, a teasing smirk playing on my lips.

I had chosen him not because he was the most handsome man I had ever encountered, but because I assumed I would never cross paths with him again in this vast city. I didn't want to know his name, and I didn't want him to know mine. This was a temporary distraction. My way of seeking revenge and showing Julius that he meant nothing to me anymore. Tonight had become a game, and I had led us to this moment. But Lucas had broken the rules by revealing his name, wanting to hear me yell it, and yell it I did.

"I told you mine." His lips brushed against my jawline as he spoke, sending shivers down my spine. I had to fight the effect he was having on my body. I had never reacted this way to someone before. It was both exhilarating and unnerving.

"That was your choice. You broke the rules, but I prefer to play by them." I winked, stepping back out of his reach.

He narrowed his eyes for a moment before straightening up, reminding me of his imposing 6'2" stature. He had a lean physique, not the bulky bodybuilder type, but one that exuded strength and agility. His thick eyebrows furrowed slightly as he crossed his arms once again.

"Fine then, I'll call you Rose," he declared.

"Rose?" I tilted my head in confusion.

"For your rosy red hair," he explained, a hint of a smile tugging at the corner of his lips.

"Real original." I rolled my eyes playfully. "Goodbye, Lucas."

I hurriedly made my way out of his apartment before he could pull me back. My heart raced with the memories of the night. I couldn't believe that someone as captivating as Lucas had chosen me out of all the women vying for his attention at the bar. It was a confidence boost I desperately needed.

During my high school years, I had struggled to tame my wild, curly red hair. The frizz was relentless, earning me cruel nicknames and subjecting me to relentless bullying. But I had persevered. I excelled in my studies, even if my social skills lagged behind. And now, I was on the cusp of graduating with my engineering degree from my dream school.

It was in my first year of college that I met Hailey. We instantly clicked, and she became my guiding light, helping me break free from my shell. She gave me a makeover that transformed not just my appearance, but also my confidence and ability to interact with others. Hailey was like a fairy godmother, or perhaps a god-sister. I dialed her number as I stepped into the elevator.

"Oh my God, Olive! How was it?" she exclaimed with excitement as soon as she answered, as if she had been eagerly awaiting my call.

"Hailey! It was uh-mazing," I replied, a smile spreading across my face. "Come pick me up. I'll send you my location. I'll spill all the details in the car."

"I'm on my way. And don't you dare leave out a single juicy detail!" I could hear the jingle of her keys in the background.

Is it wrong that a small part of me secretly hopes I see him again?

I woke up with a pounding headache, the result of last night's alcohol-fueled escapade on an empty stomach. Regret washed over me as I realized I should have eaten before drowning my sorrows. Today, anger outweighed heartbreak when it came to Julius. He had wasted my time and left me feeling used. I had no intention of sparing him another thought. Let him continue his affair with Clover, for all I cared. They deserved each other.

Dragging myself out of bed, I felt the room spin, but I was determined to make it to my Calculus III class. I quickly threw on my blue Columbia hoodie to ward off the chilly September air, grabbed a pair of leggings and my trusty running shoes, hoping a jog would help clear my hangover. With my bag slung over my shoulder, I jogged towards campus, feeling bile rise in my throat twice along the way. I powered through, determined to clear my head before reaching class.

I arrived just in time, slipping into a seat near the back as Professor Dune entered the room and began setting up. Calculus had always been a subject I enjoyed, but Professor Dune had a way of dampening my enthusiasm. He insisted on solving problems his way, even when he was wrong. Challenging him was out of the question, as he couldn't bear to be proven wrong. I needed to survive this class. Hailey's text message provided a welcome distraction from the ongoing lecture.

Hailey: Lunch at the quad today?

I quickly replied, grateful for the chance to vent.

Olive: Sounds great! Professor moody pants here are driving me insane.

Hailey: Drop his class. There's still time. Or maybe see if you can switch professors?

Olive: Maybe. I'll talk to my advisor. I can't stand this ass clown.

The hour dragged on as Professor Dune continued his nonsensical ramblings. I couldn't be the only one questioning how he had become a professor. Finally, class was over, and I bolted out of there, making a beeline for my advisor's office, hoping to find her. I had never visited her office before, as we usually communicated through email or in her classroom. As I reached for the door, my phone buzzed with an incoming call from Julius. I rolled my eyes in annoyance, only to have the door swing open and smack me right in the face, knocking my phone out of my hands.

Just my luck! Now I'll need to buy a new one.

Clutching my nose as blood gushed into my mouth, I cursed my string of bad luck. The guy responsible for my misery today looked at me with horror. His dark circles and overwhelmed expression gave away his freshman status. I remembered the pressure to be perfect during my own first year of college.

"Are you okay? I'm so sorry!" he exclaimed, rushing to my side and offering tissues he had pulled from his pocket. They looked clean, so I took them, pressing them against my nose and leaning forward. "Please, let me take you to the on-campus clinic."

I shook my head, trying to convey that I was fine, but I suspected I had bitten my tongue when the door collided with my face. My nose didn't feel broken, but looking at the poor guy, I figured it wouldn't hurt to get checked out for his peace of mind. Besides, it was free for us students, anyway. The guy seemed nice enough, despite his accidental tendencies. His jet-black hair was neatly parted down the middle, framing his face. He had a pale complexion and wore a black shirt with matching pants. Stylish, black-framed glasses adorned his face, accentuating his clear blue eyes. He was quite handsome for a freshman, and now I felt more embarrassed than anything. I pointed to my phone, signaling for him to retrieve it, and he did.

"Damn, it's broken. I'm so sorry! I'll get you a new one," he swore as he walked me to the clinic. Grateful that he had inadvertently saved me from having to deal with Julius, I shook my head, declining his offer.

We arrived at the clinic, causing a stir among the nursing students who were just starting their clinic hours. They hurriedly led me to a room down the hall, as the guy accompanying us explained what had happened. He assured me he would leave after speaking to the doctor on my behalf. I couldn't help but feel like he now thought I was unable to speak.

"Good morning, Ms. Brewer. What brings you in today?" The doctor began, but his words trailed off as he looked up from my chart. "Oh, my." He quickly grabbed the rolling stool and examined my nose. "What happened?" He turned to the guy standing beside me.

"I wasn't paying attention and accidentally hit her in

the face when I opened the door. It was a complete accident, I swear!" the guy explained.

"Well, the good news is that your nose doesn't appear to be broken. We'll clean it up for you. Are you experiencing any pain or injuries elsewhere?" The doctor asked, and I stuck my tongue out, pointing to it. He wiped it several times, inspecting it.

"The bad news is that you've bitten your tongue badly. There's a significant hole in it," the doctor informed me. I let out a sigh and rolled my eyes. *Of course.*

"Let me go get a couple of nurses," the doctor said as he discarded his gloves and left the room.

"Dude, I am so sorry! I feel terrible. Give me your address, and I'll bring you a new phone later today," the guy said, holding his phone out for me to type my address. I raised an eyebrow at him, wondering if he was joking. He was still a stranger, and I wasn't about to give him my address, no matter how attractive he was. I shook my head at him, and he continued to hold out his phone.

"Okay, how about you tell me where and when I can meet you?" I typed, suggesting the quad at noon. That's when Hailey and I usually meet, so I wouldn't be alone. He read my message and nodded.

"I'll see you there then, Ms. Brewer," he said with a smile before leaving, just as the doctor and nurses returned to the room.

I kept my gaze down, feeling incredibly embarrassed at that moment. I could hear the doctor explaining to his team what needed to be done as he took a seat in front of me again. He put on his gloves and got to work, leaving me with the taste of metal and rubber in my mouth as he examined my injured tongue.

"There we go. Good as new. It'll be sore for a few days, so try not to strain it too much. I'll print out some aftercare instructions for you," the doctor said.

Great, I thought sarcastically. I wonder if those

instructions will tell me when I'll be able to speak again?

After leaving the clinic, I found an empty table in the quad and pulled out my laptop. I typed out the most polite email I could manage to my advisor, hoping to switch my class. It was already 11 o'clock, and the sun was high in the sky, warming my skin with its bright rays. The door incident and the doctor's visit had caused me to miss my other morning class. So, I had to send my professor an email explaining the situation and asking for today's assignments. I attached a picture of my aftercare instructions with the date printed on them as proof.

Sighing, I closed my laptop and closed my eyes, allowing the sun to soak into my skin. The warmth filled me with a sense of calm as I enjoyed the beauty of nature around me. However, my peaceful moment was interrupted when a gigantic shadow loomed over me, forcing me to open my eyes. It was Julius, looking down at me with what seemed like anger in his eyes. I scowled at him, cursing the freshman who had caused all of this. Now, I couldn't even yell at Julius. Instead, I had to sit and listen to his excuses. I opened my laptop, already typing out my response to him. I knew exactly what he was going to say.

"Liv, I am so sorry," he began.

'No, you're not', I typed back.

He furrowed his brow as he read my message. "You're not even going to talk to me now?" he said, sounding frustrated.

'Nope', I replied.

"This is childish, Liv. We need to talk like adults," he argued.

Too bad, I typed.

"Are you serious? Liv, I love you. Please, let me explain," he pleaded, leaning forward as if he wanted to kiss me.

'I don't love you anymore. Leave me alone!' I responded, my anger and hurt evident in my words.

"Of course you still love me. You can't stop loving

someone overnight," he insisted, reaching for my hand. I pulled back before he could grab it.

I can and I did. Fuck you! I typed, refusing to cry in front of him.

"Liv! She meant nothing. She seduced me. Please, you have to forgive me!" he begged.

I don't have to do shit. Now leave me alone before I scream. I threatened him.

"You wouldn't," he challenged.

Wanna bet?

He narrowed his eyes, trying to determine if I was bluffing or not. "You're being ridiculous. We need to talk for real, Liv. You can't avoid me forever," he huffed before finally walking away. As soon as he was gone, I let myself fully succumb to the tears I had been holding back. I was torn between anger and heartbreak. He had taken my virginity, and he had sworn he loved me. But what kind of love involves a third person in the relationship? What he had done was unforgivable.

"Olive, what's wrong?" Hailey's voice reached my ears before I spotted her. She had tied her dark brown hair up, showcasing her natural beauty. I handed her my aftercare instructions so she could see that I couldn't speak yet.

Julius saw me. I sighed, my frustration clear.

"Ese hijo de puta. Did he bother you?" she asked, scanning the crowd for him. She was ready to give him a piece of her mind. I shook my head to show that he hadn't bothered me much, but then gestured with my fingers that he had a little. Hailey almost growled in anger as she crossed her arms and sat back, clearly ready to confront him.

"When I find him, he'll never hear the end of it," she promised me. I nodded in appreciation. But she didn't have to. Hailey ate her lunch while I sipped on a smoothie from a strawless cup, my stomach growling. I couldn't eat yet with my tongue still numb.

"Hey, I'm glad you're here. As promised, a new phone,"

the freshman from earlier appeared at our table, holding out a box with the latest iPhone in it. I immediately rejected it, pushing the box back towards him.

"She won't even let me buy her one. I doubt she'll let a stranger do it," Hailey pointed out, pointing her fork at the phone. "Who are you?"

"The idiot who did that to her," he replied, gesturing towards my face.

"Well, idiot, who did that, how about you leave the phone and run? Then she won't be able to give it back to you," Hailey laughed, earning a glare from me. Lavish gifts were not my thing. I preferred to earn expensive items myself to avoid feeling let down by life.

"My name's actually Leo," he said with a smile.

"Well, Leo, she will not accept it," Hailey stated firmly, and I nodded in agreement.

"Please, I feel so bad. I mean, look at you! I made you bleed. You literally can't even talk right now," Leo pleaded. "Please, take it. It'll help me feel better."

After some hesitation, I eventually nodded. I would take it, but only as compensation for the pain and inconvenience he had caused. I wasn't entirely comfortable with it, but I needed a phone at the moment, considering he had broken my previous one. Perhaps I could trade it for an Android that suited my style better.

"Yes!" Leo exclaimed with a smile. "It's already programmed. I cloned your old phone, so everything is now on the new one. I also added my number in there, just in case you need anything," he added, causing Hailey to laugh once again.

"Leo, what are you doing?" Another random freshman appeared out of nowhere. He had light brown hair, sun-kissed golden skin, and hazel eyes. Where were all these attractive freshmen coming from?

"Hey, Kade. Meet Olive. I was just about to invite her to join us this weekend. What do you say, Olive? It'll be a sizable group, with seniors and juniors as well," Leo said, his eyes pleading for me to say yes.

"We'll be there, Leo," Hailey answered for me with a wide smile. I turned to face her, clearly annoyed, which only made her smile widen. "I'll have her text you later for the details."

"Perfect. See you guys then," Leo said before leaving.

Olive: Here's a text. I guess the phone does work.

I sent a text to Leo to see if he had really left me his number and not a fake one. Although I wasn't sure what the point of it would be. I trusted men less and less.

Leo: Of course, it works. :)

Guess I'm going out again this weekend. *I wonder if I'll run into Lucas again?*

Chapter 2

Olive's P.O.V.

The rest of the week passed with no issues. I avoided Julius at all costs, taking different routes to my classes and even arriving early to the ones we had in the same building. Leo hadn't texted me since Monday, and I started to think that he had forgotten about our plans for today. Honestly, I wouldn't have minded, as I was certain he only invited me out of pity.

Thankfully, I could now talk with minimal pain as the swelling had finally gone down. I felt grateful to have my voice back and to be able to thank my advisor for miraculously getting me out of Professor Dune's class. She managed to enroll me in Professor Lewis' class, which was my last class for the day.

Leo: Hey Olive. Can't wait to see you tonight! We're going to The Tunnel Nightclub in Manhattan. We're all meeting up outside the dorms if you want to come with us. Otherwise, you can meet us there at 9.

Well, it seemed like he hadn't forgotten.

Olive: Sounds like fun. See you there!

I sighed, pushing away the insecurities that were trying to brew inside me. I set my phone down and focused on the lecture. Professor Lewis was an excellent teacher. She explained things well and encouraged questions. I found her class refreshing and a hundred times better than Dune's.

"So, where are we going tonight?" Hailey asked, waiting for me outside my class, having the same schedule as me today.

"The Tunnel Nightclub. Have you been there before?"

"Are you kidding? That place is amazing. It looks like some old warehouse during the day, but at night they transform it into a fun-filled venue." Hailey practically screeched with excitement as she linked arms with me. "We need to get you looking sexy for tonight, and I know just the dress."

"Hailey, no," I whined, foreseeing hours of torture in the name of beauty.

"Olive, yes," she said sternly. "It's rare that I get an excuse to dress you up. Besides, Leo may be a freshman, but he's hot as hell, and if you don't plan on pursuing him, I just might." She winked at me.

"Go ahead. I believe my days of one-night stands are behind me," I admitted, unable to shake Lucas from my thoughts. He had set the bar too high for any man that would come after him. I doubted I would ever encounter someone as skilled as him again.

"Already? After just one?" she complained.

"Yes," I affirmed.

"Stop pulling at it," Hailey scolded me as I tugged down at the hem of my dress for the millionth time since leaving the penthouse.

"It's too short. I feel like my ass is hanging out." I complained.

Hailey had dressed me in a tiny black dress that glowed in the light from the glitter littering it. It had thin spaghetti straps and was tight against me, like a second skin. I felt as if my boobs were about to spill out of the top while my ass fell out of the bottom. I was so uncomfortable, but Hailey refused to let me change. She even locked the door and took my key, so I couldn't get back in.

"That's the point, Livie. You look ready to devour." She

bit the surrounding air, acting like I was a meal.

"Stop," I laughed, linking our arms as we approached the doors of the club.

"Damn." I heard Leo whisper under his breath as we approached. His eyes dragged over my body, making me blush as he obviously checked me out. "Glad you guys could make it. We're waiting for two others before we go in. Let me introduce you to everyone."

He walked us over to a small group of guys with a couple of girls. The guys all looked like catalog models with chiseled faces and toned muscles. The girls looked like runway models with long legs and perfect bodies. They had high heels with straps wrapped around their calves and dresses as short as mine, if not shorter.

"Guys, this is Olive and her friend Hailey." Leo gestured to us. "Girls, this is CJ, Kade, and Willis." He pointed to the guys. Then he extended his hand to the girls and said, "This is Claire and Shelby."

We all nodded at each other a little awkwardly before a loud motorcycle caught all of our attention. I watched as the motorcycle parked in front of us with two people sitting on it. The person on the back got off first, removing her helmet and allowing her long black hair to cascade down around her. She was absolutely stunning, with pale skin and light blue eyes.

"Finally! Took him long enough," Kade complained, looking at the driver of the motorcycle, who took his helmet off to reveal an all too-familiar face. His intense brown eyes met mine before roaming my body with the right corner of his lips turned up in a smirk.

Lucas.

"Isn't that...?" Hailey started, unable to finish her question as I nodded in confirmation.

Leo greeted him, sliding their hands across one another into a bro hug, and said, "Nice of you to finally join us."

"Sorry, I had to take care of something." He gestured to the girl with a smirk. An innuendo if I ever heard one. I don't know why the thought of him with her made my stomach and I. "This is Hailey and that's-"

"Rose," Lucas interjected, causing me to shake my head.

"That could have been your chance to learn my name." I looked up at him, not shying away or showing him any of the jealousy I was feeling. I discreetly squeezed Hailey's arm for support, still having it linked with mine.

"It would have been too easy. I want *you* to tell me." He stepped closer to me. He was here with another girl, yet was shamelessly flirting with me. It turned me off faster than anything.

"You guys know each other?" Leo raised a brow in question.

"You could say that," I answered, having Lucas nod his head.

"Shall we go in now that everyone is here?" CJ pointed to the door, clearly over this awkward interaction.

"Yeah, let's go." Leo draped his arm over my shoulders, guiding me away from Lucas and into the nightclub.

I never thought I would run into him again.

The place was a chaotic mix of flashing lights, dimly lit and filled with the overpowering scent of alcohol and sweat. The bass thumped, reverberating through the floor as lights danced around us. The deafening volume drowned conversations out. Leo turned his head, leaning in close to my ear to be heard.

"Want a drink?" he asked, prompting a nod from me. "What's your poison?"

"Surprise me!" I shouted back, struggling to be heard over the music.

Leo grinned and made his way to the bar. I could feel Lucas' gaze on me, but I refused to meet his eyes. He was here with someone else, and I shouldn't be on his radar, even though it's exactly what I craved. I yearned for him to whisk me away, behind the building, reminding me of the pleasure he could bring. *No, you horny bitch. He's here with someone else.*

I bit my lip, attempting to divert my thoughts away from him. Leo returned with a colorful cocktail, revealing his perception of my drinking preferences. He assumed I couldn't handle strong drinks or that I rarely indulged. He had the wrong impression, but I accepted the glass with a smile.

"Thanks," I said, but before I could take a sip, Lucas swiftly replaced it with a shot of Fireball. I furrowed my brows at him, but he wasn't looking my way. His gaze was fixed on Leo, shaking his head subtly.

"That's not her drink," he yelled over the music to Leo.

He wasn't mistaken, but I didn't appreciate the fact that he already knew my preferences. How did he even find out? I never disclosed my preferences to him the last time we were together. In fact, I had been downing tequila for most of that night.

"How would you know what I like?" I questioned, downing the shot without protest.

"I know exactly what you like," he replied, his face serious, yet a hunger gleamed in his eyes.

A blush crept up my cheeks at his remark. He wasn't lying. He knew precisely what I enjoyed that night without me uttering a word.

Trying to avoid Lucas tonight would prove to be an impossible task.

He wasn't mistaken, but I didn't appreciate the fact that he already knew my preferences. How did he even find out? I never disclosed my preferences to him the last time we were together. In fact, I had been downing tequila for most of that night.

"How would you know what I like?" I questioned, downing the shot without protest.

"I know exactly what you like," he replied, his face serious, yet a hunger gleamed in his eyes.

A blush crept up my cheeks at his remark. He wasn't lying. He knew precisely what I enjoyed that night without me uttering a word.

Trying to avoid Lucas tonight would be impossible.

Lucas' P.O.V.

There stood Rose, a vision in her little black dress that left little to the imagination. Her fiery red hair, now sleek and straightened, cascaded down her back, adding an extra touch of allure. Those red stilettos, perfectly matching her hair and lipstick, screamed confidence and sex appeal. She was hotter than hell, and I couldn't tear my eyes away.

Leo, being the clueless guy he is when it comes to women, handed her some fruity drink, thinking it would suit her taste. Polite as ever, she accepted it with a smile. But I knew better. I swiftly swapped her drink for my own, knowing that she craved the burn of alcohol down her throat. And boy, was I right. She downed it like a pro, not even flinching. Since that night, she had taken up permanent residence in my mind, and I couldn't shake her loose.

No other woman had ever excited me the way she did. Her body was a work of art, and those unexpected tattoos on her side only added to her mystique. The ink started below her breast and traveled down to the top of her thigh, a tantalizing glimpse into her wild side. I could only imagine that she got them done without even batting an eye. She was tough as nails, unlike any other girl I had ever encountered.

It was her fearlessness that first drew me to her that night. The way she stood up to that big, drunken idiot without a trace of fear was a sight to behold. And the game she played with me afterward only fueled my desire for her. She wasn't like any other girl I had been with before. I doubted she even knew who the hell I was, and that only added to her allure. She wasn't after me for my money; she came for me because I was the most intimidating man in the room, and she loved the challenge.

I couldn't for the life of me understand why she was

here with someone like Leo. She was way out of his league. Leo wouldn't know what to do with a woman like her if she slapped him in the face. Sure, he's my best friend, but when it comes to girls, he's a complete idiot. He had nothing to offer her except his wallet. I had no idea how he managed to get her here, but I wasn't about to let this opportunity go to waste.

I had to pick up Lisa from her apartment in New Jersey, which made me fashionably late. She's lucky she's my sister. But she needed a night out after the shit week she had, so I didn't mind being her chauffeur. Plus, Leo always had a soft spot for Lisa. He's had a crush on her since we were six, but thankfully, she never paid him any mind. I didn't want to be caught in the middle if they ever hooked up and had a messy breakup.

"Care for a dance?" I asked Rose, relishing the sight of her cheeks turning a delightful shade of pink.

"Shouldn't you be dancing with your date?" she snapped, catching me off guard. I couldn't help but laugh. Was she jealous?

"She's my sister, not my date," I whispered into her ear, trying to drown out the blaring music.

"Yeah, sure, and I'm a rockstar," she replied, rolling her eyes with a hint of skepticism.

I shrugged, making my way toward Lisa. Maybe Rose would believe it if Lisa confirmed it. Lisa already knew about Rose; I had called her on Wednesday, bitching about how Rose had taken up permanent residence in my mind. Lisa teased me, wondering if she could be the one to finally tame me. But she was dead wrong. I knew I needed to have her again, to fuck her senseless and get her out of my system. I had no desire for another relationship after the shitstorm I had been through.

"Hey, do me a favor and go tell Rose who you are," I casually asked, pulling her away from Kade's feeble attempts to capture her attention.

"So, that's really her, huh?" She snatched her phone and snapped a selfie, capturing Rose in the background. Zooming in on the picture, she expertly checked her out without being noticed.

"Luke, she's hot." She playfully smacked my chest with the back of her hand.

"She thinks you're my date."

"Why didn't you tell her I'm your sister?"

"She didn't believe me," I shook my head, frustration laced my tone.

"Don't worry, I got you." She winked at me, effortlessly flicking her black hair over her shoulder as she made her way towards Rose. They had a conversation, and I couldn't help but wonder what she was saying. When they finished, Lisa returned to me with a smile.

"I see why you can't get her out of your head. Good luck, brother." She patted my back before heading to the dance floor. *What just happened?*

Rose walked towards me, giving me hope that she would take me up on my offer, but instead, she grabbed her friend and dragged her to the dance floor. Eshay by Dassy started playing, and Rose and her friend danced seductively, fully aware of the effect they were having.

Rose paid me no attention, as she enjoyed herself. I couldn't help but grin with amusement as I watched her. She was incredibly attractive, and she had caught the attention of other guys too. I saw them try to approach, but she pushed them away whenever they touched her. She made it clear she wasn't interested.

"When did you meet her?" Leo joined me, holding his scotch.

"Last week."

"It's not like you to still be hung up on someone after a week." He swirled his drink.

"I know." I couldn't tear my eyes away from her as he spoke.

"Damn, man. I thought maybe I had a chance, but if she's slept with you, there's no hope for me," he dryly laughed.

I usually avoid pursuing girls. Leo likes to avoid any tension between us, but in this case, I had her first.

"Sorry, Leo. Where did you meet her, anyway?"

"On campus, I accidentally bumped into her, or more like I whacked her with a door. I ended up hurting her and breaking her phone," he groaned, explaining their encounter. I chuckled at his clumsiness. Usually, he only ended up hurting himself, not others.

"I'm surprised she still talked to you after that."

"You and I both," Leo sighed. "Fuck, man. I was really starting to like her. You know, she refused the phone I got for her because it was too fancy?" He shook his head in disbelief. She didn't care for extravagant gifts. I made a mental note as I continued to watch her while sipping my drink. I noticed other girls checking me out, but I ignored them all, even the bold ones who approached me. My eyes were fixated on my Rose and her stunning figure.

I observed as a larger man approached her. He grabbed her waist, but she pushed him away. He was too drunk to take the hint and came back, grabbing her hips again. I started walking towards them, ready to intervene if needed. Little did I know she didn't need my help.

"I said get your hands off me before I kick your ass!" she yelled at him fearlessly. This guy was twice her size, even with her stilettos on, yet she threatened him as if he were a small teenage boy. The guy laughed, clearly not taking her seriously. I approached, prepared to pull him away from her.

"Come on, babe. Don't be like that. You're dancing with your friend like that because you wanted a man to come to you. Well, here I am, baby."

Just as I was about to reach them, I witnessed her pull her fist back and deliver a punch right to his throat, surprising everyone. She followed it up with a kick to his side and a punch to his kidney. It was evident she had experience in fighting.

Damn, this girl is full of surprises.

Chapter 3

Olive's P.O.V.

I found myself staring down the towering figure before me, gasping for air. Growing up, my dad, a former MMA fighter, had taught me everything he knew about self-defense. He always emphasized the importance of being able to defend myself against anyone, regardless of their size. And now, faced with this situation, it seemed his teachings had paid off. This wasn't the first time some creep at a club had tried to overpower me, but it was the first time I had fought back right on the dance floor.

As security fought their way through the crowd, panic began to set in. If charges were pressed against me, I could kiss my scholarship goodbye. My mind raced, desperately searching for a solution, but the alcohol had clouded my judgment. Just as I started to panic, a familiar tattooed hand grabbed mine, pulling me through the throng of people.

"I'll make sure she gets home safely," Lucas called out to Hailey, deftly guiding us through the crowd and out the side exit. "Come on, we need to get out of here."

He tossed me a motorcycle helmet and effortlessly mounted the bike. I stood there, momentarily stunned, as security guards shouted after us. Hastily, I put on the helmet and climbed onto the bike behind him. Unfortunately, my dress rode up, revealing more than I intended, but there was no time to fix it. I clung tightly to Lucas's waist, desperate not to fall off as the vibrations of the bike coursed through me. The wind whipped harshly against us as we sped through the streets.

We arrived at his apartment building, a familiar sight. Lucas parked the bike in the side garage, and I quickly dismounted, tugging my dress down and running my hand through my hair to regain some composure. Handing him the helmet, I watched as he removed his own, shaking his hair loose. Damn, just looking at him gets me all hot and bothered.

"I thought you were taking me home safely," I finally spoke up. He chuckled, a mischievous glint in his eyes.

"I did. I got you home safe. My home," he replied, winking as he walked past me. I stood there, momentarily stunned, before deciding to follow him. Part of me wanted to demand that he take me home immediately, but there was an undeniable allure to the idea of going back up to his apartment and letting him fuck me into tomorrow. I trailed behind him, heading towards the elevator that led to his place.

"So, when exactly were you planning on taking me home?" I asked as the elevator doors closed behind us.

"Whenever you want me to," he leaned in, causing me to take a step back, my back pressing against the elevator wall. We locked eyes, the tension between us palpable. The elevator doors chimed, opening once again. He swiftly turned, striding down the long corridor towards his apartment. The last time I was here, we were too busy making out to pay attention to the surroundings. Now, with a clearer mind, I couldn't help but notice the pristine, well-lit halls, exuding an air of luxury. This place must cost a fortune to rent. I wonder how much.

Lucas unlocked his door, the sound of the lock clicking echoing through the hallway. Without sparing a glance in my direction, he stepped inside, leaving the door ajar as if inviting me to follow. I hesitated, my mind racing with doubts and second thoughts. Maybe I should turn around, call an Uber, and escape from this place once again. The nagging feeling that this was a terrible idea gnawed at me.

"You coming?" Lucas poked his head out, his brow raised in a challenging manner. "Or are you too scared?"

Scared? Not a chance. I mustered up all the confidence I could and walked into his apartment, even though every fiber of my being screamed that it was a mistake. He closed the door behind me, the click of the deadbolt sealing our fate. There was no turning back now.

"Want a drink?" he offered, his voice casual as he made his way towards the kitchen. The apartment seemed different, larger than I remembered. The kitchen boasted shiny, untouched appliances, giving off a modern vibe. While the white walls added a sense of brightness and spaciousness. But also an emptiness that made it feel like a show home rather than a place someone actually lived in.

"Some water, please. Thank you." I accepted the cup, watching as he took a sip from his own glass. His eyes never left me, his gaze fixed on the rim of his glass, making me acutely aware of his scrutiny as I drank.

"Where'd you learn to fight like that?" he asked, placing our empty cups in the sink.

"My dad taught me," I replied, trying to sound nonchalant.

"No kidding?" Surprise tinged his voice.

"He was a professional MMA fighter in his twenties. He started teaching me when I was 13."

"That's impressive. Think you could take me down?" He closed the distance between us, a spark of excitement igniting within me.

"Probably. Guys are always overly confident in their skills." I couldn't help but smile playfully.

"What if I told you I fight for a living?" His voice dropped, a seductive undertone lacing his words.

"I'd call bullshit. Your hands haven't seen any action recently. Your knuckles aren't bruised or bleeding," I observed, making him chuckle.

"I quite like you, Rose." His thumb grazed my lip, tilting my chin up. "I plan on fucking you until the sun rises, unless you tell me otherwise."

My breath hitched, a swarm of butterflies fluttering in my stomach. Heat pooled between my legs at his words, and I knew deep down that he meant every word. I bit my lip, locking eyes with him, but the English language seemed to escape me at that moment. What are words again?

His words, laced with desire, hung in the air between us. "If you keep biting your lip," he murmured, his warm breath fanning over my lips, "I won't be able to contain myself."

The anticipation of his touch made me ravenous, craving the sensation of his lips against mine. Succumbing to the desire, I bit my lip once more, silently granting him permission to proceed. A seductive smirk danced across his face, a silent acknowledgment of my consent, before he crashed his lips against mine. The intensity of his kiss sent shivers down my spine, while his hands firmly gripped my hips, effortlessly lifting and placing me on the kitchen island. Eagerly, I parted my legs, inviting him to position himself between them, his hands exploring my curves with a possessive touch. With a skillful flick of his tongue, he parted my lips, delving into the depths of my mouth, evoking a soft moan of pleasure from me. The sensation of his touch and the taste of his lips overwhelmed my senses, rendering me powerless to resist.

Reluctantly, his hands left my ass, traveling up my thighs, pushing my dress higher. As his finger traced the path along my dampening slit, concealed by my underwear, he couldn't help but remark, a mischievous smirk playing on his lips.

"You're already so wet for me." His words, dripping with desire, fueled the fire within me, eliciting another moan of pleasure. "I want to know what you taste like, Rose," he whispered, his voice filled with longing.

He gently guided me until I was reclining on the counter, the cool air teasing my exposed core. With a deliberate motion, he slid my underwear off, exposing me completely. His tongue traced a path up my slit, igniting a chorus of loud moans to escape my lips. The grip of his hands on my thighs tightened, drawing me closer to his face, as he skillfully devoured me with expertise and passion.

"Fuck Lucas," I moaned, my fingers entwined in his hair as he skillfully brought me to the brink of ecstasy. My hips swayed against his eager mouth, his finger sliding inside me intensified the pleasure coursing through my veins. The sheer electricity of his touch threatened to shatter me from within, each stroke of his finger and suck of his mouth pushing me closer to the edge. With a few more deliberate swipes and a couple more tantalizing sucks, I succumbed to the overwhelming pleasure, my body convulsing as I tumbled over the precipice of bliss.

"Shit, I'm cumming!" I cried out, my core clenching around his finger, buried deep inside me. Waves of pleasure surged through my body as Lucas diligently licked me clean, his hunger for me clear. I knew he wasn't finished with me, and truth be told, I didn't want him to be.

He effortlessly lifted me off the kitchen island, his powerful arms cradling my ass, and carried me to his couch. It seemed that our fucking would continue throughout his entire apartment. I watched with anticipation as he removed his white shirt, revealing his beautifully inked skin and chiseled abs. Leaning over me, his lips met mine, a delicious wrestling of our tongues. The straps of my dress slipped off my arms as he skillfully slid it down my body, bunching it together over my stomach. Without a bra, my hardened nipple was instantly met with his eager mouth, sending waves of pleasure coursing through me. The intensity of the sensation caused me to arch my back involuntarily, pressing my breasts further into his hungry mouth.

"God," I moaned, my voice filled with desire.

"Not God, darling, Lucas," he teased, his tongue tracing a path along my neck. I rolled my eyes playfully, eliciting a singular laugh from him. Without hesitation, he stood up, shedding his pants and boxers, leaving them discarded on the floor. His gaze locked with mine, a smirk playing on his lips as he positioned the thick head of his shaft at my entrance. With a swift, powerful thrust, he drove deep inside me, catching me off guard and causing a surprised cry to escape my lips. The rhythm of his thrusts quickened, our skin slapping together. The room filled with the harmonious blend of my moans and his grunts. As he skillfully played with my clit, his thumb adding to the explosive sensations, I felt myself approaching the edge once again.

"Don't stop, Lucas!" I pleaded, my voice filled with need, as I reached the pinnacle of pleasure, my release washing over his throbbing length.

He swiftly turned me around on the couch, reentering me from behind, his desire for me unyielding. I knew I would be sore tomorrow, but in that moment, all I craved was the intoxicating connection we shared. Lucas kept his promise, fucking me well into the night, our bodies fitting perfectly with one another. By the time morning arrived, my body ached and my legs felt weak. The need to relieve myself pulled me from the warmth of the bed, despite the uncertainty of my ability to walk.

Naked, just as I had been the night before, I made my way across his room, unashamed and unbothered by my exposed state. After all, Lucas had seen every inch of me. As I washed my hands and splashed water on my face, I caught a glimpse of my reflection in the mirror, my body littered with dark purple hickeys. *When did he do that?* There was no hiding them, causing me to sigh. Opening the bathroom door, I found Lucas sitting up in bed, his back resting against the headboard. That sexy smirk of his greeted me as I approached.

"Hey Luke, we need to talk," Leo opened Lucas' door, surprising us all. I screamed and ran back inside the bathroom, feeling absolutely mortified that he had seen me fully naked.

"I'm so sorry!" Leo yelled quickly, closing the door with a surprised slam. I groaned, covering my face with my hands, hoping it could somehow erase what had happened.

"You can come back out now. He's gone," Lucas laughed at me from the bed.

"Not funny," I scolded him as I opened the door.

My eyes scanned the room for my dress, but then I remembered it was in the living room, along with my underwear in the kitchen. I grabbed one of Lucas' larger t-shirts and slid it on without asking, feeling frustrated that he hadn't bothered to lock the door.

"I like the way my shirt looks on you," Lucas wiggled his eyebrows suggestively.

"Don't start. I don't think I can handle any more of you," I warned him, holding a finger up. I searched the room for my phone, but it was nowhere in sight. Lucas laughed again, finding everything so amusing this morning. He got up, put on boxers and a pair of sweats. I was thankful he left his shirt off, giving me something delicious to look at. We both exited the room, my cheeks now even pinker than before.

Leo was sitting on the couch where we'd been intimate three out of the seven times last night. I swallowed nervously as I scanned the room for my dress.

"What'd you wanna talk about, Leo?" Lucas asked, heading for the kitchen to start a pot of coffee. "Rose," he called me by his made-up nickname, tossing my underwear to me out in the open. He had no shame, and it was embarrassing me to no end. I could feel the heat rushing to my cheeks as my blush deepened. Leo watched the exchange too, his cheeks slightly pink with embarrassment as well. I went back to the room to put on my underwear while trying to eavesdrop on Leo's conversation with Lucas.

"I wish you would have told me she was here. I wouldn't have barged in," Leo scolded Lucas.

"That's not what you came for. What's up?" Lucas asked him.

"I was going to ask you to leave her alone, but I'm too late," Leo sighed. *Is he talking about me?*

"Why?" Lucas asked.

"We'll talk about it later."

I stepped out of the room just as my phone rang. I heard it ringing in the living room where Leo was, but I couldn't see it. Leo moved, revealing that my phone had fallen between the couch cushions. Julius' name was flashing across the screen, causing me to groan in agitation.

"Everything okay?" Leo asked, concerned.

"Yup, just dandy," I replied, unable to look him in the eye, still embarrassed about him seeing me naked. Lucas had come up behind me without me noticing, grabbed my phone, and saw the name. Since Leo cloned my phone, Julius' contact picture still showed him and me together. I hadn't changed it yet, not giving it much thought. Lucas furrowed his brow before he answered the call. I went to grab it, but he held it out of reach, leaning back away from me.

"Hello?" he answered, making my stomach somersault inside me. I looked at Leo for the first time, silently asking for help, but he just shrugged his shoulders. I rolled my eyes, turned back to Lucas, and raised a brow at him as I held my hand out for him to give me the phone.

"Yeah, hold on. She's right here," Lucas said, handing me the cellphone with a cheeky grin, winking at me as if it was all fun and games. My hands were getting clammy, knowing Julius would ask me a million and one questions now. None of which I wanted to answer, or should have to.

I pressed the phone to my ear, mustering up a casual tone. "Hello?"

"What the fuck, Liv! Who was that?" Julius's voice seethed with anger, even through the phone. I could practically envision the contorted expression on his face, a face I had grown all too familiar with during our relationship.

"It's none of your concern," I snapped back, my frustration bubbling to the surface.

"The hell it isn't. You're my girl."

"I stopped being your girl when I caught you balls-deep in Clover. So fuck off, Julius, and stop calling me." With a huff,

I ended the call, not wanting to waste any more time on him. I grabbed my dress from the couch and hurriedly made my way to Lucas's room to change, not uttering a word to either of the men in the living room. I needed to release this pent-up frustration at the gym. The sudden urge to punch something was overwhelming. I wished my dress was longer, providing some semblance of comfort and protection.

As I got dressed, I sent a quick message to Hailey and called for an Uber. I couldn't stay here any longer. Lucas had me under some kind of spell, and I needed to break free. I couldn't afford to get involved with a guy like him. He had the power to shatter my heart if I let him. There was nothing here for me except a temporary pleasure, and I had to remind myself of that.

"Leaving already?" Lucas's voice broke the silence, and for a fleeting moment, I thought I detected a hint of disappointment in his eyes. But just as quickly, it vanished, replaced by his usual nonchalant demeanor.

"Yeah, I need to go," I replied, my tone matching his casualness.

"Sorry again about earlier," Leo chimed in, his head hanging low. I could sense his genuine remorse. He really was a sweet guy.

"Let's just pretend it never happened," I told Leo, but my gaze lingered on Lucas as I spoke. Maybe it would be easier if I could convince myself that this was all just a figment of my imagination. The intense pleasure he had brought me felt like a distant dream. Lucas closed the distance between us, his touch gentle as he lifted my chin, forcing me to meet his deep brown eyes. He leaned in, planting a soft, tender kiss on my lips. It was a stark contrast to the passionate and hungry kisses we had shared the night before. This one was warm and gentle, causing my heart to flutter in my chest.

"Goodbye, Rose," he whispered, before turning to join Leo on the couch, not sparing me another glance.

I don't know why it infuriated me, but it did. I double-checked to ensure I had everything I needed before leaving. It was better to wait for the Uber outside, away from him. I walked out without saying a word, accidentally letting the door slam shut behind me. I couldn't let this happen again. The mix of emotions inside me was overwhelming - the lingering desire for Lucas, the anger towards Julius, and the uncertainty of what lies ahead. But one thing was clear - *I need to stay clear of Lucas.*

Chapter 4

Lucas' P.O.V.

Last night was amazing. I had finally gotten Rose in my bed again where she belongs. She was as beautiful as I remembered, if not more so. The sounds she made as she moved her body had me so wrapped up in her. My dick twitched thinking about it again.

She'd gotten onto me last night for trying to dance with her when she thought I had a date, but it seemed she was in a relationship, or so I thought when I answered her phone. I wanted to ruin it, and make her solely mine. I wasn't expecting to hear the asshole had cheated on her. Who would ever be stupid enough to do such a thing to a woman like her?

I wanted to keep her here with me, but I had to watch her leave. I wanted to spend the morning with her, having her as my breakfast. Again, she left in a hurry, as if spending any time with me was too much to ask of her. I was here to please her and nothing more. I felt my stomach drop when she looked at me as she responded to Leo.

Let's just pretend it never happened.

Were those words directed at me, too? How can I pretend it didn't happen if it's all I can think about?

"Why'd you want me to stay away from her?" I asked Leo, needing to redirect my brain.

"I was hoping to get a chance." He shrugged, but I could tell he was feeling down about it. It was probably a dick move on my part to steal Rose from him last night, but I couldn't help it. She drives me nuts. I hoped sleeping with her one more time would get her out of my system, but somehow it's gotten her further in.

"Sorry, Leo. Hate to sound like a child, but I saw her first." I winked at him, making him give me a small smile. I pushed his shoulder with mine, almost making him fall over. "Let's go get some breakfast at the little cafe you like so much. Maybe your favorite barista is working." I wiggled my eyebrows at him. He's always been shy when it comes to making a move on a girl. By the time he gathered his courage, someone else would already have claimed her. Leo's a great guy, just needs a little more confidence.

"Yeah, alright." He sighed. He's going to be insufferable today with the moping.

"Let me get changed, then we can take the car."

Maybe she's still outside.

I hurriedly put on clothes, dragging Leo out of the apartment, hoping to get a last look at my Rose. I was too late. She was gone again. I wish I could have gotten her number, but maybe it's best I didn't. This girl is bad news for me.

"Good morning. What can I get for you two?" The barista greeted us as we approached the counter. I elbowed Leo, trying to get him to say something to her. She flashed us a smile, her blue eyes looking over at me. I rarely come up in line. Normally, I meet Leo here and he has my coffee already ordered. Leo leaned forward, dazzling her with his flashy smile.

"Hey, Carly. Can we get two black coffees, please?" Carly pried her eyes away from me, smiling back at Leo.

"Of course. Can I have your name?" She asked me as she wrote Leo's name, already having him memorized.

"Luke." I told her the name I prefer for strangers to call me.

"Got it. They'll be ready soon."

To avoid the feeling I was trying to upstage him, I let Leo pay for the coffee, even though I could have done it myself. I took a seat at the table and watched as Leo waited at the counter for our drinks. In order not to jeopardize his chances, I stayed away. I hope he finds the courage to open his mouth and say something to her.

"Here." He shoved the cup of coffee in my hands, almost making it splash on me. He looked pissed.

"What happened?" I asked, slightly annoyed at his outlash. He scoffed, sulking in his chair, sliding down until his head hit the back of his seat. I looked down at my cup, seeing my name, but beside it was a phone number with a note.

Call me. -Carly

"Shit, man. I swear I didn't do anything." I shook my head.

"I know you didn't. That's what's so annoying. You don't have to do anything to get a girl." He sighed, sinking even lower in his chair. He was in a bad mood now, and I know it won't go away soon.

"Sorry, I can't do anything about it." I shrugged, thankful for the caffeine now coursing through my system.

"Yeah, whatever."

A flash of red hair walked by us, instantly drawing my attention. The girl slowly turned, filling me with disappointment when it wasn't my Rose. I can't believe how badly I want to see her again already. It's been less than an hour, but it feels more like days.

"You've got it bad." Leo smirked.

"What?" I snapped my focus back to him.

"You had hoped she was Olive." He pointed to the redhead.

"Olive?" I curled a brow.

"Dude, the girl you were with this morning."

Olive. I smiled, loving the fact I now knew her real name.

"She's Rose to me." I smirked, taking another sip of my coffee. Leo rolled his eyes, still in a crap mood. My phone buzzed in my pocket, and even though I know she doesn't have my number, I somehow hope it was her.

Lisa: Well?

Nope, just the annoying sister.

Lucas: Well, what?

Lisa: Uh, hello? Red head, feisty, beautiful, absolutely perfect for you. Any of this ringing a bell?

I rolled my eyes, reading her text. I don't know what she is expecting.

Lucas: What about her?

Lisa: You're so annoying. What happened? Is she still with you?

Lucas: She left this morning. Leo came in.

Lisa: When will you see her again?

It's a question I'm asking myself. I want to see her again, but I don't know how I will. Last night the universe lined things up just right for her and I. I doubt it'll do it again. This was my one chance to get further than last time, but I'm in the same boat. Her in my mind, but not in my arms.

Lucas: No clue. Hopefully soon.

Lisa pestered me for a while longer, but eventually I ignored her million and one questions, some of which I didn't even want to ask myself. Leo sat pouting a while until I realized Leo was the key to seeing my Rose again. Although, how do I get him to help when he's in a mood?

"I'm gonna go. I am meeting up with the guys to work on a stupid group project." Leo rolled his eyes.

"Want me to come help?" I offered, feeling bad for him, but also hoping for a run in with Rose.

"You want to see her again." He shook his head.

"No, I want to help. I promise I won't leave your side. I'll even train my bladder to go when you go." He smirked with a breath of air when I winked at him.

"Alright, man, but you better help."

"Aye, aye, capitan." I hadn't been on campus since I graduated in the spring. I should have figured she attended Columbia. She must be as intelligent as she is sexy. I wonder what she's studying. My phone rang as we were getting into the car. I answered through the car system, making the mistake of not looking at the collar ID before I did.

"Lucas?" Dad's voice boomed from all around me.

"Hey, Dad." I made a face at Leo, making him smile and shake his head disapprovingly. "What do you need?" Dad only ever calls when he needs something from me. It's never for a friendly chat or even a check in.

"I need you and your sister to come home for dinner tonight. I have a meeting with the Camilo family. They are bringing their daughter, who is around your age. I need you to keep her happy while I get her father to close on a deal."

There it is. The big favor.

"Seriously, Dad, I hate when you do this shit. I don't feel like entertaining some random girl." I rolled my eyes, turning onto the interstate.

"Don't give me that crap, Lucas Alexander!" He scolded me. "I know of the many girls you take back into the apartment I let you live in. I'm not asking you to sleep with her. Just keep her out of our hair until I close the deal." I gripped onto the steering wheel tightly, showing the whites of my knuckles.

"The deal is you come when I need you, and I don't go through with the arranged marriage I have set up for your sister." He reminded me, only causing my blood to boil.

"Yeah, I got it. I'll see you there." I hung up before he could say anything else. My fist pounded into the steering wheel, causing the horn to blare, but it didn't feel like enough.

"Does Lisa know?" Leo asked, not knowing of the deal I had made with my dad before the phone call.

"Of course not. Don't you dare tell her either," I seethed.

"I won't," he promised.

"I'm going to drop you off and head to the gym instead. I need to punch something that isn't my car."

"Understandably. If you need me, let me know."

I was grateful to have Leo. We may have a 5 year age gap, but he was the closest friend I had. He knew me the best, and he was the most loyal person I knew. I nodded my head at him.

After I dropped him off, I headed to the on campus gym. They have great punching bags in the back no one uses. I snatched Leo's student ID to get in.

There weren't too many people here so early on a Saturday, making it easy for me to spot her beautiful red hair in a topknot. She was punching and kicking away at a bag with nothing but a sports bra and yoga pants. She's damn sexy.

Time to get her number.

Olive's P.O.V.

I had finally cooled down from the anger plaguing me this morning. Now I was hitting the bag in front of me to get Lucas out of my head. Even though he made me mad this morning with his stupid stunt, I couldn't shake him from my mind. I kept picturing those intense brown eyes staring at me.

I must be under some spell because I swear I can smell his cologne right now. It was almost like he was here. I felt someone was watching me, but I refused to see who it was. Going to the gym and seeing guys there who just wanted to flirt with girls made me so angry I wouldn't allow anyone to talk to me. I saw a figure from the corner of my eyes step around me. They grabbed the bag from behind, holding it steady for me. Putting all of my strength into it, I punched the bag with the intention of them being able to feel the power behind it through the bag. I didn't ask them to hold it. I was doing fine by myself.

"Damn, Rose. I didn't know you could punch so hard." His voice halted my next punch midair. I leaned to the side to see around the bag, finding those brown eyes looking back at me.

"What are you doing here?" How did he even get in here? Does he go here too and I'm just now seeing him for the first time? How is it possible I keep running into him out of nowhere?

"I needed to let out some steam, but I never imagined you'd be here doing the same," he explained with a half smirk. *Damn you and your god-like looks.*

"Holding the bag isn't the way to let your anger out."

"My anger disappeared the moment I saw you, Olive." He winked at me, using my real name for the first time. My name never sounded better than when it left his lips.

"Olive, huh?" I arched a brow at him. He nodded with a playful smirk on his lips.

"I like it, but I think you'll always be my Rose." My body wanted to step closer to him, to feel his warmth near me again. My brain, on the other hand, kept yelling about how terrible of an idea it would be. It left me rooted in place.

"I'm not yours," I finally blurted out.

"You're *only* mine." He gave me an arrogant smirk, making me punch the bag as hard as I could. He had to take a step back from the force.

"I'm *no one*'s," I snapped back, taking the tape off my hands as I walked off. I wanted to be nothing but mad at his proclamation. However, I'd be lying if I said his words didn't give me butterflies. Those words shouldn't make me happy, but they did. I wanted to be his, but it's way too soon to be with someone else. Julius and I had been in a relationship for over a year. I need more time to heal, to get to know myself again. I can't be jumping into another relationship, no matter how sexy the guy was.

"Rose, be mine. At least for the night?" He whispered into my ear from behind me. He had caught up to me easily with his long legs.

"Not in the mood, lover boy." I continued to walk. His hand clamped around my wrist, and I felt his calloused fingers as he turned me to face him. He softly brushed his knuckles across my cheek, and the sensation sent a chill through my body. He gazed at me with such an intensity I thought I'd implode.

"Please, I want to take you out. You don't have to do

anything else with me," he whispered to me, leaning down closer to my face. I could breathe in the air as he was exhaling. I swallowed hard, trying desperately to contain myself.

"Out where?" I asked with scrutiny. I don't want him to know I wouldn't mind another night of the heaven he brings me.

"To dinner. Let me feed you, and then you can decide what we will do after. If you say to take you home and leave you alone, then I will," he promised. I stared at him for a while, thinking over his offer for a few seconds. Despite knowing I should say no, the word refused to leave my mouth. I know I should walk away and do my best to stay away from him, but I could not bring myself to do so.

"Fine," was what actually came out of my mouth. He gave me the most beautiful smile, making my heart literally skip a beat.

"Give me your phone, Rose." He held his hand out. I furrowed my brows at him for a moment. "You need my number."

I pulled my phone out of the side pocket of my yoga pants, slowly placing it in his hand, watching him fiddle with it for a minute. When he handed it back to me, it showed he had sent himself a text. Not only that, but it showed the name he saved himself under. **The man who makes you scream.** He leaned forward, capturing my lips with his before I could say a word. My legs wanted to give out from under me with the sheer pleasure his lips brought me. Lucas' arm wrapped around my waist, both melting me into him and holding me upright. When he pulled away, I had to suck a breath in.

"I'll see you tonight, Olive." He smiled widely at me before he stood up straight. He pushed his hair back over his head again. I'm beginning to like it when he does that. He walked off, never having hit the bag he claimed he came for. He left the gym, giving me one last glance when he got to the door. The corner of his lip twitched up for a second before he went outside. I let my heart slow back to its normal pace before heading to the locker room to shower and change.

"I can't believe you said okay. I am so excited for you!" Hailey screeched after I told her what happened with Lucas.

"I can't believe I did either. Maybe I should text him and say I got sick." I bit at the inside of my cheek, getting nervous suddenly. I hate first date jitters. *Wait, is this a first date?*

"No!" Hailey quickly took my phone before I could text him anything. My phone vibrated in her hands. "Looks like he's asking for our address." I saw Hailey type it in before hitting send. She held onto my phone a moment longer, before I got it from her.

"You're no fun, Liv. Live a little. You're a free woman now. If you want to be with Lucas, then be with Lucas. If you wanna fuck him, then fuck him. Don't worry about what anyone else is gonna say," she lectured me.

"It's more like I'm scared this means more to me than him. Hailey, I just got my heart broken. I am still healing."

"Let him heal you, then. No one said you had to heal by yourself." She grabbed my hands. "Just promise me you won't hold yourself back, overthinking about everything."

"I'll try."

Hailey and I hung out for a while at the apartment, talking and watching TV together. A knock on the door had us both wondering who it could be. Hailey answered, since it would more than likely be for her, with this being her apartment.

"Oh? Lucas sent you something." Hailey smiled as she returned with a large white box tied with a neat bow and a card. "Open it! I'm dying." I grabbed the card first, needing to know what he said.

Hope you don't mind, but I picked something out for you to wear tonight. -Lucas

He bought me something to wear? My heart raced as I untied the bow, slowly opening the box. There was a deep green dress folded neatly inside. I pulled it out, seeing it was a floor length, a-line dress with straps that hung off my shoulders. There was a long slit on the side of the dress going up to mid thigh.

"It's beautiful!" Hailey sounded more excited than me right now. This dress told me so much. One, we were going somewhere fancy. Two, Lucas has money I don't know about. Three, he felt I had nothing appropriate to wear tonight. And four, it told me how bad of an idea this was. I do not know what I'm doing. I am so out of my league here.

"Go shower now! I'm doing your hair and makeup. You're going to have every man's attention tonight."

Where are you taking me, Lucas?

Chapter 5

Olive's P.O.V.

"There, all done." Hailey stepped away from my face, allowing me to see myself for the first time since she started.

She had styled my hair in a pinned up bun with a few loose strands on the front. She did my makeup flawlessly, adorning red lipstick on me. I could barely recognize myself. I looked beautiful and the dress fit me like a glove. Somehow Lucas knew my size better than myself. Hailey let me borrow for the night a pair of her black heels that clasped at my ankles. I could feel my stomach turning. The swirl of butterflies in me was making me nauseous. My hands felt clammy, making me want to wipe them on the dress. My heart was racing from the nerves eating me up inside.

"You look beautiful." Hailey whispered as we both stared at me in the mirror.

"Thank you, Hails."

The ring of the bell had my heart hammering faster. Hailey raced to the door. As I grabbed the small black clutch purse she let me borrow for the night. I stepped out of the room to see Lucas in a 3 piece suit, looking fine as hell. That's a mental image I'll save for later. He gave me his signature smirk that melts me to my core. His eyes checked me out from head to toe.

"Beautiful," he boldly stated as he held his hand out for me to take.

"I won't be out all night," I told Hailey as I stepped past her through the door.

"Have fun, and don't worry about me." She pushed me out with a gleam of excitement in her eyes. I silently followed Lucas out of the building to his car. He must have money, seeing as he showed up in a Lambo. He held the door open for me to get in like a gentleman. I felt my cheeks flush at the gesture as I entered the car.

"You clean up nice." I finally said, as he drove us. "Where are we going to make me dress up so nicely?"

"My dad's house." He answered causally.

"You dress up nice to go to your dad's house?" I arched a brow at him, thinking he was joking with me.

"He has a dinner meeting tonight, which means a fancy meal, fancy clothes, and a boring business talk. It may be selfish of me, but I brought you to save me from a hellish night." He grabbed my knee as he spoke, sending a spark of energy through me.

"Are you sure I should come? It sounds like you're making me crash this dinner." He gave me a cheeky smile, letting me know how right I was. I smacked his arm scoldingly.

"Lucas!"

"It's fine, I promise. Trust me, Rose. I would never embarrass you." Something inside of me inclined me to trust his words. I sighed, trying to gather even more courage, but failing as the nerves took over instead. I'm meeting his dad, while crashing his business meeting.

"I could kill you," I muttered to him, making him laugh.

"Thank you, Rose," was all he said as we pulled up to a large iron gate.

Lucas pushed in a code, having the gate creek open for us in protest. It led to a long driveway that circled in front of an enormous house. Better yet, let's call it a mansion. I did not know Lucas came from money. I honestly didn't care about it, but at the moment, I found it intimidating. What if they have a table set with all kinds of silverware I don't know how to use? You know, like the mini fork, the one no knows what it's used for. Lucas parked, coming to my side, opening the door for me again. He held his hand out, helping me out of the car. He led me up the 5 steps to the front door, passing by a familiar blue car. Where have I seen that car before?

"Good evening, young Mr. Porter." An elderly man with a gray mustache and an air of sophistication about him greeted us.

"Hello, James. Where are they?" He handed James his keys and jacket as he spoke.

"In the front room, sir." He motioned to the room in the back left corner. Lucas grabbed my hand, placing it in the nook of his arm, before walking behind James. He slid the French doors open for us, revealing a small group of people. All eyes landed on him, and then on me, but mine were stuck on an all too familiar face.

Clover sat in a lounge chair by herself. Beside her was an older woman and man I recognized as her parents. Lisa, Lucas' sister, whom I met last night, sat on the couch beside a more serious man with the same blue eyes as Lisa. His jaw ticked in obvious anger, but he said nothing about me. Hell, he seemed to pretend I didn't exist. Lisa tried to suppress her smile not too well. She found this amusing. I gripped onto Lucas' arm tightly as Clover eyed me.

"Olive, sweetheart, is that you?" Clover's mom called out to me, breaking the long silence.

"Yes, hello, Mrs. Camilo," I greeted her with a sweet smile.

"You look so beautiful! I didn't know you'd be here." She came up to me, embracing me in an awkward hug. I'd met her many times when she would come to the apartment to visit Clover. We would all talk, eat, and shop together. It was usually Clover and her mom did the shopping.

"I was sad to hear you had moved." Clover obviously didn't tell her why, and I would not be the one to reveal what a bitch her daughter was.

"Yeah, I'm sorry I didn't tell you myself."

"Ronda, Malcolm, this is my son, Lucas, and it seems you

are acquainted with his guest," Lucas' father finally spoke.

"So lovely to meet you, Lucas. This is my daughter, Clover. She and Olive were roommates until last week," Mrs. Camilo explained.

"Nice to meet you," Lucas said with a curt nod. He was also being polite, but I didn't miss the quick second of anger that crossed his face as he looked at Clover.

"Shall we start dinner now that everyone is here?" Lisa suggested, trying to save us all from any more of this.

"Yes, please, follow me," her father responded.

We all headed to the next room. The table sat 12 despite there only being 7 of us. I did not know where to sit and, to my horror, the tiny fork stared at me from the table. The urge to take a step back and run away and hide was very strong as I approached the table. I won't give Clover the satisfaction. Lucas thankfully led me to my seat, pulling it out for me, and pushing it in as I sat. He was a proper gentleman. He took the seat beside me, but then they directed Clover to sit beside him. Her parents sat across from her and Lisa sat across from Lucas and I. Of course, Lucas' dad sat at the head of the table looking out at the rest of us.

His gaze lingered on me, but I made sure not to show any intimidation. I kept my gaze fixed on the odd painting above the fireplace. I couldn't make out what it was, but it was slightly off-putting. Lucas squeezed my thigh under the table, trying to give me some encouragement. I turned to look at him, seeing him wink at me with a little smirk. I rolled my eyes, but couldn't help the small smile tugging at my lips.

Lucas' dad talked business with Mr. Camilo shortly after we all finished eating. He invited Mr. and Mrs. Camilo to the cigar room to talk more, leaving Clover out here with Lisa, Lucas and I. I bit my tongue not wanting to say anything to Clover.

"So Lucas, tell me about yourself." Clover rested her chin on her palm as she stared up at him.

"Why?" He asked coldly. I was loving the attitude.

"Aren't you supposed to keep me entertained?" She asked with a raised brow. "I can always let my parents know I'm ready to leave."

"I hate snobby girls. These dinners are insufferable. I hate girls who cheat with other girl's boyfriends. Oh, and I love redheads." My mouth dropped open as he listed these things quickly, numbering them off with his fingers. I couldn't believe he was so bold, but I absolutely loved the words he spoke. He made my heart swoon further for him, even though I told it not to. Did he say he loves redheads? Was that aimed towards me? Clover gasped, just as shocked as me.

"Just so you know, Ollie." She used the nickname I hated. The one she came up with because she said it sounded like a guy's name. "It wasn't the first time." She was referring to when I caught her with Julius. My hands fisted, but I didn't react to her words. She was trying to hurt me, and she succeeded, but I won't show her.

"Just so *you* know, Clover." I turned my gaze to her. "He was sleeping with me, too. Does that make you sloppy seconds? Or maybe just desperate?" I pursed my lips, pretending to contemplate it. "No, that's not right. It makes you pathetic."

"Ugh! I am not pathetic. What's pathetic is the way you keep dating guys for their money. You met Julius at one of my parties. You knew he came from money and stole him from under me. Now here you are throwing yourself at Lucas because you think you caught a bigger fish." She shook her head like she was disappointed in me.

"Ha! That's a laugh. Stole him from under you? He threw himself at me. He begged me to go out with him. After his insistent badgering, I finally agreed. Sorry, he wasn't interested in you in that way. Guess he wanted something easy to do while he waited for me." I gave her a fake smile, batting my lashes at her the way she did when she flirted with guys. She always looked so stupid when she did that.

"She didn't throw herself at me. I begged her to come

tonight. She's here because I asked her to be," Lucas interjected, grabbing my hand from under the table and kissing the back of my palm. I wasn't expecting the action, so I blushed. Lisa suddenly burst into a fit of laughter, making us all look at her puzzled. She shook her head, reigning in her laughter. It took her a minute, but eventually she stopped, clearing her throat before explaining.

"Christ, this is some daytime drama shit. So what I'm understanding from this is you slept with her boyfriend multiple times while they dated, because what? You wanted to prove you were better? All he did was make you the side piece. Honey, the side piece is worse than being rejected. It means he gets from you what he wants, but still makes his girlfriend the priority." Lisa shook her head disapprovingly as she explained. "Now here you are, thinking that saying you slept with her boyfriend more than once is something to brag about. *Oh, Honey.*"

Lisa had me cracking a smile at the way she was putting Clover in her place. I wasn't sure she liked me much when we met yesterday. She asked me a million questions, walking off suddenly without another word.

"I...But she..." Clover couldn't seem to form a sentence anymore. She was stunned and flustered, and I was so happy I could see this moment right now.

"Could you let Julius know I don't plan on getting back together with him the next time you guys are having sex? Cool, thanks." I knew Julius was probably still sleeping with her. I also knew she probably didn't know he was trying to get back together with me.

"You're such a liar. He doesn't want you anymore," Clover hissed.

"You think so? Let's see." I pulled my phone out, ringing Julius' number, placing it on speaker for everyone to hear. He picked up on the second ring. Julius answered the phone almost immediately.

"Liv, baby. Thank God you came to your senses." Julius'

voice actually sounded relieved.

"I certainly came to my senses tonight." *About what a fucking liar you are.*

"Come to my place and let's talk about it, Liv. I love you. It meant nothing, I swear. I only want you." Julius was making this so easy.

"Julius, I want to make something very clear. You are not the man I thought you were. You are a disgusting pig who had no respect for me or our relationship. I will *never*, never, Julius, get back together with you. We are done. There is no *us*. I am not your girl, nor will I ever be again. I called to tell you I will be blocking your number. Don't find me, and if you see me on campus, avoid me." I hung up before he could say anything, blocking the number.

"Damn, Rose. That was hot." Lucas smirked at me, moving my hair back over my shoulder. His fingers tickled my exposed skin, making me flush again. Clover was stunned silent. There was nothing she could say after that. She was a stupid, spoiled girl. I can't believe I ever thought she was my friend. Her lips were pushed together into a thin line. She was mad with her eyes narrowed at me. She wanted to fight. I've seen that look before in people who were about to attack.

"Go ahead, Clover, hit me, and see how fast you land on your ass," I dared her, because I wanted an excuse to hit her without getting myself in trouble. Self defense would be the only way to do that. To my disappointment, she didn't move.

"Clover, sweetheart, we are leaving now. Olive, it's always so nice to see you," Mrs. Camilo called from the entryway of the dining room.

"You as well, Mrs. Camilo." I gave her a small wave with a smile. Clover got up with a humph, storming out. I could hear her mom calling after her, asking what was wrong. I dare her to say something about this. She'll only make herself look bad. No, she'll stay silent, festering in her frustrations.

"Lucas, a word," his dad called from his office.

"I'll be right back, beautiful. Don't go anywhere." *I*

wonder what they're going to talk about?

"You did well tonight, considering," Lisa said with a nod of approval.

"Thank you. I think?"

"You're the first girl he's ever brought home. I know it may have been nothing fun or romantic, but it was huge for Lucas to bring you here. Just keep that in mind, okay?" She clearly wanted me to see Lucas in a better light. She didn't have to say anything. I was already seeing him differently. The sweet gestures throughout the night were enough to make me like him even more. I need to be careful, because I am not sure he likes me as anything more than someone to sleep with. I bit my cheek, trying not to ask her anything about Lucas' love life. It's not for her to answer.

"Okay. I'll bear it in mind," I answered her.

I could hear some faint yelling coming from the direction of Lucas' father's office. My body stiffened, holding myself back from going and opening the door. I hate hearing people yell. My dad and mom would fight a lot growing up, and usually in my presence. The fights would always involve them yelling at one another. Most of the time it ended with dad throwing something across the room, sometimes throwing a punch at my mom. Dad always had a bad temper, exasperated by his fighting career.

Dad was abusive with mom, and after she couldn't take it anymore, she left us. She had me swear not to get with a man who couldn't handle his anger right before she disappeared from my life. I was 10 at the time, and dad was gone at one of his fights. I stayed home alone for a while before dad arrived. He was furious, hitting walls and calling her name like it would make her appear before him. He became a real drunk after that.

"Don't worry, he's fine. Dad always huffs and puffs, but does nothing, at least not when there's company. Lucas knows how to get under his skin," Lisa assured me, but it didn't calm the nerves in my stomach.

"Lucas, I'm not done!" I heard his dad yell, making me instinctively flinch.

"But I am!" he yelled back, slamming the door behind him.

He stormed towards me with his hand extended out to me. I flinched as we went to grab me, despite knowing he would not hurt me. He furrowed his brow for a moment, obviously hurt by the way I had reacted.

"I won't hurt you, Rose. I was going to grab your hand. May I have it, please?" His deep brown eyes stared into my blue ones with concern as he held his hand out. I cleared my throat, feeling a bit embarrassed and still on edge. I extended my hand towards him, letting him take it and lead me out of the house.

"Nice seeing you again, Liv," Lisa called from behind me, throwing me a wink. *Liv* was always Julius' nickname for me. I hate that he's left a negative connotation to one of my favorite nicknames. I gave her a wave in return, unable to call back to her, knowing my voice would sound weak.

"Lucas!" His father yelled after us, but Lucas didn't turn. He walked us out so fast I was practically sprinting to keep up with him. He grabbed his coat before James could, ushering me out of the door. It was almost like he had set off a bomb inside, and was trying to get us out before it exploded.

The chilly night air hit me hard, snapping me out of the trauma induced anxiety I'd been feeling. Lucas opened my door for me again, but his movements were fast and harsh. I got in, having the door slammed behind me. He slammed his own door after he sat. He punched his steering wheel in anger, making me flinch again.

"Lucas?" I cautiously called his name. When he turned to look at me, meeting my eyes, he quickly composed himself again. He slid his hand over his hair, pulling back the loose strands. "What happened?"

"It's nothing, just my father being my father. I am sorry I scared you, Olive. I didn't mean to."

"Back to Olive, huh?" I smirked at him, trying to calm

him with my flirting. He smirked back, licking his lips.

"Which would you rather I call you? Rose or Olive? Your name is beautiful. I don't want you to think I don't like it." He took my hand from my lap as he drove us away.

He kept it in his own, squeezing it and occasionally bringing it up to his mouth to kiss. I thought about it for a moment; I had grown fond of him calling me Rose. He's the only one that ever has. Around him I don't feel like shy, traumatized Olive. I feel like a beautiful Rose with sharp thorns that could hurt.

"Call me Rose," I finally answered him, making him smile so big as he stared at the road ahead.

"Well, Rose, where to now? I promised you we'd go where you wanted afterwards."

"Take me home," I said, seeing his shoulders slump and a frown form on his face for a second. "We need to change before we go where I want to take us."

He immediately smirked again, his mood lifting. He wanted to spend more time with me, or maybe he's hoping it ends in sex again, and was only disappointed when he thought it wasn't going to. I wish I knew what he was thinking.

"Where are we going?" He raised a brow curiously.

"It's a secret. You'll see." I winked at him with a giggle.

"Can't wait. I think I have some spare clothes in my trunk for me, if you don't mind me getting changed in your apartment."

"That's perfect." I nodded.

Chapter 6

Olive's P.O.V.

We pulled up to Hailey's apartment building not long after. Lucas opened my door again, handing the keys to the valet. We walked by the doorman, Scott, who greeted me with a smile. He was a round man with a very sweet temperament. Everyone loved Scott.

"Good evening, Ms. Brewer." Scott tipped his hat as we walked by.

"Hey, Scott!" I smiled widely at him. "Has Hailey left?"

"No, ma'am. I have not seen her come down."

"Okay, thanks."

We made our way up the elevator. Lucas had a backpack strapped over his shoulder with his spare clothes inside. When the elevator doors dinged, we stepped towards the penthouse. I fumbled with the key for a moment, not having opened this door very often. I felt embarrassed until the door finally opened. I didn't expect us to be greeted by such a sight. *What the hell happened here?*

"Hailey?" I called out to her as I approached the bomb that had gone off in the kitchen. The place was a complete disaster. "Hailey, did you try to cook again?"

Hailey cannot cook to save her life, but she still tries anyway. She swears she needs more practice, but I think she's cursed. Everything stops working when she touches it in the kitchen. I narrowly avoided being splattered down on by some odd substance that clung to the ceiling. Lucas was suppressing his laughter behind me, picking up what looked like an attempt at brownies, maybe?

He eyed it curiously, looking at me with pressed lips. He was trying to be polite by not laughing, but he couldn't hold it in anymore. His laughter filled the apartment and my heart. It was the best sound I had heard in a while. His laugh was perfect and fit him exactly right. It was contagious too, making me laugh alongside him.

Hailey stepped out of her room with a towel on her head, clearly having stepped out of the shower. She looked at us both as we reined in our laughter. Her cheeks blushed deeply when she looked at the kitchen and then at Lucas. She didn't care that I had seen it, as I've seen it many times. She, however, cared that Lucas saw it.

"Hailey, I've told you to stop trying to cook. What even happened?"

She narrowed her eyes at the standing mixer like it had done her wrong by existing. She pointed at it with narrowed eyes. "That cursed thing happened. It was going great until I used *that*. All I did was plug it in and start it, only when I lowered it, it threw the batter everywhere."

"Hailey, did you turn it on with the mixer part still up?" I asked her, seeing where she went wrong.

"Yeah." She nodded.

"Hailey, you're supposed to have the mixer in the bowl before you turn it on, and always on low to start." I shook my head at her.

"Oh, that makes more sense." She blushed. I laughed, hugging her tightly.

"I love you, Hailey. Thank you for trying to make my favorite."

"I wanted to know how everything went. I figured we could eat brownies while we spoke, but obviously it was a terrible idea. You go do what you need to do, and I'll clean up here." She pushed me towards my room. "You too, Lucas." Lucas gave me a smirk as he followed me to my room. I bit my lip in anticipation, wondering if we can keep away from each other as we change alone in a room behind a closed door.

"Could you get the zipper for me?" I asked Lucas after I locked the door. He came up behind me without a word, letting me feel his presence before his hands ran the length of my back. His fingers grabbed the zipper, dragging it down slowly, drawing the moment out. He then kissed my exposed back, making me take a deep breath. I enjoyed the feel of his warm lips on my skin. He slid my dress off my arms, making goosebumps erupt where his fingers touched.

"You're so beautiful, Rose. I'm sorry I made you endure a dinner with Clover. I didn't realize who she was to you." He sighed as he leaned down and kissed the nape of my neck. His arms wrapped around my now naked torso, pressing my back against his chest. He inhaled my scent as we stood there for a moment in silence.

"It's not your fault. I am sorry I dragged you into my stupid drama." I rolled my eyes at the memory of Clover.

"I didn't mind hearing you put her, and your piece of shit ex, in their place." He kissed my neck again. "God, you're so perfect, Rose." I let out a small laugh at the notion of me being perfect.

"Far from it." I shook my head. Lucas quickly turned me to face him. His eyes were hungry as they stared down at me.

"You. Are. Perfect." He slowly enunciated each word, as if trying to engrave into my mind. He then leaned down, giving me a kiss I hadn't experienced before, one that stole my breath away. "Let's get dressed. I'm curious to see where you want us to go."

Lucas released me, turning to his bag and grabbing his clothes. I was still lost in the earth shattering kiss as I stood there a moment, watching him. When I finally collected myself, I got dressed in a long black shirt and yoga pants. I planned on showing him what I could do tonight.

We were going to the underground fighting club I found in my first year at Columbia. I'd heard some guys talking about it on campus and checked it out myself. I am well known there now, having won countless fights. It was a good way for me to make decent money. I stopped going when I started dating Julius because he didn't think it was appropriate for me to be fighting. I turned to find Lucas fully changed in a dark top and bleach washed jeans. He was handsome no matter what he wore. He eyed me curiously, trying to get a read on where we were going from my outfit. I doubt he'll guess it.

"Hailey, we're leaving now. I'll be back later." I told her, finding her still in the kitchen with most of the mess already cleaned up. She saw what I was wearing and smiled real big.

"Give 'em hell." She winked at me with a smile. She knew how much I liked to fight. I know it's contradictory to want to fight when you've seen abuse before. It makes no sense I would flinch at Lucas, but not in a ring with someone who is actually trying to hurt me. I think it's the fact I know I can hurt them back. Fighting gives me back my control.

"Thanks, Hails." Lucas looked even more intrigued now as he followed closely behind.

"Are you going to tell me where we're going now?" he asked me when we got to the elevator.

"No, you'll see when we get there." I gave him a playful smirk, taunting him a bit. He did something tonight he has apparently never done before. Lisa said I was the only girl he'd brought home, so I want to show him a part of me few people have seen. If he gets scared away because of this, then it was never meant to be more than just sex.

"You're gonna have to tell me where we are going so I can drive us."

"Nope, I'll direct you." I winked as I stepped out of the elevator, leading the way back to the valet.

"Leaving again, Ms. Brewer?" Scott asked, surprised.

"Yeah, one last stop before I call it a night. I'll see you tomorrow, Scott."

"See you tomorrow, Ms. Brewer." Lucas didn't get the chance to open my door this time, as the valet did. I got in without protest, but Lucas didn't like he wasn't the one to open my door. I could see it in his stiff posture as he took his seat, eyeing the valet.

"Go straight and take a right on 74th," I told him, snapping his attention back to me.

I guided us the entire way there, having us pull up to the abandoned warehouse where they were meeting today. The location always changed to keep the cops from finding the place. Today's location was a large abandoned warehouse with poor street lighting.

"Where have you taken me, Rose?" Lucas seemed amused as he looked around.

"Come find out." I smirked, opening my door, quickly stepping out with a giggle. I ran ahead towards the side door of the building.

He locked his car, speeding to catch up to me. He grabbed my hand, interlocking our fingers as I led us in. I wasn't sure what he wanted from me anymore. Does he want more than just sex? I mean, do you usually hold hands with someone you're only hooking up with? This feels like something you do when you're dating. Are we dating?

I led us down to the side door where a big, muscled man waited. I spoke the words, allowing us access past him. As we got down to the basement where the action was, you could hear the cheers of the excited crowd. In front of the basement door stood another large and extremely muscular man. He had a shiny bald head with beautiful ebony skin. He flashed me a smile as he recognized me.

"Hey Carter," I greeted him with a smile back.

"Twinkle Toes, you're back!" he said excitedly. "Are you fighting tonight?"

"You know it! Let Davis know for me?" I asked him. Davis was the man in charge of the fights.

"He'll be happy to hear it." Carter pulled up his walkie. "Yo, Davis, you're never going to believe who's back." It should be obvious to Lucas what this place was now, if it hadn't been already. I was nervous to turn and look at him. What if he thinks this is too weird? Or what if he's put off by strong women? I finally gathered the courage to look at him. My chest tightened at the sight.

Lucas' P.O.V.

Rose finally turned to look at me. Her beautiful clear blue eyes captivated me even more. I smiled down at her, excited to see her fight. She took me somewhere I'd never been before. It surprised me she knew of such a place, and by the looks of it, they knew her well.

"Who is it?" The man I'm assuming is Davis came over the walkie talkie.

"Twinkle Toes." Carter's smile widened with excitement.

Twinkle toes. I wonder how she got a fighting name like that. Doesn't sound very aggressive, but she's respected enough to be known by these men. With an excited response like that, she must be a good fighter. My Rose has pricklier thorns than I thought.

"No fucking way! I'll be right there." Davis sounded as excited as Carter. Rose squeezed my hand, turning to me again.

"I hope you don't mind that I leave you for a little while tonight. I wanted to show you somewhere special to me," she explained, making my heart swell. *Fuck, I'm really liking this girl.*

"I don't mind at all, as long as I get front row seats to your fight." I winked at her, causing her to blush.

"Is this your boyfriend?" Carter sized me up with his eyes. He looked amused by our interaction.

"He's-" Rose stared, but I interrupted.

"Yes, I am." I surprised the living hell out of Rose, and even myself. I've never proclaimed myself someone's boyfriend, but I felt the need to stake my claim here and now. I hoped she wouldn't call my lie out. She went to say something, but the door flung open behind Carter, revealing a tall, muscular man. He was probably in his 40s with long blonde hair in viking braids. He turned his lips up as he sported a wide smile, looking at my Rose.

He wrapped his arms around her, carrying her in a big bear hug. Rose didn't let my hand go, squeezing it as he squeezed her. Davis put her back down with a pat on the head. Normally, I'd be jealous if a guy hugged my girl like that, but Davis looked at her more like a daughter than anything else.

"Damn, twinkle toes, it's been too long. You disappeared off the face of the earth." Rose sighed, scratching at the back of her neck nervously. "I know. I'm sorry, but I'm back now. At least for a couple nights a month, if you'll still have me?"

Davis let out a laugh, placing his hand on Rose's shoulder. "Of course we'll have you back! You're the best fighter I've had down here in a while. Although, there's been some competition since you've been gone. Don't worry. I'll start you off midway, work you back up to the top."

"Sounds good." Rose smiled. I could see she was filled with excitement. She was antsy, ready to be in the ring already. I love seeing this side of her. I don't think anyone would ever guess she had this fierce fighting spirit. She seems quiet and reserved when she's out, yet she's anything but. She's a spitball of fire, my flaming Rose.

"Let's go, kid, you'll go on next. Your boyfriend can hang with me," Davis told her, opening the door behind him.

There were three rings set up down here. Each surrounded by their own crowd. The cheers were loud, along with the music. The lights were bright over the ring, but the rest of the place was dim. Bets were being placed at each fight, encouraging the crowd to cheer for their fighter harder than before. There were men and women in each fight. No refs, no bells, no rules, true underground nature.

I felt nervous thinking of Rose getting hurt, but when I saw her face, I knew I couldn't deny her this. She looked like she was staring at a Christmas tree full of presents. She appeared excited, hungry, and ready for it. I couldn't help myself, grabbing her chin, turning her towards me. I captured those perfect lips of hers with mine in a tender kiss.

"Go get 'em, Twinkle Toes." I whispered in her ear, making her blush.

"You better be cheering me on," she told me as she walked off to the ring Davis directed her to. He hung back with me, waiting for the current fights to end.

"Have you seen her fight before?"

"Not in a ring," I told him, thinking of the way she handled the man at the club last night.

"You're in for a treat." Davis smiled as he kept his gaze on the now finished fight.

"Oh, man!" The guy with the mic near the DJ booth caught everyone's attention. "We're in for a treat tonight!" he continued. "Our next fights are reigning champion Mercy the Merciless versus Don Juan in Ring One. In Ring Two, we have Donny, the tomb, versus John, The Lightning kid. And in Ring Three we have returning champion Olive Twinkle Toes versus Dana the Cobra." The crowd went insane at the mention of Rose's fighting name. *Returning champion, huh?*

"Why do you guys call her twinkle toes?" I asked Davis, yelling through the roaring of the crowd.

"You'll see. She's light on her feet, and extremely fast, dancing around her opponents. She doesn't get hurt much in a fight either, but she deals a lot of damage." Davis explained. We made our way towards Ring Three to watch Rose.

Davis parted the crowd for us, earning us the spot right by the cage. I saw Rose enter the ring with her hands taped, and a guard in her mouth. She shook her body as she jumped, loosening up. Her opponent was a larger woman with heavier muscles. She had short black hair and a serious look of determination on her face. Rose focused on her fight, jumping between her feet on her toes. I smiled, thinking of her name.

"Let's get their fights started!" The announcer said as "Can't Be Touched" by Roy Jones Jr.

Rose and her opponent circled the ring, staring at each other. Rose kept her arms raised and ready. She had tied her hair back, showing off her high cheekbones and firm jaw. She looked radiant in that ring. Cobra lunged at her, but Rose spun around her, simultaneously punching her right in the side. Cobra would attack and Rose would dance around her. It was beautiful to watch the way she commanded the ring. She beat Cobra easily, only taking one punch the entire time.

"Come with me. We'll meet her over there." Davis signaled with his head, having me follow him through the thick crowd. Rose's ring had the largest crowd.

My girl is amazing.

My girl. I need to make her my girl.

I saw Rose in the distance, taking her mouth guard out. I rushed to her, grabbing her and spinning her around. My lips met hers as I kissed her again before pulling back and smiling at her proudly.

"You were amazing." Her cheeks had the most beautiful shade of pink as I put her back down. I rubbed the spot her opponent had hit gently with my thumb. She didn't wince, so I figured it wasn't too tender. Davis cleared his throat, getting both of our attention. He had an amused look on his face as he stared at us.

"Great job, Twinkle Toes. Let me know when you wanna do it again this month. Hughes has your money at the exit. It's great to have you back." Davis patted her on the back as he walked away. Rose turned, looking back up at me with those beautiful, enormous eyes. She pulled her hair tie out, shaking her head to let her hair loose. The way her hair fell around her shoulders had me wanting to take her back to my place and fuck her hard.

"Where to now?" I raised a brow at her as I wrapped my arm around her waist and pulled her flush against my chest.

"Your place?" She bit her lip, obviously feeling the same way I did. I nodded with a smirk on my face.

"You're perfect, Rose. Absolutely perfect."

CHAPTER 6

We reached the car rather quickly after Rose collected her chunk of cash. I opened her door, watching her climb in. I may have sped a bit as I raced us to my apartment, ready to devour this woman beside me. The woman who I can't get out of my head, no matter how hard I try. She's consuming me whole, soul, body, and mind.

We entered the elevator in the garage, but I couldn't wait any longer. I closed the space between us, pinning Rose against the elevator wall. She stared at me for a moment before meeting my lips. For once, she was the one to start the kiss. I hungrily licked at her lips, sucking, and nipping at them. Her breasts pressed tightly against my chest. I gripped her hips as I parted her lips with my tongue.

I reluctantly broke our kiss when the elevator doors opened again, keeping my hands on her sides, guiding her through the hall. I kissed her neck from behind as we walked. She was panting with the lust I knew was growing in her. When I made it to my door, I unlocked it from behind her, stepping into the poorly lit entryway with her.

The sound of someone clearing their throat made my blood run cold, knowing exactly who was waiting in the dark for me.

Shit, this won't end well.

Chapter 7

Olive's P.O.V.

Lucas froze stiff behind me as we both stared at the tall blonde in his recliner. The trench coat she wore had nothing under it, I am sure. She was stunning, with sharp features and wide eyes. She held her head high in confidence. It did not embarrass her to be sitting there in just a trench coat. Her legs were crossed, showing off their beautiful length. She was like a model in her beauty and perfection.

"Janessa," Lucas let her name slip from his lips, causing my chest to tighten.

I was an idiot to think he liked me. He has options and I'm only one of them. I had opened up to him today, letting myself feel so alive with him by my side. Being back in the ring was amazing, and I had been riding high since we left the warehouse. Reality slapped me hard in the face in the form of a stunning woman. She got up, her eyes clearly assessing me, not impressed by what they found. Despite feeling like an ugly toad beside her, I held my head high, refusing to show her any weakness.

"Hello, Lucas. I was hoping to have some fun with you tonight. I'll wait for you in your room while you take care of the trash." She crossed her arms, staring at me.

My anger was high, but it's not like I can say anything. I don't know how Lucas feels about me. He could very well choose her over me, so I refuse to make a fool of myself by saying otherwise. I scoffed, stepping out of Lucas' hold, shaking my head as I backed away. I don't need to hear him send me away. The small hope I let myself have about Lucas and me being anything more than fuck buddies is already crushing me enough.

I watched Lucas grab Janessa by the arm. I knew this was a bad idea. My heart had been crushed again. This was supposed to be a one-night stand, and instead I let myself catch feelings. I focused on my rage instead of the hurt I was feeling. As I reached for the door, Lucas beat me to it. He opened it, only rubbing salt on my wounded heart. I kept my head held high as I went to step out. However, Lucas threw Janessa out instead. She stared at him, stunned. In fact, we both did.

"The trash is out now," Lucas said before closing the door on her face.

To say I was feeling triumphant was an understatement. The corners of my mouth turned up in joy. For some reason, he had picked me over the model of a woman who had thrown herself at him. The moment of elation only lasted for a second as I realized he had a naked woman in his chair a second ago. How did she even get in? How often does this happen to him? Am I another one of those girls?

There were too many questions floating in my head, and although I wanted to ask them all, I knew he wouldn't want to answer them. The hunger I had for him earlier had died, leaving me with insecurities. He turned to face me after he locked the door.

"I'm so sorry, Rose." He pinched the bridge of his nose like this was all too much of a headache.

"How about I go home?" I asked him, using a more demanding tone.

This showed me how vastly out of my league he was. I can't handle this roller coaster anymore, even though I'm the one doing it to myself. When he said he was my boyfriend at the warehouse, I had let myself daydream, but I shouldn't have. He had accepted me fully, even calling me perfect for being a fighter. Now I know it was all just words.

"Rose." His voice was almost pleading as he looked at

me. He cupped my face with his hands. "Are you sure you want to go?"

"You're a busy man. Maybe having another woman to handle isn't the best idea for you. I'll see myself out. Thanks for an interesting night, Lucas." I took a step back, reaching for the door again.

Part of me hoped he would protest and ask me to stay, but as I opened the door, he said nothing. I left toward the elevator again, thinking maybe he'd chase after me, but he didn't. It proves to me how little he cares. I'm sure he's probably calling Janessa right now to get her back. He probably only kicked her out because he had started his night with me. At least he's loyal in the sense he stays with the girl he started the night out with.

The elevator doors opened, revealing Leo's sweet face. He had replaced his glasses with contacts. He styled his black hair beautifully, and he had piercings I'd never noticed before. For a more professional appearance, he must take them off while on campus, as he had a multitude of them.

He had his bottom lip pierced, a round ring around the corner of his mouth. He had a dangling cross earring on his right ear and a cuff in the cartilage. His left eyebrow had a piercing as well, ultimately giving sweet Leo a not so sweet look. He looked so different right now. I found myself staring at him. Leo furrowed his brow at me in surprise as he recognized me.

"What's wrong, Olive?" He pushed off the wall he'd been leaning on. I shook my head, not wanting to admit anything .

"Nothing's wrong." I gave him a sad attempt at a smile. He studied me for a moment before pulling me by the hand into the elevator.

"I'll take you home, and you can tell me what's actually bothering you." I noticed he wasn't asking when he said this, causing my heart to flutter for a moment.

He'd only seen me three times, and texted me throughout the week, but despite the short time frame, he could pick up on my sadness easily. Could Lucas see it too, and just not care? I sighed, but nodded my head at Leo. I figured Leo came from money as well, seeing as he got me the newest iPhone as a replacement for the one he broke. Besides, usually rich people flock together like birds. Lucas, coming from a rich background, meant his friend's probably would be too.

Leo didn't drive a Lambo, he drove an orange McLaren. Like Lucas, he held the door open for me to climb in. He closed it with a serious look on his face, making my stomach turn. I hadn't seen Leo look this way before. He was mad, but about what? I had no clue. He pulled out of the garage, driving at the speed limit.

"Tell me what Lucas did. I'll kick his ass," Leo finally broke the silence.

"He did nothing." I sighed.

"Then what happened, Olive? You looked like you could cry earlier." His hands gripped the steering wheel tightly as he spoke.

"There was a girl waiting for him in his apartment. I'm pretty sure *all* she was wearing was a trench coat," I started.

"Did he kick you out for her?!" Leo raised his voice, making me flinch a bit. "I'm sorry. I didn't mean to yell." I just shook my head again.

"You're fine, but no, he didn't kick me out. He kicked her out. It's just... I don't know. I'm stupid, and thought this could be more than it was. It's nothing, and I'll be fine. I need to keep my distance from Lucas. He's got other girls to play with, and I don't need to involve myself with him anymore than I already have." I chewed on my cheek as I finished confessing my inner thoughts. Leo nodded his head in understanding. I saw his piercing flick from side to side against his lip. He played with it as he was thinking about what to say.

"Lucas is my friend, my oldest and bestest friend. He's been around a lot of women this last year. He's not a serious relationship kind of guy anymore. Usually, he only ever sees a girl once and then never again. The fact he took you out again for a third time means something, but who knows what? I'm not sure. I know it's not like him." He continued to play with his lip piercing as he paused for a moment. "Janessa is the only person he's had around for a while, but she's more of a bed warmer. She goes in and out of town a lot on business. So when she's in town, she pays him a visit. Janessa is the closest thing he has to a serious relationship and if he kicked her out for you...well, he likes you more than I thought."

I let his words process in my mind a while longer. If that was the case, why didn't he say anything? Why didn't he ask me to stay? Why didn't he try to explain, or even chase after me when I left? It honestly wouldn't have taken a lot of convincing on his part. Yes, Leo may be his friend, but even he doesn't truly know how Lucas is feeling.

I won't do this to myself any longer. I don't need to be questioning myself or my worth. My focus should solely be on finishing this year of college, making it on the dean's list again, and not dating. Julius tore my heart out, and I honestly need to give it a break before I let Lucas pulverize it.

"Maybe, but I doubt it. Honestly, I need to focus on my studies. I just got out of a terrible relationship, and I don't need all this drama in my life." I rolled my eyes at it all.

I don't want to be this pathetic girl pining over some playboy, thinking I could be the one to change him. I am nothing to him but another girl he's slept with. Lisa's words made me think it was more than that. I was stupid to let my brain get carried away when he introduced himself as my boyfriend. I'd be extremely dumb right now to let Leo's words sway me again. *I won't be seeing Lucas again.*

"I understand." Leo nodded. "Just remember, I'm not Lucas, so don't stop seeing me, too." I smiled at his remark.

"Don't worry, Leo. I'll still reply to your texts and see you around campus."

"Maybe hang out once in a while too?" He curled a brow suggestively.

"As long as you don't bring Lucas."

"Deal." He smiled widely at me, making my crumbled heart piece back together a bit.

"Thank you, Leo."

"What for?" He furrowed his brow as he pulled up to the front of Hailey's apartment building.

"For this. For taking me home and listening to my problems." I leaned over, kissing his cheek before getting out. I giggled as I saw his cheeks flush for a moment. It would appear Leo is the innocent type, despite his current look. He cleared his throat before he spoke.

"Anytime, Olive." He smiled at me again. Such a sweet smile.

"Call me Liv," I told him before stepping out of the car. I want to reclaim my nickname from the memories of Julius. Refusing to let him ruin that for me, too.

"Okay, Liv. Text me when you've made it inside your apartment, so I know you're home safe," he told me, as I closed the door. I nodded my head at him through the window. My phone buzzed as Leo drove away. The name on the caller ID brought all kinds of mixed emotions. What does he want now?

My dad's name continued to flash across my screen as he called. It surprised me to see him call me so late. It wasn't like him to be up at this hour. The timing caused me to worry, making my mind race with worst-case scenarios. I swiped the green call receive button as I entered the building.

"Hello?" I answered.

"Livie, are you okay?" His voice sounded so concerned.

"What? Yeah, I'm fine." I furrowed my brow in confusion as I pushed the elevator button. "What is it? What's wrong?"

"It's your mother." I froze stiffly at the mention of her name. I understood why she had left dad, but I never understood why she had left me, too. She never called, sent letters, or even tried to visit me. She abandoned me like bad luggage, which I guess to her I was. The mention of her made my chest tighten.

"What about her?" I bit my cheek nervously, as the anticipation built inside me for his answer.

"She's sick, Livie... cancer." He sighed. "She called me, wanting to speak with you. She's in a hospital in Brooklyn, in hospice. You need to go see her."

The world seemed to stop all around me. My chest felt so tight it was as if an elephant were sitting on top of it. The air was escaping me and forgetting to return. I know I haven't spoken to her in over a decade now, but it doesn't mean I don't still love her. I'd even thought of trying to find her recently. Never did I expect she would be dying.

"Did you hear me, Livie?"

"Yeah, I heard you, dad. Text me the hospital details and I'll see her tomorrow." I somehow made my voice work again.

"I will. I am sorry, Livie. It's all my fault." Dad's guilt was well placed, seeing as he's the reason she left us to begin with. Of course, he didn't cause her cancer, but he made me miss having a mother around during my formative teen years, when you need your mother the most.

"I'll talk to you later, Dad. Goodnight." I ignored his admission of guilt completely, because I certainly would not comfort him about this.

"Goodnight."

The nurse showed me the way to mom's room. I had stopped by the gift shop on the way up as if it were calling me to make more poor decisions. I stupidly bought a stuffed bear with the words 'get better' scribbled on its heart. She's literally in hospice, which means there is no 'getting better'. I didn't notice when I got it the heart actually said something, but now it's too late as the nurse is opening the door to her room.

I swallowed hard, entering the cold, feeling the need to grab a jacket. The hospital air was stale and frigid, carrying the scent of rubber gloves, antiseptic, and rubbing alcohol. It was eerily silent on this wing, aside from the beeps of the monitors. As I entered, I saw mom sitting up in her bed with her legs dangling off the side. She was staring out of the large windows which encompassed most of the wall. The sun was shining brightly, giving her a better view of the garden outside.

"Mom?" I called out to her, feeling strange saying it again.

She turned slowly, letting me fully take in the sickness which was eating away at her body. Her body was nothing but skin and bones. She had a colorful scarf tied around her head to hide her balding scalp. She also had no hair on her face, no eyebrows or eyelashes. Her skin was almost an ash color, having lost its rosy tint she used to carry on her cheeks.

I remember mom being so beautiful, with long curly hair like my own. Only she knew how to maintain it. Her dark green eyes, which used to hold a shine, now looked so dead inside. The smile she gave me was clearly forced, only making this situation even more strained.

"Olive, is that you?" Her voice cracked as she spoke.

"Yup." I stepped further into the room.

"You've changed so much! You've grown into such a beautiful woman."

"Yeah, people change when you don't see them for many years." I knew the comment was snarky, but I couldn't help myself. She may die, but what she did to me was still shitty... cancer or not.

"I'm sorry, Livie." She sighed. "I wanted to get you here for selfish reasons. I need to apologize to you." She coughed, and it didn't stop until she coughed some blood out of her mouth. She grabbed the tissues beside her. "Sorry."

"An apology is not enough after you abandoned me. I need more. I need an explanation." My tone was demanding.

I was hurting her, I could see it, but I didn't care. My heart keeps taking more and more damage. I don't know how much more I can handle right now. I need closure, and the only way I'll get it is if she can explain her actions in a way I can understand, a way I can get behind.

"I know it wasn't right to leave you behind, but at the time, I knew it would be better for you to stay with your father. He never hurt you, and I knew he never would. I couldn't take you with me when I left because I had nowhere to go. I lived on the streets for about a year before I could finally get a job and a place of my own. My plan was to come back to get you once I was stable enough." She looked me deep in the eyes as she recounted her tale...the one I'd been curious about all my life.

"It scared me to reach out to your dad and have him find me. I would sleep with a gun under my pillow in case your father came for me. He swore he would kill me if I ever left him. I'd taken self-defense classes, but I knew they wouldn't do much good against your dad. The fear of your father finding me kept me from sending letters or making phone calls." I nodded my head to let her know I was still listening. When I got older, I realized that was probably the case. She never contacted me for fear of dad finding her, but I could never be certain.

"I filed papers with the court, but since I never filed police reports against the abuse your father caused, there wasn't much I could do. They couldn't prove abuse, and with me barely making enough money for just myself, my lawyer knew we wouldn't win custody. I should have fought harder for you, Livie, but I was so scared. I was young and stupid and frightened, so very frightened." A tear streamed down her face as she spoke. "I am sorry for leaving you behind, for being so weak. I am sorry for not being strong enough to come back and get you, and for not fighting for you harder."

I was silent, letting tears fall from my eyes. My chest felt like it was caving in on itself, unable to stand the sheer bittersweet moment. I have waited years to hear this story, to hear her apologize. I always pictured finding her and having this moment, and then getting to know each other again, creating a new mother-daughter bond. That's been stolen now, by the cancer plaguing her body.

"I didn't just call you here for this. I want you to get yourself checked, Livy. This cancer runs on my side of the family. I missed a few screenings, which caused them to catch it too late. It's breast cancer." She wiped at her tears, looking up at me. "Promise me you'll get checked for the gene, and if you have it, you will go to all your screenings. I know I've been a terrible mother, but please Livie, learn from my mistakes," she pleaded. I couldn't take it anymore, getting up and wrapping my arms around her. I held her tightly against me, feeling her arms wrap around me as well. We cried together for a while, a very long while.

"I promise I'll get myself checked," I finally told her after we both had calmed down.

"Good." She nodded, twirling my hair in her fingers.

I spent the afternoon catching up on years worth of stories. I felt the most whole I've felt in a while. It was nice having mom here in front of me, getting to know her again. We laughed and cried, and sometimes we did both. It wasn't until my phone buzzed a few times that I noticed the time.

"Who is it?" Mom asked as she saw the face I made as I looked at my phone. It was Lucas. I had forgotten he had my number now.

Chapter 8

Olive's P.O.V.

The man who makes you scream: What is my Rose up to today?

I have yet to reply to his text, staring at it for hours, deciding on whether I should text back. I had ignored it earlier because I wanted to focus on mom. Now back at Hailey's penthouse, we were both weighing my options.

"He could very well like you. I mean, look, he's texting you the very next day," Hailey argued. She was obviously on team 'get together with Lucas'.

"I don't know, Hails. I feel like I should just avoid him right now. Between school and my mom, now isn't the time for a boyfriend." I sighed.

"Fine, no boyfriend, but you can still sleep with him. Didn't you say he was the best sex you'd had?" She tapped me with her elbow playfully.

"Yes, but I'm worried I'll get too attached. I keep hoping it will be more, but it shouldn't be. It's complicated with him, and I don't need that."

"Ay pues, uncomplicate it. Do what you did the first night, make it only about sex, no going out. No meeting each other's friends or family, just plain old hooking up. Keep the texts to a sexual nature, too," she suggested.

"I don't know, Hails. It feels like I'd be playing with fire." I was reluctant, but sex sounded so good right now. I need a distraction from mom's current condition and I know Lucas could provide me with the best kind.

"Just do it one more time and if you feel like you can't keep your feelings separated, then break it off. Don't leave him hanging." She was laying it on thick.

"Fine," I finally caved. "But what the heck do I say? 'Sorry I took so long to reply. I was busy with my cancer ridden mother' seems like too much of a bummer." Hailey squeezed my hand, feeling sympathy for me. Her face showed me she wished things could be different. I wished the same.

"How about you say you were having some 'me' time?" She wiggled her eyebrows suggestively.

"You want me to tell him I'd been masturbating for the past couple of hours?!" I caught on to what she was saying. She laughed at my reaction.

"Well yeah. I bet he'd find it hot." I let out a laugh at her antics, but decided it was probably the best way to go. I need to keep this conversation centered on sex.

"Fine, but I'm taking this to my room," I told her, getting off the couch.

"You're no fun!" she complained.

Once I got into my room, I locked the door and sat on my bed.

Olive: I was taking care of myself.

I sent the text with a blush on my face. I bit my lip as I waited for him to see it and reply. The suspense was killing me as I saw the three dots appear, letting me know he was typing a response.

The man who makes you scream: Picture, or it didn't happen ;)

I stared at the text, slack jawed. Was he calling my bluff, or did he just want a kinky picture? My heart raced and my stomach pooled with a mixture of nerves and lust. I bit my lip as I undressed, deciding to do what I had said I had already done. I fished my toy out of my underwear drawer.

I somehow propped my phone right, timing a picture just right. I took a few as I pleased myself, somehow getting turned on more, knowing he'd see these pictures. In rapid succession, I sent them as I continued to play with myself, not yet having found my release, but feeling it get close as the vibrator pressed against my clit.

The man who makes you scream: Fuck, Rose. What are you thinking of while you touch yourself?

His texts were getting me hot as I inserted my toy inside myself. Lucas sent a text at the same moment. It was a picture.

The man who makes you scream: I'm thinking of you pleasuring yourself.

The text read under a picture of his hand, caressing his erection.

Olive: I'm thinking about how good it would have felt if we could have finished what we started last night.

I was thinking of Lucas and his sensual touches. Of his hot lips and large hands which know exactly how to touch me. I do hate how I keep yo-yoing back and forth between wanting to stay away from him and wanting him to fuck me every which way.

The man who makes you scream: I would have made it worth your while. I would have undressed you in the living room, before sitting you on my table and eating you for dessert.

His texts were only dampening my core further.

The man who makes you scream: After you would have cum on my face, I would have kissed you so deeply you would taste yourself on my tongue. I would have carried you to my recliner and had you on your knees bent forward. Can you guess what I would have done next?

I felt my breathing and my pace quicken as I read his texts, imagining the things he was saying.

Olive: You would have gripped my hips firmly as you stretched me with your dick. I would have moaned loudly at how good it felt to have you inside me. Then you would have thrust inside me, inevitably making me scream your name.

I could feel myself getting close to reaching my peak, pulling the vibrator back out to my clit.

The man who makes you scream: Shit, Rose. I would have kept thrusting into you after you came again. I would have had you stand and bent you over the arm of my couch, inserting myself back inside you as I played with your sensitive clit, until you clenched my dick again as you came. Eventually, I would have joined you over the edge.

I started a voice recording, feeling myself getting close. I moaned low into the phone, letting his name slip between my lips as I came over my fingers and the vibrator. As my breathing came back to normal, I stopped the recording and sent it to Lucas. About 5 minutes later, I got a picture message back. It was of Lucas' cum all over himself with a text message under it.

The man who makes you scream: That was the hottest thing anyone has ever sent me. I hope you know I'll be saving this for all eternity ;)

I felt myself blush with a heat of embarrassment washing over me. I didn't think about him saving these things. It felt nice knowing he found it so hot. I'd done nothing like this before, and it was fucking hot.

Olive: Just as long as no one else hears it.

The man who makes you scream: Don't worry, Rose, it's for my ears only.

I cleaned off, leaving him on read because I had nothing else to say. I was going to keep this strictly sexual as Hailey advised and see how it goes. Neither my heart nor my head won't get ahead of me again.

The man who makes you scream: Want to get a bite to eat tonight?

He texted again, trying to confuse me with his forward advances, making it seem like he wants more than sex, even though he doesn't.

Olive: No thanks, but I'll come over for a nightcap if you want ;)

Strictly sex.

The man who makes you scream: It is like all you want

me for is sex 3:)

Olive: You catch on quick.

Normally, I would have dissected his text, wondering if he wanted more. I would have obsessed over what he meant by it, but now that I've kept it just about sex, it didn't matter. I am convincing myself all I want from him is sex, and only sex.

The man who makes you scream: My apartment, 8 o'clock. Wear something easy to slip out of.

Olive: See you then.

If I keep telling myself it's just sex, maybe my heart will believe it, too.

Lucas' P.O.V.

Lucas: It is like all you want me for is sex. 3:)

It slightly hurt me by how quickly she had turned my invitation down for dinner. If Janessa hadn't interrupted yesterday, we could have spent all night together. I longed to have her near me when I woke up again. Noting Rose's unease with Janessa, I backed off. I didn't think chasing after her would be the right move, because I doubt she would have believed a word I said, anyway.

Rose: You catch on quick.

Now I feel like I made the wrong choice. I feel her pulling away from me. I'll have to work my way back, but the only way to do it is to do her. So I'll give her what she wants, and then I'll give her more.

Lucas: My apartment, 8 o'clock. Wear something easy to slip out of.

Rose: See you then.

I texted Janessa last night and broke off this long-standing friends with benefits. It slipped my mind she was stopping by last night, and it messed everything up. I won't let something like that happen again. Besides, Janessa may be beautiful, but her personality has always put me off. She's way too arrogant, calling my Rose trash.

I hated the way Rose left last night, and I had planned to make it up to her, but she kept me waiting for a couple of hours before responding. Then we got off track with the hottest sexting. Now I see she would have turned me down anyway, no matter the time of day in which she responded.

I got up to grab a snack from the kitchen, practically tripping over Leo's guitar case. He said he would come by and pick it up last night, but I guess he forgot. I grabbed an apple, hearing the crisp crunch as I bit into it.

Lucas: Your guitar is still here.

Loe: Yeah, I got sidetracked last night. I'll come get it tonight.

There's no way I'm letting anyone ruin tonight. I will have no surprise, or planned visits, tonight.

Lucas: Not tonight. I have plans, get it before 8.

Leo: Another girl or Janessa?

I don't know why his question highly irritated me, but it did. He used to ask me that question before and it wouldn't bother me. I don't know why it does now. Maybe because Rose isn't the option?

Lucas: Neither. It's Rose.

Leo: Leave her alone, Lucas. She wants more than just sex.

I don't know where Leo gets off telling me to leave her alone. Where did he even get the idea she wants more? She literally told me, in not so many words, she wants only sex from me. I want more, and I have to get her to want more, too.

Lucas: So do I.

Leo: Bull!

Lucas: No crap here.

Leo: I'm coming to your apartment now.

With a shrug, I put my phone on the counter face down. I headed to my office, needing to get some work done. I know Dad will breathe down my neck more now since I pissed him off last night. He didn't like that I had brought Rose with me.

He told me the only reason he didn't kick her out was because she actually knew his guests. My anger boiled when I thought of him mistreating my Rose. I told him I wouldn't be his puppet any longer, and I had no more patience for this game. I warned him if he attempted to marry Lisa off, I wouldn't be taking over his business.

I bit the bullet and started my business during my sophomore year. I made my first million a few years ago. Managing both my company and Dad's keeps me pretty busy most of the time. Being with Rose had distracted me yesterday, making me fall behind. I'll get caught up and then get ahead on the paperwork, leaving me time to focus on her. About 20 minutes into my work, I heard my door open. I had given Leo and Lisa keys to my apartment; they were the only two I trust or want in this apartment.

"Lucas?" I heard him yell out.

"In my office."

He entered, looking upset. Something had made him mad, but he was trying to hold it back. He has a bad habit of playing with his lip piercing when he's upset, and the thing was swinging like a pendulum. I sighed, already seeing I won't be able to get this work done with his current mood. He came to talk about something.

"I'm going after, Olive," he proclaimed, shocking the absolute hell out of me. It took me a moment to collect my thoughts and respond.

"You're what?"

"I'm going to ask Olive out. I was going to leave her alone when I thought you would make her happy, but after I saw her last night, I decided I'd take my chances with her," he informed me. I'd never seen Leo so determined. My stomach was twisting in knots. I don't want to fight with Leo, but I'm not letting him have Rose, either. She's mine, and I plan to make her admit it tonight. I furrowed my brow at him, letting him see how serious I was, too. I stood up, walking to the other side of my desk.

"I'm not giving her up, Leo. I've already made her mine."

"You need to let her go, Lucas. You're only going to hurt her, and she doesn't deserve that. She looked so sad when I ran into her in the hall." He shook his head at the memory.

"You saw her last night?" So he had come for his guitar, but ran into Rose on the way.

"Yeah, we talked about you as I drove her home. She's hurt, and at first I tried to make excuses for you, but after she left my car, I had this nagging feeling in my stomach. She doesn't deserve to be hurt by you, so I decided I'll actually try for once. Lucas, you're my best friend, but I've seen the way you have been treating women here lately, and it's not what Olive deserves." He was firm in his belief. He stood proudly, his head held high. Normally I would have been proud of him for standing up for himself and going after what he wanted, but what he wants is what *I* want.

"I hear what you're saying, Leo, but I don't plan on backing down. So, I guess all that's left is for Rose to make her choice. I hope you're prepared if you're going to challenge me for her heart, my friend, because I plan to go all out," I warned him, making him nod his head, not backing down.

"I don't doubt it, but I have my ways, too. I know it will be stupid of me to hope this doesn't affect our friendship." His face fell for a moment. "I just hope we'll be able to fix it in the end."

"You're still my best friend, Leo. I won't hold it against you if she chooses you. I hope you'd feel the same way." He nodded his head in agreement. I extended my hand for him to take, and he did. We shook, as if promising those words.

"We need rules," he blurted. "We can't interrupt one another. Like if we know we have plans with her, the other can't butt in."

"Sounds fair. As you know, I have plans with her tonight at 8." I nodded.

"Okay, so I'll stay away. I'll tell you if she and I ever have plans."

"If it's just hanging out, then it's free game, but if it's a date or a hookup, we'll keep away," I added. Otherwise Leo would get a lot more time with her than me, since he sees her on campus sometimes.

"Agreed." Leo nodded. "May the best man get the girl." Leo left, shortly after, taking his guitar with him. I watched him leave, feeling anxious now. I don't want to lose Leo as my friend, but I also can't stand the thought of not having my Rose.

The rest of the afternoon was spent finishing my paperwork. I ordered dinner, finishing right at 7. I took a quick shower before Rose showed up. I had my pants on, with a towel draped over my bare shoulders as I dried my hair with it. The doorbell rang, making me answer it with my still damp hair.

My Rose stood before me. She was early, looking fine as hell.

Chapter 9

Olive's P.O.V.

    I over-thought about my outfit about a million times. Not wanting to dress up for a hookup, but also not wanting to look like a slob. Deciding on something to wear felt like an impossible task until Hailey entered the room. She gave me a sweet, sleeveless, dark blue sundress which was both cute and casual. It was just right.

    There was no need for me to do my makeup, since all we would do was have sex. I kicked myself in the ass when I realized I had shown up early because the traffic was lighter. Lucas opened the door, shirtless, with damp hair, clearly having just showered. He looked hot as hell, as usual.

    I caged my bottom lip between my teeth, admiring his chiseled abs and tattoos. The heavens must have sent this man down with how damn handsome he was. His sexy smirk was ever present as he reached for my hand, pulling me into the apartment. The moment the door closed behind me, he pinned me against the wall beside it. He leaned his face down, a few inches away from me. The feel of his breath fanning across my face sent my heart thundering against my chest.

    "Couldn't wait to have me, could you?" The raised brow on his face showed I had inflated his ego. I shrugged my shoulders.

    "Not necessarily." Our eyes never broke apart, captivated by one another. He let out a laugh as he stood straight, letting my body cave in disappointment when he stepped away.

"I see," he said before walking away towards the kitchen.

My lungs strained as I tried to take a deep breath to calm my nerves. Did I upset him? Trailing him into the kitchen, I watched him put a dish in the sink. As he rested against the counter, he turned his body towards me with his arms crossed in front of him.

"How do you want to do this, Rose? What are we?" His questions caught me off guard. Is this him making sure we are on the same page? Does he think I'm trying to trap him or something?

"I don't know, hook up buddies?" I shrugged my shoulders. "You're a much needed distraction. I'm here to let you do what you want with my body, as long as you make me scream your name the way you do."

I struggled to keep the warmth from rising to my cheeks, trying to avoid a blush. I had never uttered such words in my life, and it made me feel so out of place. My hands moved nervously behind my back as I avoided eye contact, instead focusing on the pattern of the tiles on the counter.

"Are you sure? You're willing to let me do whatever I like to your body as long as it brings you pleasure?" He took a step closer, making me feel slightly intimidated. I know there's still a lot I don't know about sex with my limited experience. Lucas has a ton, which made me feel inferior. I was eager to learn all I could from him, to determine what I like and don't like, so I had to allow him to take control. Even if I am not convinced it is the right thing to do.

"I'm sure," I spoke confidently, finally lifting my head to meet his eyes. The look he gave me made my stomach swirl with butterflies in anticipation. He had the look of a wolf ready to consume its prey, and I wondered whether giving him absolute power over me may not have been the best decision. Inching closer towards me, he removed the towel from his shoulders and cast it onto the counter. His powerful arm came around me, gripping my waist and holding me tightly against his chest.

"Don't worry, Rose. I'll bring you all the pleasure imaginable. No other man will come close to making you feel the way I do. You won't be able to look at them without thinking of me," he promised, making me shiver with his words.

I swallowed hard, feeling way over my head right now. Lucas slid his hand down behind my thigh, lifting my leg up and wrapping it around his torso. His hand carefully slid under my dress, securely grabbing my exposed thigh as he leaned me back and tenderly kissed me with his burning lips. His kiss filled me with an intensity I have never felt before, and as he squeezed my thigh, his fingertips dug into my skin. Without breaking our kiss, he picked me up, wrapping my other leg around his torso.

As I embraced him, I placed my hands on either side of his face, deepening the kiss and squeezing my thighs tightly around him. I thought he was taking me to his room, but I was mistaken. Instead, he took us to a room I hadn't been in before. He pushed me against the wall of the dark chamber, lifting my wrists above my head as he fiddled with something above me. It was difficult to make out what was happening, but I could feel something encircling my wrist before it was let go. He did the same to my other hand, making me realize he had tied me up.

My heart raced with the thrill of something new. I was nervous, but mainly excited as I wondered what he planned on doing to me. He slowly released my lips and moved his mouth down my neck, planting gentle kisses on my collar bone before tugging my strapless dress and bra down. His hands slid all my clothes off me in one fluid movement. I was fully exposed, standing against the wall, gripping the binding around my wrist, needing something to hold.

Lucas stepped away from me, turning on a dim lamp as he opened a drawer, returning with a toy I had never seen before. I swallowed hard again as excitement and nervousness swirled together inside me. My core became warm as I envisioned the many things he would do to me. With the muted light, I could make out the curves of his face, his expression one of ravenous hunger.

He licked my chest up to my neck, forcing his tongue into my mouth. His lips gave me the hungriest kiss yet. I felt out of breath as he pulled away. He ran his finger over my slit, reveling in the wetness pooling in my folds. The slightly cold silicone of the toy slid between my wet folds as he rubbed it outside of me. It vibrated when he turned it on, circling it around my clit with a teasing motion. Never breaking eye contact as he did it. He watched me closely as my breathing picked up.

"You're so damn sexy, Rose," he whispered into my ear as he sucked on my earlobe for a second. He inserted the vibrating toy inside of me, surprising me as he used it to pleasure me. He pulled the toy in and out of me, sliding it out to rub against my clit. His pace was slow, teasing me further. The pleasure grew inside me, leaking out between my thighs. "You're dripping wet for me, Rose, but I haven't heard you moan once. Don't hold back on me," He instructed me, making me realize I had been biting my tongue this whole time.

He quickly inserted the toy inside me again, causing me to gasp. He then kneeled down in front of me, flicking his tongue over my clit. I couldn't hold back anymore, and moaned emphatically, as he wanted. I saw him smirk with pleasure as he continued to flick his tongue over my bundle of nerves. My back arched in pleasure as he sucked on it, causing another louder moan to escape my mouth. My hands gripped onto the binds harder as I swayed my hips. Lucas moved the toy inside of me as he continued to eat me. Eventually, he pulled the toy out, having it vibrate on my clit as he inserted his tongue inside of me instead.

"Fuck Lucas, don't stop." I moaned as I felt myself getting close.

He quickened his pace and applied pressure with the toy on my clit. It didn't take long for me to fall over the edge with a high-pitched moan. Lucas licked it all up like he'd been starving. His lips glistened with my pleasure as he looked back up at me. He slid the toy further back, reaching my ass. My cheeks puckered, never having had anything near them. The toy slid between my ass cheeks, with the slickness of myself, on it.

"Relax, Rose." I heard Lucas tell me as he felt me tense.

I took a deep breath, trying to calm myself about having a toy near my rear end. When Lucas noticed my muscles were still tensed, he sucked at my throbbing clit, making me moan. I focused on the sensation, letting my body turn into a puddle in his hands. He rubbed the toy around my puckered hole before slowly inserting it inside me. It felt uncomfortable as hell at first, but Lucas kept me focused on the pleasure he was giving my clit. After a moment, I had gotten used to the feel of the slim, small toy inside my ass. Lucas left it vibrating in me as he stood up, taking his pants and boxers off.

His enormous shaft stood at attention, making me lick my lips in anticipation. My arms were still high above me, keeping me from grabbing onto him. My legs wrapped around his hips as he lined himself up with my entrance. He pushed inside me, making me feel full between the toy in my ass and his dick in my front. His quick thrusts made me yell with pleasure. The vibrations from the toy with Lucas' thrusts had me reaching my next peak quickly.

"*Lucas!*" I yelled his name as the waves of ecstasy crashed over me. He didn't stop slapping into me, taking the hardened bud of my nipple in his mouth. His hips swirled in a circular motion, wiping around the walls of my core. I felt him hit a special spot, making me quiver over him. He pounded into me harder and faster than before.

"Tell me only I have ever brought you this kind of pleasure, Rose. Yell my name again," Lucas spoke in his sultry voice as he continued, causing waves of pleasure to flow through me.

"Only you, Lucas." I moaned as I swayed my hips over

him.

It was true. I know I have only had two sexual partners, but I know even if I had more, Lucas would probably still have been the best one. His experiences gave him an upper hand over the rest. He wasn't afraid to experiment, and he had no shame, which made you feel less self-conscious. I didn't feel ridiculous or judged by him. He wanted to bring me pleasure anyway he could. He quickened his pace inside me, feeling me getting close again.

"Come with me, Rose." He whispered in my ear, causing goosebumps to erupt as I came, tightening my walls around his shaft. I felt his warm seed spurt deep inside me at the same time.

"Lucas." I let his name slip from my lips as I came crashing down. Lucas quickly untied my hands and removed the toy from my rear, as everything felt fuzzy. My head was spinning in pure ecstasy, but I saw stars as I went limp in Lucas' arms.

"Shit," I heard Lucas swear under his breath before everything went dark.

My eyes felt heavy as I stirred. My hands rubbed against the silky material of the softest sheets I'd ever felt. This was not my bed. I knew as much, but I could not remember where I was before I went to bed. The smell of his cologne wafted into my lungs as a powerful reminder of where I was and what had taken place. I was in Lucas' bed alone. I found my phone on the nightstand, checking the time to see it was 1 o'clock in the morning already. I grabbed the sides of my head as I sat up, feeling it pound. My head throbbed, and my arms felt so sore. Lucas quickly appeared at my side.

"I'm so sorry, Rose. I went too far." He bit his lip anxiously, looking me over. "Here, take this, and drink the whole glass." He handed me some painkillers with a tall glass of water. I took it, chugging the refreshingly cool liquid after.

"What happened?" I asked him hoarsely.

"Your blood pressure plummeted after the high I

brought you. I am sorry, Rose. I got carried away." He looked so riddled with guilt as he watched me.

"Are you kidding? It was amazing." I smirked at him. I didn't want him to feel bad because of my inexperience. Honestly, what he did was incredible and I wouldn't mind doing it again. Some of the worry faded from his face as he chuckled. His intense eyes softened on me for a moment.

"How are you feeling?" he asked.

"Fine, aside from a headache." I shrugged, looking around the room for my clothes. When I couldn't find it, I looked at Lucas again. "Where are my clothes? I need to get going."

"Rose, no. It's late and you need to rest before you move." he said sternly.

"It's fine. Hailey can come get me, and she'll watch over me," I assured him. It would be better for me to stay here, but I know it will only muddy the waters again. I have to remember this is only for sex. Sleeping here won't help me keep focus on that. Lucas looked sad, but in the blink of an eye, it was gone, making me wonder if I had imagined it.

"Fine, but I'll drive you home and make sure you make it inside," he told me sternly.

I nodded my head, mainly because I didn't want to bother Hailey this late. Even if this whole thing was her idea. He disappeared for a moment, coming back with my clothes. I got dressed with him, watching the entire time. He pulled a shirt over his sweatpants, looking comfortable and yet still so sexy. I will keep a mental picture of him in sweats and store it next to the mental image of him in his suit yesterday. Lucas held his hand out for me to take, but I shook my head. Holding hands seemed too intimate.

When I didn't grab his hand, he placed his arm around my waist, grabbing my hip on the opposite side. He held me firmly, making me realize he wasn't wanting to hold my hand. He was trying to give me something to hold in case I felt faint again. I bit my lip, feeling guilty as he walked us out of his apartment. We made it to his car with no trouble. I still felt a little lightheaded, but it was small.

The car ride was silent and uncomfortable. I felt like I should say something, but I wasn't sure what. Lucas must have been feeling the same way. I think he still felt guilty as he bit at the back of his finger on the arm resting on his door. He looked so handsome even when he was worried. His face was serious as he drove. I could tell he was trying to think of something to say, too. We reached the apartment building without either of us being able to exchange any words.

Lucas opened my door, helping me out. This time, I took his hand when he offered it. He gave it a squeeze when I did. He appreciated the fact I accepted it this time. We walked in silence to the elevator, but by then I couldn't take it anymore. I had to say something or I would lose my mind in this quiet. I wasn't the only one feeling this way, as we both spoke at the same time.

"I'm sorry I-" He started.

"I truly enjoyed-" We both laughed at each other.

"Don't feel guilty, Lucas, and please don't apologize. I enjoyed myself and I would hate to have it ruined with a memory of you feeling guilty over it," I told him, not able to look him in the eyes as I did. He grabbed my chin, gently lifting it until I met those intense chocolate eyes. He leaned down, kissing me so tenderly. It wasn't like the kisses we share when we have sex. It was sweet and gentle and had my feelings mixing up again.

"Thank you, Rose. I'll do better next time," he whispered to me as the elevator doors opened. He walked me to the penthouse door, watching me unlock it and enter.

"Goodnight, Olive." I heard him say as I closed the door.

I leaned against the door for a moment before I turned and looked through the peephole. I saw him in the elevator, leaning back against the gold rail. He looked sullen as the elevator doors closed. I sighed, trying to shake the need to comfort him.

It's just sex.

"Have you made an appointment yet?" Mom asked me as I sat on her bed, eating the jello she told me she couldn't stomach.

"It's the weekend, mom. Doctor's office isn't open," I reminded her.

"Promise me you'll call first thing tomorrow." She looked so concerned as she met my eyes.

"I promise. Don't worry, Mom, I'll get it done." She nodded her head, closing her eyes again. She looked exhausted today, but any time I would offer to leave, to let her rest, she'd wake herself back up. I didn't want her to wake up and not find me here.

"I'll be right back, Mom. I'm going down to the cafeteria to get something else to snack on. Keep resting." I kissed her forehead before leaving. It took me a good minute to find the cafeteria, getting lost in the hospital about a million times. Why are hospitals so hard for me to navigate? I pushed open the doors, finding a couple of things that looked rather good. I paid, but as I was about to leave, I heard a familiar voice call my name.

"Olive?" I turned to see Leo sitting at a table by himself near the doors. I furrowed my brow at him, not expecting to see him here.

"Leo?" I cocked my head to the side.

"What are you doing here?" he asked me as I walked towards him.

"Visiting my mom. What about you?"

"Visiting my dad." He looked down for a moment.

"Is he okay?" I asked, feeling something was wrong.

"We're pulling the plug on him today," he explained, crushing my heart.

I placed my things down on the table, grabbing his arms

and making him stand. He furrowed his brow at me for a moment, but I wrapped my arms around him in a tight hug. I felt him melt into the embrace as he wrapped his arms back around me. I held him close for a while, knowing he needs more than this, but it was the only thing I had to offer.

"I am so sorry, Leo. I had no idea." My voice barely carried in the air, with my head resting against his chest.

"It's okay. Thank you, Olive." He sighed. "He's been on life support for a year now, but there's no improvement. Mom finally decided it was time," he explained.

"I am so sorry," I said again, sounding like a broken record, but what else is there to say? He squeezed me for a moment before letting me go. I let him go too, but neither of us stepped back, keeping the space between us small.

"Is your mom okay?" he asked, and I wasn't sure how to answer. I didn't want to tell him she had cancer. He has his own problems to worry about today.

"Leo, it's time." I heard a familiar voice call from the silver double doors. I turned to see Lucas in the doorway, looking at his phone.

"I'm coming." Leo told him, making Lucas look up. Confusion, worry, and guilt crossed his features quickly.

"Rose, are you okay? Are you still dizzy?" He took a step towards me, stopping himself as he saw Leo.

"I'm fine, not here for me. Don't worry," I assured him, turning my attention back on Leo. "I'm sorry, Leo. I'm here if you need to talk."

He nodded with a sad smile. He wrapped his arms around me again, hugging me one last time before leaving. Lucas hung at the door for a second longer, watching me for a moment before he followed Leo. I picked my things up, heading back up to mom. Leo stayed in my mind. I'll be in his shoes soon. Mom doesn't have much time left. When I arrived, they told me her condition was declining, and we would be lucky if she made it through the week.

Every free moment I have I'll be spending here with

her. I will only leave her side to go to class. I may even skip a couple this week. Like my English class and perhaps the easier math class I have. A heavy sigh left me as I wondered how anyone deals with losing a parent. I'll have to check in on Leo tomorrow. I am glad he had Lucas there for him. It's important to have people around you when you're going through something major.

"Ew, mom, no!" I laughed as she tried to tell me the story of my conception. "No, child should *ever* hear how they were made."

She laughed with me, causing her to cough hard. I poured her a glass of water, and she took it with shaky hands. I went to my morning classes today, but my mind had stayed on mom, and then on Leo. Honestly, I was so distracted. It was like I hadn't attended class at all. I emailed my professors and let them know what was going on. They were all very understanding and compassionate, giving me my assignments ahead of time. I was working on one as mom and I spoke.

"What about you, sweetheart? Do you have a special boy in your life?" She raised a brow.

"Not exactly." I blushed, thinking of Lucas. How would I describe him to mom?

"Oh? Who did you just think of?"

"His name is Lucas," I admitted. "But he isn't interested in a relationship, at least not a serious one."

"Are you? Wanting a serious relationship?" she asked, curiously. I just nodded my head.

"Yeah, I do, but not yet."

Mom and I spoke for a while, where I told her all about Julius and what had happened. We spoke about how he took my virginity and catching him cheating on me. Mom joined me in trash talking him until we were laughing again. She coughed every time we laughed. It was breaking my heart to see her this way. She rested her eyes after our talk, feeling exhausted. I hated seeing cancer eat away at her body. I finally got her back to only get maybe a week with her. There's too much to talk about, to fit it all into one week.

    I felt my phone vibrate in my pocket, snapping me from my depressing thoughts. The name flashing on my screen made my chest hurt.

Chapter 10

Olive's P.O.V.

Dad had called, but I ignored it. I didn't want to talk to him right now, especially not by mom. It's his fault I missed all these years with her. It's his fault she had to run away. How could he ever hurt her like that? I watched mom sleep, wondering how she endured him for 10 years. She was strong in her own way.

I used this time to call my doctor and get myself checked. She placed an order with the hospital I was at to take my blood and have it tested. I would have the results in two weeks, and we'd talk about options once she had them. She then scheduled me for a breast screening at the end of the month. I checked in on mom again, seeing she was still asleep.

"Sorry to bother you, Nancy." I spoke to the nurse at the round desk. "Can you please let my mother know I went to get my blood drawn if she wakes up wondering where I went?"

"Of course, darling. No problem." She answered in her sweet southern accent. I'd only ever heard it in movies, having lived in the north all my life. It was adorable to listen to.

"I am glad you got it going," Mom told me the next day.

She had slept for the rest of my visit Monday, but I had stayed by her side anyway, only going home once it had gotten dark. Neither Lucas nor Leo had texted me yesterday or today, which was fine. I know Leo is going through a lot, and I'm sure

Lucas is by his side. I didn't text them myself, feeling like I would be a nuisance right now.

"She told me I would get my results in a couple of weeks."

You might not be here to hear them.

The thought had my chest squeezing in pain. A depressed and overwhelmed feeling clutched at my heart. I wanted to cure her cancer. I wished there was something I could do for her, but there's nothing. My phone vibrated once, letting me know I had a text.

Leo: How's your mom?

He just lost his father, but he was checking in on me. He shouldn't be worrying about me.

Olive: Not well. How are you holding up?

I asked him, wishing there was more I could do or say to make him feel better. I've only known him a week, but in that week I've seen Leo had a gentle heart. He's kind, and he's funny. He's clumsy, but still somehow cool.

Leo: Not well.

Olive: I am so sorry, Leo. Is there anything I can do for you?

I have a lot on my plate right now, but I would add on to it, if it would help him.

Leo: Distract me.

Olive: No problem! Are you wanting memes? Dark humor? Or maybe a rundown of my life? Lol, kidding about the last one.

I will scour the internet for the best memes to make him laugh, but not really sure what his sense of humor is.

Leo: Actually, the rundown of your life seemed the most interesting of my options. Haha.

I slapped my forehead so hard I almost woke mom back up. She stirred for a moment, taking a deep breath. She was still beautiful despite her graying complexion.

Olive: Oof, I would need lots of alcohol and about 3 hours of your life. Lol.

Leo: I'll bring the alcohol if you tell me what you like to drink, because I clearly don't know.

He referred to his choice of drink for me at The Tunnel Nightclub on Friday.

Olive: Deal! Bring Whiskey, I need to feel the burn, and whiskey always gets me talking about deeper things in life. Hospital roof sound good?

I honestly don't think I've ever opened up about my past to anyone, aside from Davis. Hailey knows the most about me, but even with her I hadn't told her about my mom or dad until last week when I found out mom had cancer and needed someone to talk to.

Leo: Yeah, that's fine. I'll come around 7 tonight. Hope it's okay. Lucas is coming too. I haven't been able to get him to leave me alone.

Another loud forehead slap had mom stirring. I am sure my forehead is red now. I sighed, because telling Lucas about my life feels different from telling Leo. It feels more intimate which I am not a fan of.

Olive: In that case, I'm going to need more alcohol.

Leo: No problem. Thank you, Olive. I appreciate this.

That was enough to make me feel better about the whole thing. I took a deep breath, letting the nerves fly away.

Olive: I got you, Leo! Also, call me Liv.

Leo: Okay, Liv. See you at 7.

I refocused on my schoolwork, not trying to fall behind in my senior year. It feels impossible to get out of the hole you dig if you miss too much work or class.

🌹

"There she is, the woman of the hour," Leo greeted me with open arms as I walked through the roof door.

I wasn't sure if the door would lock behind me, so I left a wooden block as a wedge. Leo greeted me with a big hug. I felt his arms wrap around me and squeeze me tightly. He inhaled deeply, slumping his shoulders, sniffling as he pulled away. He was trying to bite back the tears. I could see my future in him right now. I'll probably be the same way in a week.

"Do I get one of those too?" Lucas asked with a smirk, his arms held open.

I pondered over it for a moment, but Lucas didn't give me much of a choice. He took me in his arms, squeezing me gently. I melted into the hug, wrapping my arms around him, too. His sandalwood and vanilla cologne attacked my lungs, making me dizzy with lust for a moment. I was the one to pull back first, when I realized this hug had become a long embrace.

"Okay, where's the whiskey?" I asked, looking around.

Lucas handed me the bottle.

"No glasses?" I asked.

"Nope. The bottle is for you. Leo and I are drinking beer," Lucas explained, holding up a 6 pack.

"Perfect." I smiled. I opened the bottle, chugging a good amount, feeling like I incinerated my chest. Lucas and Leo stared at me with wide eyes as I downed a quarter of the bottle in one go.

"Damn," Lucas muttered with a smirk, as if he enjoyed seeing the way I could handle my liquor. Leo, on the other hand, had his brows slightly furrowed with concern.

"Where do you want me to start?" I asked Leo, because tonight is about making him feel better, even if it's at my expense.

"At the beginning, tell me about your childhood." Leo smiled. Poor guy probably doesn't realize he's asking for the worst years of my life.

"Okay, one second." I drank more whiskey, to their surprise.

"Is it that hard for you to open up?" Lucas raised a brow.

"You'll see. We should probably sit." I pointed to the folding chairs set out here, probably by staff members. After we each took a seat, I took a deep breath and dove right in.

"I grew up in New Hampshire, in a small house on a

winding road. We didn't have close neighbors, and looking back at it now, I know it was on purpose. My father didn't want others hearing the screams." They both looked at each other for a moment as I stared at the ground. I took another swig.

"My mom, dad, and I were only ever a picture perfect family in public, but behind closed doors my father would abuse my mother. I am not sure when it started or why, but as long as I can remember, they would fight. It always started with yelling, leading to things being thrown, and eventually him hitting her."

"Olive...Liv, you don't have to. I'm sorry I didn't realize." Leo shook his head.

"No, it's fine. It's too late now. I've already drunk quite a lot." I smiled. "Anyway, my dad was an MMA fighter, so his punches were always hard. One time I got in front of my mom, trying to keep him from hurting her, but in his fit of rage, he pushed me away to get to her. I hit my head on the corner of the kitchen counter, splitting my forehead open." I touched the scar, remembering the warmth of my blood flowing down my face. I have to continue this story now that I have started it.

"A month after the incident, mom left us. She didn't take me with her and she never contacted me again until last week. Dad raised me from the age of 10 until the second I turned 18. He taught me to fight, and he taught me how to be safe, but the man showed no affection. Not a single hug or a simple I love you. He was cold, and for the first few years, he was determined to find my mother. I had to take care of myself since he had turned into an alcoholic. Eventually, he realized he wouldn't find her and gave up. Which only dove him deeper into the alcohol." Leo and Lucas were so quiet, they were listening attentively. Leo looked at me with deep concern while Lucas had his hands fisted beside him, looking mad as hell.

"My 8th grade year a teacher noticed my giftedness and had me apply for a scholarship to a private high school with a high rate for getting kids into Ivy League colleges. Dad sobered up around then, realizing he was failing as a father. He had to drive me to the high school since it was so far and they didn't have buses. I would get picked on a lot by the students there, since I was the scholarship kid who came from nothing." I picked at the string poking out on my pants, feeling the need to fidget with something as I spoke.

"I hate people like that. Money doesn't make a person. I am sorry you went through all of that, Liv," Leo told me, reaching for my hand and squeezing it.

"Thanks, but *they* definitely believed differently. I did well in my studies and worked part time to save for college for most of high school. Eventually, I got my acceptance letter to Columbia, and it made it all worthwhile. I was pretty sheltered in high school because of my lack of friends. So I never attended a high school party, or even had a boyfriend. Hailey was the one to burst me out of my bubble freshman year of college." I smiled at the thought of her.

"She took me to my first party where I had my first kiss over a stupid pass the card game. The guy made the card fall so he could kiss me. His name was Adam, and he was a senior. He tried to get me to do more, but I refused, and when he didn't take no for an answer, I beat the shit out of him."

"Of course you did." Lucas smiled at me proudly, making me smile too.

"I am, to this day, still not allowed to any parties on sorority row." I let a laugh out. "Hailey still found other parties for us to attend, and during the second semester of freshman year, I met Julius." I sighed, remembering the feelings I held for him once upon a time. "He was my first boyfriend, but I was still a virgin and I didn't want to hand it over after having held on to it for so long. We dated and eventually he asked me to be his girlfriend. I stupidly said yes, and in the spring of sophomore year I slept with him for the first time. I should have known he had been cheating on me. What guy would be with a girl for a year and be fine and dandy not sleeping with her the entire time?"

"If it were with you, I would be," Leo quickly responded, making me blush a bit.

"Almost a month ago I walked in on him fucking my roommate, Clover, for God knows how many times. He tried to tell me it meant nothing, but it didn't matter. I don't forgive unfaithfulness, ever." I looked at Lucas as I said this; I am not sure why I felt the need for him to know this. He nodded his head for me to continue.

"That's when Hailey offered for me to stay with her and forced me out to the club where I met this one." I pointed to Lucas with a smile. "It was meant to be a one-night stand to show Julius, and myself, I was just fine."

"Okay, wait, so you're telling me I'm only the second guy you've slept with?" Lucas asked with a shit-eating grin.

"Yes, that's right. Don't get a big head about it. Anyway, I met you and saw him again, and here we are." I summarized.

"Wait, you didn't say why you're here. What's going on with your mom?" Leo cocked his head to the side.

"My dad called me the night you dropped me off," I told Leo. " He told me my mom had gotten a hold of him. She is in hospice here. I wasn't sure if I wanted to see her after the way she left me, but I couldn't deny the little girl in me who wanted her mother. My mom told me her side of things and now I'm using the little time I have left to catch up and talk as often as we can. She has breast cancer, and she's having me get screened. They took my blood yesterday and I'll have results in a couple of weeks, but she doesn't have too much time left. She probably won't be around by the time I get them."

Saying it out loud killed me, making my heart shatter. A dot of water fell on my pants, making me think it was raining until I realized it was a tear. I had begun to cry without noticing. Leo knelt before me, pulling me into a tight embrace. I only cried harder in his arms. I hadn't realized how sad I had been. Between telling them my life story, the alcohol, and the embrace, I was letting everything out.

"We're here for you, Rose." Lucas' voice came from

beside me. He wiped at my tears as Leo continued to hold me.

"I'm sorry. I am supposed to be comforting *you*, Leo." I sniffled as my tears slowed. He pulled back, letting me go. I wiped the rest of my tears with my sleeve.

"You already have. I am sorry I had you spill your life's secrets to us. I honestly wasn't expecting it to be that way. You're such a bright person. I assumed you'd tell me these wonderful things about your life. Liv, you're amazing! Considering the things you've been through, I am surprised you're still able to smile so beautifully. You even care enough to comfort someone you met a week ago. Thank you," he whispered before kissing my forehead, surprising me. His lips were soft and warm, and I could still feel them on my skin when he pulled away.

The rest of our time was spent talking about frivolous things. We laughed at Leo and Lucas' expense as they retold embarrassing stories of one another. They wrestled with each other playfully when they got upset about the very embarrassing stories. I let out a loud laugh at them, making them stop. They both smiled at me with their arms around one another.

"I better head back down. Mom will probably wake up one last time before going to sleep again."

"Can we come?" Lucas asked.

"Yes, I would love to meet your mother before we can't." Leo added, getting a slap to the back of the head by Lucas.

"Idiot, don't word it like that," he scolded him. I laughed again, feeling at peace for once. Maybe it was the alcohol in my system, but I nodded my head.

"Okay, but don't be loud, and remember, she has cancer. She doesn't look her best." I pointed my finger at them in a sort of warning.

"Yes, ma'am." Leo saluted, making me chuckle again.

"Come on, then." I walked them down to her room.

We were all definitely drunk as we stumbled a bit. Lucas and Leo sounded like schoolgirls with their giggling and shushing. They sobered up when we got to my mom's room. They stood straight, clearing their throats and pushing their hair back. The two of them were almost like twins with the same mannerisms.

"Mom?" I called her name softly. I found her sitting up in her bed with a thick book on her lap.

"Hey, Livie, I was wondering where you wandered off to." She smiled sweetly at me.

"Are you feeling up to meeting a couple of my friends?" I asked her shyly.

"Are you sure? You want me to meet them?" She looked so happy, almost as if I had told her she wouldn't be dying this week.

"Yeah, I mean, if you're up for it." I picked at the sides of my fingers as I spoke.

"Of course!" She smiled, sitting up straighter.

"Come on in, guys," I called out to them. "Mom, this is Leo and *this* is Lucas." I pointed to each of them.

"Oh, I see." Mom raised a brow, appraising Lucas since she partially knew what he was to me. "It's lovely to meet you handsome young men. I am Abigail Rose, Olive's mother. You can call me Abi." I forget mom's maiden name is Rose. It's funny Lucas calls me Rose.

"The pleasure is all mine, Abi." Lucas gave her a dazzling smile, making my heart skip at the sight.

"It's nice to meet the woman who created Olive," Leo added with his own sweet smile.

"You both seem polite enough, but sadly, I don't have enough time to get to know you better. So, let me just say if either of you hurt my baby girl, I will crawl out from my grave and drag you down to hell with me." Mom scared me for a moment with the casual way she just threatened them.

"I wouldn't dream of hurting her," Leo responded first.

"You have my word. I'll do nothing but please your daughter," Lucas assured her, making me blush deeply.

"Good." Mom nodded at them both. We spent another

hour together, the four of us talking. It was nice seeing mom get to know them both. I have to be sure to bring Hailey tomorrow. I need mom to meet my best friend too.

"We should go. It's getting late," I told mom, seeing her yawn for the 5th time now. She didn't want us to go, but I knew she was growing tired.

"Are you sure?" She asked, almost sadly.

"Yeah, but I'll be back in the morning." I kissed her forehead as I told her.

"Are you sure you should be missing so much school?" She was concerned about my studies.

"Yes, mom, it's fine. I've already spoken to my professors," I assured her. "Get some rest. I'll see you tomorrow."

"Okay, Livie. Goodnight."

"Goodnight, Mom."

I closed the door to her room behind us. Okay, now how do I say goodbye to these two?

Chapter 11

Lucas' P.O.V.

I couldn't get my thoughts straight ever since Rose told us her story. I was glad I tagged along. I never would have believed she had such a sad story to tell. She's so strong and resilient. I think I understand why she's like that now. I wanted to be angry at her mother for abandoning her, but how can I be? Her mom is a victim too, and now she's dying. The only person to be pissed at is her father, and I plan to find out who he is exactly. I'll rain hell down on his life for what he's done.

Rose stood before us, her head was held high, but her eyes were on the ground. She was thinking. About what? I'm not sure. Leo was the first to speak. He had been through hell these past couple of days, and being with Rose was the first time I had seen him relaxed.

"Thank you for tonight, Liv. Know I'm here for you, whatever you need. We half orphans gotta stick together." I know he was trying to be funny, but it was poor timing. Her mom wasn't dead yet, and bringing it up made Rose's face scrunch for a moment. I slapped Leo upside the head again, giving him a 'you're so stupid' look as I stared at him.

"Sorry." He scratched at the back of his neck.

"It's fine." She gave him a small smile, but I could tell it wasn't real. I stepped forward, grabbing her hand without asking. I couldn't hug her earlier because Leo had beaten me to it. So, I pulled her flush against my chest and wrapped my arms tightly around her. I kissed the top of her head before I spoke.

"You're amazing, Rose," I whispered into her ear,

wanting her to know how I looked at her. "Text me when you need me, and I'll show up."

"We'll see you later," Leo called to her as we walked off. Leo was silent as we made our way to my car. I could tell he was deep in thought, but I wasn't sure what about. There's so much happening right now, it's impossible to tell what's going on in his mind. He stopped walking for a moment, making me stop to turn and look at him.

"What's up?" I furrowed my brow at him in concern.

"Do you think she regrets telling us?" His piercing was moving left and right over his lip again. He was worried she'd push away now, and honestly, I was too.

"Probably," I admitted. "But don't worry, we'll make sure she keeps talking to us."

Leo nodded his head before we continued walking. The ride to his house was quiet as Leo stared out the window the whole way. I know he's sad about his father, but we all knew it was coming. It wasn't as big of a shock as it was when his father had his accident. I know it still hurts, but I think it helps him know it was coming.

"Want me to spend the night again?" I asked him as we pulled into his circular driveway. The place was dark inside, letting me know his mom called it a night already. It was Leo and his mom since his brother, John, died in the same accident that put his father in a coma. Last year was hell for us all, with the loss of John and Ivy.

John was my age, and we had a ton of classes together in high school and college. Leo and he were my two closest friends. John was a great guy, the life of the party. He was the man every girl wanted, and every guy wanted to be. He was the best wing man too. The image of him lying peacefully in his casket still haunts me, as well as Ivy's, and now, the image of Mr. Darius will haunt me. Their father was always this big man with a large heart and a glorious smile. You would think nothing would have been able to hurt him, but a semi can do a lot of damage to anyone, in this case, three someones. My heart still aches thinking about Ivy and John.

"No, it's alright. Thanks though." He sighed as he got out of the car, closing the door behind him. I turned the car off, getting down myself. "I said no, Lucas." He rolled his eyes at me.

"I know, I heard. I'm ignoring it, because I can tell you still need me." My elbow hit his side lightly, trying to be annoying.

"Whatever." He rolled his eyes, but I saw the smallest tug at the corner of his lips. He appreciated it.

I walked inside with my hands in my pockets. The nostalgic scent of Leo's mother's perfume, which always lingered in the halls like a ghost, greeted me as I entered. Growing up, I'd spent more time here than in my home. I knew these hallways and rooms better than my own.

"We're not sleeping on the same bed." He pointed at me.

"Awe, but you're such a good little spoon," I teased him, causing him to blush the slightest bit. I let out a laugh at his innocent reaction.

"I am not. These arms are meant to hold, not be held." He flexed his biceps, which he's clearly been working on. I poked it, pretending to inspect it.

"If you say so." I shrugged, heading up the stairs, leaving him to chase after me to say something else.

"I say so," he whispered so as not to wake his mom when we passed her room. Leo's room was at the end of the hall. He usually stays on campus in his dorm, but with everything that happened, he's been staying here for his mom this week. In the same way Rose has been staying at the hospital with her mother. I felt my chest tighten at the thought of her hurting.

"Let's go to bed." Leo threw one of his pillows at me. He had a giant king bed with black sheets to match the black walls. He had a dark gray leather couch to the side of the room. I'm guessing I'll have to claim it as my bed tonight.

"Fine by me." I threw the pillow down on the cold couch and jumped on it. "Tuck me in, daddy," I joked. Leo sighed, clearly getting annoyed with my antics, but that only made it better.

"Here, you can use this." He threw me a small throw which barely covered my shoulders and my feet at the same time.

"Where's my goodnight kiss?" I puckered my lips at him.

"Go to bed, Lucas. You're being annoying," he spoke in a stern voice, only making me smile with amusement. I felt my phone vibrate once before stopping. I fetched it from my back pocket to see I had a text from Rose. My heart sped, surprising me at how excited I could be to get a text from her.

Rose: Can you meet with me tomorrow? I need some good sex.

I couldn't help the shit-eating grin on my face. I heard Leo's phone vibrate next. His face illuminated by the blue light of his phone, revealing the same grin on his face. Did she text him too?

"Who's bothering you so late at night?"

"It's Liv. I guess she isn't regretting telling us," he answered me without prying his eyes away from his phone.

"Oh, yeah? What did she say?"

"She's glad she could help make me feel better." He smiled again as he typed a response.

Two can play that game.

Lucas: You know I'll come whenever you need me, my not so innocent Rose. You gotta do something for me first.

I smiled, waiting for her response, but all I heard was Leo's phone vibrating a few more times, as my text stayed on delivered. Is she choosing to talk to Leo over me? I felt a pang of jealousy as I looked Leo's way.

Rose: What might that be? O_o

Lucas: You have to wear what I tell you.

Rose: (-_-;) um, depends. What it is you're wanting me to wear?

I noticed Leo's vibrating had slowed, letting me know she was focusing on our conversation now.

"Who's got you smiling?" Leo caught on now.

"Rose," I answered him, as I typed my response. I wanted to tell him she wanted to hook up again, but I also didn't want to be a dick and cause him more heartache right now.

"What are you guys talking about?" He arched a brow at me as he pulled the sheets over his shoulders.

"You sure you want to know?"

"Maybe?" He wasn't sure. He was curious, but he wasn't sure he was ready for the answer.

"I'm just giving her advice on what to wear," I told him a partial lie, to spare his feelings.

"Oh, okay. I mean, that's weird." He shrugged his shoulders.

Lucas: I'll send it to the penthouse tomorrow. I know a place we can go to have sex that is unbelievable.

I love dressing my Rose. I know exactly what to put her in to make her feel as sexy as I think she is.

Rose: I don't know, Lucas. I just want something simple right now.

Her text had my chest tightening. I guess she's going through a lot right now to want to try something new.

Lucas: I understand, Rose. Perhaps another time. Tell me where you want me and when. I'm yours ;)

Rose: Thanks, Lucas. Tomorrow, your place, around 7?

Lucas: Sounds good to me. I'll come get you.

Rose: Okay. See you then.

Rose: Thank you for not being weird after I told you my story.

Lucas: Me? Weird? Never. ᕙ(ò_óˇ)ᕗ

Rosa: Is that you flexing? X'D.

Lucas: You like it?

Rosa: mmm, yeah totally, those little lines are definitely doing it for me ;)

I let out a laugh by mistake, gaining a glare from Leo.

"Sorry." I held my hand up. I turned to my side, so I didn't have to see his eyes on me again.

Lucas: Goodnight, Rose. I look forward to touching your

body again.

Rose: Goodnight, Lucas.

I closed my eyes, feeling a little too excited about tomorrow now. There are so many things I want to do to her. I hope she gives me control again.

Olive's P.O.V.

I had a hard time going to bed last night. Lucas' texts had my heart racing with excitement. I had a stupid grin as we texted last night, which I later got onto myself about. I can't let myself get too attached. He wants nothing serious, and fooling myself into thinking he does will end in my heartbreak.

This is just sex.

"Mom, this is Hailey." I had convinced Hailey to come up during her lunchtime to meet mom. She, of course, accepted, excited to meet my mother. "She's my best friend and current roommate."

"It's so nice to meet you!" Hailey smiled sweetly, giving mom an unexpected hug. Hailey has always been very affectionate. She attributes it to her being latina. She tells me Spanish is the language of love, and love involves a lot of affection.

"It's lovely to meet you. Thank you for caring for my Livie." Mom spoke with her eyes still wide in shock.

"It's no trouble. I very much enjoy having Liv with me. She's tons of fun, and like a sister to me. She's great!" Hailey's words had me blushing a bit. I thought of her as a sister too, but I'd never told her. It was nice to have it confirmed.

"I'm glad to hear it. Please tell me more stories about my baby girl. Ones she may not have been so inclined to share with me herself." Mom was fishing for information, making me suddenly regret bringing Hailey. We sat and talked for about an hour before Hailey had to go back to Columbia for her afternoon classes. Mom had enjoyed getting some juicy gossip about me from Hailey. It was odd, but I liked how she knew all these new things about me now.

Leo: Think you can come down to the hospital garden for a little while?

Leo's text had surprised me as mom slept. She'd been sleeping a lot here lately. Every little thing would exhaust her and even though she fought it hard, the exhaustion was consuming her. I could see death approaching soon, tearing me up inside.

Olive: When? Now?

Leo: In 5 minutes?

Rose: Yeah, okay, see you then.

I responded as I headed out of the room towards the elevators. It took a good 5 minutes to get to the garden from where I was. When I arrived, I could see Leo standing under the shade of a massive tree. The weather was beautiful with the warm sun and cool breeze of a soon approaching autumn.

"What's up?" I asked him as I hopped next to him. He turned, giving me a bright smile, making my heart skip. Leo looked even more handsome with all his piercings on display. He had the top section of his shaggy hair tied back so it didn't fall on his face. He looked damn good right now.

"I wanted to talk to you. It's probably bad timing, but I wanted to get this off my chest and I wanted to tell you in person." He kept his clear-blue eyes on me.

"Okay, I am listening." I said wearily, because when someone wants to speak in person, it's usually serious.

"I genuinely like you, Olive. Liv, I mean. You're absolutely amazing, and I want to take you out on a date, but I know you have something going on with Lucas. I am not trying to make you my girlfriend yet, so I don't care that you do. I want you to see I'm an option, too." He spoke clearly, never once breaking eye contact.

His words surprised me. I didn't know Leo felt this way about me. I wouldn't have believed it if I hadn't heard him say it. The fact that two extremely hot and rich men wanted my attention was shocking to me. I am not sure I can handle it. I don't know how I could go about dating one while sleeping with the other. Leo's piercing moved side to side as I contemplated his offer. He was nervous, very nervous.

"I don't know, Leo. I just got out of a long relationship last week. My heart needs time before I jump into another one. I don't want to lead you on into thinking we would be anything more anytime soon," I admitted, trying not to be too harsh.

"I'm okay with that. I just want a chance to take you out on a date. It could be just one, and then you can see if you want to go on another one with me or not. We don't have to put any kind of label on it." He stepped closer as he spoke to me.

I could feel the heat radiating off his body from his proximity. He lifted his hand, grabbing a lock of my hair and placing it behind my ear, letting his fingers graze my face. I felt a light blush tinge my cheeks, because I did find him attractive, even if he was a couple of years younger than me.

"Say yes, Liv. Please." He grazed the back of his knuckles against my cheekbone.

"Okay, just one." I held my finger up. Leo smiled so wide the corners of his eyes wrinkled. He was beautiful when he smiled.

"Thank you, Liv." He leaned in, kissing my forehead with his hot lips. I couldn't help the way my heart raced. "Tomorrow okay?"

"Um, yeah, it should be fine." I nodded, still feeling his lips on my forehead.

"Perfect. I won't keep you long. I know this time with your mom is important," he said, making me like him a little more now.

"Thank you, Leo."

"No problem." He held my face with his hands, letting his thumb rub against my jaw line. I felt myself leaning towards him.

God, I must be hornier than I thought. What's wrong with me?

"Leo?" I whispered his name.

"Yeah?" He leaned further down towards me, our noses almost pressed together.

"Was there anything else you wanted to say?" I asked, feeling my heart race with excitement.

"No, that was all," he whispered to me, letting me feel his breath fan across my lips.

"Okay, I'll see you tomorrow," I told him, staring at his lips, not moving a muscle, even though I was saying goodbye in not so many words.

"See you then."

His voice was so smooth, like velvet. He stepped back, pulling away before he did anything. I felt my head spinning with emotions as I watched him walk away. I was seeing him differently now, noticing how broad his shoulders were. How tall and absolutely handsome he was, too. *Shit, what is this?*

I headed back towards mom's room, trying to get rid of the itch Leo left behind. I was glad I would see Lucas tonight, because I need the tension released now.

"Olive, sweetie?" Nancy called me over from the nurses' station when she saw me step out of the elevator.

"Hello, Nancy. What can I do for you?" I asked her, leaning my arm over the counter of the desk.

"Did I just hear a handsome boy was kissing you in the garden?" She arched her brow.

"Nancy, how the hell did you even hear about it so fast?" I asked her, astonished. I knew she was the best nurse at knowing every rumor or gossip going about these walls, but still, that was way too fast. "We weren't kissing. More like he was asking me out on a date while being super close to my face."

"Mhmm, sure, sweetheart. Just be careful with these boys. They can be cruel," Nancy cautioned me as she bit into her juicy nectarine.

"I hear you, Nancy. No need to worry about me. I already know how cruel men can be," I informed her.

When I walked into the room, mom was sitting upright. She looked pale, grayer than usual. She had a puke bucket in front of her, letting me know she was nauseous today.

I sat beside her on the bed, rubbing her back as she dry heaved over the bucket.

"Everything okay?" She asked me, like she wasn't about to hurl.

"I'm fine. You're the one almost throwing up." I wrinkled my nose at her. She rolled her eyes at me.

"Something is bothering you. Tell me." She was trying to get her words out before gagging again.

"Leo asked me out on a date. I said yes, but I don't know how I feel about it. Lucas and I have plans tonight, but I know he wants nothing serious. Leo seems like he would, and I don't know if I'm ready for it. Now I feel guilty for going to be with Lucas tonight and then going on a date with Leo tomorrow. It feels kind of slutty." I bit at the inside of my cheek as I thought about it further.

"Oh sweetheart, you don't owe either of them your full attention. You're not their girlfriend, and it's okay to date more than one person as long as they are both aware of it. Let Lucas know tonight. You're not limited to one person until they ask you to be," she assured me right before she threw up.

I rubbed her back, trying to make her feel better as she hurled. I hated seeing her this way, suffering for no reason. Her words stayed in my head, trying to make myself not feel guilty. She was right, neither of them own me. Currently, I'm not anyone's girlfriend, so I could date Leo. Lucas and I can stop what we are doing if I get a boyfriend.

"Thanks for the advice, Mom." She nodded her head, unable to speak at the moment. I will have to tell Lucas tonight. I hope it doesn't ruin the mood.

Chapter 12

Olive's P.O.V.

After spending all day with Mom, I arrived home around 6. I quickly showered, not wanting to smell like the hospital when Lucas picked me up. I know I need to disclose that Leo and I will be going on a date tomorrow, but I wasn't sure exactly what I would say. How do I even bring it up? I don't figure I would just blurt it out, but I feel like that's exactly what I'll end up doing.

I dressed in my cute matching lace set of black bra and underwear, thinking maybe Lucas would like it. I felt bad for turning him down to taking me somewhere for sex. It sounded exciting, but with Mom's declining health, I couldn't get myself to agree to it. I am not exactly in the mood for something thrilling right now. I wore a simple blush pink sundress, because I wanted to feel Lucas' hands sliding up my thighs from under it. Hailey was out with a study group right now, allowing me to get ready without her trying to doll me up more. I smiled, thinking of her excitable self when it came to my dating life. Is Lucas considered part of my dating life if we aren't technically dating?

I heard the bell chime, racing towards the door to see who it was. I could see Lucas standing in the hall through the peephole. He looked so handsome in a simple t-shirt and bleach washed jeans. His hair was slicked back as usual, and he stood with his hands in his pockets, looking sexy as hell. I opened the door, greeting him with a smile.

"You ready to go?" He inquired as he checked me out,

licking his lips as he did.

"Actually, Hailey is going to be gone for another couple of hours. Do you want to come in instead?" I suggested, because I was ready to jump his bones right here and now.

Lucas smirked with only one corner of his lips turned up. He looked damn fine when he gave me his half smirk. His eyes devoured me as he continued to look at me before stepping into the apartment. I closed the door behind him, turning to find him in my personal space already. His hand gripped my hip, bringing me closer to him. His other hand cupped my face, letting his thumb rub over my lower lip. He leaned down so his face was leveled with mine.

"Tell me, Rose, what would you like me to do to you tonight?" He whispered, allowing his minty breath to hit my nostrils.

"Before we start, I need to tell you something," I quickly spoke, gathering my courage and biting the bullet.

"Okay, I'm listening." His thumb stopped rubbing my lip, instead rubbing my cheek. He didn't move away, staying right in front of my face.

"Leo asked me, today, to go on a date with him tomorrow, and I told him I would. I know we're not exclusive, but I wanted you to be aware." I quickly let the words escape me, feeling my heart race in anticipation of his reaction.

He was quiet for a moment, making me wonder if he had actually heard me. He then leaned forward and kissed me so passionately my knees quivered. His tongue licked at my bottom lip, asking for permission to enter. When I opened my mouth, his tongue slid in, dancing over mine as it explored my mouth. I moaned in pleasure when he sucked my lower lip back.

"Thanks for letting me know, Rose. Don't worry, I don't care, as long as I get to have you at night," he practically growled in my ear.

I nodded my head, leaning to the side to expose my neck to him in hopes he would grace it with his tongue or mouth.

He obliged by tracing my neck with his lips ever so softly. He then sucked on my skin so viciously I knew I'd need makeup to hide the mark. His mouth moved down to suck at my cleavage. I couldn't help the moan that escaped me as he pinned me against the wall. His strong arms wrapped around my waist as his mouth met my neck again.

"Lucas..." I whispered his name, ready to feel him deep inside me.

"Yes, Rose? Tell me what you want." He let his finger graze over my jawline lightly.

"Take me right here against the wall." I told him, wanting him to hike up my dress, and insert himself deep inside me.

"Gladly." He smirked at me with slanted eyes.

I can't express how fucking handsome he is. He leaned down, taking my lower lip into his mouth, sucking on it for a moment. His hands slid under my dress, dancing around the hem of my underwear. He hooked his finger over it, slowly pulling it down, allowing me to kick them off. He unzipped his pants, pulling them down enough to release the holy grail of dicks. My eyes widened as I was reminded of its size. I could see him smirk at my reaction.

"Are you ready for me, Rose?" he whispered in my ear.

I nodded my head, unable to speak at the moment. My breath felt frantic as he carried me up against the wall, holding onto the back of my thighs tightly. I felt his dick align just right over my entrance, causing me to hold my breath as I braced myself. He didn't thrust himself quickly into me as he had done previously. No, this time he went slow, pain stinkingly slow. I could feel his eyes on me the entire time he did it. He was watching me carefully, making me feel hot.

I gripped onto his shoulders as he reached his special spot inside of me. I felt myself take a breath when he swayed me over him. Before I knew it, he was thrusting hard into me, making me slide up and down against the wall. I moaned loudly, digging my fingers deep into his upper back, right by his shoulder blades. Lucas let one of my thighs go, somehow still keeping me up, as he pulled my dress down to reveal my lacey black bra. He pulled it to the side as well, letting my breast out. My nipple only hardened further from the cold air conditioning in the penthouse. Lucas flicked it with his tongue a few times before sucking on it.

"*Shit, Lucas!*" I moaned, grabbing a fistful of his hair, pulling him further into my breast.

His tongue circled my nipple as he continued to suck on it. His thrusts were rhythmic and pleasure inducing. I felt myself getting close already as he continued. Even with him buried so deep inside of me, I couldn't get enough of him. I want this, always. I want him. The feeling scared me, because I know I can't have him. This thing we are doing is becoming addicting, and I need to be careful. His hands grabbed my ass cheeks, slightly spreading them, bringing my attention back to this euphoric moment.

"I'm getting close," I moaned as I felt myself reaching my peak.

"Fuck, Rose, your moans are everything and more. Cum with me," he told me as he thrusted faster inside me.

I yelled his name as I found my release over his enormous shaft. I felt his seed hit my cervix as he came with me. He stayed deep inside me, resting his head on the nape of my neck as both of us caught our breath. He kissed my neck tenderly, once, twice, three times. His eyes stared deeply into my own as he pulled back.

"I could do this forever," he admitted to me, not looking away for a second. I blushed deeply, feeling his dick go flaccid inside me. His words reminded me he only wanted sex.

"It's becoming addicting for me, too," I admitted, biting my lip slightly. Lucas licked his lips, giving me his devilishly sexy smile.

"Good." He kissed me out of nowhere, a kiss so passionate I was melting into his arms. "Let's get cleaned up."

With him still inside me, his hands held me close, as he

carried me towards the living room and into my room. He sat me on the bathroom counter as he slid out of me. He bit at my lower lip before starting the shower. I hadn't expected him to want to shower after. We had never done that before. I didn't move from the spot he sat me down on. I somehow felt frozen watching him in his naked glory. His muscles were well toned and strong. His skin held an almost gold undertone with a very light tan. He was like a Greek god sent down from the heavens for me to ogle over.

Lucas walked back towards me, his eyes still looking hungry. He helped me out of my dress, maintaining eye contact with me the entire time he undressed me. He kissed me again. It wasn't like the kisses he would give me before or during sex. It felt almost intimate, but I am sure I'm reading too much into it. He kissed my chest next as he took my bra off. He then kissed my neck again, right over the spot I am sure will be purple tomorrow.

He grabbed my hips, lifting me off the counter, placing me on the floor gingerly. He grabbed my hand and took me into the shower. Are we about to have shower sex?

Lucas' P.O.V.

I walked her to the shower, wanting to pamper her as best I could. I want her to see I can do more than just have sex. She needs to know I can be that guy for her. I can be a guy who takes her on a date like Leo. He told me he was going to go after her, but it's still like a slap to the face to know he actually asked her out. She said yes, which only twisted my stomach further. I need to step up my game if I don't want to lose.

I pulled Rose into the stream of the large double-headed shower above us. I ran my hand over her face gently, pushing her hair back as it got wet. She was even more beautiful when wet. Her ice-blue eyes stared deeply into me. It felt like she was looking into my soul, trying to determine if I was good or not. I hope she sees I can be. I want her to see me, to really know me. She might be one of the few who could truly accept me for me. I ran my fingers through her hair before grabbing her shampoo, lathering her beautiful red hair.

"I can do that just fine on my own," she complained to me.

"I know you can, but let me do it just this once." I felt her staring at me, but I didn't look away from her hair. "Please," I added for good measure.

"Fine, just this once," she caved, making me look as delighted as I felt.

I rinsed her hair out, running the conditioner through it next. Her hair was so beautiful and soft. I enjoyed watching it curl back up, even under the water. She was absolutely stunning, and she didn't even know it. Her stupid high school made her feel like less than she was. I want to show her she's better than any of those people. I'll find every single one of her classmates and show her off to them. Let them see how beautiful and unattainable my Rose is now.

I could see her closing her eyes as she relaxed into me. I pulled her against me, letting her back rest against my chest. My arms wrapped around her waist, letting my head rest over her. She let out a soft, relaxed moan as she sank further into me with her eyes still closed. I let my right-hand trail up and down over her arm. She was so relaxed for a moment; I thought she had fallen asleep. I kissed her shoulder, making her open her eyes. She blushed a little as she stood straight up again.

"I think I'm done," she quickly said, stepping out of the shower with such speed you would think a meteorite was going to hit this very spot.

I felt my shoulders slump in disappointment. She's still pulling away, and I was so sure I was opening her up more. I washed myself, stepping out to a towel being handed to me. Rose had dressed herself in an oversized t-shirt with some short shorts as pajamas. She looked hot, even in her current attire. Her wet hair was tied in a loose bun at the very top of her head, almost like a pineapple.

"Here," she told me, shaking the towel for me to take, but I shook my head.

"Dry me, Rose." I smirked at her again as she looked at me, unsure.

She furrowed her brows, making me believe she would deny my request, but to my surprise, she didn't. She opened the towel, drying my arms first. Her hands moved down to my chest, skipping my groin, and going for my legs instead. She was sensual as she rubbed my dick dry. She knew exactly what she was doing, and I didn't mind it one bit. I grew hard as she continued to rub me.

"Are you planning to take care of me?" I raised a brow at her, teasing her the only way I know how, through sex.

"Maybe." She raised a brow back at me with a slight hunger in her eyes.

She knelt before me, causing my heart to race. She looked even sexier, like this. Her eyes locked with mine as she licked my dick like a popsicle. She made it twitch with excitement, growing even harder by the second. When she took the tip into her mouth, I groaned in pleasure. She seemed to like the sound as she sucked harder. I could tell she was inexperienced, and it made me wonder if this was the first time she'd done this.

"Rose, you don't have to do this if you don't think you can. I won't be disappointed," I assured her, not wanting her to feel like she has to do it now that she started. She shook her head at me, pulling my dick out of her mouth.

"I want to try, but I don't know how good I'll be. I've never done this before," she admitted shyly, making my heart soar. She was willing to do this for me. She was willing to let my dick be the first to fuck her mouth.

"I'll guide you, Rose. You feel fucking amazing, but tell me if you want to stop. I swear I won't be upset." I tucked a loose strand of her bun behind her ear. She nodded her head before taking my dick back in her mouth.

"Breath through your nose, and try to lean your head like this." I moved her head so I wouldn't gag her as easily. She sucked on me as she moved her head back and forth. "Fuck, Rose, that feels great." She was encouraged by my words, taking more of me into her mouth. I felt her gag against me, but she worked through it, letting her eyes water slightly. I moved her head a bit more to help, feeling her relax a bit more, letting me know it worked.

"I'm going to move now, okay?" She nodded, with me still inside her mouth.

I grabbed the sides of her head as I thrust gently and slowly into her. The sounds of her sucking me off were the most enthralling thing I heard tonight, aside from her moans. I moved faster and deeper, seeing she could take it. I fucked her beautiful mouth, trying to find my release quickly for her sake. Tears were streaming down her face, but she refused to call it quits. She was determined, and she was honestly doing a great job.

"I'm going to cum in your mouth, Rose. Think you can swallow it for me?" I asked her as I got close. She nodded her head, groaning. The idea of her swallowing me had me excited, and I found myself cumming inside her mouth a few thrusts later. I saw her swallow it before she wiped her eyes and stood straight. She had a small smirk playing on her lips. She was proud of herself and so was I.

"That was incredible, Rose. Thank you." I kissed her forehead, making her blush.

"Thought it only fair after I worked you up," she explained. "You better go before Hailey gets here."

She was like this Yo-Yo I couldn't control. One minute she was my delicate Rose, and the next she was pricking me with her thorns. I was hoping to have more time with her, to cuddle her, to sleep beside her. She still wasn't ready for that. I stepped closer to her, caging her between my arms against the wall.

"You sure you don't want me to stay and cuddle?" I

winked at her, but she only laughed like I had made a joke. I'd never been laughed at before. It was not a feeling I liked.

"Yeah, I'm sure. It doesn't suit your style." She shook her head, still with a look of amusement, at my expense.

"I'll make anything my style for you, Rose," I told her seriously.

She froze for a moment before shaking it off, raising a brow, unconvinced by my words. I sighed, but got dressed, deciding she wasn't ready to believe me yet. Tomorrow she'll go on a date with Leo, but she'll have reminders of me throughout it.

Sorry Leo, I never said I would play fair.

Chapter 13

Olive's P.O.V.

It was time for my date with Leo already, and I had no idea what he had planned. I honestly was feeling odd about it. I kept trying to get my head into the right mind frame, but it somehow kept going back to Lucas. Last night's events kept playing in my head. He seemed so serious when he, in not so many words, said he'd change for me. I know I was reading too much into it. He probably didn't want to leave.

"You look cute." Hailey snapped me out of my thoughts.

I had worn a floral patterned, light pink dress with a small jean jacket and wedged sandals. Hailey had done my makeup, giving me a more natural glow. She said I needed to look more of the innocent girl next door type for this date. I didn't see why. I should just be myself, not some innocent version. A lot of makeup was needed to cover up the marks Lucas had left as well.

"I don't know Hails. Is this okay?" I sighed, not feeling very excited.

"Yes, go out and explore. See what you like. Julius was only one guy. You need to see what else is out there, aside from Lucas. Don't feel guilty and enjoy yourself!" she scolded me, knowing me all too well.

"Yeah, okay," I reluctantly caved to her words. Suddenly, the doorbell rang, having Hailey squeal with excitement as she raced to the door. I walked slowly behind, seeing Leo standing at the door, dressed nicely. He had a pair of slacks on with a button-up shirt. He was a more casual formal, which worried me for where we were going.

"You ready?" He smiled widely at me.

"Yup." I nodded, grabbing my small brown purse off the hook by the door.

Leo held his arm out for me, which I took with a slight reluctance. This date would start once I took his arm, and I was feeling pretty nervous about it. I was worried the makeup would melt around my neck, revealing the deep purple mark Lucas left me last night. I would almost think he did it on purpose. My hand grabbed the nook of his elbow, beginning our date.

"Where are we going?" I asked him.

"There's a new restaurant I want us to try. My mom's friend is the chef there," Leo answered me as he opened the car door for me. I was worried he'd take me somewhere fancy.

"That's cool." I smiled at him as he closed the door.

I took a couple deep breaths, trying to calm my nerves before Leo entered his car on the driver's side. He drove us to a very elegant-looking restaurant with glass walls near the entrance and very modern decor inside. We were sat quickly despite the large crowd waiting in the foyer. It made me feel bad for them all. I don't enjoy having so much privilege.

"This place looks very nice, don't you think?" Leo asked me as he opened the menu before him.

"It's very elegant, that's for sure." I opened my menu, wanting to pass out from the sheer lunacy of the prices. "*Leo!*" I scolded him. "This is way too much." I shook my head crazily, still astounded.

"Don't worry about it. Remember, the chef is friends with my mom." Leo tried to ease my worries, but I didn't like the idea of him spending so much money on me. I stared at the menu a while longer, unable to decipher what half these dishes were. I also still couldn't stomach the prices of most of them.

"Leo, I honestly don't know what to order." I bit at my lip as I kept looking at the menu with furrowed brows.

"I can order for you, if you like. I think I know what

you'd want." He offered, and I quickly nodded my head, trying not to make a fool of myself here. Leo ordered some food I couldn't pronounce when our waitress came by with some white wine. I'm surprised they allowed him to order, considering he's not 21. I also despise white wine.

"What do you like to do for fun, Olive? Surely going to parties isn't the only thing." He winked at me. I laughed, shaking my head no.

"Yeah, definitely not. I like to read. I love to go on runs. Hikes are my jam, as well as camping. I also like to fight." I was on a roll, and had forgotten to stop myself before the last one.

"Fight?" He raised a brow in question.

"Mhmm, like in a ring," I explained, trying to avoid his blue eyes.

"Hmm, I can't picture it," he mused as he took a drink from his glass. I hadn't touched my wine except to taste it, and confirm I still hate it. He didn't take his eyes off me the entire time. So I think he caught how offended I was by his words. I'm definitely a fighter and I thought I gave off an intimidating aura, but I guess not.

"What about you?" I asked him.

"I like to watch sports at the stadium. I love watching scary movies. Also, I like to spend time with my friends playing football or soccer. You know I actually have a baseball scholarship?" He raised his brows at me like I should be impressed, which I was.

"That's awesome. I want to see you play one day."

"I would like that." He smiled back.

Our plates were brought out, and I wondered where the rest of the food had gone. The portion was likely to feed a small child, moreover an adult. I couldn't believe how expensive the food was for so little of it. I picked up my fork, wondering what exactly it was Leo had ordered us. The meat was very tender, cutting like butter against the knife. It looked good, but tasted a little too gamey for me. I ate it all, not because I was hungry, but because I would not have Leo waste any money.

Leo paid for the overpriced food, making me feel guilty, but he didn't think of it at all. He left a nice tip, which gave him a plus in my book. He grabbed my hand, leading us out of the restaurant and towards a busy strip mall across the street. I hate going shopping. I never did much shopping as a kid or a teen. Now, as an adult, it's the last thing I want to go out and do. I mainly order clothes online because I hate feeling like other people are watching what I pick to wear.

"What are we doing now?" I asked him.

"Thought we could look around and see if there was anything you liked," he offered.

"I hope you're not planning on buying me anything else. The meal was very expensive, Leo!" I scolded him and his poor use of money.

"Liv, you don't have to worry about it. Money isn't an object I have to worry about," he assured me, making me feel slightly disgusted with him for a moment.

"Tell me you didn't just say that." I stopped walking, forcing him to take a step back so he wouldn't pull me forward.

"What?" He seemed genuinely confused.

"Just because you have a lot of it doesn't mean you need to spend so much of it. For example, our food just now, aren't you still hungry?" I asked, hearing his stomach rumble.

"Maybe a little, but I am fine." He shrugged.

"That was way too much money for too little food. I am not trying to be ungrateful, but I also don't like to spend too much money." I sighed, feeling this date wasn't going the best.

"I understand, Liv. I am sorry I made you feel uncomfortable," he squeezed my hand as he spoke. He meant it, but honestly, Leo didn't know me well at all.

He still has this nice, sweet and innocent image of me in his head, which is very inaccurate. I feel like it's the version of me he wants, this non-existent one. Leo is sweet, and he's been through a lot with his dad. I know I can lean on him, but honestly, I don't know if he understands me well enough. This date has proved it to me.

"How about you pick where we go next? Obviously, I'm not doing the best job," Leo laughed nervously as he scratched at the back of his head. I looked around, trying to think of where to go, when I saw it in the distance. The dim lighting inside with the neon sign overhead called to me. *Jimmy John's Arcade.*

"Let's go there." I smiled up at him as excitement rolled through me for the first time. Leo smiled back at me as he noticed where I pointed.

"Are you sure that's where you wanna go? I won't go easy on you," he teased, making me laugh.

"I'm sure."

To make my point, I pulled him by his hand towards the arcade with a giggle. The familiar scent of sweat, Windex, and whatever was spilled onto the dark blue carpet, soaked up by the padding underneath for all eternity, hit me as I entered. I took a deep breath, transporting myself back to when I was a teenager and would go to the arcade Friday nights with my only friend, Ian. I had been determined to beat the high score on Pacman.

Leo and I played many 2 player games, from street fighter to racing games. Leo wasn't kidding when he said he wouldn't take it easy on me. He was good at these games, making me question how often he'd been to an arcade. I didn't lose every time, but Leo definitely had more victories than me. I laughed at his comments and the way he tries to block my view to win a few times.

"Cheater!" I pushed him playfully. "I could have won if you hadn't covered my eyes."

I laughed as I complained. My cheeks hurt from all the smiling. I looked at my phone, realizing we'd been here for almost two hours now. I had wanted to get back to mom before two o'clock but now it was three. I looked at Leo with my smile fading.

"I need to get back to my mom," I sadly admitted.

"Oh my gosh, I am so sorry, Liv. I know it's important

you spend as much time with her. Let's go. I'll take you to the hospital right now."

He walked so quickly I practically had to sprint to keep up. I appreciated that he wanted to get me back to mom so fast. Leo was a sweet and caring guy, and although the date had not gone well at first, it ended wonderfully. The arcade was what we needed to let loose and enjoy each other's company.

Leo stopped right by his passenger side door. He leaned down towards me, getting so close to my face again. I didn't move as he leaned in, letting his lips meet mine. I was curious to see how they would feel. They were soft and warm, like plush marshmallows. The kiss was short and sweet, leaving me with a light blush on my cheeks.

"Thank you for today, Leo." I smiled up at him as he opened the door for me. He shook his head no at me, making me furrow my brow for a moment.

"Thank *you*, Liv. I know it was not going great until you took us to the arcade." He smiled at me, shaking his head no. "Let's get you back to the hospital."

My phone rang as he came around to the driver's seat. It was the hospital.

"Clear!" I heard the doctor's shout from Mom's room.

They had us wait in the hall right outside her door. All I could see through her room window was her limp hand dangling off the bed. Leo held me close to his chest as I cried, waiting for them to tell me she was okay. I knew her time was coming, knew it would be before the end of the week, but it still shocked me to get the call. The doctor shook his head, calling her time of death, killing me inside. I turned, burying my face in Leo's chest. I couldn't look anymore. It wasn't enough time. *This week was not enough.*

"I'm so sorry, Liv," Leo whispered to me as he rubbed my back soothingly.

I couldn't speak. All I could do was silently cry. She may have been gone for half of my life, but she was still my mom, and getting to know her again this past week has only made the pain worse. I wish I had more time with her, but cancer is a scary and unexpected thing. Leo led me away, telling the nurses to send any paperwork to my house. He placed me in his car and drove me home in silence. He said nothing, but he held my hand the entire way.

"I'm here for you, Liv," he assured me. "I know part of what you're feeling."

"Thank you, Leo." My voice cracked from not having used it but to cry for the last hour. We got to the penthouse where Hailey was waiting for me with my favorite blanket and hot tea. She wrapped me in her arms, soothing me like an older sister.

"I got it from here, Leo. Thank you," she told him, as her way of getting him to go.

"Text me if you need me, Liv," he said from the doorway, kissing my forehead before he left.

Hailey let me lay my head on her lap while she ran her fingers through my hair, letting Disney movies play on the TV for comfort. The tears had dried up inside me, unable to produce more. I felt oddly numb...numb and weak. The doorbell rang, surprising us both, but I didn't have the energy to even lift my head off her lap. Hailey got up, running to open it. I couldn't hear who it was, but I heard whispers before the door closed again.

"Who was it?" I asked, not seeing her but feeling her in the living room.

My head was lifted and placed back on a lap, but it wasn't the cushiony soft lap of Hailey. No, my head was met with denim and hard muscles. I turned, looking up to see Lucas. He ran his fingers through my hair with a deep look of concern on his face. His eyebrows were slightly furrowed, as if seeing me in pain made him uncomfortable.

"What are you doing here?" I asked him.

"I'm here for you, Rose. Shhh, watch your movie. It's the best part." He pointed to the TV, but I kept looking at him, trying to make sense of this. Why'd he come here for me? There's no sex in this, no gain for him, yet here he is. Not only is he here, but he's here comforting me. I felt myself relax as he continued to play with my hair, his eyes fixed on the screen before us.

"This is my favorite one," he told me, making me turn to look at the TV to see what had been playing. It was Lilo and Stitch, which is one of my favorites too.

"Mine too," I whispered, keeping my eyes on the screen now.

Lucas continued to rub my hair and my arms, relaxing me so much I must have fallen asleep. I woke up in my bed, but I wasn't alone. Lucas laid beside me, his hand over my stomach, but his body was on the other side of the bed. I think he was giving me space while letting me know he was here. I found comfort in him, scooting closer, wanting to feel his warmth more. His sleepy self didn't mind, as he cracked a small smile.

It was only three in the morning, but I was having a hard time trying to go back to sleep. I kept picturing mom's face when I was little and then mom's face yesterday. She always had the most beautiful smile. I'll have to plan a funeral or a memorial or whatever it is. I have no idea what I'm doing, considering I've never had to handle something like this before. Lucas rubbed my stomach with his thumb.

"What are you thinking about?" He asked me in a sleepy tone.

"How to plan a funeral."

"Come here." He pulled me closer to him until both his arms were wrapped around me and my head was in his chest. "Don't think about that now. We'll figure it out together with Leo. We just helped do it for his dad so we can help with your mom. You're not alone, Rose. Go back to sleep."

He rubbed my arms, soothing me with his touch and his

words. He brought me enough comfort to lull me back to sleep. I dreamt of mom, waking up with a couple of tears streaming down my face. Lucas wiped them away before I opened my eyes. He stared deeply at me, holding my face in his hands. He pulled me towards his lips, kissing my forehead tenderly.

"Good morning, Rose."

"Morning." I whispered, unable to call it a good one.

"Do you feel up to eating?" I shook my head no, not having the energy to get up or even chew. I also had little appetite.

"I figured as much, so I made you this. You still need something in your stomach." He handed me a green smoothie, making me sit up.

"Thank you, Lucas. This is very considerate of you."

I took a sip, worried it would taste terrible, and would have to drink the whole cup because I am too polite. Thankfully, despite its color, it was very delicious. I gulped it down without a problem, feeling a little more energized now. I was still mainly feeling numb emotionally. It was an odd feeling, one I knew I needed to be careful of. I can't fall into a depression again. My phone buzzed on my nightstand, causing me to jump as it broke the silence. I grabbed it, seeing Leo's name.

Leo: Lucas told me you need help planning your mom's service. I'm coming over in an hour. I'll bring the binder my mom made. Don't worry about anything, Liv. We got you.

Leo's text made me feel a little better. It was nice knowing they were here to help. I hated that Leo had gone through this. It was tragic for us both.

Olive: Thank you, Leo. I honestly appreciate it. I doubt I could afford most of it.

My phone rang with an unknown number. I rarely answer unknown numbers, but I felt compelled to answer this one.

"Hello?"

Lucas looked at me curiously. I could tell he wanted to

know who was on the phone.

"Hello, my name is Daniel Warren. I'm a lawyer from Frank and Fran. Is this Abigail Rose's daughter, Olive Brewer?" A man asked, filling me with worry. Why would a lawyer be calling me?.

"Yes, this is her."

"I am so sorry for your loss, Ms. Brewer. I am..I was your mother's lawyer. She has left a will, and you are the primary beneficiary. Is there a time you can stop by my office today so I may read it to you? I know you're dealing with a lot, but her will has her plans for her burial and money to cover it," he explained, suddenly making me feel antsy to get to his office right away.

"Yeah. I'll be right there. Is there a way you could text me the address?" I asked him, getting off the bed and scrambling through my drawers.

"Yes. I'll send it right away. Again, I'm so sorry for your loss."

"Thank you. I'll see you soon."

I hung up, quickly changing. Lucas found his way to me again, grabbing my sides and turning me to face him.

"What happened?" He furrowed his brow, concerned for me.

"It was my mom's lawyer. I need to go to his office. Mom left plans for her burial and he needs to read her will to me." I explained. "Can you let Leo know not to come yet? I am not sure when I'll be back. I'll text you both whenever I get home again."

"Want me to come with you?" He offered, but I shook my head.

"No, I'll take Hailey. Thank you, though. Go be with Leo until I get back."

"If you say so, my Rose. Please, text me if you change your mind or if you need *anything*."

"Okay." I nodded as he leaned down and captured my lips in a very tender kiss.

"I'll see you later."

He left my room with me staring at his back. He was devilishly handsome even with his tousled bed head. I enjoyed watching him walk away. His ass was a pleasant distraction, my eye candy of sorts. I shook my head, snapping myself out of the Lucas spell. *I need to go.* I grabbed Hailey and had her drive us to the lawyer's office. A sweet receptionist, who gave me sad eyes when I told her who I was here to see, greeted us.

"Ms. Brewer?" A younger guy came out to the lobby for me. He looked to be in his late 20s with dark brown hair, groomed neatly to the side.

"That's me." I stood, following him to an office in the back which read Daniel Warren.

"As I said on the phone, your mother has plans laid out for her burial. Of course, you don't have to follow her plans, but it was what she wanted."

"I want to do what she wanted," I assured him with a nod.

Hailey held my hand as Daniel read the will. Mom wanted to be cremated and have part of her ashes spread at the top of her favorite trail. She hoped I would keep an urn with the rest of her wherever I would like. He informed me mom had a half a million dollar life insurance on her before she developed cancer. The money would go entirely to me. My mouth dropped open. I had never had so much money in my life!

Daniel gave me names of excellent accountants and investors, but Hailey told me she knew some she would rather I use. Mom had a flat she had purchased which now belonged to me. He gave me the address and the spare key. I also got Mom's classic 1966 convertible Ford Mustang. I felt like Mom had left me too much, and I wondered how she had amassed all these things.

"I am sorry for your loss, Ms. Brewer. Your mother was truly a wonderful woman. I know she was a part of a lot of volunteer organizations. They'll probably be reaching out to you throughout the week to let you know if she had left any personal items with them." Daniel told me.

"Thank you." I got up from the chair, feeling this meeting was over. Daniel wrote the address of Mom's place down for me, as well as where the car was parked.

"Your mother planned everything out, didn't she?" Hailey shook her head in surprise.

"Seems that way."

I quickly texted Lucas and Leo to meet me at mom's place. I want to get this planning done, but I also want to see where mom lived. Hailey drove us there quickly, speeding past yellow lights, and skipping some stop signs. I told her I may be in a rush, but I wasn't looking to die. She laughed at my comment and continued to drive like a madwoman. Mom's flat wasn't very far from Lucas' apartment, actually. *Go figure.*

"Ready?" Hailey asked me as we stood before the burgundy door of my mother's flat.

"I think so." I nodded, opening the door slowly. A strong and nostalgic smell hit me hard, one I haven't smelled since I was ten. It was mom, her perfume she apparently had not changed throughout the years. Mom didn't smell like this at the hospital, and it is so comforting, yet painful, to smell it right now.

The place was absolutely stunning. It was cozy with an open floor plan. There were many dead plants hanging, as well as ones on planter ladders. I'd have to get rid of those. There was so much sunlight in this place it warmed my heart. The kitchen was beautiful, with shelves instead of cabinets and a large kitchen island with a couple of bar stools. The soft, round rug in the living room made me want to take my shoes off and dig them into its fibers. The bed was on a loft to the right, up the stairs. There was no door and could be seen over the rail. It was the only thing upstairs, if you can even actually call it an upstairs. I could see it from the couch if you looked up and right.

The place was wonderful, and I couldn't believe Mom

lived here by herself for so long. I can't believe *I'll* be living here. It was nice to feel close to Mom again. Hailey and I sat on the large circular couch, staring at the glass coffee table beside us.

Time to wait for Lucas and Leo.

Chapter 14

Olive's P.O.V.

The knock on the door had me jumping off the couch. I opened it to find Lucas and Leo standing tall. They were each a good foot taller than me, but normally I didn't care. When they're together, standing side by side with their arms crossed, I totally care.

"Come on in." I gestured for them to step in as I moved aside.

"I brought names of crematoriums and funeral homes." Leo held up a thin binder as he stepped in first.

"Thank you." Lucas stepped in after him, kissing the top of my head as he entered. Leo looked at him with narrowed eyes, to which Lucas just shrugged.

"This place is nice," Leo said as he spun around the center slowly, looking around.

"It's homey," Lucas added.

I closed the door, feeling a little scrutinized by these two here. They live in large houses, and are standing here in this quaint loft saying it's nice. I took a seat, grabbing the binder from Leo. We all called different places and got prices as well as asked about urns. All 4 of us made calls and wrote down information. Eventually we found a place that was nice, affordable, and held a wake before the cremation.

"I need to find out who all of mom's friends are to invite them." I bit at my lip as I wondered how I would go about it. I am not exactly sure how to find her friends since I don't know the name of a single one.

"I can help," Lucas offered.

"Yeah, he's great at finding people online and tracing friendships and stuff." Leo nodded in agreement.

"Awesome, thanks."

"Anything for you, Rose." His statement had me blushing for a moment. I started wondering why he was here. Is he being kind or is he wanting something later? I hope he isn't expecting anything, because I know I'm not ready yet.

Lucas hopped online, finding mom's social media and then finding all her closest friends for me to contact. We set the service for tomorrow at 2. I'll spread her ashes around sunset at the coordinates she wanted. It was closer to evening now as we finished with most everything. Just needed to contact a couple more of her friends.

"You guys want food? I can order something." I offered.

"That sounds great!" Hailey called out. "Get some Chinese food from the place we saw around the block."

"Okay, I'll walk there and grab it," I told them as I headed for the door.

"I'll come with you," Lucas and Leo spoke in unison. Hailey did a terrible job of suppressing her smile at their offer.

"No, it's fine. I want to be alone for a little while."

The air had a chill to it with the sun setting. It woke me up and made me feel something more than this numbness deep inside me. I held my arms as I walked, fighting the nip in the air. The sidewalks weren't as crowded here, making it a nice quiet walk. I chewed on my cheek as I thought about mom. What did she like to do, or where did she like to go? Had she been to this place before?

I opened the door, hearing a chime over my head as I did. The workers behind the counter greeted me in unison. I gave them a small smile and a curt nod as I made my way to the counter and looked over their takeout menu. I was so lost in thought I hadn't noticed a man approaching me.

"That looks good." Leo came up behind me, pointing to some noodle dish on the menu.

"Leo, I told you I wanted to come alone." I sighed.

"I know, but I also know you don't need to be alone with your thoughts right now." He didn't look at me as he spoke, keeping his attention on the menu.

He was looking out for me, the same way Lucas must have looked out for him. I watched him from my peripheral, admiring his jawline and soft lips. He was a very handsome guy, and it killed me how attracted I still was to him. Our date hadn't exactly gone to plan, but he was a good guy. I think if there was to be a next time, I would have to plan it out. I'm not sure Leo has ever been with someone who wasn't rich before.

"Thank you," I whispered to him.

"I'm here for you, Liv. I know what you're going through. Still going through it myself. Don't shy away from me, okay?"

Leo wrapped his arms around my waist from behind, placing his chin on my shoulder. I leaned into his chest, enjoying the comfort he was bringing me. The moment was cut short as the worker came to take our order at the counter. We placed our order, and of course Leo refused to let me pay.

"You wouldn't have had to spend so much if we hadn't come over, so let me pay, okay?" He squeezed me again as he spoke.

I nodded my head, because it honestly wasn't much. I think Leo likes to express his affection through gifts and monetary objects. I am not one to enjoy such things, but I know he does it with good intentions, so I'm trying to get used to it. In fact, Julius never gave me much of anything, despite being pretty loaded.

The worker brought our food to us in two bags. Leo grabbed them both as I thanked the man, leaving a tip. I chased after Leo down the sidewalk, grabbing one bag. He raised a brow like I shouldn't have taken one, but I raised one back.

"You're too much, Liv." He smiled at me.

Leo had a very sweet smile, one which made you feel the same joy. I smiled back at him, batting my lashes, even though it's not a thing I normally do. The moon was half full tonight, with clouds constantly covering it, causing most of the lighting to come from the streetlights. Leo held my hand as we walked, interlocking our fingers, and giving it a light squeeze.

"I'm sorry our date was horrible, Liv, I didn't think it through. I didn't have *you* in mind. Like I did, but I didn't. I wanted to give you new experiences, but I should have realized it wouldn't be the experience you wanted." Leo sighed, referring to the restaurant and trying to take me shopping.

"You're right, but I know you meant well. Maybe next time, I'll plan it out and you can pay for everything," I joked, making him chuckle.

"Next time, huh? So I didn't totally fuck it up?"

"Yeah, you didn't totally fuck it up." We reached the loft in no time. Leo held the door open for me like a gentleman, allowing me to enter before him.

"After you, my lady." He bowed his head in the slightest, making me let out a laugh.

"Are you okay?" Lucas asked me, being the first to see me enter the loft.

"Yeah, I'm fine. I got the food." I held up the large bag, which was quickly taken by Leo.

"Correction, *I* have the food," he said with a cheeky smile as he placed both bags on the table. I wonder if going on another date with Leo is a good idea or not?

"Hailey!" I yelled at her as she continued to mop, swaying her hips side to side over the blaring salsa music. "Hailey!" I yelled again when she didn't hear me.

She was humming along as she helped me clean mom's loft the next day. Eventually, I gave up on yelling, tapping on her shoulder instead. She turned with a smile, grabbing my hands, and trying to make me dance with her. I wasn't in the mood. There was a lot to get done before the service today. I

CHAPTER 14

shook my head at her, making her pout for a moment before she grabbed the stereo remote and muted it.

"What's up?" She cocked her head to the side.

"I need to go get the flowers for today and take them to the funeral home and sign the release papers for mom's body. Do you want to come with me?" I bit at my cheek, hoping she would say yes. I didn't want to be alone.

"Of course!" She nodded, dropping the mop and giving me a big hug. "Let me clean myself off first." Hailey and I ran around town for a while, just getting what was needed. I signed the papers, avoiding looking at mom's body. It felt odd knowing she was there, but not truly there.

"I am sure you're tired of me asking, but are you okay?" Hailey turned to me as we entered the elevator. I stared out at the hall, seeing a familiar pair of broad shoulders. He turned, spotting me at the same time. *What's he doing here?*

Leo was wearing a pair of khaki slacks, loafers and a baby blue button down which accentuated his beautiful eyes. His hair was tossed in a messy way, but you could tell it was done purposefully. He looked extremely handsome, and as his eyes landed on mine, I felt almost exposed under his gaze. He arched a brow at me, recognizing me too, before the elevator doors closed.

"Earth to Olive!" Hailey waved her hand in front of my face.

"Sorry, Hails, I don't know how I am, honestly. I am sad, overwhelmed, and all around numb. I hadn't spoken to her in 11 years and then we had this week, and now she's gone. It's killing me, but I know I'll be fine. I did fine when she left me the last time."

My last sentence sounded colder than I meant it to, but it was the truth. Mom had left me a while ago, and I survived fine without her. I know I'll be okay, just sad for now. Hailey stayed silent until after the elevator doors opened again.

"Liv!" I heard someone yell from behind us before we reached the exit doors.

I turned to find an out of breath, Leo, making his way to us. He jogged over to Hailey and me, who stared at him in surprise. He stood straight as he reached us, giving himself a moment to catch his breath before he spoke.

"I thought that was you." He smiled at me.

"So you ran down two flights of stairs because you *thought* it was me?"

"Well, yeah." He chuckled nervously, scratching at the back of his neck. It's his nervous habit. "I wanted to make sure you were okay."

"You did all that to make sure I was okay?" I was surprised by the effort he had put in. "You know, you have my number. You could have called."

"I enjoy seeing and talking to you in person, so of course, I'll run down two flights of stairs to see you." His answer made me blush, and my heart swoon. It was sweet, and I hadn't noticed he felt this way about me.

"What are you doing here anyway, Leo?"

"My dad's business wants to buy this hospital. I've been in charge of the company since his accident. I was touring the entire facility with a group. It's *really* boring."

"It sounds important. Shouldn't you get back to it?" I raised a brow.

"Probably." He sighed, slumping his shoulders. "Can I get a hug from you to keep me going?"

I smirked at his request, rolling my eyes happily. I opened my arms towards him to show him my willingness. He grinned merrily as he wrapped his well toned arms around my waist, leaning down so his face was in the crook of my neck. He kissed me there, surprising me with a rush of emotions I wasn't expecting. His face stayed there a moment before pulling away.

"Thank you, Liv. Text Lucas and I when you're ready to spread your mom's ashes. We'll be there, I promise," he said as he jogged back to the group he had run away from.

Honestly, I was surprised to see Leo or to hear he was in

charge of his dad's business. I didn't think about those kinds of things with his father passing away. A lot of responsibility ended up falling on Leo's shoulders. I feel he's too young to be worried about this kind of stuff. He looks like he knows what he's doing, which makes me wonder how young these guys are when they are taught to run a business. How long had his father been grooming him to take his place before his accident?

"I like Leo. I think he's very sweet and very smitten with you." Hailey smiled at me as we walked towards the door again.

"I think I like him too." I admitted.

"Stop fidgeting, you look good," Hailey scolded me as I pulled at the collar of my black dress. It felt like it was choking me, but maybe it's just the panic inside. I don't know how to do this. I have never held a wake before. Thankfully, it wasn't one of my experiences.

"Do you think they'll show?" I asked Hailey, worriedly.

"If they were her close friends, then yes, they'll show."

Surely enough people emerged out of the woodwork. They introduced themselves to me with sad smiles as they entered. The room was small with a few chairs for us to sit and view mom, who I had dressed in a white sundress I'd found in her closet. She looked stunning with her makeup on. You would think she had fallen asleep. As everyone arrived and greeted one another, I thanked them all for coming and asked if there were any memories of mom they wanted to share. It didn't take long for someone to volunteer knowledge of her.

"Some of you already know me, and some are fresh faces. I'm Linda. I was Abi's first friend in New York about a decade ago now. Abi looked so scared when I first laid eyes on her. She had just arrived from New Hampshire and had no idea what she was doing. After getting to know her and seeing her stay at the homeless shelter I volunteer at, I offered for her to stay with me. She and I bought the loft she lives in together. She got her life together, going back to college and investing her money well. When she got tired of my shit, she bought my half of the loft from me." Linda laughed along with a few others, who must know her well. "To Abi!" She raised her glass of water.

"To Abi," everyone joined.

People continued to go up and talk about mom. She volunteered a lot, mainly at the women's shelter. She ran charities, was very smart and apparently funny. Mom was loved by every friend here. Not a single one of them had a complaint about her. I felt oddly proud, but also jealous she flourished so well without me. I was her daughter and I doubt any of them knew about me when they first met her. How long did she wait before telling them about me?

"She helped me get out of my abusive relationship, having been through it before. She told me the right words to keep me from returning to him again. I've lived outside that man's cage for 5 years, all thanks to this woman." She gestured to mom. I think her name was Penny. "I can't express how much I needed her at that time. It hurt me to see her hurting over her daughter." Her eyes landed on me.

Things continued on for a while. Sob stories, funny stories, touching stories. They were all beautiful, piercing my heart deeply. I was hugged and kissed goodbye as they all left when mom was taken to the crematorium. A few promised to come visit me at mom's loft, and one even lived in the same building.

"That went well." Hailey smiled at me, hugging me again. Hearing all those stories, seeing the life mom had lived these past few years, had helped me heal a little. I felt a sort of bittersweet feeling in my chest.

"Yeah, it did." I nodded. I jumped when I heard my phone buzz on the table, breaking the silence. Hailey and I both giggled at my reaction.

Lucas: We're headed to the spot now. We'll wait for

you here. We didn't want to cramp the wake. It felt more like something for you and your mom's friends to share.

Lucas' text made me feel even better. I was feeling all the love from everyone.

Olive: Thanks, we'll be up there soon.

Thank you for everything you did for me at the end, mom.

Chapter 15

Olive's P.O.V.

My phone buzzed way too early in the morning for my liking. I groaned as I reached for it with closed eyes. It has been a week now since I spread mom's ashes with Lucas, Leo and Hailey. I started going back to regular classes and thankfully hadn't fallen too far behind.

"Hello?" I answered, not caring I sounded hoarse from sleep.

"Good morning, am I speaking with Olivia Brewer?" An elegant woman's voice came through. I cleared my throat, sitting up on the bed more.

"This is her. May I ask who I'm speaking with?"

"Hello, Ms. Brewer, my name is Tammy and I'm the genealogist who performed your BRACA gene test."

My heart stilled and my palms sweat as I awaited for her to continue. Do I have the gene?

"I am sorry to inform you. You carry the BRACA gene. You have options, and it isn't a certainty you will get breast cancer, you're just more likely than others. I suggest having regular screenings. The results were sent to your PCP as well, and she should reach out to you to explain your options further. Do you have questions for me?"

I was frozen for a moment, letting the line go silent. I had the gene, just like mom. It was scary to think. I pictured mom's withering body and then imagined myself looking the same. I swallowed hard before I answered.

"No, no questions. Thank you for letting me know."

"Of course. Have a good day, Ms. Brewer."

"You as well."

I hung up, sitting up on my bed, staring at the indigo wall across from me. I had officially moved into Mom's loft yesterday. This was my first night sleeping in this bed. I was all alone, trying to digest this information.

Lucas: Open the door. I'll be there in two minutes with breakfast.

The text surprised me, as I wasn't expecting him today. Lucas and Leo both had been very helpful and comforting throughout this whole thing. Lucas felt like a completely different person. It was a side of him I never imagined I'd see, and it had definitely muddied the water again. I opened the door as Lucas appeared before it.

"Good morning, Rose. I have your favorite." He smiled widely at me as he stepped inside. He wrapped his arm around my waist, pulling me towards him, before his lips met my forehead. He hadn't kissed me, hit on me, or tried to have sex with me since mom died. I think he was trying to respect my grieving.

"And what is my favorite?" I asked him, closing the door, and turning to him.

"Banana nut muffin, and a caramel frappe." He produced the items on the table as he spoke. He wasn't wrong, either.

"How'd you figure that out?" I raised a brow at him.

"I have my ways." He winked at me, taking a seat at the small round table pushed against the wall between the living room and kitchen.

"Hmm, I am not sure I like that." I took a bite of my muffin with a smirk on my face.

"I think you do." He leaned forward, rubbing his thumb over the corner of my lips at the crumbs.

"How do you know I wasn't saving those for later?"

"I'm terribly sorry. I'll leave your crumbs alone."

"Good." I nodded, taking another bite and intentionally getting a lot of crumbs around my mouth.

"I lied." Lucas told me as he leaned forward and *licked* the crumbs off the corner of my mouth. I froze as he did the same to the other side. My lungs filled with deep breaths, loving the sensation of his tongue against me. I hadn't noticed I had missed it until now.

"Lucas." I let his name slip as a kind of warning.

"Yes, Rose?" He leaned back in the slightest, having our noses barely touch.

"Kiss me," I whispered, hoping he wouldn't hold back.

"Are you sure, Rose?"

I nodded my head, within seconds feeling his hot lips on my own. I was so hungry for him. A week without him had apparently been too much for my body as it quivered for more. Lucas held the back of my neck, deepening the kiss further. His tongue swept over my bottom lip before he caged it between his, pulling back with it. I moaned as he did it, opening my eyes to see the hunger in him as well.

"Take me, Lucas," I told him, grabbing his face and pulling it back towards me. He didn't fight it, running his hand up my thigh, squeezing it around my hip. He kissed me further, sliding his tongue into my mouth. Our tongues wrestled with one another for dominance. Lucas broke our kiss first, moving his lips down to my neck above my collarbone. My breath came out shaky as the pleasure pooled inside me. My breathing was heavy with lust as I held onto the back of his neck, pushing him deeper toward me.

He grabbed my legs, pulling me with my chair towards him. My legs wrapped around his waist, with me practically on his lap now. He slid his hand under the oversized shirt I had worn to bed. There was no bra on, allowing him to squeeze at my breast. I moaned, feeling taken over with lust between his mouth on my neck and his hand on my breast.

"Lucas.." I moaned his name, almost pleading, causing him to smirk against me.

He stood with me attached to him as he carried me to the couch. His large hands slid my shorts and underwear off while I took my shirt off. He pulled his pants down enough to release his massive manhood. I licked my lips happily as he used it to spread my wet folds. He slapped it against my clit, causing me to yell in surprise.

I gripped onto the top of the couch as Lucas grabbed both my legs and held them up against his chest. He inserted himself into me with ease, slapping against me quickly. I moaned loudly as he continued his rhythm. He was thrusting into me with a force both painful and pleasurable. He was hungry for me too, like he'd been starving this whole week, and I was the first meal he was having.

"*Deeper, Lucas*!" I almost yelled, feeling myself getting close already.

Lucas obliged my request, forcefully thrusting against me until I was seeing stars. I yelled with a high-pitched squeal as I came against him with my legs still pressed against his chest. He continued his rhythm, forcing me to ride out the waves of ecstasy. He came deep inside me a few minutes later, making me moan again as his seed hit my cervix.

"Fuck, Rose. I've missed you." He groaned as he kissed me passionately again.

"I could say the same." I smirked at him, feeling a pleasurable high I hadn't felt in a while.

Lucas kissed my neck, then my stomach, before he stood back up, sliding out of me. He handed me some tissues to clean myself up with. He was so damn handsome, the way he pushed his hair back over his head. His tattoos were damn sexy, moving with his muscles. I heard my phone vibrate again, making me sigh as I saw the number. So much for staying in this blissful high.

Lucas' P.O.V.

My Rose had let me have her again, and I was floating way above the clouds. I had missed being deep inside her all week. She needed time, and frankly, I would have waited longer if I had to. I stopped seeing all the other girls in my life the moment I decided to make Rose my own. There's no competing with her. She's perfect. I watched as she grabbed her phone, sighing at whoever was calling her. I curled a brow at her curiously, but she didn't oblige my curiosity with an answer, instead of answering the phone, holding a finger up at me.

"Hello?" she answered. "Yes, she told me this morning." Another pause, as whoever was on the other end of the line responded to her. "I understand, but I would rather not do that if it's avoidable. I know I'll need to be screened more often if I don't, but I don't feel a mastectomy is the route I want to take."

My heart stopped as I picked up the words she was saying. I quickly sat beside her, wrapping my arm around her waist and taking her free hand with my other one. She almost pushed me away, but decided against it. I was grateful, because I'm currently doing this more for myself than for her. She can't be sick. She can't die on me.

"Yes, I understand. I won't miss any appointments." Another pause, as I strained to hear the other half of this conversation. "That's fine. I'll see you tomorrow then."

She hung up with a heavy sigh before she leaned into me. I was glad she was leaning on me, but my mind was still trying to process everything. How am I supposed to help her with this? I could find the best oncologist and get her seen right away.

"I'm sorry," she said, grabbing her shirt and putting it back on first, making me let her go.

"What's going on, Olive?" I used her real name to let her know how serious I thought this was.

"Olive, huh?" She smirked at me for a second before it fell with a sigh. "My mom had me get tested for the breast cancer gene before she passed. I got my results this morning. Lucky me, I have it." She rolled her eyes at her last statement. I swallowed hard. The news wasn't good, but at least she didn't have cancer already. It's good she got tested, and now she can stay ahead of it. I could see the worry and stress plaguing her at the moment.

"I'm glad you got tested. You can't miss your appointment." I warned her.

"Yes, I know."

"Good. Do you want me to come with you tomorrow?" I offered because I would love to take her. I want to be there for her.

"No, it's fine. I don't know if they'd let you." She laughed, making me smile a bit. Her laugh is beautiful, like chimes in the wind.

"Okay then, I'll drive you there. What time is the appointment?"

She thought about it with her arms crossed, staring at me. She couldn't decide. I was feeling upset, worrying over her as she stood there, deciding whether to let me in. I was tired of this game. I want her now.

"Fine, it's at 9 tomorrow morning," she informed me, easing some of my tension.

"Okay, I'll come pick you up around 8:15. I'll bring breakfast."

"Thank you," she muttered under her breath, but I caught it. "I need to get ready for class, so I'll let you let yourself out. Thank you for breakfast."

She headed up to her bed in the open loft. She was actually going to get dressed. I didn't want to leave, so I stayed, leaning against the wall, and watching her change above. Her tattoos had a white bandage on the top over her ribs. She had added onto it and I didn't even notice until now. I was enthralled inside her. I didn't pay enough attention. I wonder what she got?

"What are you doing, Lucas?" She had noticed me standing here, staring at her.

"Watching my Rose." I winked at her with a smirk. She rolled her eyes, but there was a smile playing at the corner of her lips.

"Well, your Rose isn't *your* Rose, and she has classes to get to," she corrected me as she hurried down the stairs. "Goodbye, Lucas."

"I'll give you a ride," I offered her, hoping she'd say yes. Maybe she still wants to spend time with me the same way I want to spend time with her.

"No, thanks. I have the car mom left me, and I've been itching to drive it." She had this excited look on her face, like a small child about to play with their favorite toy. Who am I to deny her fun?

"Fair, I can relate." I nodded as I stepped closer to her again, closing the space between us. My arms wrapped around her beautiful waist, bringing her flush against my chest, feeling her breasts press against me. I leaned down so her lips were a few centimeters away.

"What are you doing?" she asked, slightly annoyed, but she didn't pull away. Instead, she stared at my lips, making me smirk.

"Getting my goodbye kiss, of course."

I let my lips graze hers as I spoke, making her take deep breaths as she tried to remain calm. It made me happy to see I could make her have such a powerful reaction to me. I gently kissed her soft, plump lips, parting them with my own as I held her face with my hand.

"Go out with me, Rose." I didn't phrase it in a question. I wanted her desperately, but she shook her head in my hands.

"I can't."

"Why not?"

"You're not serious about me. I'm just another one of the girls you see." She shrugged, stepping away from me this time. Her words crushed me, but I kept my playful smirk on my face.

"But I am serious about you, Rose." I rubbed my knuckles over her cheek. "Come on, just one date?'

She was clearly thinking about it, chewing on her lip. I wasn't sure which way she'd lean, so I stepped closer again. I grabbed her hand and kissed her knuckles as I looked into her icy blue eyes.

"Say yes, Rose. Please?"

She sighed, like this was the hardest decision she's had to make. I felt myself winning her internal battle as she bit her lip. Looking into my eyes, she gave me the smallest of nods. I smiled so widely, excited she had said yes. I grabbed her and spun her in a hug before placing her on the ground again, kissing those sweet lips one more time.

"Thank you, Rose. You won't regret it," I promised her, already thinking of the perfect date.

"Yeah, yeah. I hope you know since you're not exclusive, I don't plan to be either." She raised a brow at me, dropping my excitement a decibel.

Was she talking about Leo? I know they went on a date the day her mother died. Had it gone well, despite how it ended? It's not like Leo told me the details. I'm glad they haven't slept together yet.

"I'll see you later. I need to go or I'll be late." She dragged me to the door as she talked, pulling me into the hall and locking her front door. "Just text me when you want to have that date. Bye, Lucas."

She waved at me, running down the hall before I had time to collect my thoughts. I couldn't decide if I was excited or anxious. I am glad my Rose said yes, but I wish I was the only one in her life right now.

Chapter 16

Olive's P.O.V.

Lucas had asked me on a date again. I wasn't sure how I felt about it at the moment. I know I want it, but I'm also scared to get hurt again. Despite trying to keep it just about sex, I liked Lucas too much. I tried to tell my body to say no, but what came out was yes. On the drive to school, I slapped myself stupid.

The car was a damn dream. It drove so well and with the weather being nice; I had put the top down, feeling the wind whip my hair around. It probably wasn't my brightest idea. I had to tie my bird's nest of hair into a high bun when I arrived. I ran to my class, cutting it close, but somehow still making it on time. Professor Johnson greeted me with a small smile. All my professors had expressed their condolences. They had been keeping an attentive eye on me.

Class was quick, and oddly easy lately. I am not sure if it is because Professor Johnson is such a brilliant teacher, or because I got so far ahead in our textbook last week when I needed something to do. I had been losing my mind thinking of mom, and I thought math would make for a great distraction. It worked. As long as I was doing math, mom wouldn't pop up into my head. I guess it took too much of my brain power to solve the math problems to leave room for anything else.

When I stepped out of class, I saw Leo with his black stylish glasses and his hair half up. He gave me a wide smile before hugging me. I gave him a one-armed hug back, since my other arm had my book.

"You look cute today," he told me, squeezing the bun on my head.

"Not at all." I shook my head.

"Don't be that way. Accept the compliment." He nudged my shoulder playfully.

"If you say so, thanks."

"Do you have a class next?"

"Not until 1."

"Wanna go hang out? It's nice outside today. We could sit at the quad and enjoy the weather," he suggested.

"Thanks for the offer, but I need to go see Hailey. Maybe some other time?"

"Yeah, okay." I could hear the obvious disappointment in his voice, causing me to feel bad.

"Let me call her and see if she's even home. If not, I'll come hang out with you."

Leo smiled widely at my words, nodding his head. He looked like an adorable child. I called Hailey when we stepped out of the elevator. It turned out she was out with her dad right now. I'll have to wait until later to tell her about my results. I want her to come with me to my screening, but this isn't something I want to say over the phone.

"I'm all yours, Leo." I smiled up at him as I put my phone away.

"If only." He gave me a smile, but it didn't reach his eyes like usual. I wasn't sure what he meant.

"So what now?"

"Follow me." He grabbed my hand, pulling me towards a larger tree out in the quad. He took a seat, pulling me down beside him as we looked out at everyone walking by. "Ever since you told me your story, I've been watching people and wondering what their's are."

He stared out at the crowd as he spoke, as if to make his point. I watched too, seeing many people heading to class, lunch, or home. One was almost jogging as she struggled to keep her items from falling all over the ground.

"You honestly don't know what's going on in someone's life, let alone what they've gone through. Not everyone wears their trauma on their sleeve." I squinted, watching the girl run towards the music building.

"Wanna play a game?" Leo asked randomly, going from deep to playful.

"Uh, yeah, sure. What is it?"

"I'll pick someone, and you tell me what you think their back story is," Leo explained.

"Alright, who's the lucky victim?"

"Him." He pointed to a guy in the distance with large headphones over his black beanie. He wore a faded shirt and baggy pants.

"Okay. Um, his name is David, and what you wouldn't expect about him is he isn't listening to rap. No, David is actually listening to heavy metal because listening to someone scream in his ears helps him not to scream at others. He goes out late at night and cruises around on his bike, trying to find the best place to draw. He enjoys sitting at the beach off the rocky cliffs because of its beautiful scenery, but it also holds some danger. David still goes home to see his parents. His mom still does his laundry, but he forgot to take his clothes last weekend, which is why he's wearing a faded shirt he hasn't worn since high school."

"Okay, I can get down with that backstory. Why David though?" Leo grabbed his chin in thought.

"I don't know. He looks like a David," I shrugged. "My turn to pick."

I scanned the crowd, trying to find someone who might be hard for him. My eyes landed on a taller girl. She had her back turned to us, but she wore a short black skirt with a red tank top and red high heels. She looked like she was ready to go out and not to class. Her dark brown hair was straight, reaching above her lower back.

"Her," I told him with a mischievous gleam.

"Easy. Her name is Francesca. She comes from a wealthy

family. She's daddy's little girl who gets everything she wants. Only one time, daddy couldn't get her the one thing she wanted, a guy she thought she liked. She got so mad she retaliated by trying to get with his best friend. When he rejected her too, she spread vicious rumors about the pair. Many people believed them, causing everyone to avoid them. The best friends found solace in each other, which only angered her further. She tried to get between them, drugging the guy she originally wanted at a party." Leo had an unreadable expression on his face as he looked at the girl.

"She took him to a room and had sex with him in his drugged state. The best friend found them and had to fight her to get her off him. No one believes a girl can rape a guy, so to everyone there, they assumed the best friend had gotten jealous and took the frustration out on her. They deemed him an abuser of women, causing him to have to drop out of high school and finish his senior year online. While his friend spiraled in college, almost not being able to graduate. Francesca got away with everything, because no one would believe the best friend. He, however, was charged with assault, but his mother got it dismissed."

"Jesus, Leo." I shook my head. "What makes you think that's her story?"

"I know her." He shrugged. I stared at him so fast, my neck hurt. I tried to replay everything he had told me.

"Leo, were you the best friend in this story, or the original guy?" He met my eyes with a look of surprise on his face. He was almost shocked I had pieced it together.

"The best friend." He sighed. I wrapped my arms around his neck instantly, pulling him against me and squeezing tightly like I could piece him back together from his trauma.

"I'm sorry you went through that. I know you would never hurt a woman. Fuck her. I'll go beat her ass right now," I told him with his cheek pressed beside mine.

"Thanks, Liv, but I'm okay now. She can't say anything here without bringing up secrets of her own."

"Leo, who was the original guy?" I pulled back, looking into his eyes. I think I know the answer, but I hope I'm wrong.

"He wouldn't like me telling you."

"It's Lucas, isn't it?" I felt my chest tighten, and my heart break as I saw Leo's expression change.

"No way," he tried to lie, but he's a terrible liar.

"Okay, good. Still, I am sorry for whoever your friend is." I let him believe his lie worked, but secretly I was fighting back tears for Lucas. I looked back at Francesca, waiting for her to turn her skanky ass face our way. I wanted to memorize her face, so if I ever got the chance, I could punch her right in the nose. I wanted to exact revenge like no other. I hate her worse than Julius and Clover right now.

"I knew a girl named Francesca back in my high school. She was a freshman when I was a senior and even joined in on bullying me. She was a spoiled little shit, too. The school wouldn't put up with her anymore, having her kicked out. Last I heard, she had to move out of state, because no other school in New Hampshire would take her. Francescas must be a real breed of bitch." I shook my head.

"I can stand behind that statement."

We both watched her with murderous intent until she turned, revealing an all too familiar face. Her sharp nose and thin lips made me flash back to when she stole my clothes from the locker room, making me walk out with nothing but a towel to the office. She even tried to take the towel, but I had a tight grip on it.

"Holy shit!" My mouth dropped open. "She's the same fucking Francesca."

"Are you serious?" Leo sat up, looking at me more intently.

"Yeah, I would recognize her bad nose job anywhere."

Her eyes landed on us, causing the corner of her lips to turn up mischievously as she approached. Leo stiffened beside me as he noticed her. I hated that she had caused him so much trouble. I could tell it traumatized him, showing a slight fear of her.

"I got this, okay?" I told him, squeezing his hand before I stood up, approaching her too. Her eyes were fixed on Leo as I stood in front of her. She spared me one small glance before trying to walk past me. I grabbed her arm, pulling her back to me.

"Franny, you better leave him alone." I used the nickname she hated. The girls in highschool would bully her too, because she pissed off queen B one month. She narrowed her eyes at me, trying to place me. It took her a second to remember, because of the vast changes to my appearance.

"Holy shit, Brilo Liv?" She smirked like she was happy to see me.

"Olive, actually." I squeezed her arm tighter until she flinched.

"Let me go, before I yell."

"Go ahead. No one's going to care. They'll look at you like you're crazy. In fact, by all means, please yell," I egged her on.

"Whatever, let me go. I see my boyfriend. He's calling me over." She pointed to Leo.

"Funny, I am pretty sure Leo is dating me," I lied.

"As if he'd stoop to your level."

I pushed her back a few steps before running over to Leo and straddling his lap. He looked at me, a bit confused for a moment, before I crashed my lips against his. It probably wasn't the best idea, but I wanted her to see. I wanted her to leave him alone. The sound of her scoff was like music to my ears as her heels clicked away against the sidewalk. I pulled back, looking her way to make sure she was still walking.

"Shit, Liv. You can't do that to me," Leo groaned. I felt the bulge of his excitement between my legs, making me quickly hop off him.

"Sorry. I didn't want her to think she could come bother you. She said you were her boyfriend, so I told her we were dating." I slapped my forehead lightly, shaking my head. "I'm sorry, I shouldn't have said that." Leo laughed, a big smile gracing his face.

"Don't apologize. I truly enjoyed it, and the lie." He winked at me, making me blush for a second.

It was kind of hot. I didn't think Leo had it in him, but it wasn't the same way Lucas set me aflame. I know mom said this was fine as long as they knew of each other, and neither of them have asked me to be their girlfriend, but it still felt wrong. It still felt kind of slutty kissing Leo after I had kissed Lucas this morning. Hell, we had done more than kiss.

How do people deal with these guilty feelings when they date more than one person?

Hailey twitched her leg beside me, full of nerves, even though I should be the one freaking out. She bit at her thumbnail as we waited in the doctor's office for her to return. She had done my screening yesterday and asked me to come in today. Lucas had gone with me yesterday, being a significant support, so I brought Hailey here with me today instead. I didn't think she would panic on me. She was raising my anxiety up.

"Hailey, stop, you're making *me* nervous."

"You should be! Doctors never call you back to the office to share good news."

I knew she was right, but I was hoping this was a 'hey you're clear, but let's discuss options' kind of visit. Dr. Payne came in, clearing her throat as she shut the door behind her.

"Olive, I am glad you could come in so soon," she greeted me, as she sat behind her desk with Hailey and me sitting across from her. "I am afraid I have some bad news, and some good news for you."

My heart was speeding with nerves, making my stomach twist, and hands feel clammy. I felt a cold sweat work its way through my body.

"We found a small mass in your right breast." It felt like

the walls had crashed down around me. Dr. Payne sounded so distorted as she continued talking. "We will need to schedule a lumpectomy to remove the mass. We'll send it to pathology to be biopsied. If it comes back positive for cancer, we'll start you on target radiation to the breasts."

"You said there was good news. What's the good news?" Hailey quickly asked, looking for her silver lining.

"Since it's so small, if it is cancer, we caught it early enough. By removing the mass, and getting targeted radiation, she should be fine. I'll schedule to remove the mass within the next few days. Depending on your results, I'll refer you to an oncologist if needed."

I knew she was talking to me, but all I could hear was womp womp like the adults in Charlie Brown. I stared at my right breast like the traitor it was. It wasn't a piece of me anymore. It was foreign, making me want to tear it off and be a cyclops breasted woman.

"Olive, let's take this one step at a time. Keep in mind your survival rate is extremely high even if this is cancerous. Try to keep a positive mind."

Unable to speak with the weight of my tongue, I nodded my head. I stood up, rushing to get out of there. It felt like the walls were closing in on me, making me need an escape. I rushed outside with Hailey hot on my tail. When I felt the sun hit my skin, I took a deep breath, not having realized I had been holding it. I kept gasping for air like I couldn't get enough of it. Hailey stroked my back, hugging me and telling me it would all be okay. I shook my head, remembering mom. Remembering how awful she felt and looked at the end.

"Let's get you home," Hailey whispered, pulling me to the car. She drove me home and laid me on the bed. "It'll be okay, Livie, I am here for you. We'll get through this. I'll be here every step of the way."

She tucked me in, patting my head. I silently cried myself to sleep, waking up to Hailey's hushed whispers. I strained my ears to listen as the fog of sleep lifted more.

"She probably wouldn't tell you guys herself, but I felt you should know. Honestly, you guys are the only other friends she has. She is going to need support, but she's going to be stubborn about getting it from you," I heard her.

I groaned as I tried to open my eyes, sitting up on the bed. I turned to find Lucas and Leo on my couch staring up at me. Lucas looked so serious, biting his cheek. Leo looked like he would cry as he looked at me. I sighed, because I didn't want Hailey to tell them. She was right. I wasn't planning on letting them know. They're not *just* my friends. Leo is trying to date me more seriously, and Lucas is sleeping with me. They don't need to be involved in this.

"Do you need anything?" Leo was the first to get up and step by my side. He was acting like I didn't know how to walk anymore.

"I'm fine." He tried to grab my side, but I smacked his hand away. "Leo, I still know how to use my legs. I have a small mass in my breast. I'm not an invalid." Leo froze, staying back as I walked towards the couch, narrowing my eyes furiously at Hailey. She shrugged her shoulders like I should have expected it. Honestly, I should have.

"What *would* you like us to do?" Lucas asked me, leaning forward on his knees.

His intense brown eyes stared deeply at me, straight to my soul. All I could see now was a man who had been hurt, humiliated, and traumatized. I couldn't stop thinking of the story Leo told me. Lucas had been raped. Is that why he is the way he is with women? Is it to gain back a part of himself?

"Go home," I told them flatly. Lucas sighed, bowing his head into his hands. He lifted his face back up, wiping it against his hands.

"Fine, but you better tell us when the surgery is. We want to be there," Lucas demanded as he got up. I have noticed he's always quick to do what I say. He's good at listening to my demands and wishes. He never argues about them, he respects them and follows them.

"We can't leave. We just got here," Leo protested. "You don't want us to go, do you, Liv?"

I felt a slight guilt at Leo's tone. He sounded sad, almost hurt that I would send him away. He wanted to stay to feel better himself.

"You heard her, Leo. She said she wanted us to go home, so we're going," Lucas answered for me, saving me from caving and letting them stay. I didn't want the attention right now.

"I will tell you when my surgery is. You can wait with Hailey. I am sure she wouldn't mind the company." Leo wrapped his arm around my waist from behind, kissing my temple.

"Fine, Liv. After surgery, I plan to stay glued to your side. I am going to pamper you, stupid," he promised, causing me to roll my eyes. He's sweet, but I don't want that. I want my space right now. I have a lot to process.

"Yeah, okay," I told him, feeling him let me go. Lucas came forward next. He grabbed my hips, pulling me flush against his chest. His eyes softened as they looked at me. He rubbed his knuckles against my cheek sweetly, making me blush. He then ran his thumb over my lower lip.

"I'll be waiting for you. Can't wait to see how you'll fight this one." He made my heart skip as he kissed my forehead. *How I fight this one, huh?* Lucas knows I love a fight and thinking of this as something I have to fight made me feel less panicked. I can fight. I can fight this the same way I fight in the ring. You're going down, breast mass!

"I always win my fights," I whispered.

"I know you do, Rose." He winked at me with a small smirk. He gave me the words I didn't know I needed to hear. He made me feel more ready for this than I had all day. I don't know how he lifts me up like this. It's something only he can do.

Chapter 17

Olive's P.O.V.

Hailey left about an hour after the guys did. I wanted to feel the sun's heat against me again, so I headed to the roof where a sweet flower garden was being grown and two lounge chairs always sat. The sun was setting, leaving the sky with a bright orange tint. I sat back with my eyes closed and my arm laid above my head. The roof door opened about 10 minutes after I got up here, disturbing my peace. I didn't bother to open my eyes and see who it was, worried it was Mom's friend who lives in this building. I didn't want to have to make small talk right now.

"This is beautiful." A familiar voice surprised me. I felt them sit in the lounge chair beside me. I peeped an eye open, seeing his broad shoulders first.

"Lucas?" I furrowed my brow as I opened both eyes. "What are you doing here?"

"I figured you could use some company."

"Oh, did you?" I sat up, no longer relaxed in the slightest.

"Yeah, I know you have too much going on in your head. Honestly, I couldn't get *you* out of *my* head." He shocked me with his revelation.

"I want to pretend like everything is fine and not falling apart all around me." I sighed, laying back on my chair again. "I keep wondering how mom felt when they told her she had cancer."

"I am sorry, Rose. I hate her cancer wasn't caught sooner. She was an amazing woman to have passed away over something that could have been cured if caught soon enough." He shook his head as if he were so mad over the fact.

"No, kidding." I sighed, staring up at the one lonely cloud floating above.

"She seemed like a wonderful woman. I know she left you when you were young to deal with a lot of shit you shouldn't have, but she was a good person when I met her."

"I am glad you got to meet her. She looked happy. She deserved to be happy after everything she went through."

"You deserve happiness too, Rose. After everything, I am sure you went through. Your mother told me her biggest regret in life was leaving you behind. She was sure your father wasn't hurting you, but there was no way for her to be certain, and it killed her. Was she right? Did your father leave you alone?" Lucas' deep brown eyes stared at me, desperate for my answer.

"When did she tell you that?"

"The next day. I went back to see her after you left, and we spoke a while longer," he admitted, making me freeze for a moment as I imagined them talking together without me. I'm not sure why it touched my heart to know he had spent more time with her. "Now answer my question, Rose. Did he leave you alone?"

"He would only ever hit me when he was teaching me how to defend myself. The only thing he was good for was teaching me to fight and being a drunk I had to take care of." I shook my head at the memory. Lucas' eyes didn't stop staring at me as he took in my words. His chiseled jaw ticked for a moment.

"I hope you were able to beat his ass."

"Not once." I shook my head. Dad is the only one I could never beat. He's the only one I refuse to fight, too.

"Sorry I brought it up."

"It's no big deal." I shrugged, too used to my trauma. It's nothing now.

"It is a big deal, Olive. Don't downplay the shit you've

been through."

I shrugged, not sure what to say. I've noticed he calls me Olive when he's being serious about something. We sat in silence for a while, staring up at the now cloudless sky which was painted a red orange with the setting sun. It was so beautiful to watch from up here.

"Beautiful," Lucas whispered.

"It truly is." I turned to look at him, finding his eyes already on me. I blushed under his gaze. He was a handsome man I knew I couldn't have. I wanted to ask him about Francesca. I wanted to know the reason he slept with so many women. He probably doesn't want to talk about it.

"What's on your mind?" He asked me, not looking away from my eyes.

"The truth?" I asked, seeing him nod in response. "Wondering why you sleep with so many women." Lucas sighed, pouting for a second.

"I'm only sleeping with you, Rose. I haven't slept with another girl since we slept together the second time."

"Are you serious?" I couldn't believe what he was saying. "What about Janessa?"

"I broke it off with her the same night she showed up. I don't want anyone else, Rose."

"It's kind of hard to believe, Lucas." I shook my head.

"I know it is." He sighed again.

It got quiet again as I watched Lucas stare up at the sky. He tapped his foot on the lounger rapidly as he thought. Eventually, he turned and looked at me. He looked so serious I had to swallow the nerves in my throat down.

"Something happened to me a few years ago. Something I don't think I've ever told anyone. It changed me, and the way I looked at women. It's the reason I slept around so much." He gave me a vague reason, which was more than I was hoping for.

"I'm sorry, Lucas. Do you want to talk about it?" I hoped he would open up more.

"Maybe another night." He looked away from me,

staring at the multicolored straps on the lounge chair as he stuck his finger between the two of them. Is he fidgeting right now? I pulled my chair closer to his, having them meet. I could smell his hearty cologne with how close we were. Lucas looked back up at me again. I could see the pain he was trying to hide in his eyes. I scooted closer to him, never breaking our eye contact.

"I am going to hold you to that, Lucas. I hope you know I'm here for you the same way you've been here for me." I leaned forward, kissing his lips tenderly. I am not usually one to start our kisses, always being worried about feeling too romantic about him. With what I know about him now, and what he's telling me, maybe it is time I gave him a real chance. We'll see how the date he wants will go.

"Thank you, Rose," he whispered, as he ran the backs of his finger over my arm. Goosebumps erupted under his touch. It was electrifying.

"Lucas, I need to know what you want from me? Am I some conquest or do you want something serious in the end?" I bit the bullet, asking him the question that's been eating away at me since he asked me on another date.

"You're not a conquest, Rose. You're so much more. I would like to be serious with you."

His answer was what I was hoping to hear, but it didn't relieve my worries. I still felt like I was taking a huge chance on liking him. It would be so easy for him to crush my heart. I still need to be careful. I think I'll need time to trust him before this feeling finally goes away.

"Okay, Lucas. I hope you know Leo feels the same way," I reminded him he wasn't the only one after me. Leo was worming his way into my heart, too. We may not have the same intensity I have with Lucas, but he's sweet and secure. I feel I can trust him a lot easier than I can Lucas. I wish it wasn't the case, but it is.

"I know. I have an idea about that, one Leo and I have discussed already. We are wondering if you will seriously date us both for 6 months and at the end of the 6 months pick which one of us you want to be your boyfriend. Are you up for it?"

His suggestion caught me off guard. I didn't realize they spoke to each other about dating me. They have a great friendship, and I was glad I wasn't ruining it. I contemplated his suggestion, and it seemed logical enough.

"Okay." I nodded.

"There are rules."

"Alright, tell me."

Lucas explained each of them would get at least one date a week. If there were to be more than one date, the other would have to have at least one more date as well. They can't interrupt each other's dates with me, which includes texting. They told me I can't share what the other one is doing or what they have planned. I don't have to share when or if I sleep with either of them. They don't want to hear and they don't care.

I feel like the bachelorette. What is this daytime drama?

Lucas' P.O.V.

My phone was by my side all day, trying not to miss Rose's call or text. I want to make sure I am there for her when she goes in for surgery. I've been looking up the best oncologists in the state, and one familiar name popped up. But I refuse to let her see him, even if he is conveniently located nearby. I hate him. He's no better than my father.

Kane Phillips is a pompous ass. He thinks himself better than the rest with his high and mighty act. 'I not only help my patients with their cancer, I help their families as well,' he said that to us at the dinner table once. I had seen him *'help'* the family before. She was bent over his desk as he *'helped'* her.

I didn't see him the same after that. He took advantage of her. He said it was the only time he had done it when I confronted him about it. I didn't believe him, but I was only

16, so no one actually cared what I had to say about him. He married the woman, as if to prove a point to me. They divorced three years later. We never saw much of her in those years. She was like this hidden secret wife. It was the strangest thing.

If Rose needs an oncologist, then I'll fly one here for her. Someone who isn't Kane. I won't have him taking advantage of her. I hope to never let her meet him, but I know she'll have to when we go on our date on Sunday. Of course, that's only if she's okay by then.

Mom's birthday is Sunday, and she likes to have a family brunch. Kane, being her older brother, means he'll be there. I want Rose to meet mom, seeing as she met dad last time. Mom is a saint compared to dad. Honestly, compared to dad, many people are angels. The man is a massive dick with serious control issues. Not to mention the anger issues he lashes out with. I make sure they're always directed at me. I would never let him hurt Lisa the same way he hurt mom, or me.

I don't think Rose realizes she and I share some of the same trauma... an abusive dad. Only my father hurt his kids too, not just mom. Thankfully, he's not a fighter with large muscles, but he does still strike a mean punch, always somewhere that isn't noticeable. I've kept him away from Lisa as often as I could. He's only ever laid hands on her once, and I quickly stopped it.

Rose: Surgery is scheduled for 9 a.m. tomorrow. It's an outpatient procedure, so I'll be in and out the same day.

Olive's text had my chest constricting. I need her to be okay. I need this to not be cancer, even if we are all thinking it is. She shouldn't have to deal with this. It isn't right. She deserves a much happier life, and I plan on giving it to her. No matter what the results of the biopsy, I plan on bringing her joy.

Lucas: I'll be there Rose.
Rose: Thanks.
Lucas: Do you need anything right now?

I know it's currently the middle of the day, but after I

left the roof of her loft yesterday, I couldn't help but miss her. She had agreed to our proposal and I'm going to be fighting hard for the next 6 months. I need to show her I'm the one for her. I need her to see how much better I am for her.

Rose: I hate to say it, but I could use some company. It's too quiet and Hailey has classes all day today.

Lucas: Say no more. I'm on my way ;)

Rose: Thanks, Lucas

I grabbed my keys, almost running to my car. With everything that has been going on I have had little alone time with her and I miss my Rose. I am grateful she asked *me* to come and not Leo. I may have driven a few too many miles over the speed limit as I made my way to her, not having been this excited in a while.

She opened her door, greeting me with a messy bun, black sweatpants and a baby blue shirt. She looked so cozy and cute. I wanted to pick her up, wrap her in a blanket, and hold her on the couch all day.

"Hello, my beautiful Rose." I smiled at her as I entered. She gave me a small smirk, amused by my antics.

"Thanks for coming. It was pretty quiet here, and it was unsettling. I'm not used to being alone," she admitted.

"I'll come over whenever you need me. All you have to do is send me a text," I assured her. "Doesn't matter at what time, either. I have a severe case of insomnia. My body doesn't get along with sleep."

"I'll bear it in mind." She nodded. "Do you wanna watch a movie with me? I was about to play a horror film, because I need some action right now more than wholesome Disney movies." Her movie choice caught me off guard for a second, but I quickly nodded my head.

"I'm down for whatever you'd like to do."

"Perfect. I'll go pop some popcorn, you go sit."

I grabbed a blanket from the little wooden ladder she used as a throw blanket holder before taking my spot on the couch. I heard her humming as she waited on the popcorn by the microwave. She tapped her fingers on the counter, making me realize we had a similar taste in music as I recognized the song, Shadow Of The Day by Linkin Park.

"I like this song." I sang along with her humming, making her smile.

"It's one of my favorites from the band. Well, one of the slower favorites. I honestly like too many of their songs. Linkin Park is the best." Rose sounded almost giddy as she spoke about them.

"I second that statement." I loved learning something new about her. If only there could be a concert to go to, but with Chester Bennington dead, there's no way. It wouldn't be the same.

"What do you want to drink with your popcorn?"

"Anything is fine," I called back. She emerged from the kitchen with a tray of popcorn, drinks, and a few assorted candies. I saw my favorites amongst them, some hot tamales. I love cinnamon flavored things.

Rose started the movie, taking a seat directly beside me. I smiled, realizing she wanted contact with me. She could have sat at the other end of the couch, but she sat close enough that our thighs were touching. She pulled her legs in, placing the popcorn bucket in her lap, and started the movie.

Rose would jump sometimes, but never scream. She somehow never spilled the popcorn either. I had grabbed her legs part way through the movie, placing them over my lap. My hands gently massaged her calves as she laid back on the couch with her head propped up by a cushion. I felt her look at me a few times throughout the movie. I had done the same, watching her when I could.

"You're cute when you jump," I teased her as the credits rolled through the screen. She threw the pillow at me from under her head. I caught it chuckling. She immediately sat up, straddling my lap. She grabbed my wrists, placing them above my head. I was curious what she was planning to do, so I let her do what she wanted without a fight. Her lust filled eyes landed on my lips, watching as I licked them.

"What are you doing, Rose?"

"Taking what I want, if that's okay?" She bit her lip, a little embarrassed by her words, but sticking to them.

"More than okay." I nodded.

Her hands were still on my wrists, above my head, as she leaned down. She pressed those rosy red lips against mine in a frenzy. She was hot and demanding as she kissed me. This passion was new to her. I quite enjoyed it as she sucked on my lower lip. I groaned, pushing my pelvis towards her center more. She swayed her hips on me, grinding against my very prominent erection now. She was clearly wanting more, but I was letting her take charge. Everything will be at her pace.

"Lucas?" She called my name, stopping for a second to look me deeply in the eyes. She was so vulnerable right now.

"Yes, Rose?"

"Can you make me forget all about tomorrow?" My chest tightened, seeing her so anxious. I was anxious, too. Tomorrow determines a lot about her life.

"I'll do my best."

I'll give her what she wants as best I can

Chapter 18

Olive's P.O.V.

"I'll do my best." He told me with a look of determination and sympathy. He could tell I was feeling anxious about tomorrow. I mean, who wouldn't be? There's a possibility I have cancer right now. *Damn mass in my breast!*

Lucas easily lowered his arms, letting me know he had been letting me keep them there. There was a deep admiration in his eyes, which was freaking me out a little with its intensity. I looked away, feeling too self conscious under his gaze. Lucas brought his mouth down to my neck, kissing it tenderly. It wasn't the usual sucking and marking he liked to do. He kissed down to the opened collar of my shirt, before sliding his hands under it and helping me out of it.

He then continued his light kisses over my torso, around my breast, and down my stomach. His hands sensually pulled my pants down at the speed of a snail, letting his fingertips tickle my skin along the way. I bit my lip, enjoying these gentle touches he was giving me. This hadn't been something I had experienced with him before. It's usually so hot and heavy, but right now, it feels really intimate.

When my pants were discarded to the floor along with my underwear, he pulled his shirt off with one arm. He leaned down over me, kissing my lips again, licking at them, and forcing them to part, allowing him access to my mouth. He nibbled at my lip lightly, sending waves of pleasure through me down to my toes. His hand trailed over my side, past my ribs, and towards the hard buds of my nipple.

My breath hitched when his fingers pinched at it, rolling it just the right way. I squirmed beneath him, wanting him to be deep inside me already. The wait was killing me, and if he doesn't get inside me soon, I'll be begging him to in a couple of minutes. He let one of his hands run down to my leaking center. His finger slid across my slanted lips, parting my wet folds. His middle finger slipped inside of me as he curled his finger in me, rubbing at the sensitive area inside, while his thumb applied pressure to my clit. I couldn't help but moan from his lips.

I felt my toes start to curl as my pleasure rose and rose. It was pooling deep inside me, getting ready to burst if I was touched just right. I could spend days locked away in a room with Lucas, doing nothing but this, and be perfectly content. He knew exactly how to touch me to make my body respond to him. He knew it better than *I* did, giving me things I didn't know I needed.

He pulled his finger out of me, standing on his feet to remove his pants. I looked into those brown eyes of his, finding them already on me. There was still a deep admiration in them, but I didn't shy away this time. My gaze fixed on his, even as he climbed over me. I didn't look away or close my eyes as his dick touched my entrance. I was pretty sure I wasn't even blinking, or if I was; it was at the same time as him.

Lucas inserted himself painstakingly slowly inside of me. When he was balls deep in me, I moaned loudly, loving the feel of him. My fingers dug into his skin deeply as I gripped onto his back. I wanted to leave my mark on him, one that was more than just a hickey. I knew I shouldn't feel this need to mark him, but I did.

"*Deeper, Lucas,*" I whispered into his ear.

I want to see how much of him I could take. I want to see what more Lucas has to offer me. He showed me exactly what he could do for about three hours this afternoon, repeatedly bringing me pleasure. He had me yelling his name many times, taking me in all kinds of ways all over this apartment. We ended it with us on the bed. We were both breathless and sweaty, causing our hairs to stick to our faces. I turned to my side and looked at Lucas, who eventually felt my gaze and turned to look back at me.

"What's on your mind, Rose?" He asked me.

"Stay here with me tonight?" I asked before I could stop myself. That is a terrible idea, and I know it. Yet, somehow, it sounds absolutely perfect.

"I would love nothing more, but could we do it at my apartment? I have some work I need to do." He cleared the hair from my face as he spoke.

"I'm so sorry. Am I keeping you from work?" I realized in all this time, I had never asked him what he did. Nor did I ask if he was working when I would text him. I know nothing about his schedule, and yet he comes any time I ask him to. Does this mean he really does like me?

"Don't worry about it, Rose. It's nothing, just some paperwork that needs my eyes to look over." He rubbed my cheek with a small smile. "Please, don't make me sleep without you after you offered for me to." He widened his eyes to make it look like they were glistening, like the eyes of a cartoon puppy. It made me smile wider than I meant to, which had Lucas smirking. He leaned forward, grabbing my chin.

"So, is that a yes?" He asked me.

"Yes. It's a yes." I nodded. "First, let me get dressed and pick something to wear for tomorrow."

"I'll get us there early tomorrow, so don't worry about anything. We will all be there for you. *All* of us." He assured me, and all I could do was nod my head at his words. "I'll go find my clothes and let you get ready."

He kissed my forehead, leaving me feeling lonely on the bed for a moment. I reluctantly kicked the sheets off me, letting the cold air hit my skin in protest. My legs were feeling wobbly from the insane sex we just had. I had never had sex for so long before. I was the same sore I'd be after running a marathon. My legs felt heavy as I got dressed, collecting some clothes for tomorrow.

I found Lucas dressed and leaning against the back of the couch. He was typing away on his phone, making me wonder who he was talking to. I guess I still don't trust him fully, despite his sweet words. The need to look at his phone, and see who he was texting, was eating away at me. I have no right and it's honestly such an invasion of privacy. I need to get over myself.

"I'm ready now," I said, stepping towards him. He immediately put his phone down, giving me his half smirk as he held his hand out towards me. I grabbed it, letting him guide me out of the flat and to his car. The sun was halfway down the sky now, getting close to setting as the evening progressed. My stomach rumbled loudly in the car, making me blush and Lucas laugh.

"I'll order us some food when we get to my place." He smiled as he pulled onto the street. He threw me his phone a second later, letting it land on my lap. I stared at him with a raised brow in confusion.

"Pick a song to play," he told me, holding his thumb over the phone to unlock it.

It was hard for me to not click on his texts and see who he was talking to. I opened his music, seeing we actually had similar tastes. I scrolled through it, trying to find the right song, feeling a lot of pressure to choose the right one. His phone vibrated in my hand, letting us both know he had received a text.

"Who is it?" Lucas asked.

"Um…what if I told you I was an android person who did not know how to work an iPhone?" I asked shyly, unsure how to see who had texted him. He laughed again.

"Just open my texts." He shook his head with a smile.

I was surprised he was giving me permission to open his texts. I figured out how to get back to the home screen, seeing the text app on the bottom. It opened and saw he had an unread message from his mom.

CHAPTER 18

"It's your mom."

"Read it to me?" He asked as he turned right on the street.

"Okay, uh, it says: Lucas, you better not start any drama with your uncle this time. It's my birthday and I want to have an enjoyable time with my family." I read the text out loud to him, feeling embarrassed. I wasn't sure if it was something he wanted me to know or not. I turned to look at him, seeing he wasn't phased by it.

"Tell her I'll do my best as long as he does." He said. I typed the message out to his mom and hit send. I wondered what was going on between him and his uncle that would warrant such a text from his mother.

"Music please, Rose," he reminded me.

"Right." I saw the list of names on his texts as I went to go back to his music app. I saw his mom's name, mine, Leo's, Lisa's and even Hailey's, but under all of them was *Janessa*. My stomach twisted, and I felt a pang of jealousy. I thought he said he broke it off. Why is her name still there? I felt my face contort in disappointment before I could stop it.

"What's wrong?" Lucas asked.

"Nothing, sorry. Just trying to navigate your phone," I lied, smiling sheepishly at him.

"If I remember correctly, Leo got you a new iPhone when he broke your last one, no?" Lucas arched a brow.

"He did, but I am honestly not an iPhone person, so I traded it out." I held up my Samsung to show him. Lucas laughed, making me smile. His laugh was beautiful, bouncing all around me in the car.

"You're something else, Rose."

I finally got to his music and decided to play Deftones. We sang along for the last few minutes of the ride. Lucas was actually an excellent singer. I had pushed my insecurities and feelings of betrayal deep down, deciding not to let it ruin my mood. I didn't know what was said on the text thread, so I won't obsess over it. It could have very well been the message that broke it off between them. I tried to trust what Lucas was telling me was true. I was having a hard time doing so. Lucas opened my door for me when we arrived, holding his hand out. I placed his phone in his hand before stepping out.

"I wanted your hand, not my phone." He shook his head. He put his phone in his pocket before holding his hand back out towards me. I took his hand this time, allowing him to pull me flush against his chest. He pulled his phone back out and fiddled with it for a moment. I tried to pull away, but he held me close.

"I know you saw her name on my phone, Rose. I have only texted my family and Leo these past few weeks. Her name is still there because she was the last girl I texted to break things off with." I blushed, knowing I had been caught looking. He turned the phone for me to see his message to her.

Lucas: What you did today was unacceptable. I know we've had our fun, Janessa, but it's over now. I am serious about the girl I had brought home tonight, and your antics pushed her away. Please lose my number.

The words I read surprised me. He was serious about me even then? I had a hard time processing what his message said against what I had believed. I was so insecure and wrapped up in my preconceived notions of him, I never gave him a chance. He hadn't hurt me and yet I treated him like he did. It was Julius who hurt me, who's now left me with this insecurity and distrust of men.

"I'm sorry. I promise I wasn't trying to snoop. I just noticed her name. Thank you for showing me." I bit my lip, feeling both embarrassed and anxious. Lucas leaned down and kissed my forehead.

"Let's go upstairs and get some food ordered."

We made our way upstairs, ordering some Mexican food. Lucas stepped into his office after he situated me in the living room with blankets, snacks, and the TV remote. I found it cute the way he fussed over me. He wanted to make sure I was entertained and didn't plan on leaving. The doorbell rang

CHAPTER 18

15 minutes later.

"Rose, could you get the door for me, please? It's probably our food," he called out to me from his office. I smiled as I got off the couch, picturing him hunched over his desk. I felt bad he had to work.

"Yeah, I got it," I called back.

I opened the door with my smile quickly fading. I didn't bother looking at the camera monitor beside his door to see who it was before I had opened it. Honestly, I assumed it was the delivery person with our food. I was surprised to find a tall, beautiful woman standing on the other side of the open door. She had short wavy green hair and a kind expression despite her tough demeanor. She wore biker boots, torn jeans, and a leather jacket. Her mouth turned with a polite smile before opening it to speak. Her dark lipstick made her teeth look so much whiter, and her skin paler.

"Hey, um, is Lucas home?" She asked, causing my heart to clench. *Another girl.*

"Uh, yeah. He's in his office working. I'll go grab him," I told her.

"Oh, it's fine. I'll get him myself." She smirked with a mischievous grin on her face. She sidestepped me, entering the place like she owned it.

She knew exactly where she was going without me having to show her. She'd been here before, seeming so comfortable, too. I felt my chest hurt again with my insecurities bubbling up again. I hated this pendulum of emotions I'd been feeling.

"Lukie!" she called out.

Lukie?

"Rachel?" I heard him respond with confusion and surprise in his tone.

I watched as he quickly appeared at the doorway of his office. He saw her and smiled the widest I had seen him smile. Somehow it crushed my heart more. She held a place in his heart and I did not know who she was. Lucas ran to her, hugging her and spinning her around in joy. My heart hurt as I watched the scene unfold before me.

"I didn't know you were coming into town! You didn't tell me." He laughed as he put her down. The smile had never faded from his face.

"It was a surprise. You're my second stop." She smiled up at him.

"Second? I've moved up on your list." She laughed, causing her face to somehow look even more beautiful. Her bright blue eyes shone as she smiled, wrinkling on the sides.

"That's as far up as you'll go. Leo will always be first on my list." She poked his forehead between his brows. I saw Lucas pout, like he didn't like that Leo came first. Now I was very curious who this woman was. She knew both Leo and Lucas. I closed the front door finally, snapping out of my daze. That was when Lucas remembered I was here.

"Rose, come here. I want you to meet my cousin, Rachel." Instant relief washed over me. I felt stupid again, assuming more than I should have. She was his cousin. I had to bite back the sigh of relief wanting to leave me.

"Hi, despite what he calls me, my name is actually Olive," I introduced myself as I made my way to them.

"My name is actually Rachel, so he didn't lie there," she told me with a smile.

"Nice to meet you."

"You too. I don't normally see girls hanging around here, or opening his door." She side-eyed Lucas, who now had a tinge of pink on his cheeks. Was he embarrassed?

"Rose is different from the rest," he said.

"Must be." The bell rang again. This time, it had to be our food.

"I'll get it. It's probably our food. You're welcome to join us as we eat. I ordered a lot," Lucas invited her.

"I feel like I'm imposing. I wasn't expecting you to have a girl here."

"You're not imposing. I was actually getting bored while

he was working," I assured her. I was curious about her, and I wanted to get to know her more. She seems extremely cool and somehow very sweet. She spun the leather cuff on her wrist as she fidgeted.

"If you're sure," she said.

I nodded my head yes. "Very sure."

We sat and ate all together. I learned Rachel is my age and goes to Harvard. In person classes are not her thing, so she mainly does her classes online, allowing her to come visit at random. She is studying early childhood education, which almost made me choke on my food. Lucas and she laughed at my reaction. She thankfully didn't take offense.

"I know it's my appearance that throws everyone off when I tell them. I'll, of course, dye my hair a natural color once I start my internship. I also have a professional wardrobe. No one will know my style unless they see me out of school," she assured me.

"I am sure you'll shock some students when they see you out of school." I laughed.

"Oh, most definitely."

"Ladies, I leave you to keep talking. I have to get back to a stack of looming papers on my desk," Lucas said, getting up from his seat with his empty plate. He kissed my forehead on his way to the kitchen. "I'll be done soon."

Rachel and I were left to have our girl talk.

Chapter 19

Olive's P.O.V.

"Tell me, Olive, how did you manage to get this guy so wrapped up in you?" Rachel asked, leaning forward, resting her chin on the palm of her hand.

"Um, I am not sure what you mean. I haven't done anything. I don't think he's wrapped up in me."

I mean, yes, he's told me he wants me and he wants to get serious. Is it shocking for his friends and family? Has he not had a serious relationship before?

"Oh, sweet girl, he most definitely is."

I shook my head, not believing Lucas, of all people, could be *that* into me.

"You're the first girl he's been serious with since Ivy," she said. I didn't fail to catch the grimace that played on her face for a split second. I furrowed my brows at the mention of Ivy. I've never heard her name before. Honestly, I don't know many of the names of the women Lucas has been with aside from Janessa.

"Who's Ivy?" I asked.

"Ivy was Lucas' girlfriend in college. She died in the same accident as John. The one that put Leo's dad in a coma for a year." She hung her head, picking at the sides of her nail beds.

"Who's John?" I asked, feeling a swirl of emotions at her answer. *Killed*. Last year was hell for Leo and Lucas. Between what I heard about Francesca and now Ivy, I am surprised Lucas is still standing.

"Geez, these guys don't tell you anything. John was Leo's

older brother." My heart stilled, aching for Leo this time. He had lost his brother last year and now his father. It's a wonder he's still so kind and energetic. How is it he can keep such a genuine smile on his face?

"I had no idea."

I let my face fall in sadness. I felt guilty for not knowing, despite having no way of getting this information beforehand. I thought of them both and wondered how they managed through last year. When Leo told me the story of Francesca; he had said they leaned on one another, probably through grief. I feel like, despite them saying it's okay, I shouldn't be dating the two of them. I don't want to cause a rift in their friendship when they need each other. I am sure they're probably more like brothers than friends by now.

"It's a sad tale, so I'm not exactly surprised they didn't tell you," she said, taking a swig of her drink.

"How long had Ivy and Lucas been together when she died?" I was curious how long his most serious relationship had lasted before abruptly stopping.

"Three years. They met in their senior year of highschool, but didn't start dating till the summer before freshman year of college."

My eyes widened in surprise for a moment. Lucas *can* be serious. He can be very committed if he wants to be. I don't know the details of his relationship with Ivy, but to have lasted three years, it must have been good. Granted, Julius and I had been together for over a year and he cheated on me. I guess length of a relationship isn't the most determining factor of how well a relationship is doing, or did.

"That's a while."

"They were happy. Lucas had actually planned on proposing to her that night. John had been distracting her the whole day so Lucas could prepare everything without her knowing. They were on their way there when they were hit."

Rachel looked like she could cry now, remembering it all. Hell, my eyes wanted to mist thinking about it. It sounded like some tragic movie scene. I could picture Lucas all dressed up with Leo at his side, waiting for her to arrive, and instead, receive such morbid news. How do you move on from that?

"He refused to date anyone. He wouldn't even look at other women. It wasn't until after a party, where there was drama with Leo and some girl, Lucas started seeing women again. I am not sure what happened, but we were all happy to see him dating again. We didn't realize he wasn't *actually* dating till a few months later. We realized he was sleeping around. He's been through a lot, Olive. You need to be careful, because he has grown exceptionally attached to you."

I felt my heart shatter and reset inside my chest. Only it didn't set back the same way. I felt deep pain for Lucas. He, indeed, has been through a lot. I am sitting here being insecure and immature about the women that used to be in his life when he very obviously told me the truth about breaking it off with Janessa. He is being serious about wanting me. I am still nervous and scared to let him fully into my heart. I don't want to be hurt the same way Julius hurt me.

I don't want to give my heart away so easily this time. Lucas may have been through a lot, but so have I. He'll have to show me he is serious about me. He can't just say it, and it can't be something his family tries to convince me of. I have to see it for myself. I have to believe it for myself. Otherwise, I'm going to keep swinging on this pendulum of insecure emotions.

"Thank you for telling me."

Rachel and I chatted a while longer, trying to keep the topics light. She told me she would be moving back to New York once she's done with her studies. She misses the noises and cold stagnant air here. She said she even misses the subway, to which I laughed.

"Rachel kept you good company." Lucas' voice came from behind me, cutting my laughter short.

"She did. She's great."

"I'm glad you think so." He kissed the top of my head as he passed by me, taking a seat beside me. He smiled at me so cutely. It was a smile I hadn't seen before. He looked so happy, like a small child full of joy.

"Did you finish working?"

"Sure did. I'm all caught up now, so you have my undivided attention. Sorry, I had to work." He looked very sad about the fact. I found it endearing he wanted to spend so much time with me he had pushed his work back.

"Don't apologize. Your job is important. In fact, you should make sure you stay on top of it. Don't fall behind on my account," I lightly scolded him. The right corner of his lip turned up in his signature half smirk.

"I'll do anything you tell me."

"Sure, you will." I rolled my eyes, not believing it.

"I'll prove it to you. Tell me what to do," he egged me on.

"Okay, fine. Tell me what caused you to sleep around with so many women." It caught him off guard. He pulled his head back a bit in surprise. His eyes held mine in an intense gaze, but he kept quiet. I figured he would, which is why I asked.

"See, not *everything* I tell you." I made my point.

"Rachel, it was great seeing you. Text me where you're staying, and I'll make sure to come hang out. Rose and I need to talk privately." He had a serious tone, making me feel like a child who was about to be scolded for being a brat. Rachel caught the tension as well as she shot me a look. She got up, giving Lucas a kiss on the cheek as she said goodbye.

"It was nice meeting you, Olive. Hopefully, I'll see more of you before I leave." She waved at me from the door. I gave her a small wave back, but my nerves were on end. I wasn't sure what Lucas was going to say, and now I felt stupid for saying what I did. What was even the point of it?

Lucas turned from the door, his attention back to me. He walked over to me with a very intimidating look on his face. I swallowed the lump in my throat from the nerves. When he got to me, he pulled my chair out, turning it to face him. His hands rested on the back of the chair as he stared deep into my blue eyes. He surprised me when he rested his forehead against mine, shaking his head so it rubbed against me. He then fell to his knees, laying his head on my lap. He looked so broken there, pulling at the strings of my heart.

"I'm sorry. I shouldn't have asked you to tell me." I sighed, running my fingers through his thick, silky hair. He shook his head in my lap. He didn't look up at me as he started to speak.

"Don't be sorry, Rose. I said I would do anything you asked, and I meant it. It's hard for me to share. The only person who knows about this is Leo. None of my family has a clue."

I am pretty sure I know what he is talking about, but I need to be sure. I want to know how he felt. I want to hear what happened to him from his own mouth, but I also don't want to push him if he's not ready.

"You don't have to tell me now. I never said you had to tell me now. You can wait, if you're not ready."

I'm such an idiot.

"No, I want to tell you. I can see it's eating away at you and I hate it. Do me a favor and keep playing with my hair while I talk. I don't think I can look at you while I tell you this story." His voice sounded so vulnerable already. He was exposing himself to me.

"I can do that." I rubbed my fingers through his hair again to assure him. He gave me a small nod before taking a deep breath.

"I went out to a party with Leo. He had lost his brother, and I recently lost my long-term girlfriend. They had passed away in the crash Leo's dad was in."

"Rachel told me. I am so sorry, Lucas," I whispered, the sympathy clear in my voice.

"Of course she did." He shook his head in disapproval. "It was Leo's senior year and thanks to some stupid girl he was being outcast by everyone, so I decided to take him out with me to a party on campus. I had a fake ID made for Leo so he could drink with me and everything. We got there and the girl who had been spreading those rumors about him was there, too. I had offered for us to leave, but Leo didn't want to give her the satisfaction." I am sure Leo feels guilty about it now. He had left that part out when told me the story.

"We partied, and I stupidly left my drink unattended. I don't know why I did that. I guess as a guy I never imagined anything would happen. After about 30 minutes or so, I started to feel weird, so I made my way to the bathroom downstairs. There was too long of a line, but I somehow managed my way upstairs, looking through the bedrooms for one with a bathroom. I found one at the end of the hall. It starts to get hazy after that. Whatever drug I was slipped took hold of me around then. I remember laying on the bed and falling asleep. I can remember the feel of small hands running along my body." His shoulders started to shake against me. I wanted to stop him, but I knew he needed to finish his story. Biting back the tears in my eyes, I listened closely. I rubbed my hand over his hair, keeping my promise of playing with it while he spoke.

"I remember trying to wake myself up, but my eyes wouldn't open any more than a slant. I would drift in and out of consciousness. My pants were pulled down with me trying to hold on to them. The feel of a hand on my dick woke me up more, but the drug was so strong, making it hard for me to move or think rationally. I recall the feeling of panic before passing out again. My eyes opened once more to the girl who had spread those rumors about Leo, jumping on my dick. I still remember how she felt since she hadn't bothered to place a condom on me as she raped me."

His voice cracked at the word rape. My lap was wet with his tears, and my own, falling down my cheeks. I didn't want to speak. I wanted to give him a chance to finish his story before I interrupted again.

"When I woke up again I found Leo fighting her off me. The details are fuzzy, but I remember worse rumors were spread about him at school. I felt like such an idiot. I couldn't believe something like that had happened to me. It wasn't possible. They didn't believe Leo, and he told me not to tell anyone either. He didn't want me to go through the ridicule, so he took the consequences of my rape." Lucas wrapped his arms around my waist, holding me close as he kept his face buried in my lap. I felt a sob leave his chest, which tore my heart in two.

"I started sleeping around with women to try and claim back the part of me she took. I wanted to prove what she did had little effect, but it was a stupid hope."

"No, Lucas! You're not an idiot. She raped you. None of it was your fault, not a single thing." I cried over him, bending down and hugging him in the most awkward way. "I am so sorry that happened to you. I am so sorry you had to go through something like that."

I held onto him for a while, letting him cry, letting both of us cry. Eventually he lifted his head and asked me to come lay down with him. We held each other close, closer than ever before, as we fell asleep together. I rubbed him mindlessly, trying to ease his troubles, despite knowing that's not how trauma works.

"I love you, Rose." I heard him whisper in his sleep.

Surely I didn't hear that right, did I?

Chapter 20

Lucas' P.O.V.

The alarm startled me awake. I had almost forgotten what happened last night. I had told my darkest secret to Rose. She had comforted me in a way I was not expecting. She stole my heart last night. It only beats for her now. I looked down to find her still laying on my chest. I remembered waking multiple times to her inching closer to me anytime she had moved away in her sleep. Her small muscular body curled nicely around me.

"Rose, we need to get up. I need to take you to the hospital." I rubbed her back as I spoke softly. She is cute when she first wakes up. Her face scrunched up in complaint with her lips in a slight pout. She furrowed her brow, annoyed at the fact she had to wake. From the few occasions I have slept all night with her, I've learned she likes to sleep in.

"Can we pretend the mass isn't there?" She groaned, making me chuckle.

"I think it's best if we get it removed. Come on, we don't want to be late." I sat her up as she rubbed her eyes. Her beautiful curls were standing in many directions, making it look like a red flamed lion's mane. I liked being the first to see her in the morning. I smiled at her, admiring her beauty. We both got dressed and fixed our hair. I found her hair routine intriguing. I saw the millions of things she had to use to tame those unruly curls. They were beautiful, but they were definitely hard to control. I wonder how she learned to care for them without her mother present.

"Are you ready to go?" I asked her, putting my shoes on by the door.

"Yup." She popped the p, drawing my attention to her lips. I couldn't help the small smirk that played on my face.

"Let's go get this thing removed."

I held my hand out towards her. She didn't hesitate to grab it, making me smile as I turned from her, leading us out of the door and to my car. I could tell Rose was nervous on our drive over as she fidgeted with her fingers. I held her hand for comfort, stopping the fidgeting, but I saw her leg twitching the entire time. She took a few deep breaths when I parked in front of the hospital.

"Are you ready?" I asked her, making her look at me instead of the large hospital building.

"Not at all." She shook her head, her eyes wide and full of fear.

"What do you do before going into the ring? Before a fight, how do you get ready?" I asked her, because this is no different. The fight is different, but it's a fight, nonetheless.

"I shake it out."

"Then let's shake it out." I wanted to help ease her worries. I didn't care about looking like a fool as I started shaking my body like a lunatic. She laughed hysterically at me, making it all worthwhile.

"I don't see you shaking it." I eyed her as I continued shaking my arms and legs. She laughed, but I saw her shake her arms and hands out. Then her shoulders and torso, and finally her legs. I saw her open and shut her hands a few times. She took one long, deep breath at the end.

"I'm ready." Her beautiful icy blue eyes held fire in them now. She was ready.

"Thank you, Lucas."

"Anytime, Rose." I kissed her forehead before getting out of the car. I raced to the other side, opening her door for her. "My Lady." She let out a laugh as she took my hand.

"Such a gentleman." We entered the hospital, heading

CHAPTER 20

for the check in. Leo and Hailey came shortly after we did. They both eyed me suspiciously. I am guessing she didn't tell them she was with me all night.

"How are you feeling, Livie?" Hailey asked her, taking her from my side and hugging her. Surprisingly, Rose didn't let go of my hand when she hugged Hailey back.

"I'm okay now." She shot me a glance from the side of her eye, as if to thank me again for helping her calm down.

"Good. We'll be waiting for you out here when you are done. I'll take you home. Everything is going to be okay." Hailey seemed to be trying to convince herself, more than Rose, of those final words. We all waited in the lobby for a bit before Rose was called back. She gave us each a hug, leaving me for last. I kissed her temple gently, before relinquishing her to the care of the nurse. *Please don't let it be cancer.*

I watched her bright red hair disappear behind those silver doors. I wished I could follow her there. My need to be by her side was consuming every part of my being. I needed to get my mind off of Rose's surgery if I'm going to make it out here in the waiting area.

"Rachel told me she paid you a visit yesterday," I said to Leo, starting a conversation to distract myself.

"Yeah, she did. I had no idea she was coming into town. Did you?" He looked up at me from the chair he deemed his. I couldn't sit still to save my life right now, so instead I leaned against the wall.

"Not a clue. She randomly showed up at my apartment. I think Rose believed she was another girl I had slept with before." I laughed at the thought before cringing at the image. "Gross."

"Liv was at your apartment?" Leo arched his brow. I noticed Hailey leaning forward in her chair, interested in the conversation now.

"Yeah, she was. She and Rachel spoke, while I finished some work." I didn't want to tell him about last night's events. He didn't need to know the details. I will eventually let him know Rose now knows what happened to me and what had caused me to sleep with so many women.

"I see." Leo nodded. I could tell he wanted to ask more questions, but thought better of it.

"She kind of told Rose about John and Ivy." I plopped on the chair beside him, finally feeling like I didn't want to climb the walls. My anxiety settled down until I saw Leo looking kind of upset.

"Why would she do that?" Leo shook his head.

"Your guess is as good as mine." I shrugged.

"Who are John and Ivy?" Hailey suddenly asked, reminding me she was there.

"John's my dead older brother."

"Ivy is my dead, almost, fiance." Hailey's eyes widened in shock. Her mouth opened and closed a million times as she tried to think of what to say.

"*Mierda.*" Now, I don't speak Spanish, but I know my swear words, and that's definitely one. "I am so sorry, guys." Hailey was upset at herself for asking. She shook her head multiple times afterwards, having some sort of inner dialogue.

"Don't worry about it. We've healed. It's been a year and a half already," Leo assured her with a small smile.

Ivy will forever hold a place in my heart. I loved her so deeply. It broke me in two to lose her. I wouldn't eat, sleep, or even move. I remember being a mess on the floor, too fatigued to even get on my bed. Leo and I grieved separately for the first few months before we came together again. We helped each other out, lifting each other off the ground, literally. Leo is the closest thing I have to a brother.

We all spoke about lighter topics as we waited for someone to tell us about Rose. Leo and I kept asking Hailey questions about Rose, which she happily obliged. I enjoyed using any and every opportunity I could to get to know Rose better. Hailey shared how she was the one to teach Rose how to maintain her curls. I smiled, thinking back to this morning.

"You guys are good for her. She's always been insecure

with guys. She's never had them pay her much attention until she started college," Hailey told us both. "She told me about your whole six month plan thing. I think it's a great idea. I just hope the one of you she doesn't choose can be man enough to still be her friend. She's starting to care for you both, and it's going to hurt her to lose either one of you in the end."

Leo and I sat silently for a while, contemplating Hailey's words. I imagined how I would feel if she chose Leo. Could I handle being around the two of them? The thought alone caused a sinking feeling in my stomach. I know I'd have to, because Leo is my best friend. It's not like I could avoid them, but I could go overseas for a little while and give myself time to get over Rose. *Yeah, I think I'll move abroad if she chooses Leo over me.*

"Are you Ms. Brewer's family?" A doctor in scrubs came out, asking us.

"I'm her sister." Hailey stood up, regarding the doctor. The doctor narrowed his eyes at her, probably wondering how they could be related when they looked so vastly different.

"Surgery went well. She's currently in recovery, where we will keep her for an hour or two to monitor her. She should be good to go home once we remove the drain. Thankfully, she won't have to keep it in. Call the office to schedule her one week follow up. Her biopsy results should come back in a day or two, but with the weekend coming up, she won't hear from her doctor till Monday, if not Tuesday. In the meantime, let her rest. She'll be sleepy and possibly a little woozy from the anesthesia. Monitor the incision so it does not get infected. Do you have questions for me?"

"When can I see her?" She asked.

"A nurse will come and get you as soon as she wakes."

"Thank you, doctor." Hailey nodded, taking her seat again. I could breathe a little easier, knowing everything went well. My breathing won't be right until we know if it's cancer or not. I hate that we have to wait another day or two to find out.

"I am assuming you're both going to go to Liv's flat

after this?" Hailey looked at us, assessing as she waited for our answer.

"I already told her I would be pampering her after surgery," Leo answered first. I figured as much, but I was disappointed it wouldn't be her and me for the rest of the day.

"I don't plan on leaving her side," I confirmed.

"Perfect."

Hailey smiled at us sweetly. I was glad Rose had such a good friend. Hailey and she were almost as close as Leo and I. I think with everything Leo and I have gone through we're bonded for life, no matter what happens. About 20 minutes later, the nurse called Hailey back. Rose had woken up. I wished I could go back to see her as well, but I was glad she at least had Hailey. I watched them lead Hailey away to the back.

I'll see you at your flat, Rose.

Olive's P.O.V.

I woke up shaking uncontrollably all over. The nurses laid warm blankets over me, even though I was sure I wasn't cold. I kept swallowing, feeling like I would throw up at any second. The nausea was something I was not expecting. My brain felt foggy, trying to recall where I was and what was happening.

Anesthesia is a strange thing. I feel like I lost time in my life. I was neither asleep nor awake. It feels like I have this enormous gap in time I can't account for. As if I closed my eyes in the surgery room and then opened them back up to find myself in an unfamiliar room. It doesn't feel like time passed between closing my eyes and opening them, but I know it did.

Hailey was at my side, holding my hand. She gave me her sweet smile, but I could see the worry behind her eyes. The nurse handed me a throw up bag when I complained of nausea. They monitored me for a little while, checking my blood pressure and seeing how I was feeling. Hailey let me know Leo and Lucas had been waiting with her the whole time, making me feel better knowing she wasn't waiting out there alone.

"Thank you, Hails."

"For what?" She cocked her head to the side.

"For being here with me. For always looking out for me. I love you."

"I think the anesthesia still has a hold of you," she laughed.

"I mean it, Hails."

"Alright, alright. I love you too, Livie."

After about another half hour, the nurse came, explaining my after care instructions. She then told me I was free to get dressed and leave. I was ready to get out of this scratchy hospital gown. Hailey let me get dressed on my own. I slowly opened the gown up, sliding it off my arms. There was a large white bandage over the side of my breast where the incision had been made. I wanted to look at it, but knew better than to tear the bandage off right now. It'll be another day or two.

I got dressed, opening the curtain to find Hailey patiently waiting. She smiled at me again as the nurse had me sit in the wheelchair. I felt embarrassed being wheeled out of the hospital, feeling it unnecessary as I was sure I could walk on my own. Leo and Lucas had apparently left when Hailey was called to my side. She told me they would more than likely be waiting for me at the flat.

She wasn't wrong. I noticed their cars whenever Hailey pulled in. She helped me out of her car, linking our arms and telling me to lean on her if I needed to. In truth, nothing hurt too bad right now, but my head was spinning from the effects of the anesthesia.

"There's the girl of the hour," Leo said. He smiled at me as we approached him and Lucas in the hall. They had both been waiting by my door, each with their own bag of goodies. I wasn't sure what was inside, but I was curious to find out.

"How are you feeling?" Lucas asked.

"Dizzy, nauseous, like the whole thing was just a dream," I shrugged.

"Let us in, Liv. I tried to pick your lock, but your door is too good. I couldn't surprise you like I wanted to," Leo pouted.

"You tried to pick my lock?" I laughed, imagining him knelt before my doorknob with his lip ring swinging back and forth as he focused.

"I wanted to get in."

Hailey opened the door with her key. I had made a copy for her. She's the only one to have a key here besides me. I haven't told dad about mom's flat or even her life insurance money. He doesn't deserve to know anything about the life she built for herself here. I had been ignoring his calls for the last week. I've always resented him for what he did, but him being my only parent, I felt I had to respect him. All I feel towards him right now is a deep anger and a brewing hatred. I can't stand him. He says he is sorry, and he has sobered up more since I've left, but there's no taking back what he did.

The moment my front door opened, I was berated by questions raining from 'are you okay' to 'do you need anything?'. Hailey had sat me down on the couch, and I watched all three of them run around the flat like panicked chickens. They doted on me, refusing to let me get up off the couch for anything.

"Unless you can somehow magically go to the bathroom for me, I'm going to have to get up," I said with a raised brow. I laughed as Leo let go of my shoulders, making an O face in understanding. I walked past him to the bathroom, seeing Lucas upstairs in my room. I furrowed my brow as I watched him. I couldn't tell what he was doing from this angle. I'll check and see what he was messing with later.

"Are you hungry?" Hailey asked me the moment I stepped out of the bathroom.

"Starved." I nodded.

The nausea had finally disappeared, giving way to a gnawing hunger. I couldn't eat before surgery so my stomach had nothing in it but acid. Hailey brought me some Spanish rice she made with shredded chicken. She said it's called *arroz con pollo,* which just translates to rice with chicken. I love when she makes this for me. It's so comforting and very delicious. It's the only dish Hailey can make.

"Thank you, Hailey!" I smiled widely at her.

"Anytime, Liv."

Chapter 21

Olive's P.O.V.

We ate and watched daytime tv together while Lucas and Leo kept running around the flat. I did not know what they were up to, but I didn't figure it was anything bad, so I let them be. They had nervous energy they needed to work through. I was still grateful for Lucas this morning. He had helped ease my nerves before surgery. I smiled, picturing him shaking his body like an idiot for my benefit.

"Hello?" I hear Lucas from behind me on the couch. I slid my head over the edge, looking back at an upside down Lucas. He was on the phone, making me curious who had called him.

"Yeah, I know. You don't have to tell me. No, he can go fuck himself," Lucas said, sounding furious.

"I told him I was done being his puppet. No, you shouldn't go either. Let him figure this out on his own." Lucas pinched the bridge of his nose, like he was getting a headache from the conversation alone. "I am serious, Lisa, do not go help him. I won't be there." So it was his sister who had called. I was curious what it was they were talking about. Who does Lucas not want to help? Why doesn't he?

"Yeah, love you, too." He hung up, meeting my gaze with a raised brow.

"Were you eavesdropping, Rose?" He smirked.

"Sure was." I gave him a cheeky smile, making him let out a laugh. He looked up for a moment with a smirk before meeting my eyes again.

"I might have to go soon. Lisa is a stubborn little shit,

and is not going to listen to me. I'll have to go to dinner at my dad's again."

"Okay, I understand, no worries. It's not like I was expecting you to stay all day," I assured him.

"I was." We held each other's gaze for a moment in silence. I couldn't look away from those brown eyes. It wasn't until Leo cleared his throat that we broke eye contact. I lifted my head from the back of the couch to find him standing before me with a drink.

"Thank you." I smiled up at him. He sat beside me on the couch, close enough to where his shoulder was touching my own. I didn't miss the fact he spread his legs apart so it would touch me.

"Don't worry, Lucas, I'll be here to make sure she's okay." Leo's comment surprised me. It was almost like he was taunting Lucas of the fact he would have to leave while Leo stayed. I saw Lucas from the corner of my eye, looking ticked. I don't think he liked the idea of leaving me with Leo.

"I am sure you will." Lucas' voice sounded strained as he responded to Leo. "Rose, text me if you need me and I'll rush out."

"Okay." I nodded, not sure what else to say.

I got off the couch, feeling the need to at least walk Lucas to my front door and give him a proper goodbye. The moment I was within reach, Lucas wrapped his arms around me. He was careful not to squeeze. I guess he was worried about hurting me. He lifted my chin up to look at him. Those intense brown eyes stared admiringly at me for a moment before his lips met mine. His kiss melted me into his arms further, filling me with a warmth I didn't realize I was missing.

"I'll see you later, Rose," he whispered to me, kissing my forehead before he let me go. I watched him leave down the hall, before closing the door. My cheeks were still heated from my blush. I put the back of my fingers on them, trying to cool them off with my freezing appendages. I turned to find Leo watching me, only making me blush more. I made my way back to the couch, only to be grabbed by the wrist and pulled down onto Leo's lap. He wrapped his arms around my waist, keeping me there.

"My turn to have you all to myself." He whispered into my ear before kissing my temple.

Hailey had finished cleaning up in the kitchen. *Arroz con pollo* is the only thing she can cook without burning it, but she still makes the biggest mess. She turned to see me on Leo's lap. She gave me a mischievous grin, letting me know she planned on leaving now, too.

"I'm going to go, Liv. I have a lot of errands to run, and I think Leo has got it from here," she called out, grabbing her keys and making her escape before I could say anything. "Love you, call if you need me," she quickly blurted from the door before closing it behind her.

Leo kept me on his lap, unwilling to relinquish me. He buried his head into my neck, almost tickling me every time he breathed out. I felt goosebumps start to erupt down my body when his lips lightly grazed over my collarbone. His nose rubbed against my neck as he continued to place small kisses on my skin. Something inside my stomach twisted, and not in a good way.

"I am so sorry you have to go through all this, Liv." Leo kept his voice low as he spoke.

"It's not your fault."

"Still."

He kissed my neck this time, and it made my body react with goosebumps, but it also made me feel weird. I knew I needed to talk to him. I needed to set this straight. Mom said dating more than one guy is okay as long as neither of them have asked me to be exclusive. In this case, they've actually asked me to date them both. I agreed, but after yesterday, I don't think I can go through with it.

Leo is sweet and respectful. He is kind and beautiful, and I would hate to hurt him. I know this isn't what I want. I don't want to come between him and Lucas. This needs to stop before it goes any further. Before Leo gets hurt. He's already been through so much. I know he will not like it, and I may even lose him as my friend, but I need to set this straight.

"Leo, please stop. We need to talk," I said, finally finding the words. He sighed, pulling away from my neck to look at me. He let me go, allowing me to take a seat beside him on the couch. I sat sideways so I could look at him better. He did the same with a raised brow. I swallowed down my nerves, trying to find the right words to say. I want to tell him how I feel without hurting him, but is it even possible?

"I know I agreed I would date you both for six months before deciding, but Leo, I don't think I can." I looked into his bright blue eyes, trying to gauge how he was feeling before continuing. "I can't date you both. I refuse to come between you two. You guys are like brothers, and you may think you like me, Leo, but I get the sense you think of me as this innocent girl."

"Liv." He was ready to convince me otherwise, but I didn't give him the chance.

"Hold on, let me finish. You're an amazing guy, Leo. I mean that! You're caring and sweet, but also tough and endearing. I want to be your friend, more than anything, but I understand if it's not something you want. If I would have met you first, I would have given you a better chance. This isn't entirely about Lucas. I am realizing I'm not the kind of girl who can date two guys. I am not comfortable with the idea, nor do I want to force myself to be."

"I can't say I am happy about it, but I understand, Liv. I figured this conversation would be coming soon. My hope was to at least get one more date with you to prove I could be that guy for you." I saw him pick at his lip piercing with tongue as he got quiet.

"I'm sorry, Leo." My head hung as I felt bad, guilty even. I didn't want to make him sad.

"You don't need to be sorry. Thank you for being honest with me. I'm not heartbroken, but I'm certainly crushed. I guess that's why they call it a crush." He let out a strained laugh.

"Are *we* going to be okay?" I couldn't help but ask. I don't want to lose Leo as a friend.

"Yeah, you may have to give me a little while to get over you, but I am not going anywhere. You need your friends, and I get the feeling you don't have very many." He poked my forehead teasingly. I rubbed it while smiling at him.

"Thank you, Leo. For understanding, and for still willing to be friends." He nodded, turning his body back to face the tv. We watched some funny movies to try to relieve some of the awkward tension around us. I texted Hailey, asking her to come back, letting her know I rejected Leo, and he could probably use a break from me. She never responded, but the rhythmic knock on the door let me know she was here.

"I'm here to relieve you of your duties, Leo. You're free to go. I've got it from here." Hailey said proudly as she pulled Leo off the couch, practically pushing him out of the door.

"Perfect timing. I actually have a business meeting I need to get to. Text me if you need me, Liv." His eyes fell on me seriously. All I could do was nod my head at him. Hailey closed the door behind him, turning her burning gaze at me. I could see her curiosity bubbling to the surface. She wanted details, and she wanted them now. I patted the couch beside me, inviting her to sit. She responded with an excited squeal as she jumped over the couch, landing next to me softly.

"Okay, spill. What happened? When I left, you two looked cozy as hell," she asked with a nudge of her elbow against my own.

"I couldn't do it, Hails. I am not that kind of girl, the one who can date more than one person. I like them both, but I like Lucas more. He opened up so much to me last night, Hailey. I don't want to hurt him, and most of all, I don't want to come between them. They have a friendship like ours, actually, probably deeper than ours. They're like brothers. I won't be the downfall of their friendship."

"Oh, Livie. I am glad you realized you like Lucas so much. I think he likes you, too. So, are you going to give him a fighting chance?" Her question hung in the air for a few minutes as I thought about it. I am still scared of getting hurt. I've only ever had one boyfriend, and he was a cheating asshole. I'm all kinds of insecure. I still have a hard time believing Lucas actually wants me. I am scared he'll realize he actually doesn't want me as he gets to know me better.

"I am going to let things take their course. If he still wants me after getting to know me better, then yes, I'll give him a chance." I fidgeted with my fingers as I answered, a nervous energy brewing in me.

Hailey squealed excitedly, pulling in for a tight hug. I winced as she accidentally hurt me, causing her to quickly let go with an apology. She handed me my medicine and curled up next to me on the couch. Hailey was definitely this big sister I never had. It made me imagine what it would have been like to have a sister growing up. I probably wouldn't have felt so lonely having someone to share my trauma with. At the same time, I wouldn't wish that on anyone. My phone vibrated beside me, surprising me with a text from Leo.

Leo: Thanks for being honest with me, Liv. Don't worry about me and get plenty of rest. You have your health to care for. I had fallen asleep shortly after getting his text, realizing I never responded. I woke up to him at my door with Chinese food and a smile, even after I had rejected him.

"Here you go," Leo said, handing me my large container of wonton soup.

"Thank you." I smiled up at him.

The container was nice and warm against my hands. I sniffed the soup, closing my eyes, and letting my mouth salivate. I sipped the broth first before eating the wontons. Leo ate beside me as we watched the scary movie I chose. I chose it remembering Leo once told me he liked to watch scary movies. I jumped a couple times, but somehow managed not to spill the hot soup on myself. Leo tried not to laugh at me whenever I would squeak.

"I think my new favorite thing is watching scary movies with *you*," Leo laughed.

"Why?"

"Because you make it more entertaining with your jumps and squeals." He smirked at me as he leaned back against the foot of the couch. He'd been sitting on the floor while I sat on the couch. His long legs were spread out under the coffee table, and his back had been against the couch. He didn't sit far from me, but not too close, either.

"Whatever, I didn't jump *that* much," I said with a blush. I winced when the couch cushion poked my incision site. Leo sat up, looking at me, concerned.

"Do you need your pain medicine?" He asked.

"Yes, please."

He quickly got up, fetching my medicine from the kitchen counter with a small glass of water. I took them, needing to feel the relief from this throbbing pain. Leo held me carefully, picking me up as gently as he could and carrying me up to my bed. He laid me down, sitting beside me. He rubbed my back and arms until I was fully relaxed, but I wasn't sure if it was okay. I don't want to make him think I changed my mind. Is it okay for him to comfort me like this? Hailey would do this for me, but is it okay for Leo to do the same?

"What are you thinking about?" He asked me curiously.

"The rules of friendship," I muttered. He let out a loud laugh. I felt the heat of my embarrassment cross my face, turning even my ears red.

"Sorry, that was very random. Look, I understand you don't want me romantically. I am not going to push you into changing your mind. I am only here as your friend now. Honestly, I've rubbed Lucas like this before. There's no romantic intentions behind it. So don't worry, okay?"

"Okay," I whispered, as I hid half my face beneath the sheets.

"I'm going to go. Text me if you need anything okay?" He

got off the bed, heading towards the stairs.

"Thank you, Leo. I am sorry if I hurt you."

"Sleep, Liv, get some rest. Don't worry about me, I'm fine." He smiled at me, but it didn't hold the same twinkle as before. I heard the front door close and knew I needed to go downstairs to lock the deadbolt. I sighed, too relaxed to want to move. I dragged my body off the warm bed, slumping my shoulder and dragging my feet down the stairs and towards the door. I felt like a real life zombie.

The medicine had only added to my fatigued state. After locking the door, I headed back up to my bed, remembering Lucas was up here earlier messing with things. I need to look around when I wake in the morning. My eyes are too asleep and fuzzy to see right. I plopped on my bed as I tucked myself in under the blanket. I fell asleep almost instantly.

The peek of orange sky from my window let me know it was past 8 already as I woke up. I was hoping to sleep in more, but I guess my body is ready to get up *now*. I sat up on my bed, remembering to inspect my room for anything Lucas may have touched or left. As I scanned the room, everything looked to be in the right spot. It wasn't until I reached for my phone that I noticed the small envelope on my nightstand. It had *Rose*, written in neat cursive on the front.

I grabbed it, wondering if he was the one who wrote the name. I would be highly impressed if it was. I opened the small envelope to find a little invitation and a gift card inside.

You're invited to Sarah Phillips' birthday lunch this Sunday afternoon at 1. Please wear cocktail attire as we will eat on the terrace.

Who the hell is Sarah Phillips? And what's with the gift card? I turned the gift card around to find the name of a very expensive couture store. Was I meant to purchase cocktail attire from here? I sighed, already dreading the shopping trip. I know who to take with me, but I still don't want to go.

Olive: Who is Sarah Phillips?

I shot Lucas a text as I headed to the kitchen for my

much needed caffeine dosage. I need to eat something before I take my pain medication again. My incision is itchy and throbbing today.

Lucas: I was beginning to wonder if you would notice the invite or not. Sarah Phillips is my mother. Her birthday is this Sunday, and she wanted to meet you. Lisa apparently told her about you. I wanted to send you a dress to wear, but I was curious to see what you would pick out for yourself. Happy shopping }:-)

His little devil face emoji was accurate. I dread shopping with a passion.

Olive: You up for some shopping?
Hailey: Always!

She immediately responded, making me laugh.

Hailey: I'm on my way!

It didn't take long for me to hear her rhythmic knock on the door. She sported a wide smile and casual clothes. Her shades were pushed up onto her head, pulling her hair out of her face. She rushed me the entire time I was getting ready, even more so when we walked out of my flat.

Hailey drove us, since I'm not meant to drive with my pain medication. She parked in front of a store with silver mannequins and fancy dresses. I honestly never go to stores like this except with Hailey. She's the only reason I've delved into this rich lifestyle. I haven't gotten the money from mom's life insurance, but even when I do, I'll be pretending I'm still a broke college kid. I don't want to squander the money my mother left me.

Hailey linked her arm with mine, sashaying us towards the large glass doors. The place was fancy enough to have its own doorman. Hailey's long, wavy black hair blew back in the wind as the doors opened before us. She was stunning with her almost golden skin which shone beautifully in the light. She had a slender face with expressive dark brown eyes. Her eyebrows were not thin, but they were well kept. She used those things to make all kinds of faces. I loved the way Hailey's face showed her emotions so plainly.

An attendant greeted us, and Hailey instantly employed their help. She named styles of dresses and brands and listed shoes and colors that would best suit me. She knew clothes better than I did, so I let her run with it. I was pulled towards the dressing room and told to strip. Dresses upon dresses were brought to me, with shoes to match.

"Well? Come out! I want to see," Hailey ordered from the other side of the fitting room curtain.

I sighed, pulling back the curtain and stepping out. There was a three-panel mirrored at the end of the fitting room hall, so you could see your clothes from all angels. Hailey had me step up and stare at myself. The pink dress was elegant, but a bit over the top for my taste. It was adorned with beadwork and lace appliques, the corset bodice sparkled to no end. It had an off-shoulder sweetheart neckline with mesh cap sleeves. The glittered flounce skirt created an A-line silhouette that ended with a mesh overlay. I wrinkled my nose, shaking my head with a no.

"Yeah, you look beautiful, but it's definitely not *you*," Hailey agreed, sending me back to the fitting room. This continued for a little while, until I saw the perfect dress. I slid into it so well, it was like it was made for me, for this moment. As I stepped out I heard Hailey gasp. We walked over to the mirror to assess the dress better together.

It was a nice hunter green that didn't wash out my complexion. It had ruche detailing at the waist and ornate cuffs which gave it an attractive finish. The asymmetrical neckline had a fold-over panel while the skirt had a high slit. It had a beautiful pleated design at the back as well. I felt so beautiful in this dress. I almost didn't recognize myself in the mirror. The material was something else too, stretchy, yet still heavy and strong. It was soft and felt devine against my skin. I looked at Hailey in the mirror who was smiling so widely it was almost blinding.

"This is the one," she said.

"I think so, too."

Hailey found me matching shoes to go along with the dress and we checked out. I had no idea how much was on the gift card, but I prayed it was the right amount. I handed the card over to the register attendant and she swiped it. I waited to hear her tell me a new total with the gift card discounted from the original. Instead a receipt printed, telling me there was still money left on this damn thing. How much had Lucas put on it?

"That was fun! I cannot wait to see you in this dress! Please let me be there when Lucas comes and picks you up! He's going to die!" Hailey's excitement only grew more with every statement. Her voice rose with every sentence to the point she was almost screeching.

"Woah, calm down. I was actually going to ask you if you would do my hair and make up for it. So, I figured you would be around when Lucas picked me up." Hailey squealed excitedly beside me. She clapped her hands like some sort of seal, making me laugh at her antics. Tomorrow is the day I give Lucas a chance at seriously dating me.

Please, let this go well.

Chapter 22

Olive's P.O.V.

Hailey styled my hair in a curled pinned low bun with a braided crown. She pulled out a few well placed loose strands of hair to give it a sort of neat, messy look. She kept my makeup neutral, accentuating my natural beauty. Hailey tinted my cheeks a light pink, painted my lips with a shiny lip gloss to make my red pop more. She highlighted my cheek bones as well as the tip of my nose while contouring the edge of my jaw and the sides of my nose.

I felt like a damn princess. My heart was racing like the flutter of a hummingbird's wings. My stomach was twisting with nerves, yet giddy to see Lucas. It felt like a stampede of horses were trudging along inside my stomach. I think Hailey could sense my nervous energy as she handed me the tube of mascara to give me something to do.

"Here, you put this on. I know how you are with other people getting things too close to your eyes." Hailey handed me the mascara with a sigh. I leaned forward to get a better look in the mirror. I always felt like I looked so stupid when applying makeup. My mouth was open, and my eyes were wide while I tried my hardest to separate my eyelids the farthest I could.

"You look stunning," Hailey cooed beside me.

"You think so?" I stared at my reflection, feeling like I was looking at a completely different person. I looked beautiful, but it didn't feel like me.

"I know so. You're going to be turning heads today." I slipped into my dress, strapping my heels on. I barely got used to wearing heels last year with Hailey's insistent need to dress me in them. She said every woman should have a pair of heels that feel like their second set of feet. I didn't get it, and I still don't.

Heels hurt.

The knock on the door had me swallowing my nerves down. My heart raced, wondering what Lucas would think of the dress I chose for myself. I felt like there was suddenly a lot of pressure on this thin fabric gracing my body. Hailey opened the door for me as I strapped the buckle of my right heel. I stood from the couch, turning to find Lucas in a white buttoned down shirt and khaki slacks. He had his hair slicked neatly back, giving him a neat elegant look.

Our eyes met after we each checked one another out. The right corner of his lips turned up in his classic half smirk. His eyes were so intense, making me blush under their heated gaze. I bit my lip, feeling nervous and suddenly very tongue tied. Lucas didn't say a word, either. We stared at each other a moment longer.

"Perfect," he whispered as he stepped in finally. He didn't spare Hailey a glance as he walked past her straight towards me. "You look absolutely perfect."

He gently grabbed my chin, lifting it up to look at him. He leaned down, granting me one of his knee quivering kisses. I couldn't help, but lean into him more for support, feeling my knees would give out from under me at any second.

"How are you feeling today, my Rose?"

He kept his hold on my chin as he asked, forcing me to look him in the eyes. He was worried about me. I could see it in those deep brown eyes.

"I'm fine," I answered almost breathlessly, like the kiss he gave me winded me.

"If at any point it gets to be too much, don't be afraid to tell me. I'll take you home whenever you want to go," he promised, to which I nodded my head. Lucas kissed my lips one more time before grabbing my hand and guiding me out.

CHAPTER 22

Hailey waved at me as I passed her by with a wink. She was enjoying this more than she probably should.

"I'll lock up when I leave, don't worry. Have fun," she called after me.

Lucas had driven a car I had yet to see. It was a royal blue Rolls Royce with a wide tail. It shone in the sun beautifully, giving it a more elegant feel, if possible. As usual Lucas opened my door, helping me into the car before making his way around to the driver's seat. I couldn't help but watch him as he walked. The slacks he wore hugged his ass in the right way. I felt like a perv sexualizing him as he walked, but the man was too damn fine.

"Okay, so tell me what I need to know about your mom?"

I clutched onto my purse, which held the small present I had gotten for Sarah. I have no idea what her likes or dislikes are, but there was no chance in hell I was going to a birthday party without a gift. It's not much, but I hoped she'd like it. Lucas smirked again, keeping his eyes on the road as he spoke.

"There's not much to tell. Mom is a pretty open book. She believes in being polite to a fault. She loves the warm sun and a cool breeze. Sun hats are her favorite, any occasion to wear one and you will find her in one." Lucas smiled as he spoke about his mother. I could tell, unlike his father, he loved her. "She's quick to tell someone when they've done something wrong. She can be pretty funny too, but she's got a specific sense of humor many don't understand. You have nothing to worry about, Rose. She's going to love you."

Lucas grabbed my hand, bringing it to his mouth, and kissing my knuckles as he drove. He never once took his eyes off the road, but we continued our conversation. He recounted childhood stories about his mother and sister. It turns out his father would abuse his mother, too. She was able to leave him with the help of her brother Kane. I didn't miss the way Lucas spat out Kane's name. I am not sure why there was so much disdain in his voice when he spoke about him. As the man who helped his mother escape abuse, I would think he would say his name with a tone of admiration.

"If you can, try to avoid Kane. He sounds and acts good on paper, but behind closed doors he's anything but," Lucas warned me as we exited the interstate.

I was curious what he meant, but I would heed his warning. There's not a chance I will be left alone with Kane, anyway. I'm going to be glued to Lucas' side, he being the only one I feel comfortable around. We pulled into this beautiful bed and breakfast. The place was huge, more of a mansion than anything. There was a gravel road leading to the gravel driveway. The driveway was circular, with a large fountain in the center that spewed crystal clear water from the middle.

Lucas opened my door, holding his hand out for me to take. I grabbed it, sliding out of the car, immediately regretting wearing heels. Heels on gravel are asking for a twisted ankle. Lucas wrapped his arm around my lower waist, gripping my hip as he pulled me close. He steadied my steps, somehow letting me make it to the front door without hurting myself.

The inside of this place was charming. There was a large staircase to the right as you entered with a large wooden check-in desk in front. Keys hung along the wall behind it, giving it a more rustic feel. Around the desk were two passageways and to the left was a large foyer with a grand piano and several Victorian style chairs and loveseats.

"Good afternoon, Mr. Porter. Your mother is waiting for you on the terrace already. Please go right ahead." The receptionist greeted Lucas, gesturing to the passageway on the right.

"Thank you, Marcus." Lucas nodded. They must be well known here. I didn't miss the way Marcus looked at me like a meal as we passed him by. I suddenly felt highly exposed in my heels and dress. The high slit exposed more skin, but it would make it easy to kick in if I needed to roundhouse someone.

"I apologize in advance," Lucas whispered to me as we stepped out of the opened French doors to the beautiful terrace. God only knows what he's apologizing in advance for. I guess I'll find out.

On the terrace stood a large white oval table, with rounded wooden chairs. The sun was bright and warm against my skin. I could hear the waves crashing against the shore before my eyes spotted the ocean. The breeze was cool, carrying with it the smell of the ocean. I closed my eyes as I inhaled, letting the air cool me while the sun warmed me. It felt so perfect outside today.

There were beautiful white potted lilies in every corner and the center of the table. The tiny fork nightmare continued as I saw it staring at me from its place on the table. Hopefully, nothing we eat calls for me to use it. I wouldn't know how to, anyway. I spotted Lisa first as she leaned against the white wooden railing facing the beach. She wore a long off-white maxi dress that showed her shoulder blades in the back. Her black hair flowed in neat waves around her, covering some exposed skin. She looked absolutely radiant, like a still frame photograph.

Laughter caught my attention, making me turn to see a tall woman with large black sunglasses and an elegant Aubrey Hepburn style sun hat. It was white with a black thick ribbon around its base. Her dress matched her hat perfectly. It was all over lace with a black silk tied belt. It was sleeveless with a round neck and filled bust, relaxed through the hips. This woman had a smile as bright as the sun. She was so elegant with her white gloves and pearl necklace. A real Audrey Hepburn herself.

In front of her was a man, in what I would guess to be his early 40s. He was a hunk of a man with large biceps, nicely hugged by the sleeves of his button-down shirt. His short black hair was styled like Henry Cavill. He had chiseled angular features and a sharp jawline. He looked intimidating, but the way he smiled just invited you in. Lucas was guiding us right to them.

"Happy birthday, Mother." He greeted her, kissing her on the cheek, but never once removing his hold on me. "I'd like you to meet my Rose. This is Olive Brewer." He introduced me as both Rose and Olive, leaving the choice of what to call me up to her, I guess.

"It's so nice to meet you, Olive." She smiled at me. I am not sure why, but my heart clenched and tears threatened to ruin the makeup Hailey worked hard on. Being here, seeing her, it made me think of mom, and it brought back all the hurt like a punch to the stomach. I swallowed back the pain, and reined my emotions in, refusing to cry in front of this woman.

"It's lovely to meet you as well. Happy birthday." I smiled back at her.

"Be civil, Lucas, and greet your uncle as well as introduce your guest," his mother scolded him.

"Yes, mother," he said with a nod as he turned to his uncle with a glare. "Kane, I see nothing has changed." I felt like there was an insult somewhere in there. Something only the two of them know as Kane narrowed his eyes at Lucas.

"This is Olive," Lucas introduced me, but before Kane and I could exchange pleasantries, he turned me around. "We haven't greeted Lisa yet. Don't want to be rude."

"Play nice, Lucas!" His mother yelled after him. Lisa turned, realizing we were headed her way. She flashed me an amused grin as she leaned back against the rail with her elbows resting over the top.

"You look nice, as always." She greeted us, but I wasn't sure who she was speaking to.

"She was talking to you. Lisa wouldn't dare compliment me. She thinks I have too big of a head already," Lucas said loudly, causing Lisa to laugh.

"You do!" She agreed. "I can't have you getting too arrogant."

"You look radiant yourself," I said, gesturing to Lisa's dress and overall self.

"Thanks, but you don't have to be sweet with me. I'm not as prim and proper as mother would like." She held her pinky out in a mocking kind of way, making me snort a laugh. She smiled at me, happy I understood her humor. "This is going to be so much better with you here. Thank you for picking one I can actually get along with."

She had directed her last statement at Lucas. I wasn't sure how I felt about the comment. I guess Lucas had a lot of women to pick from to take here, but the one he chose to meet his mother was me. I was still fighting back the emotions his mother spurred inside of me, and the realization Lisa's words brought me, didn't help. Feeling overly emotional at the moment, I began to search for a bathroom to collect myself in.

"Excuse me for a moment, I need to find the ladie's room," I said, stepping out of Lucas' hold.

"It's down the hall to the right," Lisa called after me.

I stepped inside, following her directions. Thankfully, it was a private bathroom. It was singular without stalls, allowing me a real moment to myself. I stared in the mirror picturing mom when I was younger. I wondered if mom had parties like these on her birthdays once she left dad. Did she look as radiant as Lucas' mother? Smile as brightly? I hope she did. I looked up at the ceiling, catching my tears with tissues so they would not stream down my face and ruin my makeup.

I stepped out of the bathroom to find Lucas leaning back against the opposite wall. He quickly grabbed me, dragging me to him. His strong arms wrapped around me and held me close. He kissed my forehead tenderly, rubbing my back with his thumb.

"What's wrong, Rose?"

"Nothing. I just…it's stupid." I shook my head.

"I doubt it is. Tell me."

"I was thinking of my mom. I wondered if she was able to shine as brightly as your mother after she left my father," I admitted with a sigh.

"I am sure she did. If you're really curious, you could always ask her friends. Doesn't one live in the same building as you?" He made a good point. If I was curious, I could hunt down Penny and ask her. I nodded into his chest.

"You're right. Thank you, Lucas."

"I didn't do anything, but I'll take the thank you, anyway." He winked at me as he pulled back from our hug. "Lunch is ready. Let's get you fed."

He grabbed my hand this time, guiding me back outside. He pulled my chair out for me across from Lisa. Kane sat beside Lisa, with Sarah at the end of the table. Lucas sat to the left of her in front of Kane and beside me. I felt the tense air around Lucas and Kane. It was obvious, even to me, they did not get along in the least.

"So, tell me Olive, how did you meet my son?" Sarah asked me, her shades and sunhat were off now to reveal her black hair and brown eyes. The same brown eyes Lucas sports.

"Oh, um.." I bit my cheek, feeling a bit embarrassed. I didn't want to tell his mom we met at a club. It seemed sleazy, but I also wasn't going to lie. I felt mortified as I continued. "I met him at a nightclub."

I recalled our first night together as my mind flashed with the image of him leaning back over the bar, looking out onto the dance floor. His eyes had caught mine from across the room, pulling me towards him. It didn't take long until we were dancing with one another, eventually leaving together after my little game.

"Sounds accurate." Lisa laughed, sparing her mother from having to comment. A wave of hot embarrassment crossed my face, turning even my ears red.

"Lisa!" Sarah scolded her daughter.

"What? We all know about Lucas' escapades. We don't have to pretend otherwise. I'm glad he found this one, and is taking it seriously," Lisa said with a shrug of her shoulders.

"That's a colorful way of phrasing it." Kane commented, feeling the need to add to this conversation for some reason.

"What's that supposed to mean?" Lucas snapped.

"No, we are not doing this today." Sarah quickly shut down whatever argument was about to ensue.

"I know it's not exactly the best place to have met, but I

am glad it happened. You've raised a very caring man."

I am not sure why I felt the need to tell her such a thing, but I wanted to steer the conversation away from Lucas' less redeeming qualities. I didn't want his family picking on him for what he'd done. They didn't understand it, but I do. As such, I won't let them look down on him for it. He was doing what he needed to do in order to heal, and I will no longer hold it against him. Yes, it makes me insecure and at times jealous at the amount of girls he's been with, but now I understand it better so it's easier to swallow down.

"Thank you, Olive. I am glad to know my Lucas is treating you right." She nodded with a fake smile. The slight disdain in her voice had me believing perhaps she didn't like me very much. Silence filled the air until it was interrupted by two faces I was grateful to see.

"Sorry I'm late, Auntie." Rachel's voice came from directly behind me. I turned to see her arm linked with Leo's. "Hello, Daddy," she greeted Kane. Of course, it would make sense her father would be Kane, but it somehow surprised me.

She wore a cute high low dress which started off black at the neckline, ending in white at the hemline. The black stretched into octopus tendrils over the white bottom. The wide waistband echoed with the lace-up sides perfectly highlighting her slim waist. She wore black wedges to match. It was definitely her style while still fitting the occasion.

"Happy birthday, Aunt Sarah." Leo greeted her. I was surprised to hear him call her aunt. Are Lucas and Leo actually cousins and not just friends?

Leo looked dashing in a white button-up shirt and black trousers. He matched well with Rachel. Honestly, I began to wonder if there was a color theme and I was clashing with it. I should have asked Lucas when buying my dress, but I didn't think about it. Leo took a seat beside me while Rachel took hers next to Lisa.

"Hey," he said, nudging me with his elbow.

"Hey yourself." I nudged him back with a smile.

The conversation never faltered with Rachel around. She had a way of steering it in the right direction any time it got off course. Rachel kept the topics light and tried not to let me be the center of the questioning. I was very grateful she was here today. Her presence definitely cut down the tension in the air.

Chapter 23

Olive's P.O.V.

"Rachel, how are your studies coming along? Are you still on the path to becoming a teacher?" Sarah asked her.

"Yes ma'am, I am. I start my internship next year. Everything is going great," Rachel answered with a smile.

"I wish you would have followed in your father's footsteps and became a doctor. Teachers have such a lousy job with a measly salary." Sarah's words surprised me. Hell, they surprised Rachel, too.

"It's not always about the money. Being able to do something you love everyday and call it your job is a benefit in itself. Being a teacher is noble, and yes they don't have the highest paying job, but they make a decent salary." I am not sure why I wanted to dig my grave today, but I did. Sarah's attention was now fully on me, but it was worth it as Rachel shot me a look of gratitude from across the table.

"Are you studying to become one as well?" Sarah arched a brow at me.

"No, actually, I'm studying to be an aerospace engineer." Sarah looked stunned by my answer as she held her fork, full of food, in the air, halfway to her mouth.

"Very impressive," Kane commented in her stead. "What made you choose such a field of study?"

"I've always loved looking up at the stars, but I knew I would never want to go to outer space myself. I figured why not help build the things that take us there instead? The idea of knowing something I created could one day be floating in space amongst the stars makes me happy."

"So I'm sitting at the table with a future rocket scientist?" Lisa smiled.

"I guess so," I laughed.

"Intelligent and beautiful," Lucas added with a wiggle of his brow, which only worked to widen my smile.

We all finished our lunch, following Sarah out to the shore. There were lounge chairs and beach umbrellas set up for us to use. Sarah kept her hand firmly in place above her head to hold her hat down from the cool, blowing breeze. I had taken my heels off the moment we reached sand, allowing my toes to sink into the soft warm grains.

"I know I apologized in advance already, but let me say it again. I am sorry about my mom. She can be particular about things," Lucas whispered to me as he grabbed my hand.

We made our way to the chairs taking a seat, Lucas shared the lounge seat I had chosen. I clutched onto my purse wondering if perhaps I should leave the small gift inside of it. I can't imagine she'd like it now. I wonder what she would think of it? It's probably best if I keep it.

"Happy birthday, Sarah." Kane pulled out a couple of tickets from his pocket, handing them to her. "They're concert tickets to the symphony. I figured we could go together like old times."

"This is perfect, thank you Kane." She smiled up at him like a small child. It was a sweet scene to see, making me feel a little better about her.

"Here you go, Auntie. It's from Leo and me." Rachel handed over a small, rectangular, velvet black box. Sarah carefully opened it, exposing a beautiful thin charmed bracelet.

"It's beautiful. Thank you guys."

She quickly handed the bracelet to Kane, holding her wrist out for him to clasp it onto her. I could tell Kane and Sarah had a very close sibling bond. He cared for her, and took care of her the way an older brother should. She held her hand up, twisting her wrist as she examined the bracelet now dangling off her. It was gorgeous, with two small thin charms. One charm was of a horse and the other of an ice skate. I wondered what they each symbolized. Were they tied to a memory, or did they stand for something else?

"Lucas and I did not give you something we could wrap. We had a hard time coming up with something to give you. You know, you're very hard to shop for," Lisa said with a playful tone. "We finally decided on a vacation. The three of us haven't gone on a family trip in years. We booked your favorite cabin and planned out a whole vacation for just the three of us."

Sarah's eyes began to turn pink as tears pooled, threatening to spill down her cheeks. She was emotional at the mention of her cabin. It made me happy to see how much she loved her children, despite her odd comments. She held them in high regard, expecting a lot of them, but loving them whether they met her standards or not. Now I feel like I have to give her my gift. I can't be the only one to not give her something. I knew I was coming to a birthday party. What kind of jerk wouldn't bring something?

I guess I'll choose being embarrassed over being an ass. My fingers almost shook from my nerves as I opened my purse and searched for the small gift. It wasn't anything amazing, just a brown leather-bound journal with a heavy gold pen. I held it out to her with a shy smile. I tried to fight the blush of embarrassment from my face, but it was practically impossible.

"Oh, is this for me?" She asked, very surprised.

"I felt wrong coming without a gift. I am sorry it isn't much. I don't know what you like." I told her. "It's a journal for you. I wrote my favorite inspirational quotes on the top of each page for motivation. I've always found it therapeutic to write in a journal. My mother was the one who got me started."

I pictured the millions of journals hidden away in a box in the back of my closet. They haven't been touched or looked at in a while. A lot of those memories are ones I don't want to revisit. Sarah took the journal with a polite smile. She opened it in front of me, running her hand over the saying I wrote on the front page.

"I love it, Olive. Thank you. It's very kind of you." She clutched the journal as she spoke. I think I actually believed her. "I haven't written in a journal since high school, I think it will be nice to do it again." I gave her a light nod with a warm smile.

"I'm glad you like it." The attention was drawn away from me as everyone began to have their own conversations.

"You keep a journal, Rose? Am I in it?" Lucas asked with a playful smirk and an arched brow. I rolled my eyes, but couldn't help the smile on my lips.

"Yes I write in a journal. As to whether or not you're in it, I'll never tell." I gave him an equally playful grin.

"Mmm, no fair. Maybe I'll find it and read it for myself," he said, making me lightly punch his arm.

"You'll do no such thing."

"Pretty please?" He gave me those puppy dog eyes as he asked.

"No way."

"That's fine, Rose, one day you'll let me in," he whispered into my ear, causing my heart to race.

He sounded so certain about it. I stared deep into his eyes, not shying away from the intense feelings he was bringing out of me. I know I'm falling for him already and it scares me, but I'm going to trust him. I pray he doesn't hurt me.

"I'll let you read my past journals. You can work your way up to your journal." I offered him, because I felt I could trust him with the most inner thoughts of my past.

"My journal? So I *am* in it." He smiled widely. "I will take whatever you are willing to share. Thank you, Rose."

He made me blush, not expecting him to thank me for offering him a journal I wrote when I was 8. Maybe I'll start him with my highschool ones instead. Those are the formative years after all. I felt a sort of excited nervousness at the idea of him reading my current journal. The one sprawled with my millions of thoughts about him. Honestly, it feels like this journal is dedicated solely to him.

"Yes, you're in it, but you don't get to read that particular one until you finish all my high school and previous college ones. You have a lot of reading ahead of you if you ever want to get to yours." I giggled at him.

"I can't wait." He smiled so sweetly my heart forgot to beat for a moment.

Don't hurt me, Lucas. Please, don't hurt me.

Lucas' P.O.V.

"Happy birthday again, mom. I love you." I kissed her cheek again as I said my goodbye.

I was ready to take Rose to her flat and get my first journal. I wanted to dive right in. This woman before me intrigued me greatly and getting to see into her mind was the greatest gift I could ask for.

"I love you, too. Thank you for being civil with your uncle." She squeezed my arm lovingly.

"It was nice to meet you, Sarah." My polite Rose held her hand out for my mom to shake. Mom didn't do handshakes, bringing her in for a hug instead.

"The pleasure is all mine. I hope to see you again. Thank you again for my gift," Mom said with a smile. I was shocked, and happy to see Rose had brought a gift for her. She amazes me everyday. Surprising me with something new. I guided her outside, making sure to hold her tightly against me as we stepped over the gravel.

I won't ever let her fall.

"Thank you for coming with me, Rose." I kissed her beautiful rosy lips before opening the car door for her. She blushed, which she's been doing a lot more of lately. *I wondered why.*

"Thank you for bringing me," she whispered.

I ran to the driver's seat, pulling out of the driveway quickly. I tossed my phone onto her lap with a smirk. She knew what I wanted without having to ask. She opened my music app, putting on some Lumineers as she hummed along, too shy to sing fully. Hopefully soon she'll be comfortable enough with me to sing aloud. She has a beautiful voice, one I could listen to for hours.

I parked in front of her building, opening her door for her. As usual, she accepted my hand, letting me help her out of the car. I was glad she no longer rejected it so much. She would take it any time I offered it to her now. I kissed her knuckles lovingly.

I told her I loved her without meaning to when I opened up to her about what had happened to me. I was half asleep at the time and felt vulnerable, yet comfortable enough with her in my arms to admit it. The words kind of flowed out of my mouth, but thankfully, she was asleep. She hadn't heard me. I don't want to scare her off with my strong emotions. I feel like she'll run away if I come on too strong. She's like a fawn, quick to run if she sensed danger. Not physical danger, but emotional danger. This woman can handle physical threats just fine.

"Okay, where is my first journal?" I asked her the moment we entered her flat. She let a laugh out, turning to smile at me. She was amused with me, but I was fine with it. Anything that makes her smile is fine with me.

"Hold on. I have to find the right one. Come help me," she said, leading me upstairs. She disappeared in her closet hidden beneath the hanging clothes. She pushed 4 large white boxes out. *That's a lot of journals.*

Each one was labeled with years. At least she had a system. She found the correct box, and asked me to pick it up and take it to the table downstairs. It was heavier than I thought it would be, but I managed to get it downstairs while she placed the other ones back in her closet. She's strong.

"Okay, so pretty much this box is my whole high school

life. This corner is freshman year, this one is sophomore, this one is junior, and this one over here is my senior year." She pointed to each corner as she spoke. "Start here and work your way up."

"That's going to take a while. I can't wait to read what you were like in high school." I admitted. The sheer number of journals made this a more daunting task than I had anticipated, but it meant I'll get to know her even better.

"I'm exposing myself here, Lucas." She bit at her lip as she stared at the worn journals.

"I know you are, Rose. I will treasure these, and the words you've written inside them. Thank you for giving me the chance to read them."

I grabbed her chin, pulling it up so her eyes would meet mine. Those blue eyes were like the sky on a bright summer's day, a beautiful light blue. It was easy to lose yourself inside of them. I kissed her lips with all the love I could pour out to her, only pulling away when I could no longer breathe.

I rested my forehead against her own. Closing my eyes and focusing on the feeling of her close to me. The warmth of her skin, the smell of her breath, and the heat of her lips were all things I enjoyed immensely.

"Can you do me a favor?" She asked me.

"Anything, my Rose." I opened my eyes, standing straight again.

"Can you unzip me? I can't reach it." She pointed to her back, making me smile in amusement.

"Gladly."

I slowly unzipped it, letting the sound of it fill the room. I kissed her exposed back between her shoulder blades, letting my hands push the fabric of her dress off her shoulders, kissing those as well. I saw the hairs on her arms rise as goosebumps erupted down her body. She enjoyed the feeling of my lips on her skin.

"Lucas.." she whispered my name in an almost plea.

"Yes, my Rose?"

"Will you take control again?" I knew exactly what she meant, making me smile with excitement.

"With pleasure."

My fingers found the clasp of her bra, quickly unstrapping it, pulling it down along with her dress. When I got to her hips, I made sure to hook my finger at the hem of her underwear, taking it off along with the dress. I squatted down, having her step out of it.

"Keep the heels on." I told her, finding her naked form in only heels hot as hell.

She nodded with a deep blush as she bit her lip. My dick twitched in my pants with all the blood flowing to it. Seeing her like this made me all kinds of excited. I slowly unbuttoned my shirt with one hand as she watched me hungrily. I watched her the entire time, admiring her body. I finally saw the new tattoo she had gotten on her ribs. It was a pink breast cancer ribbon with *mom* written along the side of it.

I tossed my shirt to the side as I closed the space between us. Her skin felt so smooth against my hand as I trailed it down her back towards her plush peach bottom. I squeezed it tightly, causing her to bite her lip the way she loves to do. My lips kissed her neck softly, trailing up until I reached her earlobe. My tongue brought it to my mouth allowing me to suck on it for a moment before going back to her neck, this time sucking at it as well. I loved leaving marks on her body. I wanted everyone to see she was taken, even if she technically isn't.

With her body pressed against mine, I lifted her legs around my waist, carrying her up the stairs. I placed her gently on her bed as I shed my pants. Her eyes widened as they always do when she stares at my erection. I smirked at her, letting her admire my body for a moment. My mouth landed on her breast, flicking her nipple with my tongue. She moaned as she arched her back, taking slow heavy breaths of pleasure.

"You're so beautiful, Rose."

Taking my dick in my hand, I aimed it perfectly against

her entrance. Using my tip I teased her until she was dripping wet for me. I slowly inserted myself all the way in before pulling all the way out again. I loved seeing her squirm with pleasure. Eventually, I slid right into her with a quick thrust. I stayed there unmoving for a moment, making her moan and sway her hips in a pleading manner.

I grabbed behind her knees dragging her, with my dick still inside, until she was at the edge of the bed and I was standing. I wrapped her legs around my waist holding onto her thighs as I began to thrust quickly, and roughly, into her. Her moans encouraged me to go faster, harder, until she was screaming in pleasure.

"*Fuck, Lucas!*" She moaned. "*Faster!*"

I complied happily, increasing my speed. The sound of our skin slapping against each other filled the room along with her screams and moans of pleasure. I let my finger slide between her ass cheeks. She puckered for a moment before relaxing. I played with her as I continued to thrust into her. Her moaning increased until she let out a high pitched squeal with her walls clenching against me in her pleasure. I didn't stop either, continuing my torment until she was screaming my name again.

Rose somehow gives me more stamina. I'd never gone so long before, but after a couple of hours, I finally let myself cum. I loved knowing she had my seed deep inside her, and it would be in her for a few days, even if *I* wasn't. Rose was out of breath, lying beside me on her bed. Her body glistened under the light from the sheen of sweat all over her skin.

"Stay with me?" She asked me.

"I would love to. I have to get some clothes first, but I promise I'll hurry back." I kissed her sweet puffed lips. I was rough with them while we were going at it. She loved it, so I didn't stop. I got up, found my clothes, and quickly dressed.

"I'll be right back, Rose. Anything you want for dinner? I'll get it on my way back." I called from downstairs. I saw her naked body lean over the rail.

"A big juicy burger sounds good to me." She smiled down at me.

"Alright, big juicy burger coming right up."

I left quickly, running to the car. I wanted to get back to her as soon as I could. Today went so well, I was having a hard time believing it. My eyes spotted an old beat-up pickup truck parked in front of me. My mind began to wonder what a car in such a beat-up state was doing here. I watched as a muscular man with dirty blonde hair and a scruffy beard got down from it and headed into Rose's building. He must live there, but I don't think I've ever seen this truck before. I shook my head, focusing on the task ahead.

Don't go anywhere, Rose. I will be right back.

Chapter 24

Olive's P.O.V.

I had slipped my shirt on when I heard a knock at the door. I ran downstairs with a smile, thinking it was Lucas again.

"Did you forget something?" I opened the door, ready to tease him.

My smile quickly faded as my mind registered Dad's scruff face before me. His beard had grown, but his golden blonde hair was kept in its usual slicked to the side state. He had come unannounced, somehow finding where I lived. Did he know of this place beforehand? My stomach twisted with nerves, knowing Dad was here to lecture me.

"Are you going to let me in, or do you want to have this conversation in the hall?" He asked with his arms crossed and his eyes narrowed. He had a serious tone in his voice, one I'd grown used to, but still sent a chill running through my body.

He wasn't mad, he was furious, evident by the tic in his powerful jaw. I stepped to the side, allowing him to enter despite wanting to deny him access. I felt like I was betraying mom in some way by allowing him inside. This was her sanctuary from this very man.

"Why have you been ignoring me? You didn't even bother to tell me your mother died or when her funeral was. I would have liked to pay my respects." Dad started right off the bat, not wasting a second.

"No, you don't get to come to this place and talk about her. You're the reason she left. You're the reason I didn't have her growing up. Of course, I didn't tell you. You didn't have the right to know." Overwhelmed and furious by his words, my mouth moved before I could fully think about it. Never in my life had I talked back to my father.

"What did you say?!" He raised his voice, making me involuntarily flinch. "You don't get to tell me my rights. She abandoned *you*, too. You can't blame me. It was all *her* choice."

"She left *because* of *you*! So yes, it is your fault." Even if he refused to believe it, it's his fault mom left me behind too.

"I stepped up when your mother left, Livy. *I* was the only parent you had. This is how you treat me after I took care of you?" He was yelling now, bubbling my trauma ten fold. My body felt on edge, ready to jump at the slightest movement.

"You didn't take care of anyone! You drank yourself stupid almost every night. I'd come home and find you passed out with a bottle in your hand. I had to keep the house clean and cook if I ever wanted anything to eat. Between the two of us *I* was the parent. Don't come here acting like you did me any favors. The only thing I learned from you was how to defend myself and throw a decent punch." I was surprised by the calmness in which I was able to speak these words. My anger was through the roof, but I tried not to show it. I didn't yell at him like I wanted to, not even raising my voice the slightest. My tone did not betray me as it stayed strong and calm despite my nerves.

"Livy, that's not fair. My wife had left me without a word, and a young girl to take care of. You. It was an impossible task." He argued back. I could see the anger boiling in him. His hands were fisted by his side, causing my heart to race. Would he hit me if provoked? He's the one person I can't fight back. My hands began to clam up as adrenaline coursed through me.

"Whose fault is that?" I rolled my eyes. Next thing I knew my cheek burned, stinging from the pain of his slap. The force was so great it caused my head to swivel. Tears stung my eyes, but I didn't let them fall. I turned to look at him, not touching my cheek, even though I desperately wanted to ease its burning with my cool hand.

"Get out!" I yelled at him, pointing to my front door.

"Livy, I didn't mean to. I am so sorry." He shook his head almost in shock.

It was like he was surprised he had done it. His posture changed completely along with his tone. All the anger had left him replaced by deep remorse. It didn't matter, the action was done. He had hit me, and there was no taking it back. I'd taken a blow from him many times, but it was never out of anger. It was always when he was teaching me, trying to help me improve. He'd never hit me in the face before, and definitely never out of spite or frustration.

"Get out, dad," I said again, keeping my voice leveled. "I don't want to see you again."

"Livy, don't be this way. *Please*. I didn't mean to." He kept shaking his head, as if he could shake away the fact he'd slapped me so hard across the face.

I could feel my cheek start to swell. The taste of iron was strong in my mouth, letting me know I'd bit my cheek hard enough to draw blood. I stared into his familiar eyes, noting the wrinkles on the sides. His eyes were my own, the same icy blue stare back at me in the mirror every morning.

"Just go."

Dad was slowly backing away to the door. His eyes kept staring at my cheek, filled with regrets. It didn't matter to me, he would look the same way anytime he would hurt mom. It didn't matter how remorseful he would feel after hitting her, he never stopped. He'd apologize, and be sweet for a few days, but then the cycle would repeat. I won't be part of that.

"I'm staying at the motel down the street. I won't leave until I see you again," he let me know as he hung by the door.

With one last sorrowful look at me, he left, closing the door behind him, leaving me in a deafening silence. I let my tears fall, carefully wiping them away, feeling my cheek sting even at the gentle touch of my own fingers. I found a bag of frozen vegetables and placed it carefully on my cheek, wincing as it made contact. My tears didn't stop, either. It was like I had opened a dam, and I couldn't close it back up until it ran its course.

The knock on the door reminded me Lucas was supposed to return. I didn't want him to see me like this. I didn't want him to worry. I also wasn't sure what exactly he'd say or do. I am not sure what I need right now. My heart doesn't even know if it wants to be angry, or wallow in the sadness longer. I thought of sending Lucas away without even opening the door, but it didn't seem right. After everything Lucas has shared with me, how can I keep him out? I opened the door, standing behind it, trying to hide a little longer. Lucas' sweet cologne filled my lungs as he entered the flat.

My body kept facing the door as I closed it, avoiding looking at Lucas. If I looked at him, then he could look at me. He would see my wounded cheek. I hadn't even checked it in a mirror yet, but I know it's bad. Lucas wrapped his arms around my waist from behind, leaning down and resting his chin on my shoulder. I turned my head away from him, still trying to hide what I know he will inevitably see.

"What's the matter, Rose? Did I take too long?" He asked me, kissing the nape of my neck over my collarbone. I shook my head no, worried my voice would sound too weak. He continued to kiss my neck, moving my hair away gently with his fingers. I flinched when his fingers accidentally grazed against my cheek. *Shit.*

Lucas stiffened, pulling away and turning me to face him. He pushed my hair out of my face, lifting my chin with his fingers. He examined me carefully. His intense eyes were boring holes into me like the sun's rays through a magnifying glass.

"What happened to your face?" Lucas sounded furious as he saw my cheek for the first time.

How do I explain this one?

Lucas' P.O.V.

CHAPTER 24

It was clear someone had stricken her. I could see the well known mark. I've seen it a few too many times on Mom's face. My beautiful Rose had been hurt while I was gone, and I'll make whoever it was pay for it. The mark on her cheek tugged at my heart in the worst ways.

"It's nothing," she said, trying to blow it off.

"Olive, tell me what happened." This was serious, and the fact she didn't want to tell me, only made me wonder more.

"I hate when you use my name," she sighed. "It always gets me."

"Does that mean you'll tell me, Olive?"

"Sit down, I'll tell you." She gestured to the couch for me to sit on. Her voice deflated, leaving behind whatever stubbornness she had. I liked that my using her name had such an effect on her.

I sat on the couch, grabbing her wrist and pulling her onto my lap as she walked by me. I had her straddle me, so I could look into those eyes as she told me who hurt her like this. Whoever it was, hurt her more than just physically. Her eyes were pink and puffy, letting me know she'd been crying as well. She let out a breath, letting her shoulders fall.

"Shortly after you left, someone knocked on the door. I assumed maybe it was you, and you'd forgotten something, but it wasn't. My dad found me. I've kind of been ignoring his phone calls since my mom died. He wasn't very happy about it and started to lecture me. I got mad, so I argued back. I said something he didn't like, and next thing I knew..." she trailed off as she spoke, her voice thick with emotion.

I saw the tears pooling in her eyes, threatening to spill on her swollen cheek. The anger in me was at an all-time high, but I kept my cool in front of her. I knew blowing up right now would not be to her benefit. I'd more than likely scare her if I did. I'll deal with her dad later. Right now, I need to comfort my Rose.

I pulled her towards me, having her lay her uninjured

cheek on my chest. I rubbed her back with the tips of my fingers, lightly. She relaxed into me, silently crying. It broke my heart to hear her cry like this. I hate her father as much as I hate my own, maybe even more. How dare he hit her?

"Let's go, Rose." I picked her up.

"What? Where?" She wiped at her cheeks as she pulled back to look at me.

"You'll see." I smiled at her.

"Lucas, I can't go out like this. People will think you hit me." She shook her head in disbelief.

"Just trust me, Rose, okay?" She paused for a moment, staring deep into my eyes. I am not sure what she was searching for, but I guess she found it as she nodded her head yes to me.

"Okay," she whispered. I had her change into clothes I'd seen her wear to this place before. She arched a brow at me curiously, but got dressed anyway. I was happy she was willing to trust me right now. This probably isn't the best idea, with her still having her incision from surgery so present, but I know this is exactly what she needs.

Lucas: Twinkle Toes is coming tonight.

I texted Davis as she got dressed. I had found him the next day on social media and asked him for his number. I wanted to know any time Rose went in to fight, so I could be sure to be there and watch. It didn't take long for him to respond.

Viking Man: Hell yeah! I'll put her in a good fight.

Lucas: She needs a challenge.

Viking Man: I know what I'm doing.

I slipped my phone into my pocket as Rose approached. I grabbed one of her hair ties when she wasn't looking, currently, having it hidden in my pocket for later. I held my hand out for her to take, which she did instantly. There's no more hesitation on her part when it comes to this.

I love the feel of her hand on my own. Her skin is always so soft and smooth, but her hands are rough. I didn't fail to notice the acoustic guitar she had hidden in her closet when she fetched her journals. Her calloused fingers tell me she still plays. I hope to hear her play one day. Tonight, however, I'll be reading her journal while she sleeps. Sleep has never been my friend. It's more of a distant cousin who visits from time to time.

"Are you going to tell me where we are going now?" she asked as we entered a more deserted side of town.

She'd been quiet for most of the ride, humming from time to time to the music I had her choose. I liked giving her control over song choice. It was my way of letting her know she was in charge, even if I'm the one driving. If she told me to stop, to turn, or even speed up, I'd do it. I pulled into the driveway of a worn out building. The bulking figure at the doorway let me know I was at the right spot. Rose turned to face me quickly with a beautifully bright smile on her face.

"How?" she asked happily.

"Davis told me where it'd be."

"When did you two start talking?" She curled her right brow with curiosity.

"When you last brought me, I looked him up on social media and asked for his number so I could come watch you the next time you fought, but you never did. Understandably so, with everything going on. I hope it's okay. I asked Davis to place you in a fight." I squeezed the steering wheel anxiously as I looked at her, having parked the car to the side.

"More than okay," she said with a smile. "Thank you, Lucas." I could tell her cheek was still hurting her as her smile stayed lopsided, trying not to move her injured cheek. I hate her father so much right now. How could he hurt her? He'll get what's coming to him soon. I'll make sure of it.

"Let's go, twinkle toes." I winked at her as I got down from the car. Rose didn't wait for me to open her door. She was too excited, practically sprinting to the door.

"If it isn't Twinkle Toes, herself." The large man guarding the door greeted her with a smile.

"Hello, Carter." She greeted him back. I didn't miss the way Carter eyed her cheek, and then me. "What did you do to upset Davis this time? Front door duty? Yikes." She sucked in air between her teeth, looking like the epitome of the yikes emoji. Carter laughed, a hearty laugh that shook in his chest.

"I may or may not have accidentally hit on his daughter." Rose let out a loud laugh, clasping her stomach with one hand and covering her mouth with the other. I loved the sound of her laugh more than anything. She shook her head disapprovingly as she calmed her laughter.

"How bad was the fight?"

"Oh a few broken ribs, a busted nose, and now door duty for the rest of the year." He sighed defeatedly.

"He went easy on you," she said, surprising me, because none of that sounded like an easy punishment.

"No kidding," Carter agreed. I made myself a mental note to never mess with Davis. If that's him going easy, I don't want to know what him going all out looks like.

"Go on in, kiddo. He's waiting for ya," Carter said, pointing behind him to the door. Rose stepped through, but as I went to follow, Carter grabbed me by the arm. His hand clenched tightly around my bicep, almost bruising me. "If you're hurting her, I'll kill you."

Carter's threat was serious. I could see the murderous intent in his eyes. His grip only tightened further around my arm, as if to make his point. I was glad to know Rose had guys like these watching out for her.

"Her father." I simply stated, and it seemed Carter knew about him, too. He quickly released my arm, letting me go. Rose was still walking ahead, too excited to notice I had fallen behind. I didn't mind. I liked watching her saunter.

"He's in town?"

"Apparently." I shrugged. "I'm searching for him tomorrow."

"Let us know when you find him." The emotion on Carter's face was unmistakable. He was furious and out for blood.

"Will do." I nodded before walking in and catching up to my Rose.

Let the bastard get what's coming to him.

Chapter 25

Olive's P.O.V.

I couldn't believe Lucas had taken me here. I had no idea he and Davis had stayed in touch since I last brought him here. The idea of him wanting to come and watch me fight filled me with joy. He was supporting me even before all this.

I feel stupid for not letting him in sooner than now. I can feel myself falling in love with him already, and it frightens me. I know the longer this goes on the more in love with him I'll fall. This is different from what I felt for Julius. It already feels so much more intense. I am frightened of how badly Lucas will break me if anything were to happen.

"What'd you do to her?" Davis marched past me, right to Lucas, ready to strike. In my excitement, I hadn't realized how it might look to come here with an already sweltering cheek. I raced after Davis, trying to save Lucas from the blunt force of one of his punches.

"It wasn't him. I swear!" I yelled over the thundering music and yells of the enormous crowd.

"Don't defend the asshole, Twinkle Toes." Davis didn't believe me.

"You think I'd let him do this to me? Get serious, Davis." I placed my hands on my hips, giving him a stern look, even though his gaze stayed fixed on Lucas.

He pried his eyes away for a moment to look at me. His shoulders deflated as he took in my seriousness. He sighed, wiping his hand over his face and dragging it down, pulling on the skin in the process.

"Explain." He pointed to my cheek.

He knew I would never get hit in a fight on the face. The only way for me to get hurt like this is unexpectedly. I let out a breath, staring into Davis' caring eyes. The man was large, with muscles so thick you would think they'd burst the sleeves of all his shirts. His long dirty blonde hair was in its usual viking braid. He could instill fear in anyone, yet he cared the deepest of all the people I knew. Once Davis accepts you as family, you'll forever be in his care. He'll forever worry over you. Davis was the father I wished I had.

"My dad's in town."

Davis' eyes narrowed, and his teeth clenched at the news. I'd told Davis about my father before. Shared my whole life story with the man the night I won the championship. He'd heard it all, and accepted me into the fold. I'm forever grateful to Davis for giving me this place, for his confidence in me.

"That motherfucker." Davis seemed intent on punching something with the anger boiling deep inside him. "Get up there, you're up. We'll talk about this more later."

He gestured to the ring behind him where the last fight had ended. The crowd was still energized and it didn't take long to hear them cheer, as my name was being announced. I turned to Lucas, who only gave me his playful smile as he gestured with his head for me to go. He held out a hair tie he had dug out of his pocket. I am not sure when he grabbed it, but I was grateful as I took it. I kissed his cheek before heading towards the ring, not wasting any time. My hands were taped and my mouth guard was in place. I was up against a larger man. He towered over me, forcing me to look up at him when he was near.

He had larger muscles than I, but I knew his larger body would make it easier for me. I'd found the larger they were, the more blind spots they had. Like their muscles made it hard to reach there. I looked outside the ring to find Lucas and Davis deep in conversation. I wondered, for a moment, what they were speaking about before reminding myself to focus on the fight. I shook out my feet, arms, and hands as I jumped between my feet.

I heard the announcer start the fight in not so many words, seeing the muscles flex in the man's calves as he stepped forward to kick me. I knew it would hurt to even block, so I fell to my knees, leaning back, letting his leg fly over me, narrowly missing my nose. I felt the wind, from the force of his kick, brush past my skin. I spun on my knee, swiftly standing back up behind him now. I was never one for attacking people from behind so I waited for him to turn, before I double tapped his side.

It hurt him, but he didn't slow down. He brought his fist into my stomach with a great force, causing me to almost hurl immediately. I caught my breath, spinning around him on the balls of my feet as he tried to swing at me again. I hooked my ankle around his own, pulling so he was forced to take a step out, or risk falling. He did as I assumed and moved his leg out. I used that moment, when his muscles relaxed, to pull his leg all the way out, causing him to fall forward.

He didn't stay down long, jumping back up like a springboard. He aimed for my face, but those punches are always the easiest for me to read. This guy was tough, but nothing I couldn't beat with a little effort. I twisted and spun all around him, easily avoiding his punches, while simultaneously making him dizzy. My opponents never realized the way I dodged is meant to inebriate them in a way. They lose focus when they track me as I block, making me this big spinning blur around them.

When I saw him sway on his feet without meaning to, I knew it was time to end it. I fell to the floor, sweeping his leg out from under him. When he fell to the ground, I jumped on him, pummeling him as he lay under me. I knew my punches were too aggressive, but I kept thinking of my dad and everything he'd done.

I hadn't noticed I had been announced the winner, or the fight had ended, until a large arm wrapped around my

CHAPTER 25

waist and lifted me out of the ring. My opponent laid on the ring floor, bruised and beaten as I fought against the arm holding me. I kicked the air like a mad woman, until a pair of familiar hands found me. Lucas stood before, eyes wide and concerned. He held my face, pulling all my attention to him. His thumb rubbed my uninjured cheek, while his other hand ever so lightly grazed where my father had struck me.

"It's okay, Rose. We got you." Lucas assured me.

I let all the tears pour out of me as Davis let me go, allowing me into the passionate embrace of Lucas. Lucas lifted me up, carrying me bridal style as he followed Davis to the back, past some double doors. This corridor only held a few wanderers from the crowd around the rings. Davis continued to lead us until we were in a small room away from others. I felt some catharsis as the tears dried. I'd poured all my anger out and then all my pent-up emotions. I felt like a blank slate. A dingy, almost broken slate, but a blank one all the same. I will no longer carry my father on my slate.

"I want the full story, Twinkle Toes." Davis crossed his arms as he leaned against the tattered large desk of the room–I'm convinced–used to be an office at one point or another.

"There's not much to say. He showed up, we argued, he slapped me, and then I kicked him out of my flat. He told me he was staying at a nearby motel and he wouldn't be leaving until we spoke again," I quickly explained with a nasally voice because of the stuffy nose I'd given myself from crying.

"He'll be leaving alright." Davis uttered through his teeth. "Here's your money, fireball. I'll leave you two alone to talk. Don't forget, championships are coming up soon. You need to win at least 2 more fights to enter. You interested?"

"Extremely," I answered with an excited grin.

"I'll tell you when and where." Davis left after uttering those words, leaving Lucas and me alone in this dusty old office. My heart hammered against my chest as I stared into those intense brown eyes. He looked at me so tenderly I felt I could melt.

This man has a hold over my heart and my body like no other.

"What are you doing?" I asked Lucas as his fingers slid into the waistband of my pants as he drove.

"Pleasuring my Rose," he answered matter-of-factly, like this was completely normal.

The thrill I was getting from this was higher than I thought it would be. His hand slipped further down my pants as he continued to drive, never once taking his eyes off the road. We were headed back to my flat after having a heavy make-out session in the dingy old office. I knew I was still pretty wet from it, but Lucas didn't know until now. I saw his lips turn into his sexy arrogant smirk.

"My dear Rose, I didn't realize you'd be so wet for me already." His smirk widen at his comment.

His finger slid inside me as Change by Deftones began to play in the background. My heart raced and my legs parted for him of their own accord. His finger began to slide in and out of me, at times just rubbing against the walls of my core. I couldn't hold back the moan from ripping through me, to his delight. He continued to toy with me until he got what he wanted. My heart hammered and the walls of my core clenched around his fingers as I came. I'd never been fingered in a car with someone who was driving. It was thrilling knowing anyone could have seen any time we stopped at a red light.

We couldn't get to the flat any faster, and once there, Lucas practically tore the door down to get me inside. We discarded our clothes all along the floor as we kissed. Only breaking apart to pull our shirts off. I kept walking backwards, unsure of my destination. I felt the cold leather of my couch arm against my bare thighs. Lucas pushed me back, having me fall fully onto the couch from the side. He didn't climb over me as I thought he would. No, instead he lifted my ass and placed it on the arm of the couch. He slapped his dick against my clit, making me gasp.

He teased me with the tip, rubbing it all along the outside of my center. He eventually inserted the tip of his dick inside me, only to pull it out and do it over again. The teasing had me begging for more. It wasn't until Lucas was satisfied with my pleas that he decided to fully enter me, gracing me with the immense pleasure only his enormous shaft brought me. So began our hours of pleasure.

"Shit, don't stop!" I yelled as Lucas slammed into me faster.

I pressed my face against the cold wood of my table as he had bent me over and inserted himself deep inside me. His hand played with my clit as he hammered into me. The sound of our skin slapping against each other echoed around the loft. Lucas held my bun in his other hand, lightly tugging it back so I lifted my head and exposed my neck. I moaned loudly, as the action only caused me to feel more pleasure.

"Cum again for me, Rose. Yell my name," he commanded, pressing harder against the bundle of nerves between my legs.

"Oh, fuck—*Lucas!*" I yelled out as I came, gripping my hands into tight fists. Lucas thrusted into me faster until I felt the spurt of his seed shoot deep inside me. I moaned as I felt it. Lucas didn't pull out immediately, either. He kept himself inside me, growing flaccid by the minute. We were both out of breath at this point.

Lucas never disappointed me in anything he did. Every touch, lick, and suck brought me to new heights. Lucas kissed my exposed shoulder lovingly, causing my heart to squeeze. I hadn't realized it, but I actually enjoyed being kissed there. It felt so tender and sweet, filling my heart with joy.

"You're so beautiful, Rose," he whispered into my ear before kissing my neck.

"Mmm, don't start or I'll be getting you hard again." I

bit my lip, somehow feeling like I could take on more of him. No matter how many orgasms he brought me, it was never enough. I felt like I wasn't living until we were wrapped in one another. He was like this other piece of me, making me feel whole when we were together. I can't get enough of him physically, sexually, or emotionally. *I'm so fucked.*

"Lucas?" I called his name.

"Yes, my Rose?"

"Don't hurt me," I whispered, feeling all kinds of vulnerability.

"Never," he swore. I stood up, causing him to have to step back, finally releasing himself from me. I turned to look into those brown eyes, determined to voice how I was truly feeling. I can't keep holding back if I am serious about him being solely mine.

"I mean it, Lucas, because I've never felt this way about anyone before. Especially not this quickly. You'll crush what little of a heart I have left." Lucas pressed me flush against his chest, letting our bare skin touch again. He held my chin, keeping my eyes on his.

"I promise you, Rose. I will never intentionally hurt you. You're all I want."

With those words I've been longing to hear, he kissed me so passionately it was like we were the only ones on the planet. This was our moment, one I would never relinquish. When Lucas' mouth finally left my own, his gaze melted me further. His eyes held such love I felt I could crumble beneath the weight of it.

"You're all I want too," I admitted. I know Leo told me not to tell Lucas I had chosen him already, but how could I not? "I choose you, Lucas." The smile he graced me with was unlike any other. He squeezed me tightly, holding me closer to him, if that was even possible. His lips captured my own again in another tender and loving kiss. *Yes, I'm still scared, but I won't let it keep me from living.*

"You don't know how happy you've made me, Rose. Let's

get you washed off and in bed now," he said. "You've had a long day."

Lucas joined me in the shower, washing my hair and my body for me. He kissed me from time to time, on my shoulder, on my thigh, on my stomach, and even on my knee. Every kiss was gentle and caring. This man had my heart so wrapped in him, and I don't think he even realizes it. He dried me, dressed me, and carried me to bed. I didn't miss the fact he grabbed one of my journals earlier and placed it on the nightstand. He laid me down, crawling in under the covers with me. He was sitting up, leaning back against the headboard as he rubbed my back with his left hand. His right hand held my journal open as he read it. I closed my eyes, feeling myself lull to sleep with every aimless rub. His fingers were like magic against my skin.

"Goodnight, my Rose." I heard him whisper.

"Goodnight, my Knight." I whispered back.

Lucas was my knight in shining armor. I felt like he was constantly saving me. He's always at my side when I need him. He knows exactly what to say to me to make me feel better, even knowing how to cheer me up. The stunts he has pulled and the comments he has made are things that have shown me how much he knows me, how much he understands me. Lucas is everything I didn't know I needed and more.

I need to start fighting for him, too. This isn't a one-way thing. I've decided he is the one I wish to be with, so I'll fight to make him mine. I'll fight to keep him here with me, to make him fall in love with me, too. A relationship is a two-way street and I feel I've been sorely lacking. I'm determined to do better, and I plan to.

"Your Knight?" I heard the smile in his voice. I kept my eyes closed, feeling too tired to open them again. My body was so relaxed and ready for sleep every unfiltered thought I had, felt ready to leave my mouth.

"Yes, my Knight. You've saved me a lot, Lucas, so you're my Knight in shining armor." It grew silent for a moment, but his rubbing never stopped.

"I think I like that," he said, kissing my head sweetly. "I'll be your Knight whenever you need me to be. You should know, you've saved me too, Rose."

His comment surprised me, because I felt all I've done was make him wait too long for me. I feel I've brought my own family drama into his life. He's even fallen behind on work because of me. I don't see how I could have saved him, but I didn't ask. Sleep took hold of me, not willing to relinquish me from its grasp.

I felt myself drift off into a strange dream.

Chapter 26

Lucas' P.O.V.

Rose had fallen asleep beside me, but not before filling my heart and ego to the brim. *Her Knight.* I liked that she thought of me in that way. I'd happily fight demons and dragons for her. Right now, the only demon around is her father. I'll hire a man to do some digging for me. Once I know why he's here, I'll pay him a visit myself. I won't let Rose face him again.

I opened her journal back up, picking up where I left off on her first day of freshman year. I enjoyed reading about her innermost thoughts about her life, her friends, and her classes, seeing this whole other side to Rose. It was like I was there with her. She was sharing a big part of herself with me by allowing me to read these journals, and I don't plan on letting her down.

Dear future me, (Because who says dear diary anymore?)

I hope you're doing better than me right now. This new school, although amazing academically, lacks in social etiquette. The girls are all bitchy and the boys are all immature. There is one boy who is calm and collected. Derek Nelson. I heard he's the smartest boy in our grade. I wonder if that's true? I was going to talk to him today, but I never found the nerve.

Honestly, I raced out of school when the bell rang, trying to get into dad's rusted and crappy pickup truck. Every kid here comes from money, and being the only one who doesn't, already has me at a disadvantage. I don't need them to pick on me for dad's car. I'm sure you remember our daily evening fight sessions with dad. Have we beat him yet? I hope so, because today was especially brutal. I think he's stressed about something and it's making fighting him 10 times worse.

He forgot to do the shopping again, so I had to go out this evening and buy whatever I could carry back home. Dad had drunk too much alcohol to drive an hour after bringing me home from school. Funny how we never run out of liquor, but food is always scarce.

I walked back home with the few groceries I could carry, but I managed to cook and even made enough food for him to eat. Currently, he's snoring on the couch, beer bottle still in hand. Has he stopped drinking yet? I sincerely hope so. Anyway, I better get started on all the homework my new teachers assigned. I don't know if you remember, but they told us our public education hadn't amounted to anything, and they are going to get me caught up to my classmates' level. Even though I'm there already, probably past it.

With lots of hope for the future,
Past You

First entry and I'm already feeling upset. Her father was a worthless piece of shit. What I hated most was the fact she didn't find an escape at school, but instead found more misery. It's a cruel world when both school and your home torment you. I'm surprised Rose survived all of this. I flipped the page eager to read more about my Rose.

Dear Future Me,

Today sucked ass. You remember Derek Nelson (smartest and coolest guy at this school). Well, he talked to us. Honest to goodness, just came up to me and started a conversation. He asked what school I had gone to before here. He was being nice and polite, making it easy for me to answer his questions. I should have known better than to think he was interested in being my friend. He quickly let everyone know what I'd told him.

I am a poor kid, who's mother isn't around. I'm the kid who can only afford to be here because of a scholarship. I am a fool for thinking Derek Nelson could ever be interested in me. I should know not to trust a pretty boy. They always seem nice, but in reality *they're chameleons. I've noticed popular, pretty boys are able to change their nature depending on who they are around. They can be sweet when they need to be, cruel when they want, smart when they have to be. It's all a charade and no one notices.*

Who are you really, Derek Nelson? Are you a coward behind closed doors? Are you bullied at home, so you have to find a way to be in control here at school? Or are you some kind of sociopath? Either way, Derek, you've now made it onto my shit list. It's not a very long list, but I feel like it's going to grow in this school.

Please tell me if we have good friends in the future? Tell me we've found someone who understands us? Are we dating anyone? God, I wish I could fast forward this part of my life.

Hoping you're having better luck,

Past you

I frowned as I finished reading her entry. I hated knowing on her second day things had already gone bad. How could anyone not be interested in my Rose? She's perfect in every way. I'll be looking up Derek Nelson on social media later. Her shit list will be my shit list too. Asshole. I guess it makes sense why it took her a while to trust me. I flipped the page feeling addicted to know what happens next. I felt like I had picked up a delectable book I can't put down until it's finished.

Dear future me,

Kill Derek Nelson. Formulate the perfect murder and then do it. That son of a bitch! I'm not sure if you remember, but how could you honestly forget? Derek spread a rumor in an attempt to get his attention, I followed him home. He told everyone he felt bad for me and invited me inside where he fed me. I was made out to look like some starved teenager who ravished his fridge and was awestruck by his home.

He makes it sound like I live in a shack and not a nice residential home like most. He even went as far as to say I offered him sex for money! I swear I'll murder him. I would have beat his ass if I knew it wouldn't get me expelled. I don't understand why he did it. I have done nothing to him. I've done him no wrong for him to be this way. If he's so bored, he could have told me. I would have had him meet me at the gym where I could have taught him a thing or two. Starting with how to block your face.

I want to break that perfect little nose of his. Do me a favor and look him up in the future. Invite him to the gym, pretend not to know anything and have him "teach" you how to throw a punch. When he asks you to punch, show him how it's done right in the face! God, I'm so mad. Now I'm getting picked on by all the girls. They told me I need to stay away from Derek. Actually, they told me to stay away from all the boys at school.

I hate this place. Please tell me it at least paid off and we're at our dream college.

A royally pissed off, Past You

I'm right there with you Rose, feeling real ticked off. I've been to schools like this all my life. There was a Derek Nelson or two at every school. The guy who was popular for the things he said he did or happened to him. I've been witness to these kinds of rumors before. I never paid them any mind, but I also never stopped them. My stomach twisted with guilt for not being a better person in high school.

I laid the journal against my chest, looking down at my beautiful Rose. She was sleeping so peacefully beside me. You would never guess she had been through so much. The sound of her deep breaths were soothing, helping me calm down. I hope she made at least one friend in that hell. At least one to light up the darkness.

Dear future me,

Life totally fucking sucks! Zaiden Brier threw a wad of cash at me today, asking how much I charge. He did it in the lunchroom in front of everyone. I'd never wanted to die so badly in my life! I wanted to become the chair I was sitting in. Honestly, what I wanted to do was grab the chair and hit him across the face with it.

I was mortified! Everyone either laughed or whispered more rumors about me. I couldn't do shit, except get up and leave. I told him he couldn't pay me enough to even touch him. He didn't like that very much, finding me after school, and trying to pin me down. But he quickly learned you can't mess with me. He was rubbing his wrist as I walked away from him. I could see he understood any further physical touches would result in one of his limbs being broken.

Dad didn't drink today, surprisingly, but it's because he was fighting tonight. He's getting back into the swing of things, but I know he's rusty. I'm not exactly a good spar for him. I get the feeling he'll be in the worst mood possible if he loses tonight. Please God, let him win. Let him win, make some money, be in a good mood, and maybe, actually, buy some food.

A pretty hungry, Past You

My hands were gripping the journal so hard I was sure I left an indent. Scratch Derek Nelson. Zaiden Brier is first on my list. These guys have no idea how badly their past is about to catch up to them. Karma is a real bitch, and if she hasn't dealt with them already, I most certainly will. I continued reading until around three in the morning when my eyes finally started to stick with sleep. My shit list had grown exponentially with kids who picked on my Rose. She had the worst first semester of freshman year so far.

I'll make it better, Rose.

Olive's P.O.V.

A pair of warm lips pressed against my forehead, waking me with a smile. I knew these lips well now my Knight was waking me. I felt his arms wrap around me as he pulled me closer to him. He nuzzled his head into my neck, kissing my chest where his lips could reach. I've never woken up so happy before. I smiled widely, forgetting all about my cheek until I felt the sting again.

"Good morning, my Rose," he whispered to me.

"Good morning, my Knight."

He kissed my neck this time, trailing down to my collarbone. His hand gripped my hip tightly. I loved the feel of his hand around my waist or on my hips. It always felt so possessive, and for some reason, I really liked that. He ventured lower until he was under the sheets. I giggled, wondering what he was up to.

"What are you doing?" I asked him.

"About to have my breakfast," he replied.

I felt his fingers hook into the waistband of my shorts and underwear. My heart accelerated with excitement at his words. I could already feel the slickness between my thighs. His words affected me as much as his touches did. I felt my breathing slow as I took deep, anticipating breaths. His hands slowly slid my underwear and shorts off as his fingers ran over my skin along the way.

His lips trailed kisses on my inner thigh until they met my center. I moaned when his tongue licked me at my core. Lucas licked and sucked at me, using his fingers and tongue in the most skilled of ways. I yelled his name in no time, feeling fully awake from my intense orgasm. Next thing I knew, his massive shaft was entering me before I crashed down, only raising me back up again.

"Lucas!" I moaned as he lifted my shirt, sucking at my nipple. He groaned in pleasure, thrusting faster and harder into me. I came quickly again feeling him do the same shortly after. Lucas perched himself up on his elbows, now laying light kisses all around my neck and face. He then pulled back and looked deeply into my eyes.

"I love waking up to you by my side. Thank you for asking me to stay." He smiled down at me. *Damn, you silver-tongued Casanova, making my heart swoon.*

"Thank you for staying. This is honestly the best way I've been woken up." I gave him a half smile, not wanting to hurt my cheek again. This man has made my heart swoon for him this morning. The further I keep falling for him the more frightened I become. I'm scared to lose him now that I've let him in.

Please, God, let this work out.

"Shall we eat for real?" He asked me with a smirk as he

pushed my hair out of my face.

I nodded my head, feeling him slip out of me, missing the feel of him already. It makes me feel incomplete without him inside me now. I am uncertain of how deeply woven Lucas' feelings are for me currently. I guess they call it taking the plunge, because it feels like you're free falling the entire time, unsure of when you'll hit the water. Hopefully, I never do because Lucas is everything I want and more.

I saw my journal on the nightstand, laid open, face down. He had read almost the whole thing last night, making me wonder exactly how much sleep he'd gotten. I wonder if he looks at me differently after reading how pathetic I'd been in high school. Freshman year was soul crushing. I finally got off the bed, cleaned myself off and dressed before joining him downstairs. He furrowed his brow as he looked in my fridge. His tall self had to lean down to see what was on the top shelf of my older styled fridge. His arm hung over the door as he contemplated what to eat, or make. He stood up straight, looking at me with a smirk.

"Rose, I think you need to go grocery shopping," he mused, making me blush. I placed my hand on the side of my neck bashfully.

"Yeah, I haven't had the chance. Want to go on campus with me? I have class soon, but this way we can still eat together." I suggested with a shrug.

"Sounds perfect." He closed my fridge door, holding his hand out towards me. I took it, allowing him to lead me out.

"Wait, I forgot something!" He said before I locked the door. I let him back in, seeing him grab the journal he had been reading along with the box. He smiled widely at me as he walked back out of the flat.

"I can't leave these behind. I have a lot of reading to do."

His excitement made me laugh. I couldn't believe he was actually looking forward to reading my journals. I, myself, found them cringey, painful, or outright boring. Lucas refused to take different cars, swearing he would wait for me on campus.

"I don't want you to have to wait for me," I argued.

"I don't mind, besides it'll give me a chance to see some old professors. I need to see my advisor and give him a big thanks, anyway."

"Are you sure?"

"Extremely. I can do some work while I wait if I have to." He shrugged his shoulders like this was no big deal.

"Okay then." I nodded, allowing him to open his passenger door for me to climb in.

He drove us towards campus, allowing me to pick the music again. I decided to change it up a bit and played Playinwitme by KYLE. Lucas didn't seem to mind, or if he did, he didn't voice his complaint. The drive was quick, allowing us a little more time to eat together. Lucas held my hand as we headed to the coffee shop.

"So you're not just a rock girl then," he observed.

"I'm a girl of many things." I winked at him, causing him to let out a light laugh of amusement. "I was feeling happy this morning, so I wanted more upbeat things."

"I didn't mind it. I liked it. Maybe next time I'll have you play one of my playlists. Let you get to know my music style." He wiggled his eyebrows quickly, making me giggle.

"Think I'll like it?"

"No doubt about it." He nodded.

We took our place in line, waiting our turn. We were so lost in each other we hadn't looked around us in a while. I think I heard her before he did. Her nasally voice was like nails on a chalkboard. I saw her from the corner of my eye as Lucas stiffened beside me.

"Francesca." The barista called her name to grab her drink.

I squeezed Lucas' hand, trying to remind him I was right here with him. I couldn't imagine what it would be like to be faced with your rapist out in the open like this. To know nothing happened to them, that they faced zero consequences for what they did. She grabbed her drink, turning and spotting me. She smirked for a moment, heading my way, until she saw my interlocked hand. That's when she noticed Lucas.

I took my attention off her, looking up at Lucas too. There was such anger in his eyes. His face was still, but his teeth were clenched and he was gripping my hand so tightly it hurt, but I didn't complain. Francesca froze in her tracks, which surprised me. Maybe she feels some remorse for what she did.

I thought too highly of her for a second, because after a moment her smile widened further. She continued to stalk towards us as if happy to see us. I stepped in front of Lucas as if my body could shield him from this moment. I stared daggers at her, making her unsure about what she was doing for a moment.

"Ollie, weren't you dating Leo a few days ago? You sure move quick," she commented, trying to offend me or maybe get a rise out of me.

"If I wanted your commentary, I'd ask for it. Goodbye now, Franny." I waved at her, closing and opening my hand at her.

She didn't move, standing there looking right at Lucas.

"Well, enjoy my sloppy seconds." She laughed, taking a sip of her frappuccino.

Her comment made me snap, causing me to take a step forward with my hand fisted. I had it pulled back, ready to throw hands at this bitch, but Lucas wrapped his hand around my waist and pulled me back into his chest. He leaned down, kissing my neck and whispering in my ear.

"She's not worth it, Rose. Let's just have our time together."

His words deflated me instantly. I nodded my head, stepping forward in line, ignoring Franny completely. She scoffed but disappeared when she realized we would pay her no mind. I was such an idiot bringing Lucas on campus. I had forgotten all about Franny attending this university as well.

I've only run into her the one time with Leo. I didn't think I'd run into her again.

"I am so sorry, Lucas." I whispered to him from across the table. He was so stiff, rigid even, since we ran into her.

"It's not your fault, Rose. I'm fine. Don't worry about me. Let's get you fed and to class on time. Wanna walk and eat?" He asked me as time was getting the better of us.

I nodded my head, unsure of what to do to make him feel better. This morning has made me realize how little I know of Lucas. What does he do when he needs to relieve pressure? What helps calm him? Can I do anything to help him right now?

We walked in silence as I ate my muffin. Then it dawned on me. It's stupid and small and probably won't work, but I took a big bite, being intentional to leave a million crumbs on my mouth. I turned and smiled at Lucas with a crumb coated mouth. He looked at me a moment before bursting into a chuckle.

"You look ridiculous." He shook his head, wiping the crumbs from around my lips. He bent down and kissed me lovingly. "Thank you," he whispered.

"Go get some work done at home. Don't stay on campus. I'll text you when class is over," I said to him. He shook his head no at me, holding my cheeks in his palms.

"You can't get rid of me that easily. I'll be here waiting for you when you get done. Go learn something new, Rose, and don't worry about me." He kissed my forehead this time.

"How can I not worry about the man I'm falling in love with?" I spoke the words before I could stop myself. We both froze at my admission. My eyes were wide as they met him. I couldn't believe my mouth betrayed me. "I–" There was nothing I could say to take it back now. After a few seconds, Lucas smiled the widest I'd ever seen. It made my heart skip a beat at its absolute beauty. The smile went so far as to light those intense brown eyes with a gleam of happiness.

"Falling in love, huh?" He teased me with his brows

raised. He licked at his lips when he finished speaking.

"Stop, you didn't hear that. I'm going to class now." I went to run away embarrassed, but he grabbed my wrist, pulling me back towards him. He pressed me flush against his chest, uncaring of the stares we were getting by everyone who passed us by.

"I'm falling in love with you too, Olive."

With his admission his lips met mine again in an earth shattering kiss. It was so full of love I could feel it seeping through my pores, running through my body. When he pulled away, my cheeks flushed a shade of scarlet.

"I'll see you after class, Rose." He turned me, nudging my frozen self towards the STEM building.

I ran up the stairs, needing the physical exercise so I could use it as an excuse for the pink on my cheeks. I made it to class just as the professor was starting, earning me a brow raise. It was hard to stay focused as thoughts of Lucas plagued my mind.

I wonder what he's up to now?

Chapter 27

Lucas' P.O.V.

Lucas: You on campus?
Leo: Yeah, early class today.
Lucas: So you're in class right now?
Leo: Yeah, everything okay? Do I need to leave early?
Lucas: No, everything is good. Just wanted to see what you were up to.

I was hoping to have someone to hang out with. I also wanted to talk to him about the devil incarnate. He needs to know she's here. I should have checked in on her more. How did I not know she attended this university? Perhaps I can convince them to kick her out if I give the school a couple million dollars. I would pay a billion if I needed to. That bitch doesn't deserve to go to the same school as Leo.

I hadn't seen her since the night of the incident. Her face had my mind racing back to the memory of that room, of her on me. It was a memory I try to block out a lot, but it plagues me often. There is no getting rid of it. It's a scar in my brain, something that will never fully heal. All I can do is try to avoid her for now until I can get her out of this university.

Rose did her best, trying to keep her from me. I couldn't afford for her to be on academic probation for getting in a fight on campus. Even if I wanted nothing more than to see that bitch get punched right on her nasty nose job. I did enjoy the way she tried to cheer me up by being a goof. Those crumbs around her mouth as she smiled made her look so damn cute.

"How can I not worry about the man I'm falling in love

with?"

Her voice echoed in my head, reminding me I'm the luckiest man alive. She's falling in love with me, and there was no better news for me to hear. Besides the news of her tumor not being cancerous. I hope they call her with results soon, because the suspense is killing me.

With Leo unable to come hang out, and my want to see anyone diminish, I decided to head to my car and finish her first journal. I was only to mid-September now, but I was almost done with the journal. Last night had me adding a few too many names to my shit list. I found her journal and quickly picked up from where I left off.

Dear future me,.

Today is the day we met Ian. He is new, transferring from a public school like me. We instantly hit it off, being the outcast poor kids. He is funny, and extremely kind. Plus let's not forget he's fucking hot as hell. Hottie with a body.

He asked for my number but I don't have a cell phone so I gave him my house number, since it's working this month. I am waiting for him to call now. I am trying to not lose my mind as I wait for him. I am happy to finally have someone to talk to. This has been a long month of school with nothing but teasing and rude comments spewed my way.

Can you please beat everyone's ass? I'm sure you're an amazing fighter by now. Maybe you can go around punching everyone in the nose or throat for me. Revenge is always great!

In all seriousness, try to show them how amazing we are now. Currently, they can all suck my left tit with their annoying selfs.

Feeling a little hopeful with Ian around now. Maybe things will get better.

A hopeful, Past You

Although I'm jealous of Ian, I'm happy to read that she made a friend. She needed it. I couldn't imagine being ridiculed every day and not having a friend to support you or turn to. I flipped the page, needing to see if Ian ever called her.

Dear future me,

Add Ian to our love forever list. That son of a bitch talked to me all night and kept me up so late. He was paired with Derek in lab today and I could see them hitting it off. There was a moment of small tension where Ian looked at me a bit funny and I knew Derek was telling him about the rumor he started.

Ian got up so fast, sending his stool tumbling behind him. I remember Ms. White asked what he thought he was doing and Ians response filled me with such happiness. He told her he was getting away from the plague before it contaminated him too. He told her he'd rather work with me, which she thankfully let him.

I had my first lab partner, and we worked so well together. We goofed off, but we got our work done easily. Derek glared at Ian throughout class, and I worried about him getting himself into trouble, but Ian is a pretty strong guy. He's tall with broad shoulders and large muscles for a guy his age. His piercing blue eyes are easy to get lost in.

Anyway, today was definitely a good day. I sincerely hope it stays that way.

A very happy, Past You

Okay, gold star for Ian for not falling for the rumor. Rose definitely had a little crush on him and it was kind of cute to read about it. I smiled as I continued reading about how great Ian was the rest of September. I finished the journal, grabbing the next. I checked the clock, still having about 20 minutes until she was done. I opened the journal and dove right in again.

Dear Future Me,

Ian and I went to the new arcade together today. It was an absolute blast. We've decided to meet there every Friday and play games. Whoever lost the most games had to pay for drinks and food. Thankfully, I had some extra money on me, because I lost fast.

Do we play more games as an adult? Does Ian have us play games with him still? I hope we're still friends with him. He's a great guy, and it'd be a shame if we lost touch with him.

CHAPTER 27

Tomorrow Ian and I are going to the school bonfire. We're hoping everyone will leave us alone since they'll be entertained with football. We are bringing marshmallows and sticks to roast them with. Roasted marshmallows are the best!

Dad has been busy with fighting, which is great because he's been winning. It's inflated his ego enough to keep him from drinking as much. He also bought groceries for once. We currently have a fully stocked fridge.

I'm waiting for the other shoe to drop. We both know life never stays this good.

Hoping for the best, but preparing for the worst.

A happy, Past You

Is this how she still feels? Does she think she can never be happy for long? I'll prove her wrong. I will make her the happiest woman alive. I'll give everything she asks for plus everything she needs. Starting with finding her dad.

"Hello?" Connor answered.

"Hey man, I need a favor."

"Yeah, what's up?" Connor is an old classmate turned PI. He knows how to find anyone and dig up the best dirt. I've kept his number through the years.

"I need you to find a Nick Brewer and tell me everything you can dig up on him. He's currently in town but lives in New Hampshire. He has one daughter, Olive Brewer and an ex wife Abigail Rose, recently deceased. He's a retired MMA fighter, not sure what he does for employment now. I need to know what reason he'd have for coming here to talk with his daughter. Think you can do it?" I asked him seriously.

"You know I can. How quickly do you need this done?"

"The sooner the better. Yesterday would have been great," I joked.

"I'm on it. I'll send you the bill after." He hung up, not waiting for me to utter a word. I know he'll do it and he'll do it quickly and accurately. *Let's see what you're actually in town for, Nick.* I headed out of the car back towards her building, knowing she'd be out of class soon. I should have asked what class she was in so I could have waited for her outside her door. *It's too late now.*

I hung around the entrance of the building, waiting for her to emerge. My hands were deep in my pockets and I was lightly kicking around a small rock between my feet. I miss playing soccer. I need to find a community team to join again. I haven't played since Ivy died. She was always at my games, cheering me on from the sidelines.

"I hope you weren't too awfully bored waiting on me." Her voice made me look away from the small rock.

"Your journals kept me entertained." I winked at her. "Can't wait to see what happened to Ian." She flushed pink with embarrassment. I loved seeing her cheeks turn that beautiful shade of crimson. She looked almost mortified.

"Oh God, you're already there?" She cringed.

"Sure am." I nodded with a playful smirk.

"I'm wondering if maybe I should have started you in college. My high school journals are so embarrassing, depressing, and cringy."

"No way! And miss this fun?" I shook my head at her. "I'm glad I get to read about high school you. She's quite comical." Rose groaned in embarrassment.

"I'm glad you think so, because many others didn't." She took my hand as she began to walk. I smiled, happy she initiated our hand holding this time.

"So where to now, Rose? Have another class?"

"Not until later. We have a couple of hours to kill, and I want to use them to get to know you," she said, guiding me through the familiar campus. I was surprised by her words.

"Oh? Is it because you're falling in love with me, you want to get to know me better?" I teased her, grabbing her in my arms and pulling her back.

"Asshole. I shouldn't have said anything." She shook her head as she smacked at my arm. It was cute, making me chuckle.

"We both know you didn't mean to say it, but I'm sure as

fuck glad you did." I kissed her temple, making her still against me. "Tell me what you want to know and I'll share."

"Give me your life story, the same way I gave you mine. We'll start there."

I sighed, feeling the weight of the world on my shoulders right now. She wanted my life story, but like hers, it was a sad one. It seems only fair, and the fact she wants to know everything about me, makes me jump for joy. She's starting to want me more and more with each passing day, and I couldn't be happier about it.

"Okay, Rose. Let's go to the car. I'll spill my dirty little secrets to you." I winked at her. We headed towards my car hand in hand. I opened her door as usual, allowing her to sit in the passenger seat. I took my place behind the wheel. I turned to face her, taking a deep breath before beginning my sad tale.

"I was born here in New York. My mother met my father in college and fell madly in love. They had Lisa the year after graduation and me two years after. Growing up we never needed anything monetary. Dad's business had taken off and he'd become a millionaire in no time, reaching a billion around the time I turned 7. The better his business did the worse his mood got. You'd think it'd be the other way, but not with dad. The more success he had, the more work he made for himself. We all walked around eggshells at home, trying not to trigger him in any way. There was no laughter in our home, just rigid smiles. Until I met John and Leo, anyway." I smiled sadly at the reminder of John in his casket.

"Dad and Mr. Darius became close business acquaintances, allowing John and Leo to come over often. Their home became my second house. I found myself going over as often as I could to get away from Dad. I didn't know at the time he was hurting my mom. She didn't show it, and neither did he. He kept it hidden behind closed doors, even from Lisa and I. Lisa would go with me to John and Leo's often as well. Even though she was the only girl there and two years older. Anything beats being home with Dad. Around the time I turned 12 Dad's fists found me any time I didn't meet his expectations." I couldn't look Rose in the eyes as I told my story, keeping them fixed on the sky outside my windshield.

"He hurt Lisa one night when she missed curfew by 1 minute. I yelled at him, knowing I'd get it twice as bad, but it would make him leave her alone. It was the only time I ever let him hit her. Any time she'd do something wrong in his eyes, I'd be sure to do something worse to keep his anger fixed on me. Sadly, I couldn't keep mom safe. I'd hear him rape her often, leaving her in tears and bruises, which I'd end up tending to. Dad began to train me to take over his business when I reached high school. He had me on a set path, and there was no getting off it. I didn't mind as much because John and Leo were on the same path, which meant we had a lot of classes together. They were the two who made life bearable." I remembered the stupid shit we'd get into when we were out together. *God, I miss John.*

"John and I got onto the soccer team at school, making me have games and practices kept me out of the house. I made sure Lisa would come with me to every practice and every game so she wasn't left alone at home. I enjoyed soccer, still do actually. I played all through highschool and into college. My freshman year of college, I decided I would not take over my father's business. He could go screw himself. Work until he dies. He was furious and beat the ever living shit out of me when I told him. He didn't say anything again, but only because he was scheming behind closed doors. I found a contract on his desk a month later. I felt like I was reading some kind of contract which sold Lisa off to some businessman's son. Dad was trying to marry Lisa off, and get himself someone else to take over the business." I shook my head in disgust about the contract, about all of it.

"He can't do that!" Rose interjected, causing me to look at her for the first time. She had tears in her eyes, crying for me and my past. I leaned over and wiped away at it. The swelling on her cheek had gone down, and she'd hidden the bruise beneath makeup.

"You'll find when you have billions of dollars, there's a lot you can do you shouldn't be able to. I promised him I'd take over the business if he left Lisa out of it. We made an agreement and he even made a contract for me to sign. Words of mouth are not good enough for this man. I'm stuck with his business whether I want it or not. I started dating Ivy around this time. She was like this large light in my life, keeping me from drowning in darkness. She took up every moment of my life in college, supporting me and lifting me up when I was down. She was studying business too, and she swore we would run my dad's business together so all that work wouldn't fall on my shoulders." Tears stung the back of my eyes as I pictured her bright smile, the one that always wrinkled her eyes on the side. I loved her so much.

"She came to all my soccer games. She helped my mom get away from my dad. Her heart was so pure and her spirit was unbreakable. She stood up to my dad countless times, not worried for one second if he would hurt her. He never did. I guess his fists were only reserved for his family. When mom left him, he spiraled. He began to get easily angered. Thankfully, neither Lisa nor I lived with him anymore. Still, he'll call from time to time and make us do something for him. Usually attend some kind of business dinner or meeting. That's about as much interaction as we will have with him. Lisa is frightened by him to the point she follows every one of his commands. I can't shake her out of it either." This last business dinner dad tried to pawn her off on the businessman's son, almost allowing him to date her. I, in not so many words, reminded him of our deal. He liked to remind me of the control he held over Lisa often, as if to make the point that I am controlled by him, too."

"I was planning to propose to Ivy when she died in that car accident. The truck driver was tired and on a strict timeline. He had fallen asleep behind the wheel of his semi and killed John and Ivy upon impact. Mr. Darius was the only to survive the crash physically, but he was brain dead the moment he arrived at the hospital. The news hit Leo and I hard and we wallowed for months on the ground, quite literally. I am not sure how I managed to graduate. I stopped playing soccer, stopped seeing my friends, and pushed everyone away, even Leo. Lisa had brought us back together, and that's when all the shit with Francesca started. Then came the party, and after came the countless one-night stands. The business I started made its first million in its first year, too. It's been a blur of alcohol, work, and different women, until I met you." I turned to face her again, holding her gaze for this next part. The part where she saved me.

"You pulled me out of my stupor. Everything about you enticed me, not just your beauty. The more I got to know you, the more I wanted you. The more I wanted to better myself for you. Rose, you make me want to be a better man, and I haven't felt this way in a while. You've saved me from myself. So here we are sitting in my car with me pouring my life story out to you, because I fucking love you already, even though it has barely been a month since I met you. I've fallen hard and fast for you, and I hope you know I don't plan on letting you go ever again."

Rose stared at me with wide eyes, tears still streaming down her face. In seconds her arms wrapped around my neck and pulled me towards her. She held me close before she brought her lips to mine with such intensity you'd think we'd both burst into flames. I felt all her passionate and unbridled love for me at that moment.

"Be mine, Rose. My girlfriend and no one else's."

"Thought you'd never ask." She smiled, kissing me again. "I'll be yours for as long as you want me. Only yours." She nodded. I rested my forehead against her own, closing my eyes and focusing on this moment before us.

She's everything I need in this world.

Chapter 28

Olive's P.O.V.

Lucas' story was sadder than even mine. I knew he didn't like his father, and I knew he had abused his mother, but I had no idea he had abused Lucas, too. I couldn't believe the way his father is using Lisa to control him. I need to find a way to help them both. This isn't right, and he shouldn't be able to get away with this kind of shit.

Lucas and I couldn't keep our hands off each other after he asked me to be his girlfriend. He took me to his apartment, which was closer than my flat. We had a quick round of the most passionate sex before he brought me back here for my next class. My mind was riddled with him, his story, and the feel of him on me less than an hour ago now.

I heard the way he spoke about Ivy and it hurt my heart to know he had lost someone he was so madly in love with. I'm not so insecure that I would compare myself to a dead woman. I do, however, hope one day he will talk about me with as much love. The way he described her was incredible. I need to learn how to run a business so I can help him too. I won't let him hold that burden alone.

I also need to remember how to play soccer. I'll play with him if he wants. My high school had a soccer team and I was a part of it. I wasn't the star player, but I was decent. I need to remind him of his passions and help him get back to himself. He's saved me and I'll save him, too. We'll keep lifting each other up until we are back on our feet, and then we'll support one another, so we never fall again.

"Ms. Brewer." The professor addressed me as I handed him my exam. I was the first to finish and he looked at me with uncertainty. "Are you sure you don't want to double check your answers?"

"I already have, but thank you for asking."

It always annoyed me when the teachers thought I rushed through a test. I know my shit, so it doesn't take me a million years to get it done. I know my answers are right and he'll bite his words later, or accuse me of cheating. Either way I'm done for the day now.

I headed out, finding Lucas laughing with Leo on a bench near my building. The sight made me smile. I was happy to see them bonding. I had begun to worry their relationship had strained after they both tried to go out with me. Lucas spotted me first, his smile only widened as I approached.

"Hello my beautiful girlfriend." He greeted me, to my surprise. Leo arched a brow at him.

"Girlfriend?" He asked.

"Shit, I'm so sorry." Lucas turned to Leo. I guess in his head I hadn't spoken to Leo yet. "I didn't mean to blurt it out. I wasn't trying to rub it in or anything. I was excited." Lucas panicked as he explained. I could see he was worried about possibly hurting Leo. Leo laughed at Lucas, amused by the way he was flailing about.

"Don't worry about it. She and I have already spoken. I had told her not to tell you yet. I wanted you to worry about it for a little while longer so you'd keep bringing your A game for her. I wanted to make sure you'd ask her out, but I guess you didn't need the extra fire," Leo explained, causing Lucas to turn and look at me.

"I chose you the very afternoon after my surgery," I informed him, only causing him to smile more brightly.

"I'm happy for you, Lucas. I mean it. Liv and I were never meant to be. I can see that now," Leo added, patting Lucas on the shoulder. "I'm fine, and I'm not bitter either."

"Thanks." Lucas nodded at him, then pulled me down to

sit between them. We were all talking, and joking around like close friends.

"Okay, so is this a thruple thing? Are you both sharing her?" Franny's voice cut the moment like a sharp knife.

"Oh for fucks sake, get a life, Fran. None of us are interested in you." I snapped at her, sitting up straight.

"Whatever, brillo pad. One of them wanted me enough to sleep with –" Her voice cut off as I punched her in the throat.

There was no taking it back now. I'd punched her on campus, and knew fully well she'd snitch. Her pride was wounded from my punch, but also from seeing how the two men she wanted back in high school wanted me of all people. I needed to correct this, and all I had was a threat I hoped she would take seriously.

"The only thing keeping me from pummeling you to death is the fact we are on campus. I'll leave you with a warning punch, but if you try to get me kicked out of here for it, know I'll hunt you down. You'll need more than a nose job to fix your face once I'm done with you. If you don't believe me, look up Twinkle Toes Underground on YouTube. See how willing you are to take me on after you watch it."

She held her throat as she coughed, unable to speak. There was a deep fury in her eyes, and I knew she'd only bother me more now, but her attention was averted from Leo and Lucas, and that's all that mattered. She walked off as I saw her pull her phone out. I heard the familiar rumble of the underground crowd with Baxter's voice announcing my stage name. She was looking up the video already. I smiled knowing she'd find me more threatening now. Maybe she'll be smart enough to stay away, but I doubt it. Brains were never her strong suit.

"Jesus, Liv," Leo said with a slight shock, and maybe a slight tone of disapproval. "You could get into a lot of trouble for that."

"She won't," Lucas said, smiling at me like I'd just done the hottest thing. "Thank you, Rose."

"It was my pleasure. I've been wanting to punch her since I met her." I sat back down between them on the bench, picking up where we left off before Fran interrupted. We were talking about Lucas as a child now, but I couldn't tell you how we got to this conversation topic.

"Don't let him fool you, with those tattoos and resting asshole face. He was frightened of his own shadow when he was 10." Leo laughed at Lucas' expense.

"Are you serious?" I asked, amused at the fact.

"Hey, you would have been too after that stupid movie John put on," Lucas defended himself with a slight pout.

"Awe, don't worry, you haven't lost any points in my book. In fact, you gained some," I assured him.

"Sure," he shook his head, not believing me.

I smirked at him, finding his actions quite adorable. I leaned into him, nudging his shoulder with my own. He side-eyed me for a moment, still pouting like a small child. I loved it. He finally turned and looked at me straight on, allowing me to lean in and kiss his warm lips. Lips that always made me hunger for more.

"How about you take me home and then get to work? I am sure you have work you've placed on the back burner to spend time with me." I gave him a knowing look, causing him to sigh.

"How about you come with me to my apartment and hang out while I work instead?" He asked.

"Might as well live together at this point." Leo shook his head, letting out a strained laugh.

I felt bad for being romantic with Lucas beside Leo. It's only been a few days since I've rejected him, and Lucas already accidentally let it slip that we were now in a real relationship. I bit my lip, feeling guilty. Lucas, however, smiled widely.

"What an idea," he said with a hungry look in his eye, which caused my cheeks to flush.

"I was kidding!" Leo scolded Lucas.

"Oh, I know." He didn't take his eyes off me as he spoke.

"Let's go, Rose. I have work to do." He held his hand out for me to take, even though I never said yes to coming. It did sound nice to spend more time with him, so I took his hand with a smile.

"Bye, Leo. I'll talk to you later." I gave him an apologetic look as Lucas pulled me away to his car.

I wonder if he'll get his work done with me there?

Lucas' P.O.V.

I decided to play my music this time before I pulled off campus. I wanted her to hear the artist I loved to listen to when I was trying to hype myself up. I played my Marshmello playlist, allowing his songs to play at random. Surprisingly, Rose knew some of them already, which only made me smile more as I drummed along on my steering away. Rescue Me began to play and she and I sang along together. This song felt like our song. She rescued me, and according to her I rescued her too. It's not exactly a romantic song, but it feels right for us.

"Good to know we were both feeling upbeat music today," Rose said as we pulled into my parking garage.

"I guess it goes to show how happy we both are feeling," I responded, keeping my eyes on the road until we parked.

"Lucas?" She called me, making me meet her eyes instantly. She bit her lip nervously, driving my curiosity up. I can never tell what she's going to say or ask when she's like this. Her mind works so differently from my own, yet we understand each other so well.

"Yes, my Rose?"

"Were you being serious earlier? With Leo I mean." She flushed a beautiful shade of crimson as she asked. She was still thinking about his comment of us living together. I wasn't being completely serious, but I certainly wasn't opposed to the idea, even if it would be crazy fast. Like ridiculously crazy fast.

"Maybe. Does that frighten you or excite you?" I asked her with a playful smirk and a raised brow. I was curious to know where her mind was with this topic.

"A little bit of both," she admitted, causing my heart to skip a beat in excitement. She was actually thinking about it. She had let her mind wonder what it would be like to live with me. I did the same, imagining her in my bed every morning. I would have her beside me every night and every morning. It would be a dream come true, but I know we'd be insane to do it now.

"I feel the same way, Rose. Shall we head up now?" I asked her, seeing her nod. She waited for me to open her door this time. I think she's noticed how much I like to do that for her. I popped my trunk open, grabbing the box of journals she'd given me. There's no way I'm leaving these unattended. Rose's cheeks were still tinged pink as she stayed silently thinking.

"How would you feel about having a drawer at my flat?" She asked, biting her lip again.

"A drawer?" I raised a brow at her with a smirk.

"Yes, a drawer. You've been spending the night a lot, and then you have to leave to get clothes before you come back. I figure if you're now my boyfriend we'll be having more sleep overs and I'd rather your life be easier with you having a drawer with some spare clothes in it. I mean you don't have-"

"I'd love a drawer,'" I said, interrupting her sentence. "I'll make you one too." I winked at her, making her look away as she blushed further.

I loved that I could make her feel this way. She's blushing for me, not because of what I'm saying, but because of the thoughts she's having of me. She was so beautiful with her rosy cheeks and flaming hair. I love her icy blue eyes and rosy red lips that pop against her pale skin. She's the epitome of beauty and she's all mine. *My girlfriend.* We stepped out of the elevator to my floor, heading to my door. Rose took the keys from me, opening the door. She held the door open for me, since I was carrying the heavy box.

"Such a gentle lady." I joked, making her smirk as she rolled her eyes.

"I believe you mean gentleman."

"Is there something you haven't told me, Rose?" I joked again, making her laugh.

"Mm, yes. I'm actually a very muscular large man. How could you not tell?" She joined in on the joke, making me laugh.

"My apologies, sir. Do forgive me."

"I'll let it slide this time, but don't forget who's the bigger man here," she said with a laugh.

"Yes, sir. You wear the pants in this relationship." I saluted her.

"Damn straight," she said with a nod as she closed my front door. We both laughed as I placed her journals on the closest surface, in this case, my counter top.

"Need some help there?" She teased me, to which I stuck my tongue out at her. She smirked playfully, making my heart race with her beauty.

"No, sir. I got this." I winked at her.

"Just making sure." She shrugged. "You should get to work. Stop using me as a distraction," she scolded me with a pointed finger.

"Yes, sir!" I kissed her forehead before heading to my office.

The stack of papers was high, and my motivation was low. About 30 minutes later, I felt like I was dying of boredom. I sighed heavily, causing Rose's little head to peek in through the door.

"Are you okay?" She cocked her head to the side so cutely.

"This is quite boring, Rose," I admitted with another sigh.

"How about I make it fun?" She asked, stepping into the office.

"And how do you plan to do that?" I leaned forward in my chair, interested in what she'd propose.

"For every task you get done you'll be allowed to tell me to do something. It can be absolutely anything. I have to do what you say no matter what it is. What do you say?" Rose was trusting me so much right now if she was willing to give me full control of her like this. She's asked me to take control during sex before, but this is different. This is more, and dammit if she didn't just light a fire under my ass.

"I say, hell yes." She took a seat in one of the two chairs in front of my desk, watching me work. It was distracting yet also motivating. I love the things Rose comes up with. They're always so fun and different.

"Done." I smiled up at her as I finished reviewing a contract and rejecting it.

"What's your command?" She asked with a smile.

"Come sit on my lap." I told her, pushing back on my chair so she could sit. She got up without complaint, taking her place on my lap gingerly. I liked having her there as I worked. Again, distracting, but motivating. I wrapped my arm around her waist, grabbing the next paper and reading through it carefully. I could see her reading it with me as well. I wonder if she has any interest in this kind of stuff. Another 10 minutes later and I finished, finding it adequate.

"Done." I whispered in her ear.

"What would you like for me to do next?"

"Take your underwear off and sit back on my lap." I gave her my wicked smirk.

I wanted to feel her bare pussy against my thigh with only my pants in the way. If she weren't wearing a skirt I would have asked her to remove her pants, but this is so much better. I don't know what it is about knowing she has no underwear beneath her skirt that drives me wild, but it does. She got up, stepping out of her lacey black panties. She threw them at me with a smirk, before sitting back on my lap.

"Feel free to grind against me if the urge strikes you," I said with a smile, earning me an eye roll, but I felt her legs widen in response.

I wonder how far I can take this? What will I have her do next?

Chapter 29

Olive's P.O.V.

I sat here half naked now. All I had on was my skirt and my bra, which I'm sure I'll be losing in a minute. Sometimes I want to slap myself for the ideas I come up with, but Lucas was having fun, so I can't be too mad at myself.

"Bra please." He winked at me as he finished another work task.

I see now why he puts off work for so long. It is very boring. I can't imagine having to read so many contracts and important papers daily, being careful not to let anything slide through the cracks. The smallest mistake could cost him a lot of money. I unclasped my bra, feeling my boobs bounce as I released them from their shackles. Lucas' eyes hungrily took them in. His gaze and cool breath alone were making my center dampen. I wouldn't be surprised to find a wet spot on his lap if I stood up.

"I think you're enjoying this too much," I teased him.

"I think you are too," he responded, biting my earlobe for a second. Another excruciating long few minutes, and he finished another task. I wasn't sure what he'd do once I was out of clothes to shed. I started to get up, ready to take my skirt off, but his hand held my hip firmly.

"I didn't tell you to move, Rose," he whispered in my ear. "Unzip my pants and play with my dick until I finish with the next paper." I did as he said, feeling myself get turned on as he commanded me. I slowly and sensually unzipped his pants and pulled his semi hard dick out. The more I rubbed him the harder it got, of course, reaching its large state in no time at all. I continued to rub it with my hands until I decided to play with fire. He didn't tell me I had to play with it using only my hands.

    I inched my sleek center towards him, rubbing his dick along the outside of my wet folds. I heard him groan as I continued my torment, but he never stopped me. He very obviously took longer to finish with his work this time around. When he finished, the look in his eyes let me know I was in for it.

    "Tease yourself with my dick, Rose. You can only have the tip inside of you, nothing more. You can't sway your hips either. No cheating, Rose." He grabbed my chin, kissing me with such intensity as he let his tongue explore my mouth for a moment.

    I could feel myself dripping with wetness already. I did as he said, slapping his dick against me, at times inserting the tip inside me. I wanted to hump him so badly, to sway myself against him and find a release for the pressure I was building up for him. I rubbed his dick around my clit, causing me to moan.

    "Do you want me, Rose?" He asked me in a seductive voice. I bit my lip, nodding my head in response. "Good, because I've finished working now. My last command is for you to sit on my desk and spread your legs for me." My heart raced at an almost unbearable speed as my sleekness leaked further between my thighs. I perched myself on his desk as he asked. My skirt was still on me for some reason. My legs spread for him as he asked, and I was met with immediate pleasure as his finger entered me, rubbing me in the right way.

    "Lie back and play with your breasts for me, Rose." I know he was done working and technically out of commands, but I was enjoying this too much not to listen. I laid back against his cold glass desk, allowing my hands to venture to my chest. I pinched at my own nipples, playing with them the way I liked as Lucas continued to finger me. His tongue soon joined, having me moan loudly.

His hands grabbed at my hips, keeping them still as he continued to tease me. He wasn't allowing me to find my release, letting the pressure amount to unbearable levels. Before I knew it, he stood up, aligning his dick with my entrance. In one quick move, he inserted himself deep inside me. I almost yelled out as the pressure I was feeling had me so close to the edge already. The second Lucas let go of my hips, I began to sway them desperately.

The entire time I continued to play with my breasts. Lucas was slamming into me so hard his balls were slapping against my ass a bit. I liked the feel only bringing me closer to the edge. It kept climbing until I couldn't hold it in anymore. With a loud moan, I fell over the edge, having the most intense and longest orgasm. My calves were almost cramped from it. Lucas didn't stop as he continued to thrust in me. My body couldn't seem to get enough of him as my pleasure rose again. His thumb pressed against my clit as he swirled his dick inside me.

"*Oh, god, Lucas!*". I yelled as I got close to cumming again. "*oh, fuck!*" I felt my walls clench around him as he made me cum again. This time he followed suit, filling me deep inside with big spurts of himself. It leaked out of me as he pulled out, creating a mess of our juices. Lucas cleaned us both off before cleaning his desk.

"I don't think I'll ever be able to work in this office again without thinking of you on my desk." He winked at me with a still very hungry look in his eyes.

"At least you won't be bored if you're thinking of me." I winked back, as I put on each item of clothing as I found it.

"You kill me, Rose."

"How?" I pinched my brows together in confusion, but he shook his head.

We left his office, and went to his kitchen, where he made us some peanut butter and jelly sandwiches, per my request. He sat me on his kitchen island while he stood in front me. Even though we were eating, we both still felt the need to be so close to one another. I can't keep this up. I am not sure this much sex is good for me. Lucas is seriously going to ruin me. I laughed internally at the thought.

"How's your cheek?" He asked, bringing my mood down instantly.

"It hurts to move, or smile too wide, but it isn't so bad since I iced it quickly."

"I'm so sorry, Rose. I should have taken you with me last night."

"No, this isn't your fault. Neither of us expected him to show up out of the blue. I still don't even know how he found me." I shook my head, taking my last bite of my sandwich.

"Don't worry, we'll figure it out. Do you want to stay here for now? Until he's gone back to New Hampshire?" His offer was very tempting. I didn't want to be bothered by dad again, but what if he came here? I don't want to involve Lucas anymore than he should be. I bit at my cheek as I contemplated my options.

"Are you sure? What if he finds me here? I don't want him bothering you."

"I'm sure, Rose. He won't bother me, stay with me." He was almost begging me at this point. He leaned closer to me, his lips a mere centimeters away now. When he spoke they would lightly graze against my own, almost tickling them.

"I'll stay with you," I said, causing him to smile widely. "Just until my dad leaves." I added for good measure.

"Good enough for me. Let's go get your clothes for the week." He kissed me tenderly, as he lifted me off the island, placing me gently on my feet.

"Okay, let me get my bag." I grabbed my things, looking at my phone for the first time since we got here. I saw I had a missed call. My heart stilled when I noticed who it was. Lucas had done too good of a job distracting me this weekend and today. I all but forgot I was waiting to hear back from the doctor. You would think it would be the most prevalent thing on my mind. *Do I have cancer?* Yet somehow amongst the eventful and drama filled weekend, I had forgotten all about it. Lucas noticed I had stopped moving. He approached me almost cautiously.

"What's the matter?" He asked.

"I missed a call from my doctor," I said with a shaky voice.

"Call her back!" Lucas' eyes widened in worry. He wanted answers, too.

I decided to place it on speaker phone when I was placed on hold by the nice receptionist. The hold music somehow made me more nervous. I feel it should have the opposite effect. I chewed at my nail as I waited for her to pick it up. Lucas was nervous too, only he was deadly still. All his nerves had rooted him to one spot and frozen him stiff.

"Hello, Ms. Brewer?" I heard my doctor's familiar voice on the other end.

"Yes, hello. I am so sorry I missed your call earlier," I responded.

"It's no trouble. I was calling about the results of your biopsy on the mass we found in your breast. It is what's called a fibroadenoma. It is not cancerous. You won't need any radiation or follow up treatment aside from your regular screenings." The relief that swept over me was so powerful it made me tear up.

I am okay. I don't have cancer.

"Thank you so much!"

"Of course, this is news I am glad to give. I'll see you again in 5 months for a screening and don't forget your one week follow-up with your surgeon." She reminded me.

"Yes, thank you!" My voice cracked with emotion.

"Goodbye, Ms. Brewer."

"Goodbye."

The moment I hung up the phone, I was swept off my feet. Lucas held me close, spinning around with me for a moment. When he put me back down, he immediately kissed me. It was a kiss so loving it made my knees buckle. I could feel every ounce of care he had for me in this kiss. He was happy for me. We both were. Finally, *some* good news.

"Rose, this is great! We need to celebrate."

"Depends on what you have in mind." I wasn't exactly up for partying on a Monday night.

"Leo, Hailey, Rachel, and Lisa all come over here and we celebrate together with food and some wine. Nothing wild, but something. Come on, Rose. Let me celebrate with you!" He pleaded with those adorable puppy eyes he does. *Damn those eyes.*

"Fine. I'll ask Hailey, but you ask everyone else." I pointed my finger at him. "Now let's go get my clothes." Lucas drove me to my flat but as we rounded the corner I noticed dad's pick up truck parked in front. I ducked down so fast, I almost hit my head on the dashboard.

"That's his truck," I whispered to Lucas like my dad could hear me, even though I know he can't. Lucas' hands tightened around the steering wheel.

"We'll buy you some clothes for the week. Sorry, Rose. I know you hate shopping, but it's either shopping or we go upstairs together. I can be by your side while you face your father, if you want."

"Shopping, definitely shopping." I blurted. You know it's bad when I pick shopping.

Lucas nodded, keeping his eyes on the road. I noticed he's actually a very safe driver. His eyes never leave the road, not for a second. He waits at stop signs for the full amount, making sure there are no cars coming. He even waits at a green light for a couple of seconds, in case someone decides to run a red light. I feel very safe when Lucas is driving.

He grabbed my hand, squeezing it tightly as we drove past my flat. He took me to a small shop nearby, knowing I would not enjoy a mall in the least. We ventured inside, finding some jeans, pants, and a few cute shirts. Lucas then picked out some underwear for me, being goofy and shameless the entire time. He made me laugh with his antics and for the first time in my life I didn't mind shopping so much.

"Quit,, you're going to get us in trouble," I scolded him with a smile as I slapped his arm playfully. He was playing with the mannequin, moving its hand so it was picking its nose. He was being an idiot, but I know it was for my benefit. I was falling even more in love with him for it. He'd made me smile and laugh this time.

"I think I have everything I need," I said looking at the pile of clothes stacked in my arms.

"Did you get socks? You can't forget socks. Look, these have little avocados on them. It's so cute." Lucas held a pair of socks with small cut avocados in them. His face was so damn adorable as he spoke about them.

"I forgot the socks. Give the 'cado socks." He smiled, placing them on top of my stack before taking the whole thing from me.

"Race you to the register," he said quickly before running off with all the clothes. I chased after him, giggling as I ran. I haven't had this much fun shopping since I was a small girl. Mom has always made shopping trips better, now Lucas does. We slowed as we approached the register, not wanting to get kicked out. We were now speed walking, trying to beat one another.

"I win,' he whispered to me as he placed the clothes on the checkout counter."

"I let you win," I lied. He laughed his wonderful laugh as the cashier checked us out. She checked out more than my clothes, looking at Lucas often. She ignored me completely, even though the clothes were obviously for me.

"What do you think, love? Should we get married this month or next?" He asked. My heart skipped, my face paled, and my body froze. What did he ask me?

"I mean I know I just proposed, but I can't wait to make you my wife," he pulled me close to him, leaning down and whispering in my ear. "Play along, Rose." I realized it was for the cashier. He noticed her checking him out and he wanted her to know how serious he was about me by concocting this story.

"This month, I want to be married before our child swells me like a balloon." I added we were with child, because why not? Lucas' smirk widened, liking the extra detail.

"Done," he nodded.

The cashier gave us our total with a blush on her face. She was embarrassed after our display. She handed me the receipt as we left. Lucas didn't let me pay for my clothes, despite my arguments. He used our false pretense to his advantage, saying his money will be mine anyway once we marry. My mind couldn't help but daydream about getting married. It was a thought for way down in the future, but talking about it now made me think about it. I wouldn't mind being married to Lucas.

"Thank you for making shopping fun for once," I did with a smile as he entered and sat in his driver's seat.

"It was my pleasure. Thanks for playing along with me."

"Oh, any time." I smiled. "I do have impeccable acting skills after all."

"Yes, indeed. Future Grammy winner here." He chuckled as he drove.

We drove back to his place, singing along to his music. We had a lot of the same favorite songs. He introduced me to a few, I didn't know I would end up loving. I'll add them to my own playlist later. We grabbed my bags and headed to his apartment, but as we approached his door, we noticed a person hunched over on the ground in front of his door. *Who the hell is that?*

Lisa was curled into a ball on the floor in front of Lucas' door. She held her knees to her chest with her head down between them.

"Lisa?" Lucas called to her, making her look up, showing her busted lip and bruised face. Something bad had happened, and the sight of her made me feel like I was 8 again helping mom clean up her wounds. I froze as I stared at her, Lucas did the same. He moved faster than I did, grabbing Lisa quickly, opening his door, and helping her inside. She limped, showing me she must have hurt her ankle or perhaps her leg.

It took me a whole minute to convince my legs to move again. I took a slow, heavy step towards his apartment, feeling the trauma rise in me. I swallowed the thick emotion I felt was choking me. I pushed forward, finally making it inside and closing the door behind me. Lucas had a first aid kit out, tending to Lisa's wounds already. His face was serious with his teeth clenched in anger. His nostrils flared, and his jaw twitched furiously.

"Explain," he told her in a stern voice.

"I know how to pick them." She gave a manic laugh, causing me to worry even more about her. "It's a guy I started seeing a couple of weeks ago. He believed I was seeing someone else, and didn't like that."

"What's his name?" Lucas was ready to set the world on fire to get to this guy.

"No, Lucas. I can handle this myself. I need a place to crash tonight. I don't want mom to see me like this and there's no chance in hell I would stay at dad's." She shook her head violently. I hated to see her like this. I don't understand how a man can hurt someone like this. Especially if they claimed they loved them. Hitting someone isn't love. It's not how you display emotions. Hurting someone is not a form of love. It's anti love.

"Tell me his name, Lisa." The tone Lucas used made me tense up. He was angry, and he meant business.

"Seth," she finally spoke. "Seth Reynolds."

"Got it." He nodded at her, staring at the wound on her lip. "Rose, can you finish this while I make a call?" He asked me, holding out the cotton ball with alcohol he was using to clean her wounds. I nodded my head, stepping forward. I took the cotton and began to clean her wound.

Chapter 30

Olive's P.O.V.

Lucas grabbed his phone, stepping out onto the patio, slamming his sliding door closed. I jumped unintentionally, still feeling on edge. Lisa grabbed my hand that was dabbing at her lip. She held it for a moment, making me look into her eyes.

"He's worried. I'm sorry I ruined your night." She sighed, looking guilty.

"No!" I quickly shut that down. "You didn't ruin anything. Don't you dare apologize for coming here. This is not your fault. If I ever get my hands on that guy, I'll beat his ass twice as bad," I promised. Lisa let out a loud laugh then. She smiled fondly at me.

"Thank you, Olive. You really are amazing." Her words made me blush, making me feel bashful for no reason. The look of admiration in those hurt eyes was killing me. I'm nothing inspirational, nothing to admire here.

"I'm just me." I shrugged. "Nothing amazing about it."

"That's exactly why you're amazing."

I tended to her wounds more, making her wince or flinch at times. All the while Lucas was screaming into the phone outside. It was muffled, but I could see his hand waving around as he spoke. His motions were big and fast, telling me he was furious.

"Who do you think he called?" I asked Lisa as I picked up the surrounding area. Her wounds were all clean and dressed now.

"If I had to guess, I would say Leo." She sat back in her

chair, looking out towards Lucas with me. "They're probably deciding what to do. He's venting."

We both watched Lucas a while longer, seeing him slump in the chair outside. The more I watched him, the more I *saw* him. He looked so exhausted. I wish I could help. I want nothing more than to make life easy for him.

"What's with the bags of clothes?" Lisa pointed to the bags Lucas had put down.

"That's clothes for me. I'm staying the week here." I bit my cheek bashfully.

"Oh?" She raised her brow in amusement with a playful smirk on her face.

"My dad showed up yesterday and he's still in town. Lucas offered for me to hide out here for a bit." I explained.

"I'm guessing he did that to you," she said, pointing to her cheek.

"Yeah. It's a first I won't let happen again." I felt the fight in my words and I meant it. I won't let him hurt me again.

"I wish I had your confidence, Olive."

"Call me Liv. And what do you mean? You're so beautiful, and you certainly look confident."

"Looking and being are two different things," she said with a sigh. "I hold myself well, but I'm very weak, Liv."

It's crazy to think someone like her isn't as confident as she seems. I assumed if you were beautiful, rich, and kind that you must have confidence of steel, but that doesn't seem to be accurate. I guess we all battle our own insecurities, even people we might think are perfect.

"Lisa, you're amazing too."

"Thank you, Liv, but I know you're only being polite." Before I could argue, Lucas opened the sliding door, stepping back inside. He drew my full attention instantly, making me forget everything else. His presence alone was enough to ease my nerves. I'm not sure when it happened, but I've started to feel safe around him.

"Well? What's Leo saying?" Lisa asked him knowingly,

not catching him off guard in the least.

"He's on his way. Rachel said she's stealing you away."

"Of course she is."

"Don't pretend otherwise. You love it when Rachel kidnaps you. You guys have a lot of fun together."

"I guess," Lisa sighed. "Until they get here, your Rose is mine, so go entertain yourself for a while." She shooed him away successfully.

Lisa chatted with me for a while about small and trivial things. I think she was trying to get her mind off of what happened, and I was happy to oblige. Every now, and then, my eyes would wander to Lucas, who was sitting on his recliner reading my journal. I wondered what part he was in. Did he get to the part where Ian became my best friend in high school? Is he to the part where I admit I love Ian, but would never tell him for fear of ruining our friendship? Or is he already at the Halloween party?

"You truly like him, don't you?" Lisa snapped my attention back to her.

"More than that. I'm falling in love with him." I didn't mind admitting my feelings for Lucas to her. She's his sister.

"Really?" She smiled brightly at me.

"Yes, really. He's a sweet guy, and he gets me so well. I honestly don't think I've ever fallen in love so quickly." With the exception of Ian who I liked very quickly, and began to love over the months.

"I am happy for you both. Lucas has been a mess until you arrived. Thank you, Liv, for getting my brother back for me," she said, looking at Lucas as she spoke.

"I haven't done anything." I shook my head.

"You've done more than you know."

The doorbell rang, letting us know Rachel and Leo had arrived. Lucas opened the door, inviting them inside. They didn't stay for long, grabbing Lisa with a promise of a good time. Lucas caught them at the door before they left, whispering something to them. I strained my ears to listen, but couldn't hear a word.

I wonder what he told them?

Lucas' P.O.V.

I had to tell him we would wait to celebrate Rose's good news until the weekend. With everything going on now, we could use a little downtime. I know Rose hadn't texted Hailey about yet either, so this is fine. I'll celebrate with Rose, just us two tonight.

I watched Lisa leave with Rachel and Leo down the hall. I know Rachel can bring Lisa out of her darkness better than I can. Lisa and I understand each other's pain too well to help cheer each other up. We're always there for one another, supporting and encouraging each other, but we suck at getting the other one to be happy. It's like we end up wallowing in our sadness together instead.

"Is she going to be okay?" Rose asked me, appearing beside me at the door. She peeked her head out, waving back at Lisa, who waved at her from the elevator.

"I hope so."

I need to be more mindful of her. She's always had terrible taste in men, but none of them had ever hit her before. Leo and I decided we'd pay him a visit. Let him think he's safe. Leo said he'd take her down to the police station and press charges with her. It's better to have these things documented. I don't figure Lisa would go back to him, but on the off chance she did, she'd have this report to prove his abuse if she ever needed to.

"So what now, my Rose? It's your night. You and I can celebrate your good news alone. If you're okay with that. We can celebrate with friends on the weekend."

"That sounds nice. How about we get some dinner, wine, and watch a romantic movie?" She asked, with a twinkle in her eye. *She's so adorable.*

"Sounds perfect. Preference for dinner?"

"Ooo, Italian!" She said excitedly.

"Good choice." I placed our order while Rose picked our movie. I found my favorite bottle of red wine and poured us each a glass.

"Thank God, you're not a white wine person." She let out a breath of relief, making me chuckle.

"Not a white fan?"

"Not at all." She shook her head. I love getting to know these small details about her. It's all these little things that add up to make her the person she is today. I need to know them all. I need to know her fully, to know her better.

We watched the movie and when the food arrived we ate in front of the tv continuing to watch together. Rose was now cuddled up beside me on the couch, her head on my chest and her legs over my own. She was so warm, and fit so perfectly beside me. It was like she was made specifically for me.

"Lucas?" She called my name rather sleepily.

"Yes, my Rose?"

"Can you hold me tight tonight?" She was exhausted, worn from the day. I picked her up bridal style, carrying her sleepy self to the bed.

"Good luck getting away from me tonight." I promised her. She smiled with her eyes closed and her head leaned against my chest. I tucked us both into bed. She fell asleep almost instantly, but I was still wide awake. I guess it's time to finish reading about the rest of her freshman year.

I learned Ian had become her best friend, who she apparently fell in love with. She never told him because she didn't want to ruin her only friendship. I looked up Ian on social media and I hate to admit it, but he was a pretty good-looking guy. He had hair the color of wheat with bright, crystal clear eyes. He had a handsome face and a good physique.

He seemed like a nice guy. He works with non-profit foundations and volunteers his time with the disadvantaged youths. I'm sure he'd be any girl's wet dream, so I need to be sure to keep him away. He can't have Rose back. I'm curious why he doesn't already have her if they were such close friends in high school.

I grabbed her journal reading about a Halloween party they had gone to together. People kept picking on her, so after defending her to everyone, Ian grabbed her hand and took her away. They bought a large bag of candy and spent the night eating it together from a lookout in town. She described it as being the moment she truly fell in love with him.

I'm not going to lie, seeing how this guy had a whole journal dedicated to him, made me a bit jealous. I'm pretty sure it's going to be more than one journal, too. I can't wait to read her journal dedicated to me. I want to know what she said about me. Is it as sweet as what she's written about Ian?

Halloween turned into Thanksgiving, which is apparently one of Rose's most dreaded holidays since it always makes her feel so bitterly alone. Her father would never do anything because it was just the two of them. They'd end up eating frozen dinners. This year, however, she was invited to Thanksgiving dinner with Ian. She met his whole family, and she loved them all. Ian had a warm and loving family, according to Rose.

I'm starting to get tired of reading about Ian. I skipped a couple of entries about him, figuring it would be safe to do so. I can't keep reading about how amazing Ian is. She was definitely a love sick teen at this point. I reached Christmas in no time. Her dad had forgotten to buy her something and ended up drunk on the couch again. She spent it alone and cold, because he had forgotten to pay the electric bill. She was miserable.

Ian came by her house, causing her to panic. She walked with him to keep him away from her dad in case he woke. Ian had gotten her a gift, a necklace with a blue teardrop pendant the color of her eyes. *I know that pendant. I've seen her wear it.*

I couldn't believe she still had it. It must have meant a

CHAPTER 30

lot to her for her to keep it safe for so many years. I need to buy her a gift, or should I say I want to buy her one. It has to be perfect though, so it'll take me a little while to think of it.

Rose shifted in her sleep, making me freeze until she settled back down. She seemed like she was chewing in her sleep with the way her lips were moving. It was very adorable to see. I leaned down kissing her forehead. She's so absolutely perfect. I closed her journal and held her tighter against me. Feeling her body pressed against mine helped ease my mind. For once, I actually got more than 4 hours of sleep.

I've noticed I tend to sleep better when Rose is with me. She's so warm and soft. She's this piece of me I've been missing all this time. It's like her presence alone is enough to drive away my dark thoughts, my loneliness, and my depression. I stayed asleep until I felt her try to pull away from me. I held her tight, unwilling to relinquish her yet.

"If you don't let me go I'm going to end up peeing on your bed," she warned me, causing me to chuckle.

"You can go when I get my good morning kiss," I said through slanted eyes.

"But I have morning breath."

"I don't care. Kiss me if you want me to let you go." I smirked feeling her lean forward. Her lips met mine for a split second, but before she could pull away I cupped her face in my hands and held her to my lips a moment longer. I spread her lips with my own, lightly licking her bottom one. When I felt satisfied I reluctantly let her go.

"Hurry back," I said, watching her walk towards the bathroom.

I suddenly felt so cold without her in my arms. I heard the sink turn on after the toilet flushed. She was brushing her teeth, worried about her breath. I smiled at her in amusement when she opened the bathroom door back up. She ran towards the bed, jumping on top of me with a giggle.

"When do you have classes today?" I asked her, wondering how much time I have with her this morning.

"I have a class at eleven, one and three." She smiled. "But my three o'clock one was canceled today because Mr. Burnley got food poisoning."

"Okay, perfect. I'll take you to class at 10:30 and pick you up at two. I'll run some errands while you're on campus. I know Hailey would like to see you today."

"For sure! She's already texted me a million times. We're gonna have lunch together today between our classes," she informed me.

It's important I don't monopolize my Rose. She has other people in her life and I need to make sure to give her time to see them, even if all I want to do is carry her around with me everywhere. I kissed her forehead with a smile.

"Sounds perfect." I have to meet with Connor today anyway. He's already found what I asked him to. Davis, Carter and I will pay her father a visit this afternoon. Hopefully, we can get him to leave without too much trouble.

"Breakfast?" She looked up at me through her eyelashes.

"What would you like?"

"Cereal sounds good." She shrugged.

"I'm not the biggest fan of cereal so I don't usually have any here."

"Seriously?" She seemed so genuinely surprised. I held her closer to me, looking into those beautiful blue eyes.

"Yes, seriously, but I'll go to the store and buy you your favorite cereal today if you tell me what it is?"

"Don't go now," she quickly said with a pout, making my smile widen.

"I'll go later when you're in class."

"Okay then, in that case, my favorite cereal is Special K with the strawberries in them. I love strawberries. They're my favorite." Red like her. I kissed her rosy lips, tasting the mint from the toothpaste. I think it's sweet she was so worried about her breath. I picked her up and carried her towards the kitchen, despite her protests of being able to walk on her own. I sat her on the kitchen counter, where she could watch me. Her legs swung as they dangled off the edge. She watched me while I made our omelets.

"Here you go." I handed her plate to her, and she immediately dug in.

I've noticed my Rose has a healthy appetite. She never lets any food go to waste, and I'm starting to wonder if it's because of how little food she had growing up. It still breaks my heart to think of her going hungry because her father was irresponsible. I don't want her to ever worry about food again. As much as I would love to taste my Rose's cooking, I don't want her to have to cook if she doesn't want to.

I could kill her father, and my own. They're at the top of the shit list.

Chapter 31

Olive's P.O.V.

Lucas drove me to school and even walked me to my class, giving me one last kiss before I entered. I missed him already, which only made me feel like a love-sick teen again. I remember feeling this giddy when Julius and I first started dating, but it's different with Lucas. Like everything else, it's more intense with him.

The feelings he brings out of me are almost overwhelming. I've never had anyone do this to me before, except maybe Ian. Even then, it was different. Ian was the first person to be kind to me. He showed me what real friendship could look like. I haven't spoken to him in so long. Not since he moved away. We lost touch despite swearing we wouldn't. He never replied to me like he promised he would when I wrote. I never bothered to look him up. There's no reason to, he clearly didn't want to be my friend anymore.

Class went by fast thankfully, nothing too strenuous. I hurriedly made my way to the Campus Commons to meet up with Hailey. I spotted her beautiful wavy black hair in the distance. It was so black it reflected the sun brightly. I called out her name, having her turn with a bright smile on her face. She waved at me, showing off her beautiful golden skin. I ran up to her, letting her give me a big hug.

"I feel like I haven't seen you in forever," she said with an excited smile.

"I know, I'm sorry. I've been a bad friend."

"Ha, no way! You're living your life, Livie. Now, catch me

up on everything with Lucas!" She wiggled her eyebrows at me, making me laugh.

"Oh, it's a lot, but you'll be proud." I smiled shyly, tucking my hair behind my ear. I told everything that had happened over the weekend, including all about dad. I told her about shopping with Lucas, and staying with him this week. I even told her about telling Lucas I was falling in love with him. She squealed in excitement, squeezing my arm with her hands.

"I'm so proud of you! Oh my gosh, Livie. I am so excited for you!" She seemed ready to burst with her enthusiasm.

"Thanks. I'm pretty excited myself," I admitted. "But I'm also kind of scared. Hailey, I don't understand it. I am so wrapped up in him. Like even now I want him beside me. It's overwhelming."

"It's love, Livie. It's perfectly natural. What's hard is making the feeling stay." She squeezed my hand, staring deeply into my eyes.

"But how do I know he feels the same way? What if we aren't on the same page?" I bit my cheek, fizzling with anxiety.

"Ask him, Livie. He's not a mind reader and neither are you. You need to be open to discuss these things together." She sounded so wise as she spoke, almost making me forget we were the same age.

"But what if I scare him away? What if I love him more than he loves me?"

"Then you let him catch up to you. There's nothing wrong with loving someone more. Not everything feels the same, let alone experienced the same. Those fiery locks of yours are a different red to me than to you. Don't be scared to tell him how you feel because you're afraid he won't feel the same. No one will ever feel the exact same."

Her words were heavy as bricks. I don't think I've ever noticed how wise Hailey is. She's always had a fun and positive attitude since I've known her. She's easy to talk to and easy to hang with. I have never spoken to her about these kinds of things before. I never spoke much about Julius and my relationship with her. Well, aside from when I thought I was ready to sleep with him. Hailey helped me with that, too. She's like this older sister I have never had. Like any other older sister, she was like a second mom.

"Thanks, Hails.

The rest of lunch was spent talking about lighter topics. Hailey told me her dad was going to come into town again and visit this weekend. He was hoping to see me as well so we made plans for lunch together Saturday. Mr. Medina was always kind and accepting of me as Hailey's best friend. His accent was thick, not having learned English until his late 20s. I liked it though. He's a sweet man. It's easy to see where Hailey learned to be kind from.

"Let me know how things go with Lucas," she said, hugging me goodbye.

"I will. I'll text you, so you don't have to wait so long to hear what happens."

"Perfect." She smiled. "Adios, chica." She kissed my cheek goodbye. I headed to my last class for the day, running into Leo on the way. He walked me towards class.

"How's Lisa?" I asked him.

"Could be better, but she's alright. Rachel is keeping her company until I get back. I am sorry we couldn't celebrate your good news last night. I am so happy it's not cancer, Liv." He grabbed my hand, squeezing it a moment while maintaining my gaze.

"It's okay, no worries. I know you guys are happy for me. We don't have to celebrate."

"With news that good? Of course we have to!"

"You and Lucas both." I shook my head.

"In life, there tends to be more bad news than good, so we need to celebrate anytime it comes around." I imagined the way he and Lucas probably got the news of the accident, and I realized this was probably their way of getting over that. They celebrate good news when they can because they know how bad news can be.

"Got it. Celebrate the good." I nodded, squeezing his hand back. He left me at the door of my class with a wave and a smile. I watched him leave, still feeling bad I had rejected him. He's a good guy. There's honestly nothing wrong with him, except he's not Lucas.

Class was quick, but there was a good amount of homework I needed to get done now. I'll need to try to focus tonight. Maybe Lucas can work while I work. I pictured us both sitting quietly as we poured over our work beside one another. I think even doing work with him by my side would be better. I went to text him after class, wondering where he was, but saw he had already texted me.

Lucas: Sorry, Rose, can't make it. I sent Leo in my stead. He'll take you to my place and let you in. I'll see you there.

I would be lying if I said I wasn't disappointed. I missed him a lot already, and was looking forward to seeing him. I wondered what it was he was doing that was keeping him. I looked around, spotting Leo sitting on one of the lounge chairs outside of my class. He was busy on his phone, clearly having been waiting on me for a little while.

"Did I keep you?" I asked him, snapping his attention away from his phone. He flashed me his sweet smile.

"Not really. Ready to go?"

"Yup. Sorry, you have to take me."

"Don't worry about it. I was free. Besides, now we have time to hang out a bit."

"Do you know why Lucas couldn't come?"

"No clue, but if it's keeping him from you, it must be extremely important." I frowned, thinking about what he could possibly be doing right now. I guess I'll ask him when I see him.

Lucas' P.O.V.

"Is this the place?" Carter asked as we pulled up to a run

down motel about 10 minutes away from Rose's flat.

I had never seen this place before. It was as if we had crossed some kind of magical border sending us to a different world, one of mischief and danger. Most of the buildings here were run down, with people loitering about. I couldn't help but feel more and more uneasy the further we had ventured in, but I had my sights set on confronting her father and I was gonna damn well do it.

"Yeah, that's the place." I nodded, staring up at the rusted railing on the second floor. Second floor, room 13. That's where we'll find that sorry son of a bitch.

"Let's go then," Davis commanded as he got down from the escalade he had demanded we take here. Carter and I hopped down, following closely behind.

"This is your last chance, kid. What we're about to do isn't for the faint of heart. You could get yourself in a lot of trouble if we're caught," Davis reminded me, offering me an out again.

"I'm going through with this. I need to talk to him before you guys start going crazy. It's important."

"Alright, but if he gets angry we are jumping in." Davis nodded.

"Fine by me."

We headed towards his door like sharks sniffing out blood in the water. We had our prey in sight and none of us planned on letting him get away with what he'd done. Connor was able to locate him, and the reason for which he came. I'm not sure what Rose would do with this information. Knowing her, she'd go into her savior mode, and in this situation, it wouldn't do her any good.

I knocked on the door, hearing the low murmur of a tv on the other side. I heard the mattress spring creek with relief, signifying he'd gotten off the bed. I watched as the doorknob twisted and the door swung open. We didn't wait for an invitation, marching past him. His face registered in my mind, reminding me I'd seen him the day I left Rose's flat to get clothes. His scruffy beard and honey blonde hair were styled the same as before. His blue eyes stared us all down, assessing us. I could see him trying to develop a plan of attack for the three men who had invaded his room.

"We need to talk about your daughter," I said in the most serious tone I could muster.

"You know my daughter?" He narrowed his eyes at us, probably trying to figure out how these two men behind me could possibly know his daughter.

"She's my girlfriend." Not exactly the way you dream of meeting your girlfriend's father. I don't think anyone ever imagines they'll be taking two large men to beat down their girlfriend's father on their first encounter. With a dad like hers, there's little else I'd like to do.

"What do you want?" He asked more sternly. I could see the anger festering in him. He was annoyed, and he wasn't afraid to show it. He was large like David and Carter, clearly a fighter. He must still be fighting despite his age, which is probably mid 40s. He crossed his arms, flexing his large biceps as a warning. He knew what we were here for and he wanted us to know he wouldn't go down easy.

"For you to leave. She doesn't want to see you. She doesn't want to talk. You have no right to come here and drop a bomb you know will cause her to come home before she even graduates." I shook my head at him. "She's worked too hard for that."

"What would you know?" He stepped forward, trying to strike fear in me.

"I know a lot. I know the kind of man you are. I saw it evident on her cheek." My hands fisted at my sides as I recalled the sight of her hurt face and pink eyes. "You hurt her more than just physically. You can't tell her you're having a baby. She'll come home to try to keep the baby safe. To try to keep your girlfriend safe. You haven't changed, and she knows that."

"How do you-" he started to ask, but I cut him off.

"Name your price and I'll give it to you to not tell her.

I'll tell her once she graduates." Rose can't know. She's worked too hard. The baby will be fine for a couple of months until Rose finishes college. Then she and I can go back to New Hampshire and help if we have to. I won't let Rose throw her life away because this grown ass man doesn't know how to use a condom.

"$200,000," he said without hesitation. It kind of hurt to know he would take the money rather than fight to see his daughter. Of course it was what I had hoped for, but I still hated it.

"Fine. I'll transfer the money to you. These two, however, are here to hurt you the way you hurt Rose. She has friends now, Mr. Brewer, strong ones. She's doing good here and you're ruining it." I stepped back out of the door. "Check your bank in the morning for the money. I expect you to be gone by tomorrow afternoon. Guys, I'll meet you in the car."

I began walking down the hall, hearing the door close and fists make contact with flesh. I could hear the grunting and shuffling as their fight began. I made my way down to the escalade, leaning against the black car. My eyes were fixed on number 13's door, waiting to see who would open the door. Viking Man was the first to step through followed by Mr. Clean. They didn't come out unscathed but by the look of Nick on the floor. They came out the victors. I smirked smugly as they strutted down the stairs.

"Get in," Davis told me, sounding furious. "We need to talk." That tone told me I was in trouble, but I couldn't tell you why. I opened the backseat door and climbed in. Doors slammed as they too got in. Davis turned in his chair to face me. His lip was busted and his nose had clearly been bleeding.

"You are going to tell Liv about her dad today. You aren't going to keep his secrets. She deserves to know. You have no right to make that decision for her. Don't you dare send him money! He's leaving tomorrow without a penny. I told him so already."

"How dare you try to solve this with money?" Carter

added, equally upset. I had nothing to say. My throat felt tight with my voice non existent. I thought I was doing what was right, but according to them, I had done nothing but wrong. I shook my head, trying to shake off the shock as I was caught so off guard.

"I was-" I stumbled as I tried to find my words. "She'll leave to help. She's worked so hard to graduate, going through years of hell in high school to make it to this school. If I tell her that her father is having a baby, she'll run home. She can't go back there. He's already proven he'll hit her."

"Doesn't matter. You tell her the truth and then you remind her of everything you just said. You propose solutions and you solve this together, but under no circumstances do you keep this from her. Don't ever try to buy her problems away again. She'd hate you for it."

Davis' words were strongly ringing in my head well after he finished speaking. She'd hate me for it. My intentions were good, but miscalculated. Davis is right. If Olive found out I had kept it from her, and paid off her dad to leave, she'd kill me herself. I nodded my head at Davis, unable to say anything more as his words registered what my mind failed to do on its own. Davis drove us back to our meeting point in silence. Their bloodied knuckles were clearly on display, but they didn't mind it. Maybe they didn't even feel the sting of it anymore. We arrived at the gas station we had met up at a couple hours before, allowing me to get into my own car and race towards my Rose.

I was upset it had taken us so long to get to the motel. It caused me to miss picking up Rose from her class. I am sure she wasn't exactly pleased. I hope Leo has been keeping her good company. I had told him to give her the extra key I keep in my plant jar. Rose needs her own key to my place.

I drove quickly towards my apartment, ready to see her. I waited at the red light a couple blocks away from the apartment now. The moment the light turned green, I raced forward, forgetting my own rule. I was met by a blaring horn of a pickup truck that decided to run a red light. It hit the side of my car so hard. I saw everything spin around me before it dropped onto the roof of the car, letting me know I had flipped multiple times and landed on the roof of the car. I felt my head getting dizzy as warm liquid ran through my hair and dripped onto the roof of the car, showing me its dark red. I was bleeding and my head was spinning more until my vision tunneled and gave way to the darkness.

Chapter 32

Olive's P.O.V.

"He should have been here by now." Leo sighed, playing anxiously with his lip piercings. We had both tried calling him but hadn't received a response. There was no text or call back. Anytime we tried to call, it went straight to voicemail. From there, we started to worry.

"His phone is probably dead," I said, knowing that wasn't the case. I don't know what it is, but I have this sinking feeling in my stomach that something is wrong. I couldn't tell you what it was, however; having Lucas not answering the phone was only making the feeling worse. My mind kept coming up with worse case scenarios to torture me further.

"Yeah probably," he sighed, not convinced.

"What should we do? Want to try to see if anyone else has heard from him?," I asked, hoping he would say yes, because I don't have Lisa or Rachel's number.

"Shit." I heard Leo curse under his breath before he answered his phone. "Hello?" His voice sounded so scared, like he was bracing himself for the worst news. He stood up immediately, as if the couch had caught fire beneath him. "Is he okay?....What hospital?....We're on our way."

"What is it?" I asked, feeling my heart race with worry. I felt myself taking panicked breaths and tried to calm myself until he answered.

"Lucas has been in an accident. We need to go to the hospital. Grab your stuff, let's go." Leo didn't give me a chance to ask anything more, as we practically ran to his car. He sped through the streets, straight to the hospital with a look of determination. I chewed at the side of my nail the entire time from the anxiety festering inside of me. I'm scared as hell right now. My worry and anxiety only rose more with each step I took towards the hospital.

When the double doors slid open to the emergency room, we were met by a crying Sarah and Lisa. Rachel was off in the corner, looking tortured as hell as she stared at the ground like a comatose patient. Kane was beside his daughter in a lab coat, holding her hand for comfort.

"What happened?" Leo asked before I could even find my voice.

"*That* asshole ran a red light and hit his car!" Rachel seethed, pointing at a teenage boy with a baseball cap and a look of utter horrification. He saw her finger pointed at him and he physically paled. It was obvious the kid was full of remorse and deep regret.

"He's got a bad head wound and a broken arm. They are stitching him up and taking an MRI. He's currently unconscious, but they said they would come get us when he woke," Lisa added, holding Sarah in her arms.

Leo seemed so scared, probably having a lot of trauma brought up. I can't imagine what it must be like to hear someone you love is in a car accident after you've lost people in a wreck. I am starting to understand the whole 'celebrate the good when you can' thing now. I felt so sick to my stomach thinking of Lucas being hurt. I felt like I was going to throw up.

"He's okay." Rachel looked at Leo as she spoke. "He's going to be okay."

"Rachel's right. It could have been so much worse. Lucas is going to be okay, and in a little while, we'll all be with him." Kane added, trying to persuade us all since he's the doctor of the group. We all sat in the lobby for what felt like eons before a nurse came out. We all stood up and rushed towards her. I am sure we scared her as her eyes widened and her voice shook.

"He's awake now. You're welcome to visit him two at a

time. We don't want to strain him too much at once. He's got a concussion with a large laceration to the forehead. His arm is currently pinned until we can go in tomorrow and surgically fix its fragments. Be careful not to move his arm when you go in," she explained. "Who would like to go first?"

"I would. I'm his mother." Sarah stepped up, tears in her eyes. "Lisa and I shall go first."

"Follow me."

The nurse took them down the hall past the double doors and to his room. I stood planted to my spot like the roots of a tree. I didn't want to move. Leo stood beside me, taking my hand and squeezing it as we both stared at those double doors, waiting for them to open again. Nothing needed to be said, we knew exactly how the other was feeling. Eventually, Lisa and Sarah came back out. They seemed in better spirits than before, but there was still a look of concern on their faces.

"Rachel, Leo, you guys go next." Sarah called to them. Leo gave me an apologetic look as he stepped forward. I shook my head motioning for him to go. He was his best friend and Rachel was his family, of course, they would all go before me. I'm just the girlfriend...the very new girlfriend. Sarah and Lisa had left, feeling their presence was no longer warranted now that they knew Lucas would be okay. It was just Kane and I as he waited for Rachel to emerge.

"Olive, right?" Kane asked me as he sat on the chair. I had remained in my spot this entire time, unable to move or sit. It was like my legs refused to move unless it was towards him. I turned my head to look at Kane for a moment before looking back at the double doors.

"Yes, that's right."

"I see you've managed to stick around longer than all the other girls," he mused, making me turn to look at him a bit flabbergasted.

"I see you like to stick your foot in your mouth." I rolled my eyes at him. He, surprisingly, chuckled at me.

"That was a bit rude, wasn't it? I am sorry, I didn't mean

to offend you. I'm surprised to see Lucas staying with one girl again."

"Yeah, I got that." I didn't hide the irritation in my voice. Right now, all I wanted was to see Lucas with my own eyes, to hold his hand and somehow make him better. Instead, I'm stuck out here waiting my turn as one of the last ones to see him. I'm stuck out here with Kane's unwanted commentary.

"I think I see what he sees in you," he noted in amusement.

Some time later, Rachel and Leo emerged. They seemed a bit more at ease now, too. I was ready for my turn, finally having my legs move. I brushed past Rachel and Leo, straight to the nurse. She led me down the hall right to Lucas' room. The lights were off with the exception of a small, dim lamp on the bedside table.

Lucas laid with his eyes closed. His head was bandaged around his forehead while his arm rested on a pillow with some kind of device to hold it still. My eyes watered as I took his hurt state in. *It could have been worse.* The thought made me feel like I'd shit my stomach out. I didn't want to lose him right after I found him. He means so much to me. I somehow convinced my legs to take a few extra steps towards him. I grabbed his good hand, feeling him squeeze it in return.

"I was wondering if my Rose would be coming." His voice was scratchy, almost like he swallowed glass.

"How are you feeling? Are you in pain? What can I do to help?" I asked him in rapid succession, unable to calm myself.

"Come lay with me." Lucas patted the small bed beside him. I didn't hesitate to climb in beside him carefully. I laid my head on his chest, hearing his steady heartbeat. With each beat of his heart, mine calmed. I let a tear fall, hitting his chest on its way down. *He's okay.*

"I'm sorry, Rose. I wasn't being careful. My mind was a million miles away, and I wanted to get home to you." His good hand began to rub my arm as he spoke.

"You don't have anything to be sorry about. You didn't

do anything wrong." I shook my head at him.

"But I did." His words made me pause, stopping my movements and my heart.

"What do you mean?"

"I went and saw your dad with Davis and Carter." He admitted. I sat up as best I could, looking down at his wounded state. I couldn't be mad even if I wanted to be now. "I wanted him to leave, so I offered to buy his silence, and make him leave without seeing you." He continued, making me upset at the fact he tried to offer my dad money.

"Keep going," I said, knowing there was probably more.

"He came to town to tell you he's having a baby with his girlfriend." He sighed. *Dad is having another kid?* I shook my head hysterically. This can't be happening!

He can't have another kid. He can't!

"Rose, the baby won't be due for a while and you're so close to finishing college. I know you're going to want to go back home and help care for a baby that isn't even yours, but you need to remember how much you put up with in high school to get here. Don't go back, at least not until you graduate. Please Olive! Don't go." He squeezed my hand, staring up at me like I could hurt him further with my answer.

"When is the baby due?"

"End of April. Three weeks without you there to help. Then we can rush to New Hampshire and help from there."

"*We*?" I didn't miss the fact he was offering to come with me.

My mind was still reeling from the news, trying to determine my best course of action. If I were only thinking about myself, then the choice would be obvious, but this involves more than my life. This involves the life of an innocent child. I want to say they will be okay, but I know Dad. What if he beats his girlfriend while she's pregnant and ends up killing his unborn child? I have no idea how he was with mom when she was pregnant with me. I am not sure when he even started to hit her.

"Of course, *we*, Rose. I told you, I'm never letting you go again. If you need to move back to New Hampshire to help, then I'm moving with you," he said so matter-of-factly, it caught me off guard. He'd move states with me...for me. I felt my eyes tearing up, overwhelmed by all the emotions I was feeling. I thought of how I could have lost him today and the waterworks started to flow. He's everything to me already, and it's scary how fast my life now revolves around him. I leaned forward carefully, trying not to hurt him, and kissed him gently. Yes, I was mad he tried to offer money to my dad to make him leave. I was more upset that he had planned to keep this baby a secret from me, but I still love him. In the end, he did the right thing, so I can't exactly be too upset with him.

"I love you so much, Lucas," I whispered to him as I pulled away from our kiss.

"I love you, too. So very much, Rose."

"Don't ever try to keep something like this from me again, and definitely never use your money to try to make a problem go away," I lightly scolded him.

"Yes, sir," he joked, but when he looked down into my eyes he got serious. "I won't, Rose. I promise."

I nodded my head, content with his promise, before I closed my eyes and continued to focus on the beat of his heart. The heart that keeps my Knight alive. The heart that stole my own. I don't ever want to lose him. Not ever. I'll stay by his side for as long as he'll have me. I will fight for us, and like all my fights, I'm determined to win. Our relationship will flourish. I will make sure of it.

"I can't lose you, Lucas. Please, be more careful," I whispered into the air.

"You won't lose me, Rose. I don't plan on letting you go anytime soon. That includes dying." He wrapped his good arm around me, holding me tight against him. He kissed my forehead as he squeezed my arm. I could feel the tenderness of his actions. He loves me too, and I hope it's as much as I love him. I bit my cheek as I recalled the words Hailey spoke to me this afternoon. I won't know if I don't ask. He won't know if I don't tell.

"Lucas?" He hummed in response. He was tired. I could hear it.

"I want to tell you something, but I'm worried it will freak you out. I don't want to scare you away, but I also want you to know how I feel. I don't expect you to feel the same way. I will patiently wait until you do, if that's the case."

I paused for a moment, waiting for him to respond, but he didn't. I looked up to find him peacefully sleeping. His face was relaxed, showing me a side to him I had not seen often. I'm usually the first to fall asleep, but not always the first to wake. I could count the times I've seen Lucas asleep, in one hand. I smiled as I looked at him, happy to see he was getting some rest. What I was about to tell him can wait for another day.

I carefully slid my phone out of my pocket and shot Leo a text. I told him to go ahead and leave. I'll stay here tonight with him, because there's no way I can leave his side. I let myself fall asleep beside him. It was a tight squeeze, and a bit uncomfortable, but there's nowhere else I would rather be.

I was woken up by a nurse in the middle of the night and asked to move to a little cot. They were worried about me hurting his arm, and they needed easy access to him. I hated to leave the warmth of his embrace, but I did as they asked.

"You stayed with me, Rose?" His hoarse voice woke me easily in the silence of the room. I peeked at him through my lashes, giving him a small smile. I rubbed the sleep from my eyes, stretching my body to try to wake myself better.

"Of course. I didn't want to leave you here alone," I answered him.

"Thank you," he said, giving me that delicious smirk of his. The one that made my heart soar and my core dampen.

"How are you feeling?"

"Sore, very, very sore."

"I'm sorry. I'll get a nurse and see if they can give you anything."

"Don't bother. I don't want you to leave." He shook his head lightly.

"Don't be silly. You're in pain, it'll only be a second." I got off the cot, heading towards the door.

"A second too long." I heard him whisper as I left. I found the nurse, and she said she'd be down soon to take him back to surgery. They'll be fixing his arm today. Thinking of him in surgery made me nervous even though the chances of anything bad happening were slim. When I returned to the room, Lucas seemed almost upset. He patted the bed beside him again.

"We need to talk," he said, making me all kinds of nervous.

Lucas' P.O.V.

Please, if you're willing, listen to Photography by Cody Fry as you read.

My Rose stayed here with me last night. She had slept beside me until they made her move. *Stupid nurse.* I couldn't believe she would willingly choose to sleep in a small cot like that rather than in a large bed. I want to tell her how I feel….how I *really* feel. She is everything to me and she needs to know it. I need her to know, but I'm also scared I'll frighten her away. She can be so skittish at times.

"What's wrong?" She asked, seeming shy. I didn't mean to worry her, but I need her to know I am being serious.

"Come here," I said, patting the bed again. She slowly made her way towards me.

"I'm here," she announced as she sat on the edge of the bed. I used my good hand to grab hers, holding it tight in case she tried to run away.

"I need to tell you something, but you can't run away after," I said, smirking at her sweetly, but my heart was beating quickly. She gave me a small nod in understanding, letting me

CHAPTER 32

continue. "I've told you I love you already, but I need you to know what I mean when I say that. I don't say it lightly, and I certainly don't confuse it for the attraction I have for you. You're the one thing that keeps me from suffocating in my own darkness. The person who brings me hope when the world is crashing down on me. I told you that you saved me, and I meant it. You've brought light into my life again. One that I refuse to let go of. I don't want to fall into that darkness again." Her eyes were on me as I spoke, but I couldn't look into them. I wanted to pour out my heart to her, and looking at her would only tie up my tongue.

"When I say I love you, I mean that I cherish you. That you are the most important person in my life. When I say I love you, I mean that I will be by your side always. That I will support you in whatever you do. When I say I love you, I mean that I will not let you get hurt. That I will protect you with everything in me. When I say I love you, I mean I am happy as long as I have you. Do you understand what I am saying, Olive? I love you in all sense and meaning of the word."

It was silent for a while, causing me to look up at her finally. Her eyes were pink and misted as she bit her lip. She nodded her head at me, but I couldn't tell what she was feeling or thinking at the moment.

"When I say I love you, I mean that I will give you all of me. That you will have my heart and my soul with you always." She started, making my heart swell and my eyes tear instantly. "When I say I love you, I mean that I will stick by your side through thick or thin. That I will not leave you, even when you send me away. When I say I love you, I mean that I will fight for you. That I will fight *with you,* if it's for your own good. When I say I love you, I mean that you are my everything. That I will place your needs before my own. I love you, my Knight, in all senses of the word." I nodded my head, feeling overwhelmed and elated by her confession. She was on the same page as me, if not further in. *Don't worry, Rose, I'm right there with you.*

"No running away?" she asked me.

"No running away." I confirmed, pulling her towards me. Our moment was cut short before I could kiss her the way I wanted to. The nurse had come in with the anesthesiologist, and they had begun to prep me and roll me out to surgery.

"I'll be here waiting," she promised in a hushed voice.

I nodded, still riding the high of knowing she loves me so much. I wanted to be back by her side already, but the pain in my arm let me know this surgery was necessary. They wheeled me to the surgical room, having me hop onto the surgical table. They placed the mask over my face without a word, having me breathe in deeply.

It was like I blinked and everything was over. I felt myself waking slowly. My head felt foggy and my eyes had a hard time opening fully. I could tell my mind was still trying to fight the effects of the anesthesia. The warm small hand in my hand let me know my Rose was by my side. I squeezed her hand tightly as I continued to stir awake.

"Lucas?" Her sweet voice made me smile.

"Mmm, my Rose. You didn't leave me," words slid out of my mouth like a flowing faucet. "I was worried you might have changed your mind and ran for the hills."

"Never," she said so confidently.

"Thank you, Rose." She shook her head no at me.

"No, thank *you*, Lucas. You don't know how happy you made me today." She smiled at me.

"I wonder how you'll feel when I ask you to move in with me in a couple of months?" I winked at her, finally able to open my eyes fully, and take in her beautiful face. Her eyes widened on me before she blushed deeply.

"Stop," she slapped my arm playfully.

"Just wait and see, Rose."

Rose kept me company all day. She skipped her classes and got her assignments emailed for the day. She worked on her homework and her classwork as she sat with me. I loved seeing her focus with the way she would suck her lips in when she was concentrating. Her brows would pinch at the center any time she would get confused, but it would soon unfurrow as she found her answer.

Leo stopped by again with Lisa, who seemed to be doing okay. I was still worried about her and the son of bitch that I still need to find. I hate that I can't intimidate him now that I have this thick cast on. Lisa needs help. I love her to death, but she definitely has daddy issues, and it's causing her to pick guys with large red flags. I hope she's able to break this habit before it hurts her worse.

"I still don't understand it. Once you start mixing the alphabet with numbers, you've lost me," Lisa complained as she looked at Rose's work quizzically.

"That's where you find *me*." Rose giggled as she took her work back from Lisa with a snatch of the paper.

"She's too smart for us," Leo added with a smile.

"I'm sure Lucas wouldn't be as lost as us." Lisa pointed out, knowing I actually enjoy math, and a challenge. She had Rose hand me the paper with her work. The problems were not simple, and way beyond my scope. I shook my head no.

"Normally, math is my favorite, but even this is way too complicated for me," I frowned, sad I couldn't help her with it.

"I'll teach you." She smiled, looking excited as she offered.

"Go for it."

Rose showed me how to work the problems with ease. I followed along fairly well, and it helped her in double checking her answers as she went through them again. She was absolutely perfect, and there's no way I am letting her father keep her from graduating. I'll find a way to convince her to stay and finish out school.

I'm not letting you drop out, Rose.

Chapter 33

Olive's P.O.V.

It's been a week since Lucas' accident. A week since we both admitted how much we love one another. I have been taking care of Lucas as he heals. He broke his dominant arm, and although it's adorable to watch him try to do things with his left hand, it's also sad. I end up helping him with a lot of things, which he both appreciates and doesn't like.

He's a proud man like most and all he wants is to be better already, so he doesn't have to depend on me so much. I have been staying at his apartment all week, but it was time for me to go back to my flat. I missed it, and I needed more clothes. Of course, Lucas tagged along. I didn't mind at all.

You would think that we would have grown tired of one another after a whole week beside each other, but it was very much the opposite. We wanted more of one another, and the notion of being away from each other killed us. I was happy to know I wasn't the only one of us who felt this way.

"I'm almost done with your freshman year of high school now," he informed me, as we sat on the couch. I had been working on my homework and Lucas had been busy reading my journals again.

"How do we feel about my freshman year?" I asked curiously.

"I'm growing very jealous of this Ian." I laughed, thinking he was joking, but I quickly contained it as I noticed he was not. I shook my head at him.

"There's no need to be jealous of him. He was the first

good friend, and that's it."

"If you say so, Rose."

I continued with my work and Lucas with my journal. He continued reading without complaint. I'd almost forgotten how much I had written about Ian in those journals. He took up most of my freshman year journals and almost all my sophomore ones. I'm not sure how he'll feel when he realizes Ian is still in those.

"Hey, Lucas?"

"Yes, my Rose?"

"Ian may be in a lot of my journals, but I hope you know the feelings I had for him don't hold a candle to the ones I have for you now." I turned to look at him, seeing him smile at me. He leaned forward, kissing my cheek sweetly.

"Good," he whispered.

We grew silent again as I focused. The subject matter was getting harder each week. I still hadn't fully decided what to do with dad and his news of a new baby. I don't want anything to happen to it, but I also don't want to drop out, and let my years of hard work go to waste. *Is that selfish of me? Would I be an asshole if I chose myself?*

"Rose, when's your birthday?" Lucas randomly asked, making me realize neither of us actually knew that about each other. It was odd that we would admit our love before evening knowing the basics about one another.

"Christ, we don't know much about each other," I gasped.

"Easily corrected. My birthday is April 26th."

"Mine is June 3rd," I answered him.

"A summer baby." He smiled.

"Favorite color?" I asked him, wanting to know all the little things now.

"Hmm, does gold count?"

"If you want."

"Okay then, gold. What about you, Rose?"

"Teal." It's always been teal.

"Interesting," he mused. "Favorite pastime?"

"Watching movies, or hitting the punching bag at the gym. You?"

"Reading." He smiled, holding my journal up and making me blush lightly.

"Favorite sport?"

"Soccer, of course," he answered me.

"I like to play volleyball best, but I've played soccer too. I like to watch soccer the best."

"So you'd watch me play if I joined a team again?" He asked me, almost seeming insecure as he did.

"I would love that." I bit my lip as I imagined him in a soccer uniform. He'd be hot as hell in one. I got off my spot, straddling him on the couch. My eyes and body were hungry for him. We hadn't been as sexually active with him hurt, causing me to become some rabidly horny dog. I grabbed his face, leaning down and kissing him passionately. I licked at his bottom lip, asking permission to enter. Our tongues danced against each other in a swirl.

"You stay still, and let me do all the work." I whispered in his ear as I stood up. His intense brown eyes watched me as I slowly undressed before him. I undid his pants and pulled them off him with his boxers, leaving his shirt on, not wanting to move his arm much. My hands slid onto his thighs, spreading them to allow my torso in. I took his flaccid dick into my mouth, feeling it start to grow with each suck and lick. He groaned as I continued to move my head against it. When he was nice and hard, and extremely horny for me, I stood up. I straddled his lap again, aligning my entrance perfectly with the tip of his dick.

I slowly slid down his shaft until he was deep inside me. I waited a moment before I began to sway my hips against him. My hands gripped his shoulders tightly, not looking away from his eyes as I continued to bring us both pleasure. Lucas' hand crawled up my body until it found my breast. His finger traced along the small scar from my surgery.

"You're absolutely perfect, Rose, battle scars and all."

His words drove me up, making me feel so good. Somehow, he always manages to say the right things to make me feel better about my insecurities. I had started to hate the scar on my breast, feeling it made me look unattractive. His words pushed those insecurities far away, because I know he means it. I've begun to notice Lucas never says anything he doesn't mean. I continued swaying against him until I reached my climax. I then began sliding him in and out of me, causing my thighs to burn as I continued. I kissed him passionately, leaving our mouths open as we breathed one another in. I held his head close, feeling his chin on my breasts. Before I knew it, I'd milked Lucas of all he's worth. We stayed like that for a moment longer with Lucas growing soft inside me again.

"Thank you, Rose," he whispered before kissing me again. *I love this man.*

I can't go to New Hampshire. I realize I'll be uprooting Lucas, too. He said he would move with me, and as much as I love the idea, I don't want to take him away from his family. I'll go after graduation unless something happens between now and then. I'll ask Joe to keep an eye on them for me. Joe is the man who has given me every tattoo on my body except the pink ribbon with mom's name on it. He knows how dad is, thanks to our many sessions together. A good tattoo artist is like your therapist. You lay on their chair and talk as they work. Joe was always great. In my junior and senior year of high school he got me a job to help me save for college. He also made sure I was fed dinner every night. It was more than I'd had in a while. I know Joe will watch dad's girlfriend carefully for me if I ask him to. If anything happens, I'll rush home.

I wonder if they will have a boy or a girl. I never imagined being an older sister, but I won't take the role lightly. I will shield that baby from living the same life I did. I will ensure it lives better than I did, even if it means it lives a life without a dad in it every day. It's better than one where he or she may be abused. Better no dad than *our* dad.

Don't worry, little one, I'll keep you safe.

Time flies by when you're actually enjoying life. Halloween was this weekend already and Lucas and I will have been dating for a month now. I felt giddy thinking about it. Lucas and I have not spent a single night away from each other since his accident. We alternate between his apartment and my flat. We each have our own drawer, but I honestly have 2 drawers and a quarter of his closet at his place.

"We have to match, Rose," Lucas argued with me over our Halloween costumes.

"Do we have to dress up? Aren't we too old for that?"

"Take it back. We are never too old," he argued back, making me smile with his playful tone. "Please, Rose, dress up with me?" He gave me those eyes again, the ones that always melt away my resolve. He was not playing fair.

"Fine," I sighed. "But nothing that's going to have me half naked."

"Never," he shook his head. His cast was finally due to be removed this Friday, in time for Halloween. He was excited to have it gone. He was getting tired of not being able to scratch very well with the cast on. His arm had been healing so quickly.

"What about this one?" He asked, showing me a couple of pictures of Beauty and the Beast. "You know cause, you're my Rose?"

"I get it, but there's no way I'm wearing a big poofy yellow dress." I shook my head no.

"You're right. Okay, okay, let me get serious. Let's see what would my Rose *actually* like to wear," he mused to himself as he continued to scroll through costume ideas. *I* wasn't even sure what I would want to wear. I am not one for dressing up much. Trying to come up with an original costume idea is impossible. Plus, so many of the adult women, costumes are so sexualized. Like everything is sex this or sexy that. I'm tired of it.

"I think I found it," Lucas smiled triumphantly as he turned his phone again.

"I think you did." I smiled back happily. He knows me so well. It was simple, nothing that made me look sexy or too frilly. He'll be Jack and I'll be Rose in the greatest love story. Only we'll have a happier ending, since we won't be on a sinking ship. I love the movie Titanic.

The week flew by and Lucas and I were getting his cast removed. I'm not going to lie, it was not a pleasant smell and Lucas' arm looked all pale and pruney, making me crinkle my nose. Lucas was happy to be free of the cast, finally. I gently ran my hand over his arm. He had a few scars now, but they were scars that reminded us of how precious life is. They were scars that helped us tell each other how we truly felt. They were beautiful.

"I love you, my Knight," I told him as I continued to stare at his naked arm.

"I love you, my Rose." He kissed my temple, making me smile.

"So, the party's tonight, right?" I asked him.

"Mhm, Leo is excited to go. Rachel is coming to town again, and they're going together."

"When do you think those two are finally going to tell each other they like one another?" I shook my head disapprovingly at the two. It was obvious Rachel loved Leo, and he liked her back.

"What do you mean?" Lucas was shocked by my question, like he had never fathomed the thought.

"You can't be serious? You haven't noticed the way Rachel looks at Leo? Or how she always goes to him first? How she's always at his side anytime she comes to town? Lucas, you've gotta pay more attention."

"Seriously?!" He looked genuinely surprised.

"Yes, seriously."

"That would be so awesome. Leo would actually be family. We have to get them together, Rose. Play cupid with me tonight?" He was very excited for tonight now. It made me laugh.

"Okay, I'm down."

Lucas and I devised a plan for tonight we hoped would get those two to confess their feelings for each other. It was fun scheming with Lucas. He was devilishly wicked in a cute kind of way. I loved being part of the plan making. We both got dressed in our costumes. Lucas wore a white long sleeve shirt with brown trousers and suspenders, looking like Jack. I had on the iconic purple and white dress with pink sash around my ribs. The one she wore the night the ship sank. Since it's cold in New York for Halloween, I had on the coat Jack gave Rose part way through the night.

"Are you ready, Rose?" He asked, holding his arm out for me to take.

"Ready, Jack." I grabbed it, getting into character with him.

He smiled sweetly at me as we headed out of his apartment. We decided to take my car tonight. Lucas drove the car. I made the mistake of letting him let me drive once, and I saw how scared he was. He wouldn't admit it, but I could see how rigid and pale he had become. He needs control in order to be in a car. I don't mind not driving, anyway. I hate driving in New York, so I'm fine with him chauffeuring me around. Especially if it gives him peace of mind.

We arrived at the sorority row where we planned on hopping from house to house and enjoying the different festivities at each. We paid the cover at the first house, waiting for Leo and Rachel to meet up with us. We headed outside to the backyard where different games had been set up. It was less crowded out here than inside. Lucas grabbed me a whiskey as we waited.

"Wanna play a game, Rose?"

"Always."

"I'll tell you something about myself and you guess if it's true or not. If you guess wrong you take a drink. Then we'll switch"

"Sounds like fun." I felt like I knew Lucas pretty well now. Of course, I don't know all about him. A month is not enough time to know everything, but I feel like I could make good inferences based on what I know about him.

"Okay, first statement," he said, shifting his shoulders to stand up straighter. "I was arrested once." I hadn't expected him to say that. I, honestly, had no clue and could see it being either.

"Can I ask a question?"

"Only one," he said, holding up his index finger.

"How old were you?"

"17."

"Then I say it's true." I figured a lot of 17-year-olds get in trouble. Besides, if it was when he was 17 then it meant John was alive. If John were alive, then they must have gotten into some shenanigans together.

"That is…" he waited a moment to try and keep me in suspense. "correct. I did indeed get arrested. I guess I have to take a drink since you got it right.'

"What did you get arrested for?" I asked him curiously. I can imagine it being something stupid, but I am curious to know exactly what it was.

"John and I were messing around after a soccer game and jumped a fence to get into the baseball field after drinking a bit. We were caught instantly." Lucas laughed at his past self as I'm sure the memory played out in his head.

"I could see that," I mused. "Okay, my turn. My tattoo artist taught me to play guitar." I was trying to throw him for a loop, but all it did was make him laugh.

"My one question is how many tattoo artists have you had?"

"Two." I held my fingers up as I answered.

"Then I say it's true."

"That's right, but how'd you guess?" I took a drink of my whiskey while I waited for him to answer.

"I saw the guitar in your closet a while back. I could tell you played, and I didn't figure you learned from your dad. Ian doesn't seem the type to play, and you didn't have many friends then." He knew me so well, even past me.

"I hadn't realized you knew I played. I haven't played in a little while." I need to pick it back up before my fingers soften back up.

"I want to hear you play one day." He rubbed my cheek sweetly with his thumb while he spoke.

"One day." I nodded.

"What can I do to get you to let that day be today?" He stepped forward, closing the space between us. He was trying to use this close-proximity to entice me into doing what he wanted.

"Hmm, you'd have to show me something you can do that I haven't seen before."

"Okay, deal. Wait right here," he said as he raced off from my side.

I'm not sure where he went or what he's doing, but I didn't like the fact I was now alone. I played with the drink in my hand to keep myself busy. My eyes roamed the party, scanning for any familiar faces. I could see a couple of engineering students getting plastered in the distance. They were taking shot after shot. I would have never guessed one of them as a party animal.

"Liv?" An all too familiar voice came my name.

I should have figured he'd be here.

Chapter 34

Olive's P.O.V.

Julius stood before me, dressed as Prince Charming. *As if*. I felt his eyes roam my body, and I hated the fact he knew what I looked like naked, hated that he knew what I felt like from the inside. I should have known he'd be here. He likes going to these kinds of parties.

"Leave me alone, Julius."

"Come on, Liv. You're all alone. Let me keep you company. I miss you." He tried to grab my hand, but I pulled it away.

"You wouldn't have to miss me if you wouldn't have cheated. How many times, and with how many people, did you cheat?" I asked him the question plaguing my mind since I found him deep inside Clover.

"Just once. One time," he lied with confidence.

"You can tell me the truth, Julius. It's not like I'll ever take you back."

"It is the truth," he lied again, only making me angrier.

"Go away, Julius," I sighed.

"Come on, Liv. You shouldn't be alone here."

"She's not alone." Lucas reemerged behind him, making Julius take a step back and eye Lucas curiously. He was unsure of who he was or what his comment meant. Lucas met his eyes with apathy before looking at me. He had a soccer ball under his arm, making me smile. He wanted to show me his skills in exchange for me playing the guitar for him. I ignored Julius completely, smiling at Lucas widely.

"Hello, my love." I greeted him, only trying to emphasize to Julius that I'm taken already. Lucas walked over to me, leaning down and kissing me so passionately, practically fucking my mouth with his tongue.

"Want to see my ball skills?" He asked in a lude way, making me laugh.

"Very much so."

Julius was still there, just watching. He didn't say a word or make a move. He stood there, almost frozen in shock. I guess he never imagined I would move on so quickly. Maybe he assumed I would be pining over him for a while, waiting to take him back. He's an idiot. One I cannot believe I wasted so much time with. Lucas turned, finally looking at Julius again.

"You're still here?" He asked in a taunting way. "Come on then, love. I'll show you my skills." Lucas held his hand out for me to take, and I didn't waste a second grabbing it.

He led me away from Julius, saving me again. He found a spot further off from the festivities before turning to me with a smirk. I eyed him curiously as he threw the ball down on the ground. He kicked it up onto his foot skillfully. The ball was shot up, and somehow landed neatly on his bent knee. He shot it up, landing it on his other knee. I never realized how sexy soccer could be. I loved seeing him play with the ball so well, doing things I had only ever seen in movies.

"Damn." I muttered, very impressed with him. "You're so amazing." He winked at me, catching the ball with his hands, placing it back under his arm.

"Your turn, Rose," he said, pointing to a stage with a guitar sat on it.

"No way! I'm not doing it in front of everyone!" I shook my head vigorously.

"Come on, Rose. I know you'll sound amazing. I'll come up there with you. We can sing together or if you want I'll sing, and you play." He was desperate to hear me play, and although it made me nervous, I couldn't help but give in to those eyes.

"What do you want me to play?"

CHAPTER 34

"Do you know "The Mortician's Daughter" by Black Veil Brides?"

"Yeah, but it's been a while."

"Come on, Rose. Let's go put on a show."

He grabbed my hand excitedly, dragging me to the stage. It was a small stage only about 8 ft by 6 ft or something. The guitar was perched on a stand beside a bar stool. There was a mic stand, in front of it, standing tall, yet not tall enough for Lucas. He bent down, adjusting it to his height while I grabbed the guitar and strapped it around me.

I strummed the strings and adjusted the tune, gaining the attention of a lot more people than I would have liked. I was feeling nervous as hell, but when Lucas' eyes landed on me, it all faded away. It was like it was just him and me up here with everyone else fading away. I've heard him sing in the car before, but hearing him sing into a mic with only the sound of my guitar playing was completely different. It was amazing. He had a nice voice, one that made my heart race. It was hard to explain, but his singing did things to my body I didn't know a voice could do.

It was the clapping, when we finished, that brought me back to reality. I blushed deeply, feeling so self-conscious at the moment. My blush only deepened when Lucas leaned down and captured my lips in a kiss.

"Thank you, Rose!" He smiled widely at me, only washing away my insecurities again.

I am not sure how he manages it, but he always makes me feel better...stronger. One look from him and all my troubles are pushed back, only to surface again when he's gone. Being in his presence is like feeling the warm rays of the sun against my skin. He brings me a warmth and happiness I didn't know was possible.

I woke up to my head pounding. I drank too much

playing with Lucas, Leo and Rachel. It was our own fault for coming up with a game to get Leo and Rachel to confess their feelings to one another. Our plan didn't work, ultimately resulting in a hangover from hell for no reason. I groaned, squinting my eyes at the bright light leaking in from between the curtains.

"Ugh, too bright!" I complained.

"I told you, you'd regret that last whiskey." Lucas' scruff voice made me smile, like always. He kissed my forehead sweetly before getting up and closing the curtain more for me. "Better?"

"So much better!" I nodded. He crawled back in bed with me, pulling me into his chest. His strong arms wrapped around me, so he was embracing me tightly against him. I smiled at him happily.

"Want to stay in bed all day?" he asked me with a smirk.

"Yes! A thousand times, yes." I said, with my eyes closed again. Staying in bed sounded good, staying in bed with Lucas all day sounded perfect. He chuckled at my response, squeezing me tightly against them again.

"Okay, stay in bed we shall."

Lucas spun us in one fell swoop, so I was lying on my back with him propped on his elbows over me. He smiled mischievously at me before bending down and kissing me hungrily. I knew exactly what he had in mind now, and although my head was throbbing, I loved the feeling of him against me. I won't mind this one bit. His lips left my own, trailing down my neck, over my collarbone and down to the top of my exposed chest.

"I'm hungry, Rose, and I don't mean for food." His voice made my heart flutter with excitement.

"What are you hungry for, my Knight?"

"*You*," he whispered in my ear, causing goosebumps to develop down my arms.

"*Mmm*, then feel free to have me however you like."

Lucas' intense brown eyes stared down at me happily.

He loved whenever I let him do what he liked. Hell, I loved it more. He knows so much more than I do, surprising me with things I didn't know I would like. Our experiences are different, but we both still enjoy each other in a carnal way.

"Are you sure, Rose?"

"*Very,*" I assured him.

His hungry eyes grew as he grabbed my flimsy pajama shirt and tore it open. I couldn't believe he had done it, but the action was damn hot. I had never had clothes torn off me before. He hadn't struggled to do it either, so it wasn't awkward fumbling. It was powerful and needy, and dammit if it didn't have me getting wet already.

His lips kissed the tall hills of my braless breasts as he worked his way down. He kissed my stomach, continuing to trail his lips against my skin as he pulled my shorts and underwear off together. He stood, taking his own clothes off while I watched, never breaking eye contact. His hands snaked around my thigh, pulling it towards his hip. I felt the tip of his hard shaft brush against my entrance teasingly. With his hand still gripping my thigh tightly, he thrust himself inside me so deep he hit my cervix. He stayed there a moment, unmoving, only watching my eyes with his own.

He started his movements slow, working me up more until he quickened them to the point I was screaming. His movements would die back down and then he would slowly build me back up again. It drove me mad with want and desire. The pleasure deep inside me felt ready to burst for him. He enjoyed the fact I was moaning and begging for him to go faster.

"Not yet, my Rose," he'd whisper any time I wanted more, more speed, more force, more of him deep inside me.

It was absolutely pleasurable, yet torturous. After so much teasing, Lucas finally let me reach my climax, causing a yell of pleasure so loud it reverberated through the walls. He didn't stop there either, flipping me over onto my stomach. With my face pressed against the mattress and my ass high in the air, Lucas penetrated me again. His hips slapped against my ass while his balls hit my clit with every forceful thrust. I found myself coming undone so quickly. It was like all the teasing had made it 100 times easier for me to orgasm.

The morning continued this way until I had reached my peak too many times to count. My body felt light, almost numb by the time we stopped. Yet there was a part of me that still wanted more. A part that didn't want to let him out of me. He came so deep inside me barely any of it leaked out when he pulled out. He licked my neck like an animal when we were done, making me shiver happily.

"I love you, Olive Brewer." He whispered to me, as he held me close.

"I love you, Lucas Porter."

"Move in with me?" He asked, making my heart stop and my mind race.

The question hung in the air for several minutes. I knew I needed to say something, but all coherent thoughts escaped me. I love him, and he loves me. We laid ourselves bare for one another after his accident, but we've only been together about a month. Is it too short of a time to move in together? Yet, all I wanted to do was blurt out yes. I mean, we stay together every night, anyway. What's the difference?

"No," I started, and the hurt on his face killed me. "Move in with me instead. I don't want to lose my mom's flat."

The joy that rekindled in his eyes made my heart swell. He propped himself on his elbows over me again, kissing me so deeply he stole my breath away. He smiled down at me, a smile I had yet to see before. The happiness radiated off of us in waves. I know everyone will say it's *way* too early, but it feels right. We love each other and we're practically with one another every day and night. We pretty much live together already, but between two places.

"Thank you, Rose!" He squeezed me tightly against him, almost knocking the air out of my lungs. "You've made me the happiest man." He kissed my neck multiple times, making me shiver with goosebumps.

We laid naked on the bed for a while, cuddled into each other with our legs intertwined. We were happy and content to lay there silently with one another. His soft breaths tickled my neck, sending waves of happiness through me. I loved being here with him at this moment. I didn't want to let him go, to let this moment pass.

"Lucas?"

"Yes, my dear Rose?"

"Let's go pack." I was excited to have him move in with me already.

"But…bed," he groaned.

"One more hour," I said.

"One more hour," he confirmed with a smile.

"What is this?" I asked Lucas, holding up some random black straps that looked almost like a harness.

"Hmm, I can show you later." He winked, making me throw it right at his face with a blush.

"I think I'll let you finish packing up this area," I said, moving away from what I realized were actually a lot of sex toys.

"Are you sure you don't want to see all the things I'll use on you in the future?" He gave me a playful smirk. I shook my head at him as I moved on to another area. Lucas actually didn't have much. He said all the furniture could stay, it's his dad's apartment. We packed his clothes, his toys, his office, and some small personal items he had. We were done within three hours.

"I'm starving! What about you?"

"Famished!" I rubbed my stomach.

"Let's go. I know the perfect place." He grabbed both my hands, pulling me off the ground. "I'll have someone bring the boxes to your flat. Let's go enjoy ourselves."

"What do you have in mind?"

"Trust me Rose." He smiled at me like a small child. And you know what? I did trust him. I trusted him completely.

"Okay." I nodded.

He pulled me out of the apartment, rushing me to the car. He was so excited, which only made me wonder where he was taking me. He played a song with no words but a happy melodic tune. The sun felt so nice with the convertible top down. A happy feeling deep inside me, seeping into my bones. Lucas pulled into the parking lot of a small building. I eyed him curiously as he parked. When he turned to look at me, he had a mischievous grin on his face.

"Time to play," he said, hopping out of the car and running to my side.

We walked hand in hand inside the small building. The doors opened to reveal some arcade games on the front right. Towards the back left were a ton of pool tables, where most people were right now. To the right of us was a large circular desk with vests and guns behind them. Finally, in the back, there were bowling lanes, with a concession and prize counter as well. Lucas led me towards the right. It seems we would be playing laser tag together, and I felt so excited to beat his ass. I've only ever played a few times, and each time was with Ian. I had come out victorious every time, so my confidence in winning was high. We weren't the only ones playing, of course, but we made sure to be on different teams.

"I love you, Rose, but you're going down," he whispered in my ear as we separated, entering the battlegrounds of sorts from different sides.

"If I were you, I'd start to worry about being beaten by a rose," I said as I sauntered away confidently.

Our game started, and I stayed hidden amongst the shadows. I made my way through the arena, looking for Lucas. I shot a few kids along the way, always catching them off guard. I was behind a column, hiding away as the enemy passed me by. My vest flashed before me, letting me know I had been shot. I looked around, finding Lucas' smug smirk above me. *He got me.*

I ran off, trying to hide again. Everywhere I went, Lucas would somehow find me before I even spotted him. It was beginning to annoy me at how easily he was winning. I hadn't shot him once, yet he'd shot me 5 times already. I'll get him at least once. I hid well, waiting for him to find him. I saw him pass me by, not noticing me for once. I was able to shoot him, making me jump out and do a little victory dance, only resulting in me being shot by someone else. I slapped my forehead in response, making Lucas laugh.

"I think I may win this one, Rose." He winked at me before running off. I gave chase, and the game continued this way until Lucas' team came out victorious.

"You're cute when you pout," Lucas teased me, kissing my cheek. I shoved his chest lightly in protest.

"Am not."

"Extremely cute."

We headed towards the delicious smell of food, beckoning me forward. I ordered a pretzel, a hot dog, and a red cherry Icee. Lucas ordered a couple pizza slices, a pretzel, and a blue Icee. I played with his feet under the table as we ate. I was having fun, feeling like a kid again. Lucas always had a way of making my troubles fade.

"Want to play pool next, or go bowling?" he asked me when we finished eating.

"Pool."

He nodded, taking my trash for me and then returning to collect me. He grabbed my hand and found us a table to play, setting the balls up for us as I grabbed our sticks. Lucas went first, showing me he was a master at pool. He'd almost gotten all his balls in before it was even my turn. I'd gotten a few balls in, but was having trouble finding the right shot to take with one of my balls. I felt Lucas' arms snake around me as he leaned over me.

"Try this," he said, adjusting my arms, shoulders, and

hips. He then guided me into hitting the cue ball, having me shoot my solid red into the pocket. I smiled widely, happy to have gotten it.

"Thank you," I said, turning to kiss those lips of his.

We placed our sticks back once our game was over. Lucas had won again. It seemed he was not the kind of guy to let someone beat them because they were a girl. I would be mad if I won with him not giving me his all. He seemed to understand that about me, not taking it easy on me at all. We bowled next, laughing at the amount of gutter balls I was getting. Lucas would show me how to do it, and I loved it when he did. I had honestly never been bowling before.

"It's like you've never been bowling before," Lucas teased me.

"I haven't," I said, making him freeze beside me.

"I'm sorry, Rose. I was only teasing you. I didn't think this was actually your first time." He had a somber tone as he apologized.

"Don't worry about it. I'm glad it's my first time with you." I kissed his cheek before taking my shot. It hit 2 pins, and I celebrated a little too loudly. "I actually hit some pins!" I smiled at him happily.

"You're too much." He shook his head with a smirk.

The day was amazing and filled with so much fun and excitement. I was happy Lucas thought to take me here. Although I lost at absolutely everything we did, I still enjoyed it. It was the first time I was happy to lose. Best part about losing is someone else gets to win. And in this case, that someone else is Lucas.

"Ready to go home?" He asked me, making me smile. *Home, our home now.*

"Ready." I nodded at him, following him out to the car.

Chapter 35

Olive's P.O.V.

"Are you sure you're okay?" Lucas asked from the other side of the bathroom door.

"I'm fine, go away. I don't want you to hear me puke," I said, with my head hanging over the toilet. I woke up feeling very nauseous this morning. I attribute it to the hot dog I ordered yesterday. Never order the hot dog.

"Rose, let me in. I don't care about hearing you puke, let me be by your side," Lucas begged from behind the locked door.

"No way, it's disgus-" my sentence was cut short by my vomit. The nausea faded lightly after I had spilled the contents of my stomach into the toilet. I flushed, rinsing my mouth out in the sink before brushing my teeth. I opened the door to find a very worried Lucas.

"I'm fine. It's probably the hot dog I ate."

"Lay back down. I'm taking care of you today," he commanded, making me smile lightly.

I loved it when he took care of me. I did as he said, because being in bed sounded nice, especially with this nausea. Lucas brought me crackers, ginger ale, and water. He had me lay down as he unpacked his things, making this his home too. It was crazy to me that this was *our* home now, but God if I wasn't so extremely happy about it.

"How are you feeling now?" He asked me, when he finished unpacking all his clothes.

"Better, thankfully." The nausea had died down quite a lot thanks to the crackers. The ginger ale helped, too. Lucas kissed my forehead tenderly, sitting beside me in bed.

"Good, now stay resting, and tell me what you like to do when you're feeling sick," he demanded. I could tell he was asking because he wanted to do that for me.

"Eat chicken broth and watch movies. I like to watch romance movies, or animated family movies."

"Sounds perfect. I'll be right back," he said, jumping off the bed and running down the stairs towards the kitchen.

The smell of broth in the air let me know he was warming it up for me. It was a comforting scent, bringing me a nostalgic feeling. I watched him through the railing, smiling at the fact he was mine. I know I am very lucky to have Lucas. I am not sure what I did to get a guy like him, but I am glad it happened.

"Here you go, my Rose." He gave me a warm bowl.

He didn't come lay down next to me like I had assumed he would. Instead, he set up a projector and hung a white sheet a couple feet away from the foot of the bed. He turned on the projector, showing a romantic movie on it before coming to lie beside me. I drank my broth and watched the movie with him happily. He held me close once I finished eating. Everything felt right at this moment.

"I have some bad news," Lucas sighed. I sat up so fast it caused floaties in my vision as my head spun for a moment.

"What's wrong?" I asked worriedly.

"I have to go on a cabin vacation with my mom and Lisa during Thanksgiving break. Lisa chose the dates when we gave Mom the gift. I'm so sorry, Rose." He sounded so sad as he spoke. He couldn't even look at me. I grabbed his face, making him meet my eyes. I kissed his nose and smiled down at him.

"Don't be sorry. It's important you spend time with your mom. Enjoy every moment of it with her. I'll be fine. I think maybe I'll drive back home and take the chance to check in on my dad's girlfriend and the baby." I think it would be a good idea. I definitely don't want to be here alone without Lucas.

"Are you sure that's a good idea?" He asked, probably

worried about me seeing my dad.

"Yes, I'll be fine. I won't stay with him. Instead, I'll stay at a hotel around town. I kind of miss the place." He didn't seem convinced by my words, still holding a deep concern in his eyes. "I promise, I will be okay. I won't go to his house when he's home. And I'll go to check on the baby then stay away from either of them. I'll avoid his hangouts and his house when he's there. Trust me, I know how to handle my dad. I've been doing it for a long time." I reminded him with a gentle pat to the cheek.

"Be careful, Rose. I don't need you getting hurt again."

I nodded my head, remembering the hard sting on my cheek the last time I saw my father. I swallowed down the emotion, laying back down beside Lucas. As usual, his arms carried my troubles away, allowing me to relax and nap on his chest. When I woke up, he was deeply immersed in my sophomore year journal.

"What part are you on?" I asked him, startling him just the slightest as he hadn't noticed me wake up.

"You went laser tagging with Ian for the first time. Of course, he let you win." Lucas shook his head. I think he's developing a deep- seated jealousy of Ian, which is not very healthy.

"Uh, he didn't *let* me. I won fair and square, thank you very much." I stuck my tongue out at him, making him laugh.

"Sorry, my mistake. You totally won fair and square."

"Damn straight." I straddled him on the bed, grabbing the journal from his hands and placing it on the bedside table.

"I was reading that." He smirked at me.

"I have something better for you to do." I leaned forward, kissing those delicious lips of his. My teeth caged his bottom lip, sucking on it as I pulled back from his face. My hands slid up his torso until they landed on his face. I gripped at his jaw, bringing him closer to me. His hands grabbed my hips, holding them tight as I continued to kiss him hungrily. My tongue explored his mouth as he did the same.

His hands trailed up my back to my bra strap, unclasping it in one smooth move. My shirt was shot off me and thrown to the side without a care. Our clothes were shed quickly as we continued to kiss. My body was hungry for him, as it always is. The feeling and need to have him in me has not died down this past month. In fact, I dare say, it's grown.

Lucas grabbed my legs, dragging me to the edge of the bed. He didn't waste time entering me, pumping in me quickly. His tongue licked from my navel up to my clavicle as I arched my back in pleasure. He licked at my neck next, sucking on it enough to surely make a mark appear there tomorrow. When he was satisfied there, he trailed down to my breasts. He feverishly left marks on me, littering my torso. The possessiveness of it had me feeling more pleasure than I thought it would.

"You're all mine, Rose," he whispered in my ear. He placed the back of my knees on the inside of his elbows, holding them up to my chest, essentially turning me into a ball. This position granted him deeper access to me, intensifying the pleasure that pulled inside me. I moaned loudly, only causing him to take me faster.

"Yell my name, Rose." He gripped onto my ass, spreading my cheeks apart. Not exactly sure why, but it made my pleasure escalate until I felt ready to burst.

"*Lucas!*" I yelled as I came over him.

"Fucking perfect," he told me, before kissing me so lovingly as he came deep inside me. "I don't think I'll ever get tired of hearing you yell my name." I blushed at his words, feeling a little self-conscious of the way I say his name in the midst of my orgasms. I know he's always liked it, he even named himself as *the man who makes you scream* on my phone. There's no lie there.

"Good, because I can't seem to stop screaming it when you fuck me the way you do." I admitted.

"Round 2?" He asked.

Lucas' P.O.V.

Rose was in class right now with plans to eat lunch with Hailey later. I'm taking this time to read her journals, and then hang out with Leo. Work is taken care of, having stayed up late to get it done. I hated losing time with Rose, so I have started to work at night while she sleeps. I'm awake then, anyway.

I decided to read inside the small cafe on campus that Rose and I had visited one morning. This used to be my favorite spot to get work done when I was attending here. The smell of coffee is soothing and has always helped me to focus better. I opened up Rose's journal almost to the end of her sophomore year now.

Thankfully with Ian around, she was able to handle high school better. She was still picked on, or messed with, but Ian was always by her side to comfort her or defend her. I do think Rose's first love is not her ex Julius, but this Ian guy. I hate to admit it, but I am a bit jealous of Ian. He was able to rescue her back then. I wish I could have. I wish I could go back in time and save her from her misery.

Dear future me,
He's moving. The love of my life is moving!
I hate today. I hate life. I hate everything.
He told me his parents are being sent overseas for business. He'll be moving to London for a while. He swore we would keep in touch...we both did. There's no way I'm going to lose him as a friend. I'll write to him as often as I can.
I really wish I had a phone. We would be able to talk whenever we wanted, but Dad's never seen the point in me having a phone. He says it's a waste of money. I think I'm the only high school kid without one. I'm certain I'm the only one without a computer or internet either. The only way for Ian and I to stay in touch is through the good old fashion mailing system. Which will take for-freaking-ever.
If ever there were a time I wish I had a phone, it would be

now! I feel my heart is breaking into a million pieces. I don't want to lose him. I don't want to watch the most amazing thing in my life leave. High school is going to be unbearable without him here.

Do we still talk a lot with Ian now? Is he still our friend?

A very disappointed Past You

So that's what happened to Ian. He moved. It wasn't that they had a falling out, or some kind of argument. It wasn't that Ian was secretly a dick. No, it was circumstances outside of their control that separated them. What would she do if he suddenly entered her life again? What if they one day run into each other? Would she fall for his charms? Would she leave me for him?

"What's got your panties in a bunch?" Leo's voice snapped me out of my inner spiral.

"Why you, of course, you're so hot, Leo," I joked, because I refuse to voice these insecurities. I know they're irrational.

"Mhmm." He rolled his eyes. "Seriously though, what's up with you?"

"Reading her journals and getting mad at her dad. She told us her childhood was hard, but she didn't go into specifics. It's killer, Leo. I hate knowing that man raised her." I shook my head, with my hands gripping the journal tightly.

"I can only imagine. I hate that she didn't have this beautiful upbringing like I had hoped when I asked for her life story. Honestly, I think that's why you guys fit so perfectly. You have shared trauma, and as such, think in a lot of the same ways."

"You think so?" I am sure he's right, but I had never thought of it.

"Definitely. You're both dark and twisty."

"So what are you, then? Dark and bendy?" I laughed.

"No, I'm light and airy." He smiled.

"You should be. You deserve to be light and airy."

"Don't go getting soft on me. This is usually when you tease me." He arched a brow at me.

"I know that. I just..." I sighed, pausing for a moment. "I

want you to be happy, Leo. I feel so lucky to have Olive in my life, but then I see you and feel kind of guilty, you know? I want you to find your person, too." Leo kicked my shin under the table, making me lift my leg up fast, causing me to hit my knee with the table.

"Ow, what the fuck, Leo?"

"Quit feeling sorry for me and enjoy your happiness. Of all the people I know, you're the one that deserves it. I'll find my person. I'm only 19, I have time. Maybe I'll have some fun for a little bit, and gain some experience like you did." He wiggled his eyebrows at me, making me crack a smile.

"Oh? Am I your role model, Leo?" I laughed. Teasing him has always been my favorite thing to do. It's how we show we love one another, cracking jokes at the other's expense.

"In fact, you are." His confession caught me off guard. I assumed he would joke or tease me. Instead, he made me feel important.

"Then, as your role model, let me tell you a secret." I leaned forward, looking all around us like someone was listening in. Leo leaned forward as well, getting closer so he could hear me better. "I'm the best lay there is, so if you want to learn from the best, you're gonna have to sleep with me." I blew him a kiss with a wink, causing him to roll his eyes. I laughed at him as usual.

"Ass," he muttered, but I could see the corner of his lips trying to fight off his smile.

"No, but seriously, don't go having too much fun. It gets old fast and only makes you feel lonelier." I added, being serious for once, because the last thing I want is for Leo to go down the same path as me.

"Don't worry, you may be my role model, but I'm not looking to be exactly like you. I like myself better." He winked, making me smile playfully at him.

Leo's always been easy to talk to. Someone that has always made me smile. I love playing around with him, and spending time together. He's the closest friend I have. The one who understands me better than even my own family. I hope that he's happy. I know taking over his father's business has been hard on him. I can see it starting to suck away his soul. I need him to find happiness somewhere to counteract it. I need him and Rachel to finally admit their feelings. *How did I not notice it before?* Another reason why I love my Rose. She's so attentive.

"When you are ready to find that girl, let me know. I'll help you." I offered, having Rachel fully in mind.

"I don't know if I want any of your sloppy seconds." He arched his brow.

"Never. Don't want them to compare us." I winked at him, joking around as always.

"Asshole," he muttered, kicking me under the table again.

"We need to get back into soccer. You still have a mean kick."

"They're reserved just for you. I'm not interested in soccer. It was always more Johnny's sport than mine." My chest tightened at the recollection of John's brightly smiling face on the soccer field. He was a teammate I could always count on. Our passes were flawless, with little words needing to be said. We knew each other's moves and plays, almost as if we were in each other's heads.

"Yeah, he was pretty fucking amazing."

We grew silent, a sadness falling about us. I know we were both living in the memories of John right now. I can't imagine how much Leo misses him, being his actual brother. John has always felt like a brother to me, too, but it's different. I know he's left a hole in each of us. One that's been hard to fill.

"Okay, enough with this sadness," he said, shaking his hands in the air as if he were blowing the sadness away from us. "Is there something you want to tell me about where you're living now?" He arched a brow knowingly, making me give him a big grin.

"I may have moved in with Rose." I wiggled my

eyebrows at him.

"Are you serious?" He sat up quickly, leaning forward over the table. "You guys have only been dating like a month! That's insane." He shook his head.

"It may be insane, but it's right. It feels right for both of us, so screw what everyone thinks is a normal timeline. I know I found the woman I want to be with, so why bother waiting?"

"Lucas," he said my name in a concerned tone. "Be careful. That's moving extraordinarily fast, and I don't want either of you to get hurt."

"I won't hurt my Rose. I'll only help her grow."

"I hope so."

We ate lunch together, talking about stupid stuff. He was playing some new video game he wanted me to try. We talked about the new night club we want to go to. He even mentioned the new drink he concocted, which I plan to never drink. I learned from my mistake last time. Leo makes the most delicious drinks you don't even realize there's a shit ton of alcohol. The next morning, I had the worst hangover of my life.

"I better head off to my class. Tell Liv I say hi. Let's go out this weekend, all of us."

"Sounds good." I gave him a hug before he ran off in the direction of his class.

Another hour till my Rose is back in my arms.

Chapter 36

Olive's P.O.V.

Lunch with Hailey went great. I was scared to tell her about Lucas moving in with me over the weekend, but I was stupid to be. She was so happy for me. She yelled so loud in excitement causing everyone to turn and look at us like we were crazy. We spoke about it for a little while and by the end of it Hailey had washed away all my doubts and insecurities about it being so soon. This is why Hailey is the absolute best. She never judges, just gives advice.

Class felt like it was dragging on, maybe because it was the last one of the day, and I know Lucas will be waiting for me. I missed him terribly already, even though we saw each other this morning. There's a moment when a person becomes your entire life, and I feel like I've had that moment with Lucas. He is everything I think about, all the time, at every moment. He's everything to me.

"Don't forget to work on your projects now, so you won't be trying to finish them over Thanksgiving break." Professor Devarti advised us.

Wrong sir, that's exactly when I want to do it. I am not wasting my time with Lucas. I'll work on my project and papers while Lucas is away with his mom and Lisa. Once I'm done, I'll drive up to Portsmouth and check on my dad's girlfriend and baby. It's only a four-hour drive, so it's not too bad. Not worth flying there.

We were dismissed from class, and I don't think I've ever bolted out of there faster. I saw him right outside the door, making me smile. I felt my heart beat rapidly at the sight of him. A warm, joyous feeling erupted inside of me, knowing he was here for me. He reciprocated my smile, looking just as happy to see me. He pulled me into a tight embrace before kissing me shamelessly in front of everyone.

"Hello, my beautiful Rose," he said, rubbing his thumb over his jaw.

"Hello, my shiny Knight."

"Ready to go home?"

Home, our home.

"Very much so."

He kissed me one more time before walking me to the car. We talked about class and my work. He told me what he did while I was in class. He and Leo got to spend time together and I was happy to hear it. They need more time with one another. As much as I hate being apart from him, Lucas still needs his friends, and I need mine.

"Want to cook together tonight?" He asked me randomly as he drove us home.

Home, still so giddy thinking about it.

"Ooo, that sounds good! What should we make?"

"Handmade pizza or shrimp and mango salsa, or maybe even handmade pasta?" Lucas was throwing some random suggestions out, making me smile. I looked at him, seeing his handsome profile as he drove. He was so focused on the road, despite talking with me.

"I wanna try to make homemade pasta. Sounds like a lot of fun," I answered him with a smile.

"Perfect. Let's go to the store."

"Woah, you never said anything about going to the store."

"Just the grocery store, Rose. We gotta get what we need. I'll be with you the whole time, don't worry."

"Fine," I groaned. Even grocery trips were the worst for me.

We pulled into the market, parking near the door. Lucas

held the door open for me and walked me in with our fingers interlocked. He didn't let my hand go as we walked the aisles, getting what we wanted. He played around with me as we went down the aisles, telling me jokes at times. We were checking out before I knew it, with a smile on my face. He was trying to distract me from the fact I was shopping, and he did so successfully. *He's so perfect for me.*

"I love you, my Knight." I told him as we exited the store with our ingredients in tow.

"I love you too, Olive." he locked eyes with me, staring lovingly at me. "Let's go make a mess at home."

He drove us home carefully, staying at the speed limit, and keeping both hands on the wheel as it started to pour. The rain was harsh and unexpected, making it hard to see. I was glad we didn't need to go far with home being so close. Once there, we ran inside laughing as we tried to, unsuccessfully, avoid getting soaked.

"Maybe we should change clothes first," Lucas said with a smile as we entered *our home.* I love saying our home.

We headed up stairs, changing into something comfy. I had put on a pair of sweatpants and had just taken off my wet shirt when Lucas' lips surprised me on my shoulder. He wrapped his arm around my waist and pulled me against his chest. He then kissed my neck sweetly, making it almost tickle.

"Mmm, that feels nice." I smiled, closing my eyes and leaning my head back against him.

I was focusing on the sensation of his lips against my body. He kept kissing and sucking at my neck, until my core dampened for him. He grabbed my wrists and pinned them behind my back rapidly. It surprised me, breaking the tender moment. I felt something wrap around them and felt the familiar material of his belt.

"What are you doing, Lucas?"

"Playing with my prickly Rose."

His answer caused my heart to race and my stomach to twirl. He pushed me forward, causing me to face plant onto the bed, but it didn't hurt. He pulled my pants off me, leaving me fully exposed to him, without allowing me to turn around to look at him. I felt him walk off for a moment, only to feel a blindfold cover my eyes. I bit my lip as I anxiously waited to see what he had planned.

Lucas grabbed my hips, pulling them up so I was on my knees on the bed. My shoulders and face were still firmly planted on the mattress. His tongue then began to lick at my wet folds, causing me to moan happily. His fingers entered me, circling around my walls as his tongue continued to devour me. He played with me until I was so wet I could feel it on my thighs. He didn't relent either, not until I reached my first orgasm over his face.

The blind fold only made me focus on his touch more, making everything feel so intense. I felt him grab the belt around my wrists, lightly pulling back on it. He let his dick slide between my folds, not yet entering me, but teasing me. His large shaft rubbed against my sensitive clit, making me moan loudly as I swayed my hips against it.

"Do you want me, Rose?"

"Always," I answer with a moan.

"You're so beautiful, Rose."

The words slid from his mouth as his dick entered deep inside of me. I let out a loud moan as he began to thrust against me. He slapped my ass so hard I could hear the sound throughout the room. It stung, yet only added to my hunger for him. I felt myself getting wetter, if that was even possible. I felt Lucas reach for something, but I couldn't tell what until I felt a familiar vibration over my clit. I yelled out as it caused me to reach my peak faster than I planned. My walls clenched over his dick as I came. He didn't stop either, having the little toy enter my ass. I was more prepared for it than last time, enjoying the full feeling he had created again.

Every time his dick would slam into me it'd touch a spot I didn't know I had, causing waves of pleasure through me. I swayed my hips desperately, finding my third orgasm. Lucas continued to pound into me with a speed and force unlike any other. I felt him pull out and spill his seed all over my ass. He rubbed it in with his dick too. Somehow, causing me to stay horny for him. I'm not sure why I liked his cum all over me. It felt hot as hell.

"Let's get you cleaned up," he said, taking the blindfold off to reveal his smiling face. I nodded a bit bashfully after the sex we just had. Lucas untied my hands and helped me into the shower. We washed off quickly, changing into black sweat pants and t-shirts. Lucas had tossed me one of his shirts instead of my own. He said it was an accident, but I think he wanted me to wear his clothes. I noticed he liked seeing me in his shirts.

"You ready to cook?" He asked me.

"Sure am." I nodded happily, leading us downstairs to the kitchen. *I wonder how good of a cook Lucas is.*

Lucas' P.O.V.

Cooking with Rose was lots of fun, but the cleanup was even better. I couldn't contain myself around her as I leaned her over the counter after we cleaned up and slammed into her again. She didn't mind as she moaned in pleasure the entire time, allowing me to cum inside her this time. When she turned to face me, she looked so in love my heart almost stopped.

Her beautiful icy blue eyes captivated me like no other. It's hard to describe the warm joy she makes me feel by just looking at her. I love this woman too much for my own good. She could destroy me if she wanted to, but I know she won't. She's my Rose, and I had finally climbed past her thorns and into the center of her soft petals.

"I love you, Olive, so very much." I wanted her to hear the sincerity in my voice as I said it, to notice the seriousness and the joy in which I told her. I only ever used her real name when I wanted her to know how serious I was being. She looked up at me past those long lashes, hearing my words clearly.

"I love you too, Lucas, with all my heart."

Our joyous moment only continued as we ate our homemade pasta and watched *Lady And The Tramp*. The pasta was good, only made better by the fact we cooked it together. Anything I do is always made better when done with Rose. I hate that I won't be by her side during Thanksgiving break. I know when I see her again, I won't be letting her out of my arms, or out of my bed for that matter. After dinner, Rose worked on her homework and I read her journals again. I was curious to see what happened after Ian moved. I was near the end of sophomore year now. He was due to move at the end of May.

Dear future me,

Ian has been sweet since telling me the horrible news. He doesn't want to go either, and we both wished there was a way for him to stay. We've been hanging out more every day. Any chance we got, we would sneak out together and talk. This time it was done on the roof of his house. We stared at the stars and spoke about our future aspirations.

Ian gave me the brilliant idea of becoming a rocket scientist. I want to build something that can fly into space. I want to know my creation is out there, floating around with the stars. I wasn't sure I could do it, but Ian believes me. So, I'll believe in myself, too.

What am I going to do when he's gone? Who's going to keep the darkness of my world from getting too overwhelming? So much for another nice Thanksgiving or warm Christmas. So much for having a friend in high school, for not being one against the many.

He's leaving soon, and it's tearing me up inside. Please tell me he comes back for us. Please tell me he doesn't forget about us.

A sorrowful, Past You

My heart hurt reading this. She was breaking inside when she wrote this. I could feel her raw emotions like it was happening to me. She was losing her best friend and secret first love, and it was killing her. I peered from the journal to see Rose with her pencil against her lips and her eyes fixed on her book. She was thinking and working through her problems. Ian was the one who set her down this course. He's the one who helped her see her worth first. I guess I should be grateful to him for that, but I'll beat his ass if he hurt her in the end.

Dear future me,

Sorry I haven't written to you in a while. Ian's move date had been rescheduled to earlier than originally planned. He moved away yesterday, and I didn't get a chance to say goodbye the way I would have liked. We thought we had more time, but it was taken from us quickly.

I couldn't see him off at the airport. I have no car, so instead, I saw him off at school. They picked him up early, and he knocked on my classroom door, asking to speak with me. We said our tearful goodbyes in the hallway, knowing full well everyone would make fun of me for it once he was gone. He held me for a while in his arms, and for a moment I thought of telling him how I truly felt, and begging him to stay. But, we're both minors and he has to go with his parents.

"I promise I'll write to you, Red." Those were his last words to me before he left. He used the horrible nickname he had come up with when we first met. So unoriginal, yet exactly what I wanted to hear. The image of his back leaving the double doors of the school with the sun shining so bright, will forever be engraved in my mind, I am sure.

There goes my happiness.

Sure enough, when I reentered the class, I was made fun of. They told me I was so obsessed with Ian, he had to move to a whole other country to get away from me. It didn't help the already creeping sadness in me.

A now very depressed, Past You

My heart ached for this Rose. I wished I could travel back in time and save her even then. She didn't deserve any of it. She should have been a popular choice with a million kind friends. Instead, she was tormented and bullied and had her only friend taken away.

I looked back at her, seeing her write out her answer with a triumphant smile. I sat there watching her and admiring her for the wonderful woman she is. She is absolutely amazing, and she is mine. I'll find a way to get these assholes to see her for the badass woman she is. They'll wish they would have been her friend.

"I forgot to tell you." She looked up at me quickly. "Wait, were you watching me?" She got distracted, making me laugh.

"Yes, I was. You're my favorite movie, after all." I winked at her, making her blush.

"Shut up, I am not." She fought back the smirk on her face. "Davis texted me earlier. I have a fight tomorrow night, then another one in the first week of December before the championship. Championship is right after Christmas, so no trips around then. I need you present and accounted for when I win." She gave me a happy smirk with a wink.

"I wouldn't miss it for the world, Rose."

She went back to work and I went back to reading her journal, gotta finish sophomore year. Despite how sad it makes me to read it. I need to know all about her.

Dear Future Me,

How long does it take mail to get back? I wrote to Ian the day after he left, hoping maybe he'd get my letter the first week he's there. I have been checking the mail every day since then, hoping I'll have his reply. I am not sure how long it takes, so maybe he hasn't even gotten my letter. Perhaps he got it and is now replying. There's no way to tell. I don't know what I'm going to do while I wait for him to respond. I think I'll drive myself mad at this rate.

On another note, school still sucks. Kids are still cruel, and boys are still pigs. So school is all around hell now. Home isn't much better, not that it ever was. Dad's gearing up for some big fight and he's been using me to train. I don't pose much of a challenge to him. I've got bruises all over my torso. He was pretty pissy when I got a punch in on him yesterday, so he kicked it up a notch. It kind of hurts to breathe, so sharp small breaths are the sweet spot right now.

Summer is soon approaching and with Ian gone, I have no idea what I'm going to do to keep myself entertained. Anything to keep myself out of the house. This place is suffocating and with dad being his normal asshole self, I need an escape. He's been more sober here lately, but he always goes back to heavy drinking in the summer when he knows he doesn't have to worry about taking me to school or picking me up.

Ian did leave me his bike, so I at least have it to get me places this summer. I am excited to use it. Maybe I'll find a summer job. I should start looking. Wish me luck!

Past You

I hate her dad. I hate her dad so much!

Chapter 37

Lucas' P.O.V.

"This is it!" Rose said, practically jumping in her seat.

We pulled into another abandoned warehouse, and I began to wonder how Davis found these places. Obviously, this must be highly illegal by the way they switch places and have guards, but yet I don't feel like some criminal. This is something Rose loves, and I love watching her do it.

"You ready?"

"So ready!" She yelled, before covering her mouth with wide eyes. "Sorry, I'm super excited."

"Don't be sorry. I love it." I leaned forward, kissing her soft lips tenderly. "Let's go win!" I raised my eyebrows at her, making her smile and nod. We headed in, running into Carter outside the door.

"Twinkle Toes! Wasn't sure if we would be seeing you or not. Glad to know you chose to stay." He hugged her tightly.

"Careful not to kill me," she heaved as he squished her.

"Oh, my bad. I forget how delicate you are despite your badass fighting skills." He smiled. Carter has the warmest smile of all, only making him brighter. "Go on in, Twinkle Toes."

She headed in before me as Carter met my eyes. I knew he had something to tell me, but I wasn't sure if I was about to be scolded or just asked questions. "She seems happy. Actually happy. Keep it up kid." He patted me on the back hard, making me take a step forward so I wouldn't fall.

I chased after Rose, feeling somehow accepted by Carter now. This was the family I felt I needed to get the seal of approval from. I already have Hailey's. Carter and Davis are the two I'm missing.

"Twinkle Toes!" Davis yelled from across the room. Somehow his voice could still be heard through the roaring crowd and bassy music. We met each other halfway, having Davis take Rose into another big hug. He was gentle, and even though he held her tightly, he didn't squeeze her. He did lift her up a few inches. When he put her down, he patted her head like she was a small child.

"Gave you more of a challenge this time. Are you ready for it?" He asked her with his arms crossed and face now serious. It was like he had two modes. One was his fatherly sweet side and the other was the serious ring leader or coach. It was crazy how quickly he could change between them.

"I'm always ready, Davey," she cooed, making his brow furrow. He obviously didn't like the nickname.

"I said no to that name." He reminded her, flicking her on the forehead. She rubbed it with a little pout, making me smile at her antics.

"Too bad." She stuck her tongue out at him.

"Go get ready, you little shit." He pointed behind him with his thumb and she skipped away. "You got your work cut out for you. She's going to give you hell."

"I look forward to it." I smiled as I watched her. She was already shaking off, stretching, and jumping on her feet. *God, this woman is everything!*

She was paired with another girl, about the same size as her. The girl recognized Rose, smiling widely. Not the usual reaction she gets when someone sees her. It made me a bit nervous and I think Davis picked up on it cause he crossed his arms and smiled.

"That's Dora the Bird. She's light on her feet like Twinkle Toes. I told her it would be a challenge. I hope she's ready." I felt a bit nervous for a moment, but then I remembered my Rose has sharp thorns. She's going to be fine. She's going to win this fight like all her others.

"She's got this," I assured Davis, watching the ring closely.

"I am glad you think so." He patted my back hard, the same way Carter had. I think they're trying to bruise me. Maybe I should start bulking up too. *Freaking Viking Man.*

Rose started dancing around the ring, but so did her opponent. They were maybe a little too well matched. Every punch and kick was blocked or avoided by both of them. I could see Rose thinking as she fought. She was planning her next move, calculating how best to beat this girl. Her eyes have always been very attentive, watching her opponents carefully. She always tries to find their weaknesses, they're weak points.

Rose took a step forward, and Dora took a step back. I could see something click in Rose's head, and I knew she had it now. She'd figured it out and Dora was about to get her ass handed to her. Rose took two quick steps forward, causing Dora to retreat, but the speed caught her off guard and had her slamming into the cage of the ring. Rose punched her right in the stomach, jabbing her side twice.

The music playing changed to "Lying From You" by Linkin Park, which pumped Rose up more. She backed away as Dora got back to her senses and aimed to punch Rose. She swung hard, but since Rose moved, her fist didn't make contact like she thought it would. Dora's footing failed, and she almost fell forward, having to take a step so she wouldn't faceplant. Rose used it to her advantage, punching Dora in the side again from behind. She then kneed Dora in the ass.

"Did she just corn dog her?" I asked Davis, laughing.

"I think she did," he answered with an amused smile. "It seems she's having fun."

Rose twirled around Dora, avoiding more punches and kicks. Dora was off balance and tiring quickly while Rose stayed animated. She kicked Dora in the arm hard, causing her to take a step back. She was met with the cage at her back again. Rose started to pummel her until the girl tapped out. Rose immediately stopped, holding her hand out to the girl to help her up. She helped carry Dora out, bloodied and bruised.

"You did great! Thank you for the challenge." I could hear Rose tell her. *She's too fucking perfect.*

"I'll get better, and next time I'll win," Dora promised her.

"I look forward to the rematch." Rose genuinely smiled at her, letting me know she spoke only the truth.

"Dora, go get cleaned up. Good effort." Davis gestured towards the back for the girl to go. "Twinkle Toes, you got one more fight, then it's the championship. This year we're joining with other underground fighting rings so it'll be bigger than before. Thought it would be nice to have a bigger range of fighters."

"Cool! I can't wait." Rose jumped with excitement. Surprisingly, she didn't look tired.

"I'm sure you can't. Go get your money, and I'll see you for your next fight. Glad you chose to stick around, Liv." He shook his hand in her hair. She pouted, grabbing his wrist and pulling his hand out of her hair.

"Quit, or you're going to give me an afro."

"You won't stop using that nickname, so I won't stop petting your head." He laughed, doing it one more time, even with Rose fighting him. He out muscled her, so she couldn't hold him back. I smiled in amusement at the two. I was glad to know Davis and she had a close relationship. I wish Davis was her dad. On second thought I think I'd be too scared if he were.

"Bye, Davey," Rose said, poking at him some more before grabbing my hand and running us off. We grabbed her money and headed out to the car. Carter gave her a high five as we passed him by, congratulating her on her victory.

"How do you want to celebrate?" I asked her as we pulled out of the lot.

"I have a few ideas," she said in a very suggestive tone, one that made my dick twitch in my pants.

"Don't tease me, Rose, because I'm always hungry for you."

"Good, because I am too." She leaned over to kiss my cheek. "Don't get distracted while you drive," she said, as she lifted the sports bra she was wearing, exposing her breasts. She grabbed my free hand and placed it over her breast. *Fuck, this is girl is going to be the death of me.*

Olive's P.O.V.

"You look too good to go out." Lucas whispered in my ear by our front door.

"Whatever, says the one who's too hot for his own good." I rolled my eyes at him. We were heading out to meet Leo, Lisa and Rachel –who had come into town again. We decided to try the newly opened nightclub. It's supposed to be hard to get into, but Lucas and Leo's money made it an easy problem to solve.

"Are you going to dance with me all night, Rose?" He asked me as we headed to the car.

"Maybe or maybe I'll dance with Lisa or Rachel, too." I winked at him, teasing him in my own way.

"Fine, then when you dance with them I'll dance with Leo. It'll be too hot for you to resist and you'll come begging me to dance."

"I'd actually like to see that." I laughed, wondering if Leo would ever agree. *Probably not.*

"Consider it done then." He winked at me again before pulling out of our parking spot.

The air was cold, with winter rolling in. I wonder how much snow we'll get this year? Lucas turned the heat on, pointing all the vents at me. He could tell I was freezing in my short dress, even with my coat on. When we arrived, Lucas opened my door and placed his arm around me, gripping my hip with his hand and pulling me towards his side. He did not want to let me go for anything.

Leo, Lisa and Rachel were inside already. We spotted

them near the bar once we entered. As we made our way I noticed Lisa flinch as she stood up. I know that flinch, it's the flinch of someone who's hurt. It's the flinch of someone who's been punched on the side, or stomach, a few too many times. No one noticed, and for a moment I thought maybe it was my imagination. As the night continued, I realized it was not. She didn't dance, and she didn't move unless she absolutely had to. She kept a smile on her face, trying to hide the fact she was hurt.

"Lisa, come with me to the bathroom?" I asked her, knowing I needed to get her alone so she would talk to me.

"Um, okay, sure." She got up slowly, trying not to show the pain. She did a pretty good job at it.

The line to the bathroom was long, which for once I was happy about. It gave me more time to question her. I know she's not going to open up right away and will probably deny it outright at first.

"What's going on with you, Lisa?"

"Oh, you know, nothing big. I've been working, avoiding my father, and comforting mom... the usual." She shrugged.

"That's not what I meant." I frowned.

"What do you mean, then?

"I mean, why are you hurt? Who hit you?" I asked her, no longer beating around the bush.

"What are you talking about?" She acted confused, as if I were speaking another language.

"I know that flinch. I've seen that flinch. You're hurt here." I poked at the spot I was sure she was hurt at, to make my point. She flinched, sucking air in through her teeth.

"I didn't realize you were so attentive, Liv," she complained as she sighed. "It's him again. I hate to admit it, but I went back to him. He swore he wouldn't do it again, and I stupidly believed him. This is what I get for it."

"Lisa, you're not punishing yourself like this. We're getting you treated, and then you're telling me where this sack of shit lives." I spoke firmly, making sure Lisa realized this was happening whether she wanted it to or not.

Lisa showed me her wounds in the bathroom. She had a ton of bruises around her chest. Like all over her torso, with varying colors. It let me know this had been going on this entire time. Some of the bruises had started to heal, while others were starting to darken. It made my stomach flip at the sight. I felt transported back to when I was a child and saw mom littered in her own bruises.

"Where is he, Lisa?" I asked her through gritted teeth.

"He's at my place. He won't leave, Liv. He said he'd kill himself if I left him. He won't let me have anyone over anymore," Lisa said, seeming so scared as she spoke.

"Don't worry, Lisa. After tonight he won't be in your hair any longer."

Olive: Need the coward special please.

I texted Davis and Carter. They had come up with code names for the beatings they have, and the coward special was reserved for abusive men.

Adopted Dad: I swear I'll kill that kid if he's touched you.

Davis replied almost immediately. I probably should have been more clear.

Olive: Not Lucas, not for me.

I quickly responded, trying not to get Lucas killed.

Shiny Man: We'll be there Twinkle Toes.

Carter replied.

Adopted Dad: Don't give me a heart attack like that. Send me the place and time. We've got your back.

"We're taking care of this tonight, Lisa. Let's go."

"Wait! Please don't tell Lucas!" She grabbed my wrist, looking ready to burst into tears.

"I am not keeping this from him, Lisa, but I'll give you the chance to tell him yourself. You made a mistake and hopefully it's not one you'll repeat. We're here for you and you don't need to be scared to ask us for help." I pulled her in for a hug, trying to show her all my support. "You're strong too, Lisa, so stop acting like you're not."

I didn't give her a chance to argue as I pulled us out of the bathroom and into the booming music. I dragged her over to the group, poking Lucas on the shoulder. I whispered in his ear to go talk to Lisa and to be supportive. Lisa pulled him away from the group, and I watched them while they talked.

"What's going on?" Leo asked me first.

"I'll let Lisa tell you, but Lucas and I are about to go. I have some business I need to take care of."

"Um, okay?" Leo was confused, but he didn't press the matter.

I watched Lucas hug his sister tightly as she cried. I was glad to see him hold her and not scold her. She doesn't need that right now. She needs love and support. They walked over to the group after a moment.

"We'll see you guys later. I'm stealing this one away." I told them all, grabbing Lucas' hand and marching off.

"Where are we going Rose?" He asked, surprised.

"You're taking me to go beat that sorry sack of shit to an inch of his life. Davis and Carter will meet us there. I am sure you're angry too, but let me show him that a woman can fight back."

Lucas pulled me back, and at first I assumed it was to stop me, but when I saw his smiling face I knew that wasn't the case. He leaned down and kissed me so lovingly, making me melt into him like butter.

"You're absolutely perfect, Rose. Lead the way, I'll follow."

We drove towards the address Lisa gave me, spotting Davis and Carter there already. We headed upstairs to the door, this asshole was meant to be behind. I pounded on the door with my anger at an all-time high. It swung open to a tall man with a lean physique. He had toned muscles and broad shoulders. He was a very handsome man, but knowing what he did to Lisa made him disgusting in every way.

"Can I help you?" He smiled down at me as if I were some

little present delivered to him.
> *Oh, you can help me alright.*

Chapter 38

Olive's P.O.V.

I don't understand what compels a man to hit a woman. Is it the fact that they like to prey on the weak? Do they get pleasure from it? Is there no real remorse?

"I'm here for Lisa," I told the man sternly, wiping the smile off his face completely.

"She's not here." He crossed his arms, noticing the guys around me now.

"I know she's not. I'm here to deliver a message from her to you. In all reality it's from me to you." I punched him right in the throat, making him step back into the apartment, allowing us to enter. Carter closed the door behind him, locking it to the man's horror. The guy held his neck as he coughed profusely. He looked at me furiously as he pulled his fist back. I avoided his obvious punch, returning one of my own to his diaphragm. He let out a sigh of breath with groans. I beat the shit out of him, punching him, kicking him in the groin.

"If you so much as even look at Lisa again, I'll let these two handle you next time. Maybe you'll realize not all women are punching bags. You fucking coward." I spat at him as he laid on the ground bloodied and bruised. I turned to Carter and Davis, letting them finish up here while I left with Lucas. They'll threaten him enough to where he won't talk or press charges on me. They've done this often with no cop involvement, so they know how to handle this.

"Thank you, Rose," Lucas whispered to me happily.

"Anytime. I hope Lisa learns from this."

"Me too. I can't afford to lose my sister." Lucas sounded so sad as he confessed his revelation.

"You won't."

We headed home from there, feeling all kinds of stress. We were both worried for Lisa, and even though I'd beat the man so badly tonight, it didn't feel like enough. It didn't feel like I helped her enough. Perhaps I'll teach her to fight or maybe Davis can. Maybe having control will help her. I wonder if she'd be willing to learn. Lucas held me close as he iced my fists. He wrapped my bloodied knuckles. It hurt, but I was glad I did it. It was damn worth it. I hope he gets the message.

"I love you, Olive. Thank you for what you did for Lisa tonight. I didn't know it was possible, but I think I'm even more in love with you now." His eyes bore into me, filling me with his love.

"I love you too, Lucas. So very much."

We kissed for a long while. Each kiss became more and more passionate until we were shedding our clothes and heading towards the bed. Lucas kissed me tenderly all over. It was sweet and soft. He then held me close as he gently inserted himself inside of me. He kept his chest pressed against mine and held me close as he thrusted in me. I've never had sex like this before. It felt so intimate, so loving. Is this what making love is?

I wrapped my arms around him, kissing him more. I loved the feel of having him pressed against me as he filled me with himself. I never wanted to let go. It felt like we were replenishing our souls. I couldn't get enough of him and this intimate moment. It was sweet and sensual and eventually led to an amazingly long orgasm, followed by his spurts deep inside me. With another whispering I love you, we fell asleep naked in each other's arms.

Morning came too soon, with its bright orangey hue peeking through my curtains. I squinted as my eyes began to open and focus on my surroundings. Lucas' head laid on my chest as he let out stuffy snores. He was beautiful with his peacefully resting face. I watched him for a moment before running my fingers through his hair.

"Mmm, that feels nice," he said through his raspy morning voice. I love his morning voice so much.

I continued to play with his hair while his thumb rubbed my side gently. I didn't want to move, didn't want to get up, but a wave of nausea hit me hard. I bolted out of bed so fast I scared Lucas. I ran towards the bathroom, mainly dry heaving since I had nothing in my stomach but acid. But even the acid came out of my throat along the way, leaving a nasty taste in my mouth.

"Are you okay?" He asked me as he rubbed my back.

"Yeah, I think so. I don't know what that was. It was random." I got up, brushing my teeth and washing my face. Lucas stayed by my side, still worried about me.

"Are you sure you're okay?" He asked as I turned to face him.

"I'm fine, I promise. In fact, I feel better."

I wasn't lying either. I did feel better already, like I only needed to puke once to be fine. I guess my stomach felt like being a dick this morning. As I figured, Lucas did not let me leave the bed. He gave me one of his shirts to wear with one of my underwear. He told me he loved to see me in his clothes the best.

"You look damn sexy with those on. So let me admire your body." He said, sliding my underwear on for me. His shirt slipped over me like a mini dress, exposing my thighs but covering my underwear.

"Admire away, sir." I said with a playful smirk as I sprawled myself out on the bed.

"You don't have to tell me twice."

He jumped on the bed, attacking me with his lips, nibbling at me and kissing me tenderly. While he was being careful not to jostle the bed, worried he would make me nauseous. He brought me some toast and a banana for breakfast with some water. I love having Lucas take care of me when I am sick. No one has ever done that for me, at least not since mom left me. We cuddled together, watching some movies, while Lucas played with my hand.

"You know something, Rose?"

"No, what?"

"I don't know how I'm going to survive a week without you." He sighed, thinking about his cabin trip with his mom.

"You and I both. I've grown too accustomed to you being by my side always. Plus, you've kind of spoiled me rotten." I looked up at him from his chest, staring into those adoring brown eyes. "*But* I am glad you get this time with your mom. She was genuinely touched by the gift when you guys gave it to her, so you're not allowed to pout or be sad the entire time you are there. You should, however, text me as often as you can and call me before bed every night."

"I can do that." He smiled at me, kissing my forehead. "I'm going to miss you, Rose."

"I'll miss you too, my Knight. A whole lot."

I was happy for him, glad he would have this time with his family, but I am also human and in turn selfish. I wished he could stay here with me. We will have to wait till next year for our first Thanksgiving together. I am excited to spend Christmas together at least. I need to start thinking of a present for him, but what do you even get as a billionaire?

"I'm sorry we're missing Thanksgiving together. Leo said you are welcome to come to his house and join him and his mom and his aunt who's flying down," he offered me.

"That's very sweet, but Hailey's already kidnapped me for the day. She found out you wouldn't be in town and offered for me to come to hers. Maybe I'll start my day with Hailey and end it with Leo? I don't want to turn him down after he so kindly offered."

"Sounds good to me. It makes me worry less, knowing you won't be alone." He squeezed me tightly as he spoke. "You deserve to be happy all the time, Rose."

"I don't think that's possible, but I can be happy a lot of

the time."

"Fine then, a lot of the time." He captured my lips in a sweet kiss before wiggling his eyebrows at me. "I'm going to make you happy now."

He disappeared under the sheets, making me laugh. His hands slid the shirt he lent me over my hips as his fingers hooked the waistband of my underwear. He pulled them down, kissing my legs as he did. He wrapped an arm around each of my thighs, holding them firmly. He then began to devour me with his skillful tongue and wonderful mouth. I was moaning so loudly, I'd be surprised if the neighbors didn't hear me. I lost it when Lucas sucked at my clit. I shook as I came over his face. He was sweet and put my underwear back on for me. He ran off to wash off and brush his teeth.

What am I going to do without him for a week?

Chapter 39

Olive's P.O.V.

Things come faster when you're dreading them. Tonight was Lucas' last night before he leaves for his cabin trip. We decided to spend the day together, just the two of us. There was a lot of fucking...and I mean *a lot.* He said he wanted to get his weeks worth and when he returned, he'd do it again. My legs are completely useless to me right now, having been ravished by the sex god I get to call my boyfriend.

We were talking about small silly things on the couch now. Trivial matters to keep the conversation light. We were trying to stay happy and positive, even though it felt like Lucas was taking a piece of me with him. I know I'm being dramatic. It's only a week, but still. It's a week and we haven't been apart since his accident. There's a big difference when you go from seeing someone every day, to not at all for a week.

"Favorite memory?" He asked me.

"That's a hard one," I said, tapping my finger on my chin. "The time I snuck out of my house and met a friend. We looked at the stars and spoke about our futures for most of the night. It's the night I decided what I wanted to be. The sky looked so beautiful then, too." I admitted. I didn't want to say who the friend was, worried Lucas might be jealous of Ian.

"I'll have to thank Ian for setting you down this path. Otherwise, we would have never met. However, I plan to take the best memory spot soon." He winked at me.

"How'd you know it was Ian?"

"I'm in your junior year in your journals now. I'll be

taking those with me on the cabin trip, too. I plan to be in your senior year when I return." I was surprised by the sheer number of journals he had read already. *"I'm getting closer to my journals,"* he sang excitedly like a child.

"You really are. I better start writing more while you're gone."

"I like the sound of that." He smiled.

"What's your favorite memory?" I asked him.

"Hmm, that would be the night Ivy helped my mom get away from my dad."

My chest tightened at his answer. He had a whole life before me, one where he almost married this girl. I am sure they would be happily married if she hadn't died. I squeezed his hand comfortingly as he looked down. *So much for keeping the mood light.*

"She sounds like she was a wonderful person, Lucas."

"She was, she really was." He nodded his head. We fell silent for a moment before I broke it.

"How many kids do you want to have?" I asked the next random question.

"I would like two or maybe even four," he told me. "Can't be an uneven number."

"I want two. Would you want a boy or a girl first?"

"Girl, cause she'll look like you." His answer made my cheeks burn red. He was thinking of kids with me, whereas I had been thinking of kids in general. Now I can't stop picturing it. I hope they will come out as cute as him. Hopefully, not with my flaming red locks. I am not sure they'd care for it.

"You want to have kids with me?" I asked him, surprised.

"Of course I do. I told you I'm not letting you go ever again. I've tied my life to you already. I want to marry you, have kids with you, and grow old together. We'll retire together and live on some tropical island where we spend our days drinking out of coconuts, watching the waves roll in." I imagined it as he spoke, painting a beautiful picture in my head. I want the same thing.

"That sounds perfect."

"Then we'll make it happen. Wait and see, Rose. I'll make all your dreams come true." He kissed me before I could say anything, and I knew exactly where this was headed. This time he bent me over the couch and let the slap of our skin and my moans fill the air. Every time I think I am done, he finds another way to rile me back up. I don't think I'll ever tire of him.

Song suggestion: "Love of My Life" by Avery Lynch

"Good morning, sleepyhead. Ready to see me off?" Lucas woke me with a kiss reminding me he was leaving today. I frowned, not liking the fact.

"No," I pouted, making him laugh.

"Sorry, Rose, but I'd like to be said goodbye to at the airport."

"I know, I know. I am going. I wish you didn't have to leave," I said as I got up and off the bed.

We got ready, and then headed out once we were sure Lucas had everything he needed, even the journals. We took my car so I could drive it back from the airport without having to worry. I hated having to say goodbye, but I walked him to his gate and did so.

"Be good. Spend lots of time with your mom and Lisa. Please be careful up there, and make sure to text me often. Send me pictures if you can, and call me at night. I'm going to miss you terribly. You are my everything. This week can't go by fast enough. I love you." I confessed, wrapping my arms around his neck.

"I love you too, Olive. Be careful while I am gone. Don't let your dad see you when you go check in on your future sibling. Make sure to have fun with Hailey and Leo on Thanksgiving. Text me pictures too, as often as you like about anything at all. I'll miss you, Rose."

He kissed me sweetly, leaving me wanting more as he pulled away. I didn't take my eyes off him until I couldn't see him any more, disappearing into the crowd of holiday travelers. He's out of my field of vision and away from my side for the next week. I drove home, trying not to cry. It's over dramatic, but God, did I miss him already.

I got back home safe, immediately grabbing one of Lucas' hoodies and putting it on, enveloping myself in his scent. I began to work on my projects, papers, and any unfinished work I needed to get done. It helped take my mind off my melancholy heart. It took me pretty much all day to finish my project and write one of my papers. Tomorrow I'll finish the rest and then head back home to Portsmouth, New Hampshire.

I decided to grab a small suitcase and pack enough for a couple of days. I don't plan on staying there more than one night. I packed myself what I needed, and a little extra in case of an emergency. You always want more than you need. I forced myself to eat dinner at least, but I was beginning to think I had caught some kind of stomach bug, because I was feeling kind of nauseous again.

My Knight: Made it.

Lucas' first text to me came through with a picture of him and Lisa. The cabin behind them glowed from the warm light pouring through the window. It was covered in snow making the two siblings pop out more. They sported large smiles, and it warmed my heart to see.

Olive: Have fun! I miss you already.

My Knight: Hard to have fun without my Rose :'(I miss you!

I sent him a picture of myself sprawled on the bed with my books all around me.

Olive: I dare say you're having more fun than me.

My Knight: I wish I was there with you. I miss you in my arms.

Olive: I know what you mean, but try, and enjoy yourself with your mom and Lisa. I know they could both use your happiness.

My Knight: Then I should have brought you.

I smiled like an idiot at his text.

Olive: Are you saying I'm your happiness?

My Knight: Isn't it obvious by now? You're my happiness, Olive Brewer. Now go to sleep. It's getting late, and you have a decent trip ahead of you tomorrow. No driving while you're sleepy!

Olive: Yes, sir! Don't worry, I'm a safe driver. Good night, my Knight. I love you.

My Knight: Goodnight, my Rose. I love you!

I moved my books off the bed and got myself cozily in bed. It felt odd sleeping without him by my side. I was happy knowing he was with his family safe and sound. I fell asleep thinking of him, allowing myself to dream of him. *Tomorrow I go home.*

I woke up throwing up again. I hate stomach bugs, especially when I have a long drive ahead. I'll probably have to pull over a lot more if I continue to stay nauseous. This better stop before Thanksgiving because I refuse to not feel well enough to eat Hailey's family's cooking, or Leo's.

I grabbed my suitcase and headed towards the amazing car mom left me. She made sure I was taken care of before she left, maybe as her way of making up for those long years without her. I threw the suitcase in the trunk before taking my seat. I had to adjust the driver seat, since Lucas drove last. I wish he was driving me now. Maybe next time I go, I'll take him with me and he can see where I liked to hang out.

I started the playlist I created this morning for the road trip. It was a mixture of energized music and soft melancholy tunes. I wanted to wallow in missing Lucas, but also needed to not get tired. I forget how beautiful the drive home can be with the foliage of fall. I wished I could put the top down and enjoy the sun against my skin, but the crisp cold air of New

York's November told me it was a terrible idea. The drive was relaxing, and I only had to pull over once to throw up. It wasn't too terrible considering. I need to go to the doctor when I get back.

Welcome to Portsmouth

The familiar green sign with white border welcomed me as I entered my hometown. The historic buildings of downtown came into view as I drove into town. Nothing changes much here. The ice skating rink at the Starwbery Banke Museum was open again, littered with kids who were out of school this week in preparation for the holiday.

The owner of the music hall must have had the sign fixed since I was last here, having all of its letters flash brightly again. I headed to the Water Street Inn. It's far enough away I won't risk running into dad, but close enough so I won't be driving an hour away to get into town. The historic house came into view, with its beautiful landscaping.

"Good afternoon," I was greeted as I entered the door. "Do you have a reservation?"

"Yes, it should be under Brewer."

"Ah, yes, welcome Ms. Brewer. We have you booked in room 2."

After some finagling of the computer she grabbed the key and led me to the room. I placed my suitcase on the bed and began to unpack my things. I decided I'd go pay Joe a visit first. He is the only friend I have here. If you can even call him my friend. He's more of my therapist/tattoo artist, and if you ask either, they can't be your friend. Maybe I'll have a session. I've been itching to ink my sink more.

I grabbed some lunch before heading to the Iron Works Tattoo parlor on Congress Street. The small shop between Jumpin Jay's and The Goat Entertainment came into view. Its welded sign still hung over the shop. The glass was always clean, letting me peer in before entering. I could see Joe, leaned over a woman working his magic on her ankle. I opened the door to find a new face behind the counter.

CHAPTER 39

"Welcome to Iron Works Tattoos. What can we do for you?" she asked me. She screamed hardcore chick with her multitude of piercings and neck tattoos. She had her hair dyed a faded blue with large gauges on her ears. She didn't smile much, looking at me like I shouldn't be here.

"I'm here to see Joe. I'll wait." I answered her, taking no offense to her presumptions.

I scrolled through my phone trying to find something good to add onto my numerous torso tattoos. I know in the end Joe will do what Joe wants. About 10 minutes later, the woman Joe had been working on paid and left. Joe was busy cleaning his instruments, still not noticing me. He was always very oblivious when he was focused on something.

"Joe, you got a customer!" The blue-haired girl called back to him.

Joe was a big guy, not necessarily the one you would pick to do your tattoos. His looks made you believe he didn't know the definition of gentle, but you would be very wrong, as Joe is the gentlest man around. I have never so much as felt a jolt of terrible pain when he's worked on me. His thick dark brown eyebrows, which were a shade darker than his brown hair, furrowed as he turned. He seemed upset by the fact someone had interrupted his routine. His rich hazel eyes looked almost green with flecks of gold today. He smiled as he recognized me.

"How is my beaut?" He asked about the tattoos he had made. I lifted my shirt to show it off, impressing the girl behind the counter. "Pause, that's not mine." He pointed to the pink ribbon with a scowl.

"Yeah, I know. I needed it, and you weren't exactly a close drive." I shrugged. He narrowed his eyes as he approached to investigate it further. His rough large finger traced over the ribbon as if he were trying to imagine how the tattoo had been done. He shook his head in disappointment, clearly not happy with it.

"Come on, I'll fix it. She deserves better than this." He

pulled me to his table without letting me say a word. My chest tightened at his words. He knew who it was for. He saw the name, recognized the symbol, and noticed the date.

"Thank you, Joe," I whispered as he got to work on my side.

"Start talking. I know you're dying to tell me everything that is bothering you," he said as his needle made contact with my skin. I started by telling him about Hailey and how she helped me. I then moved on to Julius and how I finally lost my virginity. He scrunched his nose in disgust at the revelation.

"Didn't need to know that part, Cherry Bomb." I hadn't heard him call me that in a long time. Sweet as a cherry with the explosive anger of a bomb, he'd explained it to me when he first gave me the nickname.

"Too bad, now you know. Anyway, I'm not done so shhh." I continued on with my story, telling him about Lucas, then Leo. I told him about mom, then Lucas some more.

"Moved in already?!" He arched his brow, surprised I would be so reckless in his eyes.

"Yes, *moved* in. It was right for us, so fuck everyone else's timeline of how things should go." I nodded with determination.

"Alright, way to blow up the norms. Continue." I told him about how dad is having a baby with some new girlfriend. I then asked him to watch out for her and let me know if he sees anything suspicious when it comes to her health.

"I'm not some secret agent for you, Cherry Bomb, so I'm not going out of my way to check on this girl, but if I see anything I'll let you know."

"Thanks, Joe."

"Alright, all done. Here." He handed me a mirror to look at it. He'd outlined the ribbon in black and added flowers to come out the center top. They were her favorites, orange tulips. He then wrote one of mom's favorite sayings from the movie Forest Gump, the one about the box of chocolates.

"It's perfect. Thank you, Joe. However, how you know

these things about my mother astounds me." I arched a brow at him curiously.

"Did she never tell you?"

"Tell me what?" I propped myself up on my elbows, extremely interested now.

"I was the one that helped her leave, kid." He grabbed the white gauze as he dropped that bombshell on me.

"You?"

"Yeah, me. We went to high school together, and we were once close friends. She was the one that got away."

"Fucking shit, Joe." My mind was reeling, refusing to process the words that came out of his mouth. *The one that got away. I guess I have one of those too.*

"Did you know where she was all this time?"

I couldn't look at him as I asked, keeping my eyes on the ceiling, trying to hold back tears. I've poured my heart out to this man many times, trusted him with everything, and he never once told me he knew mom. He never once stopped me and told me *'I know, Cherry Bomb. I know it all'*. He let me complain about how she abandoned me and how dad was an ass.

"No, I didn't. She didn't know where she was going when she left. I helped her get out and hide her steps along the way. I hid the money she saved to escape as well as a go bag. She asked me to look out for you, to save you if his fists ever turned to you in her stead. How do you think you ended up on my chair without permission at 17?" he asked me, like it should have been obvious.

"I don't know. I thought I was charming, or maybe you pitied me enough not to care." I wiped at the side of my eyes where a tear had rolled out. "Thank you for helping her, Joe." I whispered with my voice cracking.

My emotions poured out of me like a river. My tears couldn't be stopped, keeping my wrists over my eyes and wiping them continuously. I wanted more time with her... needed more time with her. I wish she could have told me about Joe herself. There's so much I still don't know about her, pieces of her I am still learning about. I tried to imagine her and Joe in high school, but it was a hard image to picture.

"Come on, Cherry Bomb, let's go get a cup of me and talk more." I laughed at his pun, a cup of joe.

"Okay, I expect all the details about you and my mom." I pointed at him as I got off his table.

"I'll be back later, Vicky, taking a lunch break."

Blue-haired girl, apparently named Vicky, nodded at him. Her eyes roamed my body, assessing me like she still wasn't sure of me. I returned her gaze, showing her I don't shy away just because someone was looking at me. She could have fucking face tattoos and I would still return her gaze. She's not hard.

Time to fess up, Joe

Chapter 40

Lucas' P.O.V.

My sweet Rose arrived in her hometown a little while ago. She had been sending me texts all day about what she was up to. I snapped a picture of the hot chocolate I was drinking beside the fire with Lisa, sending it to her with a smile.

Rose: You have hot chocolate, but I have joe.

She replied with a picture of a cup of coffee and a big burly tattooed man who looked like he could butcher people for a living. *Rose has some interesting company.*

Lucas: Should I be worried?

Rose: Ha! No way. Joe's my mom's ex, my tattoo artist and my therapist all in one. You'll meet him when we come here together.

I smiled, knowing she wanted me to come with her next time. It made me happy to know she wanted to introduce me to others. She's not afraid to show me off.

Lucas: And when will that be? I'm not a very patient man, you know.

Rose: How about the week after the championship?

Lucas: Sounds perfect. I miss you. I'll let you focus on Joe now.

Rose: I love you

Lucas: I love you too.

Rose: In case you're wondering, I miss you too.

I can't wait to have her back in my arms. I am going to devour her when I see her again. I won't let her out of my sight. She is going to be kept in bed with me all day.

"What's Liv up to?" Lisa asked with a knowing smirk.

"She's catching up with an old friend."

"That's good. I'm glad you guys are getting some time to yourself. You are so attached at the hip. That can't be healthy." Lisa gave me her unwanted opinion. I rolled my eyes at her, making her do the same to me.

"Who asked you?" I bit back.

"Don't get snappy with me. I'm saying you guys need to remember you're two separate people. You can't be with each other *all* of the time."

"You two stop it. This is supposed to be my gift, so no bickering," Mom scolded us.

"Sorry, Mom," we said in unison.

"Jinx!" Lisa pointed with a laugh. I rolled my eyes again at her.

"We're not five, Lisa."

"Oof, tell that to the laws of superstition when they come for you with bad luck for breaking my jinx." I watched her shake her head like she was so disappointed in me. I was glad to see she was still being herself after what had happened. The guy hadn't bothered her since Rose beat the ever living shit out of him. I am sure Viking Man and Mr. Clean sealed the deal. I would have shit myself if I were left alone with those two after a small girl beat me up.

"Lucas, why did you bring so many journals?" Mom asked, picking one up. I ran quickly towards her, taking the journal from her hand before she peered inside it.

"They're Rose's old journals. The ones she's letting me read."

"Hmm, that's quite a lot of them. Why is she making you read them all?" Mom's brow pinched in the middle, a bit upset.

"She isn't making me. I wanted to, and she allowed me to," I corrected her.

"I don't think I would ever want my boyfriend reading my journals. Especially not my high school ones. She's either very brave or very naive." Mom gave me her unnecessary commentary.

"Weren't you and Lisa about to go shopping?" I reminded her, ready for her to stop talking about Rose.

"Yes, we're going now. Call if you need anything, and stay out of trouble while we're gone." She pinched my cheek for a moment before heading towards the door with Lisa.

"No problem. I'll keep myself busy." I held up the journals to let her know I'd be reading. I heard the car we rented back out of the driveway and onto the narrow road which led to the cabin. I know they'll make it and be fine, but I hate thinking about them driving in the snow. I tried to push the thought out, replacing it with Rose's journal.

Dear Future Me,

Ian still has not written back. It's almost the end of June. Should I have gotten something by now?

To distract myself and to try to get out of the house I used the bike Ian left to try and find a job. Guess what? We did it! It was super random and very weird, but we have a job at the Iron Work Tattoo Parlor starting tomorrow. I was inquiring in different restaurants and fast food places when I heard a strong male voice from across the street.

"Hey, kid!" A large intimidating man called to me. I didn't know what to say, but I didn't shy away. "Come here, redhead." he called me over to me.

I crossed the street a bit wearily of the large man. I figured I could probably take him if I needed to. When I got to him, he folded his arms in front of his chest and looked down at me.

"Are you looking for a job?" He had asked me.

"Yes, I am," I answered cautiously.

"Perfect, you start here tomorrow," he told me, going back into the tattoo shop I'm almost certain I'm not even allowed inside of. I didn't say anything, allowing myself to have the small victory of finding a job. I guess we'll have to see how it goes.

A hopeful, Past You

I smiled, imagining the same large man from her

picture randomly telling her she got a job she didn't even apply for. This must be around the time she starts to get tattoos. I wonder which one she got first?

Dear future me,

Joe is the man's name who gave us the job yesterday. He said we look too nice to be greeting people, so he placed me in the back, helping clean and sanitize everything.

Joe is a big guy with many tattoos himself. He does nice work on everyone, but they complain because it isn't exactly what they asked for. Joe makes it better, so much better. He gives them what they want in a better way and they should honestly be grateful. I watched him work on a lot of people today. There were some crazy tattoo ideas and some very emotional ones as well. Joe did both jobs with the same seriousness.

I like the place. They play good music, the people all look intimidating, but are all very nice. Besides, I like getting to see how tattoos are done. I liked watching someone's skin come to life with ink. I wonder if I could get one too. It would be nice. I'd let Joe do mine. I like his work the best, even if it isn't exactly what you asked for.

Joe was annoyed with me a lot of the time. He scolded me when I did something wrong, taking it and doing it for me. I will learn, and I'll get better. I don't like doing a bad job on anything. I'll impress Joe.

A determined, Past You

P.S. Still no word from Ian. Hopefully, soon.

I loved having that picture of Joe now. It was nice to have an image to go along with the man she wrote about. I found myself almost laughing, picturing Rose in there working. I think I like this Joe already. I think I see what happened with Ian now too. He ghosted my sweet Rose. Fucking asshole. How dare he worm his way into her heart and then rip it out when he moved?

He could volunteer in all the non-profit organizations and be the nicest guy on the planet. I still wouldn't like him for hurting my Rose. I hope Rose feels the same way. Would she give him the time of day if he popped up in her life again? I would hope not, but I wouldn't stop her if she did. It's her life and if she wants to reconnect with him as a friend, then I'll bite my tongue.

Lucas: I think you forgot to say ex-boss in your description of Joe.

Rose: Oh God, you're already there?

Lucas: I'm determined to read my journals before you graduate. Trying to get through your high school years by the end of this semester.

Rose: Don't judge me too much. I'm over here blushing.

She sent me a picture of herself, with her cheeks prominently tinted a rosy red. She is so beautiful, especially when she blushes.

Lucas: I don't judge, babe. I only tease ;)

Rose: I know you do. I'm still sore from your teasing :p

The reminder of what we'd done before I left rushed all the blood straight to my dick.

Lucas: You'll be sore again when I see you, Rose. There's no getting away from it.

Rose: I can't wait.

I can't wait either.

Olive's P.O.V.

After talking with Joe for most of the afternoon. I decided to head to the bookstore. The one, according to Joe, dad's girlfriend works at. He told me her name and described her in Joe-terms to me yesterday.

"Blank skin, very plain. She's got a long neck that could use some free birds. Dark hair, and a round face that screams innocence. She's young too." He told me.

So now here I am, stepping inside some book shop to spy on dad's girlfriend. I wonder if she even knows about me? Has she seen any pictures of me? I know there is only one hanging on our wall. Any pictures with mom had been burned away when I turned 12, leaving one hanging frame of me when I was a baby, sporting a big toothless grin. I don't think she'd be able to recognize me from that picture, even if she had seen it.

I grabbed a book off a display table, flipping it and looking interested in it as I eyed the dark haired woman behind the counter. Her name was Daisy, according to the name tag. She had a round face, a long neck, and dark hair. So it's gotta be her right? I continued to walk around the store, looking at her through the shelves or past books. I hid in an aisle with my head peeking out to watch her. She would rub the small bump on her stomach every now and again, letting me know she was pregnant. *This must be her.* Joe wasn't kidding. She looked young. Probably around my age. That's so fucking gross. *Why would she be with dad?*

I forgot to pay attention to my surroundings as I watched her closely. I was looking to see if she had any marks on her. My eyes were trained at the hem of her sleeves to see if any bruises would show when they moved. She didn't seem to wince or act like she was in pain. For now, she seemed safe, and so did my little sibling.

"Red?" His voice sent a chill down my spine. It was a voice I had dreamt of countless times, only it was deeper, raspier with age. I gripped the edge of the shelf in front of me, trying to keep myself from turning immediately. I swallowed down the emotions that were building up inside me. "Is that you, Red?" *What is he doing here?*

I turned slowly, meeting those blue eyes I had once fallen in love with. He'd grown more, but he wasn't as tall as my Knight. His hair was still that golden blonde, but he styled it differently. It was long at the top falling towards his ears in a purposeful mess. It seems, like wine, he had only gotten finer with age. His eyes met mine, and I almost lost my grip on my self control.

"Ian?" I finally spoke.

"So that is you!" He smiled widely now, making my

heart race the way it used to for him. "You've changed, Red. You look great!" He added, only making me blush.

"You too," I said awkwardly as he stepped closer, invading my personal bubble. For a moment, I thought he was going to kiss me. I panicked, almost punching him before I realized he was going past me. He peered his head around the aisle curiously.

"What are we looking at?" He asked me as he scanned the place. I'd forgotten how carefree he was. I grabbed the back of his loose jacket, pulling him into the aisle again before he was spotted.

"You're going to get me caught," I lightly scolded him in a hushed voice.

"Ooo, who are we spying on?" He gave me that playful smirk of his. The one that let me know he was ready for mischief and gossip.

"None of your business." I brushed him off. As much as I have missed him, he's the one who chose to end our friendship when he didn't reply.

"Come on, Red. Pretty please?" He gave me the same smile he used to give me in high school. His pretty, please smile, I called it.

"That's not going to work anymore. I've grown, Ian." I started to walk away only to be met by dad's figure approaching the store, blocking my only exit.

"*Shit,*" I muttered under my breath, causing Ian to lean over me again to see what I was looking at. I felt the radiating heat from his chest against my back. His shirt lightly grazed my own. Before I knew it, he was pulling me back into the aisle. He took his jacket off and placed it on me, pulling the hood up to cover my hair. I placed my arms in the sleeves, only because I needed the jacket to hide.

I pushed all the red under the hood and tightened the strings. Ian leaned forward again, closing the space between us. My heart was racing against my chest, wondering what he was doing. His sweet eyes held mine for a moment before he put a book in front of me. It was a thick book, he had me cover my face with it. His hand stayed leaning against the shelf over me, covering me from the main aisle.

A few minutes passed, and neither of us moved. I kept my eyes on the book he had handed me. I was actually reading it, trying to distract myself from Ian's close proximity. It was about how to forgive those who have wronged you. I have a hard time with that one. I tend to drop them from my life and pretend they don't exist. *Seems healthy enough to me.*

"I see who you were spying on now." His voice tickled my ear as he whispered in it. "He brought her food."

I sighed, finally looking into his eyes again. Damn him, damn those eyes, and damn these emotions that are wanting to confuse the hell out of me.

"I don't want to talk about it."

"Bull. You totally want to talk about it. I can see it ready to burst from those lips."

"I don't want to talk about it with *you*. Is he gone now?" I asked him, moving away as best I could.

"He's gone." He nodded with a sad smile.

"Thanks for your help," I said, taking his jacket off and handing it back. "Goodbye, Ian." I started to walk off, only to be grabbed by the wrist and pulled into his chest. He held me tightly in his warm embrace. The one he'd give me when he knew I was going through something rough at home. His familiar scent enticed my mind and my heart. A sweet nostalgia gripped my heart tightly.

"I swore if I saw you again, I wouldn't let you go. Why didn't you write to me, Red?" My heart squeezed, feeling like it would pop soon. I pushed away from his chest, only to be gripped more tightly.

"Why didn't *I* write to you? Why didn't *you* reply? I wrote to you. I wrote to you many times actually, and every day I would check the mail and there would be nothing. It was maddening, and eventually I gave up, snuffing out the last ray of hope in my life." I pushed him hard, making his grip loosen enough for me to see his face.

"I never got one, Red. I checked every day too. I wrote to you as well, only they'd always come back as return to sender. They were left unopened." He looked at me tenderly. He didn't sound like he was lying, but it was hard to believe.

"That doesn't make sense. I never saw your letters, not once." I shook my head, furrowing my brow.

"I'll show you, Red. I kept them all." He relinquished me from his embrace, only to take my hand and rush me out of the bookstore.

"Ian, hold on," I said lightly. He was so determined he didn't hear me. He continued to drag me down the street amongst the historical red bricks of almost every building. "Ian!" I shouted his name this time. He stopped immediately, turning to face me.

"Red, please. You don't understand." He shook his head.

"*You* don't understand." I told him as I ran towards the nearest trash can and puked my guts out. All these surprises had turned my stomach sour again. I felt a large, warm hand rub my back as I puked. It was comforting. It didn't matter how much time had passed, Ian will always be Ian, and my heart will always have this bittersweet feeling towards him.

"Are you okay now?" He asked me when I finished throwing up.

"As good as I can be." I wiped at my mouth with the back of my sleeve.

"Where are you staying? I'll drive you there."

"I'm at the Water Street Inn, but I can get there just fine on my own," I told him, standing straight to try to appear better than I felt at the moment.

"Alright, I'm going to grab those letters from home. I'll see you there, Red." He ran off, knowing I was going to argue.

"Ian.no!" I yelled after him, seeing him stick his fingers in his ear to pretend like he couldn't hear me. He's still so annoyingly playful. *What's he doing here anyway?*

Chapter 41

Olive's P.O.V.

I felt antsy as I paced the room, knowing Ian would be coming here soon. I stared at my phone to see Lucas' contact. Why do I feel almost guilty for running into Ian? I didn't invite him over or initiate the conversation. Hell, I tried to get away.

Olive: You won't believe who else I ran into today.

I decided to text him about it. Then it won't feel like such a bad thing, right?

My Knight: Hmm, let's see. A high school bully who saw you today, and questioned their life decisions?

His answer made me let out a laugh.

Olive: No, although, it would feel amazing to rub my life in some people's faces.

My Knight: I give up then. Who did you run into?

Olive: Ian. He was at the bookstore when I was spying on my dad's girlfriend.

I sent the first message typing out the second when my phone started to vibrate in my hand. Lucas was calling me, no longer interested in texting about this…he wanted to talk. My heart raced with worry, making me feel like I was about to get scolded.

"Hello?" I answered wearily.

"Rose, do I need to be worried?" He sounded so vulnerable when he asked, making my chest hurt.

"No. I'm yours Lucas. There's nothing to worry about."

"Does he know?" He asked, making me realize I actually hadn't told Ian anything.

"Not yet. I didn't get a chance when I was trying to run away from him."

"That's my girl." I could hear the smile on Lucas' face. "Don't let him back in, Rose. He hurt you deeply. If I can feel your hurt from reading about it in a journal, I can't imagine how much pain you were actually in."

"I know, my Knight. Don't worry, I can handle this one myself."

"Olive, if you decide you want him to be your friend again, I won't judge you. I'll watch him carefully, but aside from that, I will be kind to him."

"Thank you, Lucas. He's actually meeting me to show me letters he said he sent. He told me he wrote to me, but the letters would return unopened with a return to sender written on them." I sighed as I plopped back on my bed, staring up at the ceiling.

"Do you believe him?" He asked, very interested in the answer.

"I don't know. I guess I'll believe him when I see it for myself."

"I love you, Rose. Do me a favor and punch him if he's lying."

I let out a laugh, smiling as I answered him now.

"I love you too, my Knight. I'll do more than just punch him if he's lying."

"Good girl, Rose." I smiled as he called me that, feeling happy, knowing we were okay. He's okay, and wants to make sure I'm okay. "I better go. I lied and told Lisa and Mom I needed to use the restroom so I could call you without them present. I better get back before the restaurant thinks I'm clogging up the toilet here." He made me chuckle, picturing him hiding away in a bathroom to call me.

"I love you, Lucas. Thank you for calling."

"I love you too, Olive. Guard your heart, and let me know how it goes."

We both hung up, and I felt a lot better after our

conversation. Running into Ian didn't feel like such a dirty little secret anymore. *I can't wait to be back in Lucas' arms.* The knock on my door had me bolting out of my bed. I opened it to find Ian on the other side with a shoe box in his hand. I stepped out into the hall, because I am not letting him into my room.

"The garden here, or our old spot?" he asked me with his charming smile.

"Garden." Going to our old spot didn't feel right. Ian isn't a liar. At least he never was in high school, so I want to believe him about the letters, but at the same time it sounds far-fetched.

Song suggestion: "The Winner Takes It All" by Mack Lorén

I led the way through the inn towards the back doors, exiting the building into the cool air. The smell of the flowers was sweet in the air with the warm sun helping to keep the cold from sinking deep into my bones. We took a seat on a metal bench in the corner.

"Here." He handed me the box, which I placed on my lap, and slowly opened. Surely enough, there were dozens of red envelopes. I grabbed one, seeing my name on it with the correct address. When I turned it over, I could see the *return to sender* scribbled on the back in familiar penmanship. *Dad.*

This entire time, I believed Ian had never written to me. I believed he didn't care about me. I let myself think our 2 year friendship meant nothing to him, yet it was my dad's fault. I'm not sure what motive he could have had to do something like this. It didn't make sense, but the proof was in my hands. My eyes watered up as the insecure teenager in me began to heal. *He didn't abandon us.*

There were so many letters, all stamped with different dates. Despite getting every single one back, he would still write. I felt a tear slide down my cheek as I stared at these red envelopes. I felt so overwhelmed with bitter happiness. Happy he didn't abandon me, but so bitter we didn't get a chance to stay in touch. *How I could have used these letters...especially that night.*

The tears were pouring out of me now. It was almost crushing me to see these letters, to know things could have been so different. I felt Ian scoot closer, wrapping his arm over my shoulders and pulling me into his side. I cried on him, clutching onto the box for dear life. I know its such a big reaction to some letters, but these weren't just letters. Back then, these would have been lifelines for me. Teenage me could have used a friend, could have used the knowledge she was wanted, even if just by one person. Joe didn't count.

"I'm sorry, Red." Ian whispered, squeezing me tight. I shook my head on his chest.

"No, *I'm* sorry, Ian. This was my dad, and I had no idea. Maybe he's why you didn't get my letters, too." I tried to think back to when I'd leave the letter in the mailbox for the mailman to take. Dad could have easily taken it.

"Red, I promise I wrote to you almost every day. You were on my mind often while I was in London. I'd search you at least once a month on social media in case your dad had somehow changed his mind and gotten you a phone." He was telling me so many things I'd long to hear when I was 16. "I worried about you daily, but I figured, or more like I hoped, you had moved on from me. I hoped you had a new best friend who was keeping you safe. Someone who was rescuing you the way I used to." His hand found my chin, lifting me up to look at him. "You were so precious to me, Red, still are." He kissed my forehead, surprising me.

"I didn't have anyone then, but I do now. I have a best friend, Hailey, and a boyfriend named Lucas. My friends aren't plenty, but the few I have are important." Ian nodded his head at my words. His eyes shimmered as he looked at me. I could almost see longing behind those blue eyes. It's arrogant thinking. Why would he long for me?

"Keep the letters. They were meant to be yours, anyway." He told me, wiping the tears from my eyes. "It may be a lot to ask for, but Red, can we be friends again?" I contemplated it for a moment. The only reason we're not is currently sitting on my lap. He didn't hurt me, dad did, *again*. I nodded my head at him, wiping my tears away.

"I would like that." I nodded my head, making him give me that wide smile I'd missed. "When did you move back to the states?"

"I moved back for college. My mom followed suit, missing Portsmouth. Dad is still overseas, but he's coming into town tomorrow.You know I searched for you when I came back, but you didn't have any social media. Your dad wouldn't tell me what college you were attending or even give me your phone number. I am so happy I ran into you Red. You should come say hi to my parents. They miss you, too. Maybe then you can fill me in on what's going on with your dad?"

He arched a brow, tilting his head towards me like he used to do when he knew I was holding back. I laughed, almost forgetting his silly antics. I couldn't believe Dad never told me about Ian coming to look for me. Given what I know about the letters now, it doesn't surprise me. Had he found me when he first came back he would have saved me from Julius.

"Yeah, okay, I'll come. Is it still the same house?"

"The one and only." He nodded. "Here, give me your number and I'll text you when dad gets in town." He held his phone out for me to take. I dug my own out of my pocket, handing it to him when I took his. I typed my number in his phone, saving myself as his preferred name for me, **Red**. When I took my phone back, I saw he'd save himself as **#1 best friend**.

"I don't know if that's true anymore." I raised a brow at him with a playful smirk.

"I'll make it true." He winked at me. I didn't realize how much I needed this closure.,, these letters. *Thank you, Ian.*

I woke up the next morning with this stomach bug still present. I guess I should be grateful it hasn't made me throw up all day long. My eyes were still sticky with sleep. I was exhausted, having stayed up late talking with Ian. We spoke in person till the sunset and then we texted almost all night.

Lucas and I texted all night, too. He didn't get much sleep. He said he needs me in his arms to get any semblance of sleep. I let him know how things went with Ian and he said he was happy for me. I don't know how true those words are. I think it bothers him a little that we're friends again. I'm not sure, but I hope not.

#1 Best Friend: Good morning, sleepy Red. If you're anything like teenage Red, then you're still asleep. In which case, I hope this wakes you 3:)

Olive: Jokes on you, I am already awake :p

I was feeling happy to have my first best friend back in my life. I feel whole again.

Olive: Good morning, my Knight. I hope you were able to get some sleep. I miss you terribly. Also, this stomach bug won't leave me alone. I'm still throwing up :(

Olive: I demand you make it stop.

My Knight: I wish I could. I miss you my Rose. Think mom and Lisa would notice if I fly back to you today?

His text made me grin so widely.

Olive: They would definitely notice. Your presence is very much noted when it's gone. I wish you could though. I need to be wrapped around you again. These next few days can't pass by fast enough.

My Knight: I need you, Olive. I need you desperately.

I was in the middle of typing my reply to Lucas when my phone buzzed with a text from Ian.

Olive: I need you too.

I sent it to Lucas before opening Ian's text.

#1 Best Friend: *gasp* She wakes before 10 now?

I laughed at his message. I used to be quite the sleepy head when I was younger.

Olive: She's grown now.

My Knight: Have fun today, and be careful with your dad. I love you my Rose.

Olive: I love you too, my Knight. Tell Lisa and your mom I say hi.

I got myself dressed for the day, ignoring the buzzing of my phone while I got ready. With my hair braided, and a thick turtleneck sweater dress and ankle boots on, I headed out.

#1 Best Friend: Look what I found.

It was a picture of a stuffed animal I had won for him at a fair the summer after freshman year.

#1 Best Friend: He's a little worn and torn, but still kicking it.

Olive: Oh my gosh! Poor little fella. He's had to deal with you for all these years xD

#1 Best Friend: Harsh.

#1 Best Friend: Come to the house at 2 today. Dad will be here then and mom's making dinner. She said she can't wait to see you again.

Mrs. Daniels was the absolute sweetest woman on this planet. She was joy and warmth bottled into a person. I missed her too when Ian left.

Olive: I can't wait to see her, too.

I snuck by the bookstore again, watching dad's new girlfriend. She was kind, and it only made me worry for her more. Kind people don't usually stand up for themselves. I hope I'm wrong. I decided to take a gamble and interact with her. I grabbed a book that looked interesting and went to check out.

"Did you find everything okay?" She asked me with a smile.

"Sure did." I nodded, smiling back. She rang me up, rubbing her stomach after she placed the book in a big.

"How far along are you?" I asked her.

"You can tell? I'm only about 15 weeks along." She blushed as she answered.

"I assumed since you kept rubbing it. You don't look big or anything." I tried to retract my rude ass question. I knew she was pregnant, but it didn't mean she actually looked it.

"Yeah. I've formed a habit of doing that now." She smiled down at her little bump as she rubbed it. "It helps me remember he's there."

"He? So you're having a boy?" My chest tightened at the news. Dad had always wanted a son, someone, to take his place in the ring. Someone he imagined would actually win.

"Yeah, we did the early blood test. I couldn't wait any longer." She giggled as she told me. She was in love with the bump. It was sweet to see.

"Congratulations."

"Thank you."

I finished checking out, grabbing my things. I should have paid more attention again. My head must be in the clouds, because in came dad. His eyes landed on me instantly, but I didn't shy away. In fact, I decided to use this public setting to have words. I marched towards him, seeing him look past me at Daisy. He looked worried. *She must not know about me.*

"How could you keep Ian's letters from me?" I started right off the bat. He opened and closed his mouth like a fish out of water for a few seconds. I caught him off guard. I guess he assumed I would be asking him about the baby or his too-young-for-him girlfriend.

"Why's that matter? It was years ago. What are you doing here, anyway?"

"I won't answer until you do." I crossed my arms. "Better hurry before Daisy wonders who I am. I don't think you told her about me. Are you trying to keep your past a secret, and start over? Make sure you don't repeat the same mistakes." I could tell I was angering him, but I couldn't help myself. I felt so bitter right now... bitter and mean.

"You didn't need to be wrapped up in a boy. It was desperate. He moved to a different country, and you needed to let him go."

"You had no right to decide that! I'm in town visiting old friends, and learning all sorts of new things about you. Good luck with the new kid. I'll be keeping a watch. If I see so much as a bruise on either of them, you can kiss your happy new future goodbye." I walked past him, and out into the fresh air, leaving behind the smell of books and coffee, and maybe a little piece of myself. *I hope he can give you a better life than me, my little brother.*

I am going to have a brother soon. I wonder if he will know about me. Will I be mentioned or forgotten...a shameful piece of his past, I guess we'll see. I made my way to Joe's shop, knowing exactly what I wanted and where. I slammed the tattoo shop door open, letting the cold breeze enter with me. Vicky's eyes widened as she watched me march straight up to Joe and hopped on his table.

"Purple ribbon beside the pink one. And a red envelope over the semicolon." I told him, not waiting a second.

"Start talking," he said as he got his instruments ready.

I told him about Ian and the envelopes. I told him how dad kept them from me with a sad ass excuse. I told him about the way I was feeling. How bitter I felt at him starting a new family and acting like I didn't exist in this new chapter of his life. I spiraled from there, talking all kinds of shit about him. I was furious and deeply hurt all at the same time. It didn't take Joe long to finish since it was two simple things.

The purple ribbon sat beside the pink one. He wrote *forever stronger than you* inside it. I liked that part a lot. The red envelope swallowed the black semicolon, as if it was coming out the envelope itself. He wrote *Life goes on* inside it. He knew why I got the semicolon. It was the only time he gave me exactly what I had asked for.

"Thanks for the therapy session, Joe. What do I owe you?"

"Go see Vicky. She'll check you out." Joe looked upset as I got up. I think he was mad over everything I'd said about my dad.

I checked out with Vicky, getting a nice Joe discount. The site stung a bit, but I liked the feeling. It distracted me from my other pain. My phone rang in my pocket, making me stop walking to fish it out. I love dresses with pockets, but these are a bit hard to get into. Lucas' name flashed across my screen, making me smile.

"Hello?"

"We need to talk." He immediately answered, sounding pissed for some reason.

What happened?

Chapter 42

Lucas' P.O.V.

Song suggestion: "Repeat Until Death" by Novo Amor

I was deep into her junior year. It had been complete misery for her. The bullying was relentless, and her home wasn't any better. She felt lost, depressed, and extremely lonely. She still worked with Joe, but she didn't count him as her friend, even though he was her only social interaction. My heart broke for her immensely. I can't imagine having to face everything she has been through by herself.

Dear Future Me,

If there even is a future for me. I guess I should say dear future whoever is reading this. I've decided today is the last day I'm going to take the harassment at school. The last day I'll spar with dad and feel his fists on my torso.

It's not worth it anymore. The ache in my chest has grown into a crater too big for me to handle. It has swallowed me whole and immersed me in its darkness. There's no light here, no hope. I'm alone, bitterly and utterly alone.

No one cares for me, not even the two people on this planet meant to. I'm unwanted, I'm tired, and so I'm giving in. I'm relenting to the voice in my head that says life will be better once I'm dead.

I can't imagine a single person who would be saddened by the news. The school may even throw a party when I'm gone. Dad would probably be mad I left a mess. I hope he regrets his life decisions as he cleans up my blood. I hope he realizes the pain he caused me and mom. She didn't love me enough to take me with her. If your own parents can't love you, who can?

Goodbye and sorry for the mess.

I think my heart stopped. Was this a suicide note? Did my Rose feel so alone she…I can't even say it. I felt tears stream down my face as I hugged the journal. *Not my Rose.* I grabbed my phone, needing to hear her voice. Did she go through with it? Did she attempt to take her life?

"Hello?" her beautiful voice answered.

"We need to talk," I said, a bit too sternly.

"What's wrong?" I could hear the concern in her voice.

"Rose, what is this entry in your junior year journal?"

"You know you're going to have to be more specific. There's quite a few of them." She laughed, but I didn't find it comical.

"The one that tore my heart out. Tell me you didn't go through with it. Tell me you wrote it down, and changed your mind after."

The line grew silent aside from her breathing.

"I did it." She sounded so small as she admitted her dark truth.

"Rose!" I couldn't help myself. "How could you?"

"I was young and alone. Life was dark and hopeless then, Lucas. You don't understand."

I've frowned on suicide all my life, but more so since losing Ivy and John. They didn't choose to die. They had their life stolen from them. Then there's people who take life for granted, permitting themselves the easy way out, because they can't take it anymore. It's unfair to those of us they leave behind.

"I know it wasn't okay. I'm not saying it was. I'm telling you why I did it." She sighed as she spoke. I could hear the sadness in her voice.

"You're not alone anymore," I reminded her.

"I know, I'm fine now, Lucas. I got help after."

"Rose, I'm sorry you ever felt so alone."

"I know," she sighed. "I'm sorry you read that. I forgot it was in there."

"I love you so much, Rose!"

"I love you too. So very much!"

"Good, because I'm never leaving you alone. You'll never feel alone again." Even if she broke up with me and sent me away, I would bother the hell out of her to make sure she never felt alone. Not in a mean way, of course, an annoying way...my way.

"I'll hold you to that." The smile had returned to her voice again.

"So tell me, what are you up to today?"

"I am going to Ian's house to see his mom and dad again. I've missed them. Mrs. Daniels invited me to stay for dinner, so I'll probably end up staying there all evening. I'll head back home tomorrow morning. What about you?"

"We're going skiing this evening, and then Lisa said she was going to cook dinner, so wish me luck. I may die tonight." I joked, hearing her laugh. *I love her laugh.*

"I'll pray for you," she teased.

"I miss you."

"I miss you, too. I am ready to be back home with you." She doesn't know this, but I plan to surprise her on Thanksgiving day. We're only here till Wednesday night. I'll be back in time to celebrate with her and be thankful for her.

"Me too, Rose."

"I'm at Ian's now. I better go, but I love you. Have fun skiing. Don't forget the sunblock."

"I won't. I love you, too. Have fun, call me tonight when you get back to the Inn." I want to hear all about this little dinner with Ian and his family. I can't help but feel a bit scared. What if she still loves him?

"I will. Goodbye, my Knight."

"Goodbye, my Rose." The line went dead, making me miss her voice already. I hate being away from her. I grabbed her journal, curious to see what she wrote next. What comes after something like that?

Dear future me,

I'm sorry. I am sorry I wasn't strong. I am sorry I almost killed us. I am sorry I am so weak and pathetic. I won't do it again I swear. As you know I got some help. I'd never seen dad so upset before. He was furious, but he was also concerned. I guess now I know he cares enough not to see me die. He helped stop the bleeding and took me to the emergency room. When I came home a few days later the blood had been wiped clean, all evidence of my attempt had been erased.

I imagined Dad cleaning it up, and I wondered how he felt as he did it. He's kinder and more patient with me than before. I guess he didn't notice how much pain I was in emotionally. He felt guilty. He hasn't had me spar, and he's been drinking a lot less. Honestly, things at home have gotten better, at least for now. I know he'll go back to normal in a week, tops. Still, it's nice for now.

I got my first tattoo today. Joe gave me permission, and so I put a semicolon under my right breast over my rib cage. It didn't end, only paused. School is better too. It still sucks ass, but at least the teachers are being nicer. The principal checks in on me every once in a while, too. I am picked on more now, but it's only done when a teacher leaves the room, or in the stairwells when no one is looking, so there's not as many opportunities for them to do it.

I am going to therapy now, every Tuesday after school. Dad actually takes me there and he stays and waits for me. I am okay now. I started going to the gym, and I'm dealing with my emotions in a better way. I won't wallow ever again. I won't.

A recovering,

Past You

I was glad to read that things had gotten easier, at least. I still couldn't believe she did it. It broke my heart to know, so when I see her I'm going to love on her like never before. I'm going to hold her and kiss her and never let her go again. *You're everything to me, Rose, and I'll make sure you know.*

Olive's P.O.V.

Ian's familiar Dutch colonial styled, white house with red shutters and bright red door came into view as I reached the end of the dirt road path. I missed this place with its lush green grass, no matter the time of year, such soft grass you'd think you were walking on clouds. I parked, taking a deep breath, and calming my twirling stomach. I don't know why part of me was scared of entering their house. I was scared of the feelings it would stir inside me again. The want for a normal family, for the loving embrace of a nice family.

I headed towards the door, knocking on the thick cold metal. I could hear Ian yelling "coming" as he approached the door. It swung open to reveal his tousled hair and kind smile. A smile that wrinkles the sides of his eyes in merriment. He was happy to see me. "Welcome back to my humble abode." He gestured with his arm to come in. I stepped past him, greeted by the toasty heat. Mrs. Daniels always kept it warm here during the colder months. The familiar scent of lavender and fresh linen hit me right in the heart. I had missed this smell. I took a deep breath, trying to fill my lungs with it.

"Livie! You've grown into such a beautiful young woman!" Mrs. Daniels rounded the corner with her gorgeous golden hair tied up in a large bun with some loose, curled strands.

She held her arms open wide for me to hug her as her grass green eyes scanned my body. I leaned in, giving her a hug back. I didn't realize how badly I needed a hug from her. She was like the mom I had been missing this whole time. She grabbed my face with both her hands, kissing each cheek before letting go.

"I'm so happy you could make it. We've missed your beautiful face over the years," she complained, side-eyeing Ian like it was his fault she hadn't seen me.

"I've missed you too." I smiled back at her kind eyes. Mrs. Daniels had a sculpted face like a model without the resting bitch face. She had a face which radiated warmth, and all that was good in the world.

"I'm making your favorite. At least I hope it is still your favorite." She smiled.

"Your lasagna rolls?" I almost jumped in excitement when she nodded. She made the absolute best spinach and ricotta cheese lasagna rolls I'd ever had. She's always said it's because of the Italian in her. "I can't wait! Thank you, Mrs. Daniels."

"Oh, honey, no. You're a grown woman now. Call me Caterina," she scolded me with a flick of her wrist.

"Okay, Caterina." I nodded, feeling odd saying her first name. She's always just been Mrs. Daniels.

"I better head back to the kitchen. Come help once you've said hello to Donald." I nodded my head, watching her walk through the swinging door to the kitchen in the back. She was a sight for sore eyes, if there ever was one. I was happy to be able to see her again. This whole family, actually.

"Come on, Dad's this way," Ian said with a smile as he took my hand and dragged me to the study. He slid the French doors open, showing his large father standing, looking over his desk. His light brown hair had grayed a bit in certain areas. He'd gained some weight, but still had his athletic physique. He was like a large teddy bear with a great big beard. His lips turned into a wide smile when he noticed me.

"Liv! Long time no see! So happy you could join us. Cat has been nonstop about how excited she was to have you over. It's like she forgot all about me coming into town." He laughed his big barley laugh, causing me to smile wider. I'd missed his laugh too, one that lightens your heart by just hearing it.

"I'm sorry. I don't mean to take the attention away from you," I apologized, feeling bad for him.

"Ah, it's alright. When you've been married for 25 years, you get to know each other too well. I know my Cat loves company, and she most especially loves company she hasn't seen in a while. I'm glad you two reconnected. Ian was such a mess when we first moved. The boy moped around the house depressed for a whole damn year." Donald shook his head in disappointment, crossing his arms. There was still a look of amusement on his face, like he found it funny.

"Dad!" Ian scolded him. "I didn't mope." He turned to me this time.

"Good to know," I giggled.

"It's nice to see you again, Liv." Donald beamed a smile at me as I gave him a small wave. Ian slid the doors closed behind us with a mischievous grin.

"Follow me, I wanna show you something." He walked ahead, going up the large stairs. He waited for me on the landing as he noticed I wasn't immediately following. He arched a brow at me. "What are you waiting for?"

"Just wondering if it's a good idea for me to follow." Probably wouldn't be cute for Lucas to hear I went upstairs to Ian's room with him.

"Of course it is. Now come on." He waved me over with his hand pleadingly.

"Fine," I caved, deciding I'll go up the stairs, but not into his room.

The stairs creaked in their familiar complaint. Even they missed me. Ian was silent and didn't look back as we climbed further up the stairs. He didn't turn right towards his room like I thought he would either. Instead, he turned left and then opened the door to the guest bedroom. He stepped inside the room and disappeared on the other side of the bed as he knelt down.

"What are you doing?" I asked from the doorway.

"Just getting something." His tone told me he was up to something, but I had no idea what. Six years can change a person a lot and I know Ian isn't exactly the same and neither am I. So, there is no telling what he's about to do. He stood back up with a triumphant haza. In his hand was a little old and dusty box. He brushed it off as he walked back over to me.

"I never got a chance to give this to you before I left, since I was picked up at school without warning. I was going to give this to you the day I was meant to leave after school." He handed me the box, and at first I just looked at it. I imagined what it would have been like to get this when we said goodbye. I slowly opened the box, peering inside with deep curiosity. The rose gold ring was braid-like in appearance and seemed almost woven together. I picked it up, noticing there was something engraved on the inside.

9/10 BFF

It was the date we had met, September 10th. With a heavy heart, I offered him a small smile as a bittersweet feeling stirred in my chest. *Our time was cut short.* I placed the ring on my right index finger where it fit perfectly.

"Thank you, Ian. It's very sweet." Ian surprised me with another hug. I forgot how much of a hugger he was. His arms felt familiar, felt safe. I'd missed this too.

"I better go help your mom before she finishes," I said, pulling back from his hug. I heard him sigh slightly, but then he nodded.

"You better wash up first. Use the guest bathroom here." He pointed behind him to the bathroom. I stepped through, admiring the ocean themed bathroom. Over the toilet tank was a little woven basket with toiletries for women, pads and tampons, both. I found it sweet of Caterina to have a basket like this for her female guests. I was washing my hands with warm water when I started thinking of the date. *Holy fuck, I'm late!* The water continued to pour over my hands as I stood there frozen. I ran through the dates in my head again, but every time I did, I came up 5 days late now. How did I not notice?

Could I be pregnant?

Chapter 43

Olive's P.O.V.

I spent the rest of my time in Ian's house with the thought gnawing away at me. Is there a baby growing in me right now? Am I going to have a baby the same age as my soon to be brother? *What should I do?*

I had such a strong urge to run out of Ian's house, buy a test, and pee over the damn stick. I wanted to know right now, right this very second. Instead, I helped Caterina with dinner. I helped set the table up with Ian, and sat to eat with them, making small talk with Donald. It was a very pleasant evening. One I would have enjoyed a lot more if I wasn't worried about carrying another life in me. I found myself looking at my flat stomach with great curiosity.

"What's up with you?" Ian asked me as we were clearing the table.

"What do you mean?"

"You seemed distracted all throughout dinner." I currently hate how he can still pick up on my emotions so easily.

"I don't know what you mean." I shrugged my shoulders, meandering towards the kitchen.

"Come on, Red, talk to me. Number one best friend, remember?" He followed me into the kitchen with his own stack of dishes. I bit my lip as I contemplated telling him. It didn't feel right. This was something I wanted to share with Lucas before anyone else. Although, I guess I should see if there is anything to share before I send him a message.

"Thinking about my dad and his pregnant girlfriend. I'm going to have a baby brother." I gave him something plausible and true, even though it wasn't what was currently making me feel this way.

"I'm sorry, Red. I can't believe he's managed to convince someone to be with him again. I am sure it's a lot to think about. Don't worry, your little brother will have someone looking out for him...you. You didn't get that growing up, but he will. You're already making his life better." Ian's words hit me like a strong punch.

He's right. I didn't have anyone looking out for me once mom left. Ian took that role when we met, plus Joe apparently was, too, but I had no idea. I'm going to make sure my little brother never goes through the same darkness I did. I'll make sure dad doesn't hurt him the same way he hurt me. He's going to have someone by his side, even if dad doesn't tell him who I am.

"Thank you, Ian," I whispered through the thick emotion in my throat.

"Any time, Red." He patted my head like I was a dog, so I playfully punched him in the side. He rubbed it, making an 'ow' face, but he was smiling.

I left Ian's house shortly after, racing to my car and the nearest store with a pregnancy test. I checked for Dad's pickup truck before I got out. There's no way I'm going to let him see what I'm buying right now. I raced inside, finding the aisle I needed and grabbing about three different early detection tests. My eyes caught sight of the self checkout counter, feeling the happiest I have ever been checking myself out. I double bagged it so it was hard to tell what I had bought.

I clutched onto the bag for dear life as I made my way to the car. My stomach was swirling with worry, making me nauseous again. I've been on birth control for a year now, and I'm always very diligent about taking it. The day after Lucas' accident, when I had stayed in the hospital, was the only time I had missed taking it. We didn't have sex for a week after, so I assumed I was fine. *I'm an idiot.*

I threw the bag in the passenger seat, of course, having its contents spill out. The box taunted me from the seat as if it were making fun of me for being so reckless. I grabbed it, shoving it back into the bag forcefully. It didn't take long to reach the Inn. Portsmouth isn't exactly the largest town.

I raced inside and straight into the bathroom, peeling open one of the boxes and taking the long stick out. I quickly scanned the directions, making sure there wasn't a certain way I needed to pee on this damn thing. My heart was racing, and all I wanted to do was pace back and forth. I peed, flipping the test upside down after, so I wouldn't be watching it for the three minutes I needed to wait. I decided to call Lucas, but this time I figured I should video call him. He can get the news with me.

I set the phone against the backsplash on the counter before calling. I was chewing the side of my thumbnail, pacing, when Lucas answered. His hair was wet, and his body was glistening with droplets of water. He had come out of the shower with a towel hugging his hips. *My Adonis.*

"Rose, what's wrong?" He furrowed his brow as he saw me.

I stopped pacing, turning to face him. I could see myself in the little box on the screen, looking like a mess with a crazed look in my eyes. It was obvious I was stressed the fuck out. I leaned towards the phone, whispering my answer as if the walls had ears and could tell everyone my secret.

"I'm late."

"You're late?" He furrowed his brow so hard it met in the middle. I could tell it wasn't clicking.

"Yes, my period is late," I explained, biting my lip after.

"Oh...OH....OHHH!" With each oh his voice got higher as if each oh was making him realize more and more. "Are you..?"

"I figured we could find out together." I picked up the phone, turning the camera so it was facing the test.

"Holy shit! Okay, I'm ready when you are," he assured me.

I could see the same wild look in his eyes, only there was more. He looked like he could almost be excited, and it made my heart race more. I picked up the test with shaky hands and a pounding heart, surprised Lucas couldn't hear it through the phone. I slowly turned it, reading positive on the front. We stayed silent, frozen in shock.

I'm pregnant.

"I'm coming to Portsmouth right now. I'll be there soon," Lucas said very seriously. "Don't panic. I love you, Rose." He hung up right after, without me saying a word. I was still stunned silent, looking at the test like it was mocking me. I opened the other two boxes and peed on those sticks, too. They were all a choir of positives.

I placed my hand over my flat stomach, immediately thinking of Daisy and how she would rub her bump to remind herself my brother was there. I can see why she would do it. My body doesn't feel any different, aside from what I'm realizing is not a stomach bug. *Is it morning sickness?*

I finally willed myself to leave the bathroom and the sight of the three positive tests. I laid back on the bed with my legs dangling off the side, staring at the pure white ceiling and wondering what exactly I would do. It'll be due around July, probably, so at least I will have graduated. It'll be hard to find someone willing to hire me when they see a pregnant belly. My field isn't exactly a woman led one. I have to prove myself and it's hard to do so as a mom.

I feel like I read somewhere employers like to hire women who are single, and have no kids, over a married mom. Moms miss work for their kids or their husbands more. They aren't one person anymore. Can I still do what I love to do, what I set out to do? I must have fallen asleep at some point amongst my contemplating, because I woke up to my phone vibrating in my hand.

****Song Suggestion as you read: "I Get To Love You" by

Ruelle*

Forcing my eyes to focus, I saw Lucas' contact flash across my screen. I sleepily answered, pressing the cold glass of the phone against my face.

"Hello?"

"I'm here, Rose. What room are you in?" he asked quickly. I sat up so fast my head spun for a moment.

"Room two," I finally answered.

I heard the phone go silent, seeing Lucas had hung up. I walked to my room door, opening it to see him making his way towards me. My eyes instantly watered at the sight of him. I missed him so much, despite it having only been a couple of days. I couldn't help myself. My legs ran towards him, and my arms crazily wrapped themselves around his neck. I held him tight as his arms hugged around my waist and pulled me close. He picked me up, allowing my legs to hook around his waist as he walked us towards my room. He closed the door behind him, laying me gently on the bed. Those intense brown eyes looked down at me lovingly as his hand pushed my hair out of my face softly. *I've missed him.*

His lips met mine, sending hot lava coursing through my body at his touch. I held the back of his neck, pressing on him so our kiss was more powerful. There was no stopping this, despite the news we had gotten. We both missed each other too much to let go now. Our hunger for one another was so intense, like an eternal flame. There was no extinguishing this fire.

"God, I've missed you," he whispered.

"I've missed you, too."

His lips met mine again, making our deep breaths the only noises heard. I let my hand slide under his shirt, feeling every dip of those perfect abs. I lifted his shirt over his head, never breaking eye contact. My heart felt complete with him in my arms again. I felt so overwhelmed with happiness, longing, and desire. I wasn't sure what to do with myself.

I wanted to feel every inch of his skin pressed against

my own, to feel him deep inside me. I longed for us to become one again. His hands gripped my sides under my shirt, pulling me to him as our kiss deepened, allowing his tongue to reacquaint itself with my own. I moaned against him, wanting more, wanting all of him. When our lips broke apart, I could see the same longing, the same hunger, reflected in his eyes as in my own.

We didn't shed clothes as quickly, instead doing it slowly and sensually. Our fingers grazed over each other's skin. Every touch was intentionally soft and sweet. Lucas held me in his arms as he aligned himself with my entrance. My breasts were pressed against his bare chest as my hands pushed down on his back, squeezing him closer to me. He slowly entered me, letting me feel every inch of him. He held my gaze before he began to thrust into me.

I have never felt so much love before. There was such love in his eyes. I couldn't look away. There was love in every touch and caress. The way he thrusted in me was filled with gentle love and care. This wasn't fucking, this was loving, and it was perfect. It was exactly what we needed after being away.

"I love you, Lucas," I whispered into his ear, holding him tightly.

"I love you, Olive."

We kept at it until I reached my orgasm with him spurting deep inside me at the same time. We were so in sync, reaching our peaks at almost the same time. He didn't let me go as we finished, either. Instead, he kept caressing my face, staring deep into my eyes. It was silent, but no words needed to be said. It was absolutely perfect. He *is absolutely perfect.* We stayed wrapped in one another for hours, only staring and caressing each other. Lucas, sadly, wasn't inside me anymore, but we were pressed so tightly against each other, it made it okay. I leaned forward, kissing his lips again. He let his thumb rub my jawline as he held my face.

"You're absolutely perfect, Rose. I am sorry I wasn't careful with you. Tell me what you want to do and we'll do it."

He broke the silence first with heavy words.

"I don't know what I want to do. We're still so young, and our relationship is still so new. Are we okay with it being more than just us before *us* even had a chance to start?" I asked him, worried about our relationship as well as my future career. Being a mom has its difficulties, the same way my career would.

"I'm okay with having a piece of each of us live in front of us. I am more than happy to raise a kid with you, to be forever tied to you. My heart would be overjoyed to see the life we created grow. We would make them the happiest child alive. We are more than capable, and I'll stay home while you start your career. I know you'll be a great aerospace engineer, and our child won't hold you back. I'll make sure of it."

My eyes watered as his words hit home. He was telling me everything I didn't even know I wanted to hear. I had no idea I wanted a child with Lucas, not until now. Now I can't even imagine not having it. I began to picture what our child would look like. My mind imagined a little boy, with strawberry blonde hair and deep brown eyes, or a girl with blonde hair and icy blue eyes. I couldn't stop imagining once I started. It was like I was sucked into a happy black hole where things actually went right for me.

"I guess we're having a baby," I finally said with a smile.

"Are you sure, Rose? I don't want you to feel pressured."

"I'm so sure. You'll be a great father, Lucas, I can already tell. A child with you will be perfect...more than perfect, in fact. You're my light and our child will be another," I assured him, kissing him again. He smiled so widely at me.

"You've given me the best gift in the world, Rose." He kissed me again, giving me the most joy I've felt in a while. I can't stop thinking about our growing child in me right now. *I'm pregnant.*

"I don't know about that." I shied away.

"Are you kidding me? It's the most precious gift you could give me. A life between you and I." He kissed me again, pushing away the hair from my face. His words were making me feel better with each statement. Lucas kissed my cheeks, then my neck, traveling down until he kissed my lower abdomen. He did it multiple times, staring happily. I loved seeing him look so happy and in love with our child already.

"Thank you, Lucas." I was so grateful he dropped everything and came here. I couldn't believe he did. No one has ever put me first like this before.

"Don't thank me, Rose. I don't need it. I'll forever be thanking you for this gift." He kissed my stomach again. I felt myself start to cry. I was overwhelmed, and it poured out of my eyes like a river.

"Shh, I'm here now, Rose. I got you...I got you both."

I cried like a small child. I was nervous about the future, but I was so happy to have him. Love engulfed my heart entirely as I started to let myself feel for this unborn child I am growing. I will never call it a mistake..*never*.

Unplanned? Yes. A mistake? Never!

Lucas' P.O.V.

Song Suggestion: "The Story" by Davis Naish

I have my Rose in my arms again. Her sweet scent chased away any and all sadness which had crept inside me in her absence. She was warm, perfect, and somehow mine. She had calmed herself after a while. I hated to hear her cry, but something tells me it wasn't because she was sad. *We're having a baby.*

I don't think I've ever gotten such elating news before today. Yes, it's extremely early... extremely. Who wouldn't be worried in this position? It's insane, yet I'm so excited. Picturing a child with Rose is something I can't stop doing now. I bet if it's a girl she'll have a sweet round face like Rose with those piercing blue eyes and fiery red hair. She'll have my nose and my lips, and maybe even my height.

I can picture a little boy with my blonde hair, but with her curls and thickness. Of course, I keep hoping they'll have her eyes, maybe shaped like mine, but colored like hers. Whatever they come out looking like, I know they'll be perfect. I'll wait patiently to see them and fall even more in love with them. I hate to admit it, because it's so soon, but I am so extremely excited. This won't ruin Rose's career either. I won't let it.

I'll be the one to stay home and care for our child. It sounds perfect to me. I would be so lucky as to be the one to put our child to sleep, to teach them about the world. I'll take care of them both, my Rose and my bud. This moment was perfect. The sex we had when I first arrived was like nothing I'd experienced in my past. The closest, I guess, would have been with Ivy, but this was different...it was more, so much more.

We're tied forever now by the child she grows inside of her. I want to link us in a more official way, too, and I'll ask her before the baby is born. I'll make her my wife, and not just my child's mother. She's my everything, and I'll give her all of me: mind, body, and soul.

"How are you feeling, Rose?" I asked her once she stopped crying.

"Overwhelmed, exhausted, in love, excited. I'm feeling too much," she admitted.

"Go to sleep Rose. I'm not going anywhere. We can drive back together tomorrow morning if you want. Although, I'd like to see the town you grew up in," I confessed, happy to be with her a day earlier than expected. *Now to break the news to Lisa and Mom.*

I had told them an emergency came up, and I had to go, but I didn't get real specific with the details, and since we were leaving tomorrow anyway, they didn't question it too much. I'm not sure how I plan to announce it to them. Maybe we'll wait a bit. I don't feel like being deflated from everyone's negative comments so soon after feeling so happy about the news. I know they'll say it's too soon, and a kid is a big responsibility. I know these things, but this is where we are, and we are going to make the best of it. I'm going to raise my child with Rose, and no one can tell me differently.

"Okay, I'll take you around town. I'll introduce you to Ian and Joe, and show you all my old hangout spots," she murmured sleepily.

"Thank you, Rose." I kissed the top of her head, caressing her arm until I felt her deep breaths.

Chapter 44

Lucas' P.O.V.

Rose had fallen asleep on my chest, relaxing me, and allowing me to find sleep faster than usual. I woke up to my Rose straddling my lap. I smirked, loving the feel of her naked body over mine. She was rubbing herself against me when she suddenly got off me at a run. She went straight to the bathroom. I hurriedly chased after her, seeing her lean over the toilet. I frowned, walking towards her. She tried to shoo me away with her hand as she vomited, but I ignored it. I grabbed her hair, holding it back for her, and rubbed her back as she threw up a little more. When she finished, she rinsed her mouth in the sink, staring at me in the mirror.

"I'm sorry you had to see that." She blushed, feeling embarrassed about it.

"Don't apologize, Rose. It's my fault for getting you pregnant. Let me be here to hold your hair and rub your back as you vomit, because it's the only thing I can do. I wish I could do the whole morning sickness part for you, but since I can't, will you let me do this at least?" I asked her, looking back at her in the mirror.

She blushed but nodded her head yes. I leaned forward, kissing her shoulder.

"Thank you, Rose. How are you feeling now?"

"Guilty."

"What?! Why?" Her answer had caught me off guard, making me furrow my brow in concern.

"I worked you up and then ran away to throw up." She

pointed to the semi hard on I sported.

"I don't care. Don't feel guilty. I'll have my way with you later, when you're feeling better," I promised her with a wink.

"Sounds good to me." I wiggled my eyebrows at her, making her giggle lightly.

"How about we get dressed and you take me to your favorite breakfast place?" I suggested with a smile.

"My favorite breakfast place would be Mrs. Daniels' house, but I doubt that is a real option. So we'll go to my second favorite."

"Ooo, who's Mrs. Daniels?"

"Ian's mom. She's the sweetest and always makes the best food."

"Hmm, I see." I need to get Rose and Mom to get along more, especially now. She should think of Mom as fondly as she does *Mrs. Daniels.*

"I want to meet this Mrs. Daniels, and Ian, of course." My curiosity was at an all-time high about Ian. What's he like in person, outside of her journals and his social media? I still can't believe her dad had kept those letters from her all this time. *I wonder if she's read any yet?*

"Okay. I'll see if they're free today."

We both got dressed as Rose texted Ian. I didn't realize she had gotten his number while here. I should have figured, but I didn't, and now I feel sour about it. I am trying not to be some controlling, jealous boyfriend, but some of her journal entries keep playing in my head about how amazing she found him. She smiled at the screen as he responded. I wrapped my arm around her waist, resting my chin on her shoulder and looking at her phone.

Olive: Can I come over for breakfast? I have someone I want you guys to meet.

#1 Best Friend: Ooo, you know I love meeting new people, and if they have your seal of approval, they must be great. I'll let mom know to make your favorites. It's still strawberry pancakes and bacon, right?

Olive: Sure is!

I wonder why she saved him as #1 best friend. I'm pretty sure that title is Hailey's now. I'm surprised Ian remembers her favorites. Her favorite is actually a banana nut muffin now, but I guess for Ian it is different. Ian knows more about my Rose than I do. I don't have to be a mind reader to know that. He got to know her for two years and I've only been around two months, but it's okay, I have a lifetime to get to know her better.

"So can we go?" I asked her, pretending not to know the answer.

"We can go."

She smiled so brightly at me, making me smile as well. There's no way you can't smile back when you see her face light up. We headed out, and Rose let me drive. She directed me as we went, pointing out buildings and places where she used to hang out. I loved seeing her enjoy telling me these things. She was so excited as she spoke about it all. By the time we got there, my mood had skyrocketed.

"I think you and Ian will hit it off. He's a very nice guy. Oh, and his mom is the absolute best! I can't even begin to tell you about her amazing cooking!" Rose was talking so fast as we approached the door. She used the black iron knocker, not holding still as she waited. She was adorable when she was excited.

"I can't wait to meet the people who helped you when you were younger."

I pulled her in, kissing her forehead sweetly at the same time the door opened. The person cleared their throat, clearly not liking the intimate moment. Rose blushed, but I turned with a smile to face the door, expecting to see the famous Mrs. Daniels. Instead, I was greeted by Ian's handsome face. His hair was longer, and his features sharper than his latest profile picture. He's one of those who looks better in person. *Oh, Joy.*

"Good morning, Red!" He beamed at her. "Who have you brought?" His eyes met mine with interest. The nickname didn't go unnoticed. He still uses it and she doesn't mind it.

"This is my boyfriend, Lucas." She gestured to me with a smile.

"Nice to meet you, Lucas."

Ian's smile remained, but it had lost some of its luster. He held his hand out to shake, and I took it. We had a death match as we shook. When we let go, I resisted the urge to open and shut my hand to shake off the hurt. He had squeezed so tight you'd think we were playing a pain game. I could see him shaking his hand off behind him, making me smile. Rose, however, saw it and elbowed me on the side lightly. *Is she scolding me? He did it too!*

"Come on in." Ian gestured for us to step inside as he moved out of the way, hand still on the doorknob. Rose stepped in first, and I followed closely behind. The house was warm and bright. It was very homey, with happy family pictures hanging on the wall. There were decorations for Thanksgiving meticulously placed throughout the rooms. I could see why Rose would have loved it here when she was a teenager. It was a loving home, one we both should have had growing up. I reached for her hand, giving it a light squeeze. Her eyes met mine in wonder, but then she smiled knowingly.

"It's lovely, isn't it?" She whispered to me, and I nodded.

"Come on, Mom's in the kitchen." Ian led the way, pushing through a swinging door. There was a beautiful woman with her hair tied in a high, tight bun. She wore a sweet pink apron as she pranced about the kitchen. The smell of bacon and coffee wafted into my nose, making this place even cozier. The woman turned as she noticed our presence and smiled widely at Rose. I could see the love she held for her and I was happy for it.

"Livie! I am so happy you came for breakfast. Seeing you two days in a row after so many years has filled my heart with so much joy," she said as she hugged Rose. "And you've brought a guest."

She finally noticed me as she pulled away from Rose. She looked at our interlocked fingers, assessing them like it was some foreign concept for us to be holding hands. Her eyes then bore into mine with a kind smile.

"I'm Caterina, Ian's mom. It's nice to meet you." She held her left hand out for me to take, making me have to let go of Rose's hand to shake it.

"I'm Lucas, Rose's boyfriend." She cocked her head to the side, furrowing her brow as I spoke.

"That's his nickname for me," Rose explained, making Mrs Daniels nod in understanding. I forgot to use her actual name, having gotten used to calling her Rose.

"It's cute," she said, but I don't actually think she liked it. "Livie, why don't you help me finish up and the boys can set the table?" She looked at me with a small smile, gesturing for me to follow Ian, and I did. Maybe it's all in my head, but I feel slightly unwelcomed.

Olive's P.O.V.

Cat and I finished making breakfast, and brought it out to the dining room. I felt the awkward tension between Lucas and Ian as I entered. I was hoping they'd hit it off, but it's taking longer for them to get along than I would like. Lucas met my eyes with a smile, causing my heart to flutter. He pulled a chair out for me and I sat happily. Lucas waited until I made my plate before making his own. He was being more than courteous. Breakfast was awkward at first, but once Donald entered, it became a big social event.

He helped make Lucas feel welcome and eased the tension in the room. I was thankful he was here. We all sat around talking and laughing with empty plates in front of us. I felt so fortunate at the moment until the bacon grease hit me, and I had to bolt for the bathroom. I could tell Lucas *and* Ian were chasing after me in concern. *There goes my delicious breakfast.* I felt Lucas hold my hair and rub my back again. I hated he was seeing all this nastiness, but I was grateful for his presence and soothing touch.

"I'm sorry, Rose." Lucas let out a sad sigh as I flushed the toilet and saw my food swirl away.

"It's okay, it's not your fault," I said, turning the sink on to rinse my mouth. Ian hung in the doorway of the bathroom as his kind blue eyes watched me, assessing me with concern. He stepped closer, itching to touch me, but restraining due to Lucas' presence.

"Isn't it?" Lucas arched a brow. I mean, yeah, in a way it is, since he got me pregnant, but that's my fault too.

"Eh, it's as much your fault as my own." I shrugged at him. He sighed, pulling me close and kissing my forehead again.

"Are you okay, Red?" Ian asked, stepping further into the bathroom.

"Yeah, I'm fine. Sorry." I blushed, hating he saw me throw up, too. I don't like people seeing me be sick, especially stomach sickness.

"Want some nausea medicine. I think mom has some somewhere," Ian offered, as he opened the medicine cabinet and began to rummage through it.

"No, I'm fine. Honest." I'm not sure what kind of medicine you can take while pregnant, but I know there's a lot you can't. I'm still feeling guilty for drinking and fighting this month. *Shit fighting!* I won't be able to do the championship. My blood ran cold and my heart rate spiked as I thought of Davis. He's going to kill me for getting pregnant so young. Forget my dad, the person to be worried about telling is Davis! *Lord, help me!*

"Jesus, Red, you're pale. Sit down." Ian pulled me from Lucas, lifting me and placing me on the counter. Lucas stepped forward, grabbing my hand again. He was worried, too.

"Should we go to the doctor?" Lucas asked me, unsure of what to do.

"No, it's fine. I'm fine. You guys are worrying too much."

"Red, you threw up and you're as white as a sheet now.

You're not fine."

"I promise I am fine. Would you guys calm down?" I was growing a little irritated with the amount of panicking they were both doing now.

"I can't calm down when you look like you're going to faint," Ian gave me his 'be serious' look, the one he would give me when I was playing around too much. I felt guilty and a little embarrassed as I realized I would have to tell him the truth to make him stop worrying. I'm not sure how he'll feel about the news, but I hope he doesn't stop being my friend over it.

"I threw up because I'm pregnant, and I'm apparently one of the unlucky few who gets terrible morning sickness," I admitted. "I'm pale because I thought of having to tell Davis."

"Fuck, I'm dead," Lucas murmured under his breath, looking as pale as me now. Ian was silent as he stared at me for a long while. He then wrapped his arms around me and hugged me tight, pressing me against him. It was like he was trying to infuse himself inside of me with how tightly he held me. I could feel the love pouring out of him, and it made my chest tighten.

"Congratulations, Red. You're going to make a fantastic mother." He pulled back as he spoke, staring deep into my eyes. "I'll let mom know you're fine." He ran off, but not before I saw a tear slide down his cheek. *Why is he crying?* It tore my heart in two and kept my mind on him even as I looked back at Lucas.

"How long do you think I should hide, after we tell Davis?" Lucas asked, holding his chin in a playful way. He made me smile and suppress a laugh.

"Years, my Knight, years."

The familiar cold air and scent of iron filled my lungs as we entered the tattoo shop. Joe was in his usual spot, hovering over some woman who was getting the cliche tramp stamp on her lower back. You'd think it would be outdated by now, yet here she was getting a butterfly.

"Joe, your pet is here," Vicky yelled back from the counter, irritating me greatly with her choice of words.

"Watch it, Vicky. My pet, as you call her, bites when provoked," Joe warned with amusement. I smirked, feeling smug he would warn people about me. "Be with you in a minute, kiddo."

Lucas and I took a seat in the chairs by the door. The leather coated cushion sank with a whiff of air as I parked my bottom on it. I watched Joe finish the butterfly on the woman's back with his tongue curled out as he focused. His tattooed muscles contracted as he finished the fine details. When he was done, he bandaged her, and left her to check herself out. He made his way towards me with his usual serious expression.

"What can I do for you, Cherry Bomb?"

"Wanna have lunch? Got a few things to talk with you about."

"I'm guessing this is the new boyfriend?" He pointed to Lucas with a raised brow.

"Yeah, it is." I smirked with a blush.

"Then let's go." Joe was like a hungry wolf and Lucas was the little bunny he was ready to chase and eat. I felt a bit bad for him, but maybe we can think of this as the test run for telling Davis. We headed out and went right next door to Jumping Jay's. The waitress came around and took our order quickly. There was a lunch rush, but they were efficient in getting our food to us quickly. *Maybe I won't throw up this time.*

"Start talking," Joe said with his elbow on the table and his eyes on his food. He stabbed his food with his fork rather aggressively before looking at Lucas.

"Um, I'm Lucas?" He said, unsure of what he meant to say. I chuckled lightly. I didn't mean to, but it was slightly funny to me how many people are intimidated by Joe when he's secretly a little teddy bear.

"Tell him whatever comes to mind, it doesn't even have

to be about you. He'll get a feel for who you are." I explained. Lucas nodded, but I could tell he still wasn't comfortable.

"Do you ever wonder how your parents felt when they found out they were pregnant with you? Like, do you think they were elated? Or do you think maybe they were sitting at a table staring at the positive test like it was the worst news of their life? I think my parents were happy, but it doesn't mean they were good parents." Lucas started as he rolled his brussels sprouts around the plate with his fork. "Being a parent is more than accepting the news and being happy about it. It's making sure you're there for your kid, and they feel loved. It's making sure you're setting a good example for them to follow. Making sure they know they can come to you with their problems, and you'll be there to help. Kids need their parents, and sometimes some kids aren't lucky enough to get parents who will pay them any mind. I want to make sure I'm a father who's good to their kids. I don't have the best role model, but I won't let that stop me."

I felt my eyes start to mist over at his words. An image of him holding our child with a bright smile flooded my mind. I never thought of how he would feel about becoming a parent, about how his trauma would affect him. He has a lot to overcome. We both do, but we'll do it together. We'll do it for our child, become better versions of our parents. I took his hand, feeling overly emotional. I squeezed it, meeting his eyes to see the sadness in him. He wants to do good, to *be* good.

"You're pregnant, aren't you?" Joe asked me with a knowing look.

"Yeah," I sighed, readying myself for a lecture.

"I better be the one you take him to for his first tattoo. Or her." He shrugged, like the news was nothing bad.

"Sure thing, Joe. Don't fuck up my kid."

"When have I ever done you wrong?" He arched a brow, taking offense.

"Never." I smirked.

Joe and Lucas talked more. Joe asked him about his

tattoos and their meaning, which were things neither of us had asked each other. He had two for Ivy and two for John. The ones he had done for Ivy were a leaf from an Ivy with a water droplet in the center. The other one was done for Ivy and John. Running along his arm were black roses tied together with a halo over them and wings around it. His other tattoo for John was a best friend's one they got together as teens. His was a crescent moon with John's name on it, and John's had been the sun with Lucas' name. They added on to it when they got older. Lucas added stars and wrote Leo's name in one. John added clouds and had Leo's name in one as well. I liked knowing these things about him.

God, we still know so little about each other.

Chapter 45

Olive's P.O.V.

"I see why you guys hung out so much here," Lucas said as he looked out towards the coast at my and Ian's favorite spot.

I would still come here even after Ian moved, but it only made me feel lonelier. I hadn't been here myself since sophomore summer. A cold breeze carried the salty ocean air to my nose, making me take a deep breath. I missed the smell. The main thing I smell in New York is the stench of garbage mixed with the urine in the alleyway. There's no fresh air in New York, just the millions of smells intermingled into one stench.

"It's beautiful," he said, wrapping his arms around my waist from behind and resting his chin on my shoulder. I loved the tickle of his breath on my neck as we watched the waves crash in.

"I'm glad you could see it. Thank you for coming home early," I told him, placing my hands over his.

"I'll come running any time you need me, Rose." I nodded, not able to say anything more. My mind focused on this moment, on the feel of him holding me. I missed him so much and it had only been a couple of days. Like him, I kind of liked knowing he'd be in my life no matter what, because of our child. We will be forever linked, even if we break up. I don't ever want to lose him, but I could live with it better knowing we have a child together.

"What do you want to do, Rose?"

"What do you mean?" I turned my head to look at him,

seeing him stare into the beautiful blue sea.

"Do you want to stay a little while longer, or go home? Do you want to confront your father? Or talk to his girlfriend? What do you want to do? Whatever it is, I'm by your side." I mulled it over, asking myself the same question. I want dad's girlfriend to know she's not alone. If he ever starts hitting her, I'll be there to help. I'll help her escape.

"Let's go talk to Daisy," I said firmly.

"Who?" He arched a brow and puckered his lips cutely.

"Dad's girlfriend."

He nodded his head in understanding. We stayed a little while longer, enjoying the view before we headed to the car. I let Lucas drive, to ease his worries, and directed him to the bookstore. We parked up front, where Lucas opened my door for me.

"Are you ready to talk to Daisy?" Lucas asked.

"As ready as I can be." I felt nervous to talk to her, wondering what she would think. Will she believe what I say? Will she heed my warnings? I hope she does.

"Did you guys find everything okay?" Daisy asked as we approached the counter. When she noticed our empty hands, she looked up at us, changing tactics. "Is there anything I can help you with?"

"In fact, there is Daisy. It's about my dad, your boyfriend." Her eyes widened as she took me in. She had been looking at me before, but now she saw me. She studied my features, probably trying to find commonalities between dad and I. She didn't wasn't too convinced and rightfully so. I look nothing like dad, taking after mom way too much.

"Your father?" She asked in disbelief.

"Yes, Nick Brewer, my father."

"He didn't mention having a daughter." She swallowed hard, probably realizing how old I am and how weird it would be to be my step-mother.

"That's exactly why we need to talk."

The sun began to set, casting a blinding light anytime

you looked out of the store's glass door or large windows. A prominent figure blocked off some of the radiance as they entered. It was hard to tell who it was at first, but as they stepped further in and away from the sun's bright light, my eyes recognized Dad's face.

"Olive, what do you think you're doing?" Dad's voice caught me off guard, chilling me to the bone. My hair stood on the back of my neck, feeling extremely exposed. I could see how enraged his expression was. His arms were crossed and flexed in anger. His eyebrows scowled deeply as he looked at me longer.

"Trying to warn her about you before it's too late."

"There's nothing to tell her, Olive. Now leave." He was trying to intimidate me.

"Or what? You'll hit me again?* I egged him on further. I wanted Daisy to see the kind of man Dad truly was.

"I would never hit you," he lied right through his teeth.

"Then what do you call the back-handed slap to my cheek the last time I saw you? I promise you that's not how you high five people."

I could see the rage rising as his muscles flexed further and his nostrils flared. Daisy was like a deer caught in the headlights. She was clearly unsure what to do or say. Her eyes darted between Dad, myself, and occasionally Lucas, probably wondering what part he plays in this.

"I don't know what you're talking about, Livie."

"It's Olive. Only people who actually cared for me get to call me Livie. I came here to warn your girlfriend about you. I want her to know if she ever needs to escape, I'll help her. She won't have to abandon her child with you to do so. You won't see either of them again, so you better make sure to hold back on those punches. I won't allow you to fuck up another child."

Dad's expression was a mixture of unbridled rage and hurt, as if my words had actually caused him damage. Did he believe he did a good job of caring for me growing up? Is he delusional enough to think he did everything he was supposed to? Surely he realizes being passed out drunk, sparing with your kid, and barely ever having food in the fridge is not a good childhood.

"Don't come back, Olive. It's clear you've disowned me as your father, even after everything I've done for you. Now you're spreading vicious rumors to ruin my happiness because I didn't give you everything you asked for as a child. You're spoiled," he spat at me. His words hurt me deeply, even though they were a bunch of lies. My anger was accessible at all times, and I was ready to show him, but I didn't get the chance as Lucas' fist made contact with Dad's jaw, swiveling his head enough to make him take a step to the side.

Oh, fuck me!

The second where we all froze in shock felt like it lasted an eternity, only to play again at double the speed. Dad swiveled back around, his fist drawn back and ready to hit Lucas in the throat. I pulled on Lucas' shirt, forcing him back so Dad's punch would miss.

Due to the lack of contact, Dad had to take a step forward to avoid falling. He had put a lot of power behind his punch. I dragged Lucas further back away from Dad. I'd like for my child's father not to be killed by my dad. Dad looked at me with narrowed eyes, and for a moment, I think he contemplated hitting me too. Daisy gasped, thrown off by the whole debacle playing before her.

"I'm calling the police," she said, rushing to Dad's side and looking at us like we were in the wrong. *Daisy, if you only knew.*

This whole thing had obviously made her believe me less. I sighed, realizing what I had set out to accomplish would not be happening. I looked at her and her little baby bump, worried she'll fall prey to dad faster now. Somehow, in my hurry to help her, I only solidified Dad's grip on her.

"We're leaving, but if you ever need to escape, ask Joe at Iron Work Tattoo for my number. I'll come help, no matter what." I hope she'll keep that information tucked safely away in her mind for when she needs it. Hopefully, the time never comes. I dragged Lucas out of the store, feeling Dad wanted to chase him down and beat him. I hurried us to the car, worried Daisy would actually call the police.

"You shouldn't have punched him," I whispered, staring out the car window at Daisy and Dad holding one another inside the bookstore as we drove away. It was like Dad was comforting her from a bad experience. One we caused.

"I'm sorry, Olive. He made me so mad. How could he say that to you?" Lucas' hand gripped the steering wheel so hard I could see the whites of his knuckles. His jaw clenched as he ground his teeth in anger. "I know I fucked up, and I'm sorry, but I am not sorry for punching him. He deserved it and he deserves so much more." I sighed, knowing I can't truly be mad at him for it. He was right.

"It was a really good punch." I smirked at him, trying not to laugh.

"You think so?" He smirked back, eyes still on the road.

"Mhm, you made his whole head turn."

"Maybe I'll fight the championship for you, then perhaps Davis won't kill me." We both laughed, lightening the mood despite what had transpired. "I am sorry, Olive."

"I know you are. Thank you for trying to fight for me." I grabbed his hand, squeezing it tightly to show him I cared. "Let's get my things from the Inn and head back to New York. I am ready to be home with you."

"Are you sure you're ready to leave?"

"There's nothing else for me to do here." I nodded.

"Then let's go home."

"Liv, pass me the tamales, please," Hailey asked me from across the table.

I reached for the warm stacked plate, passing it towards her. It touched about three different hands before making it to her. Lucas and I decided to start Thanksgiving with Hailey's family since they began earlier than everyone else. Afterward, we were headed to Leo's, where Sarah and Lisa would join us. Apparently, they get together as one big family on Thanksgiving and Christmas, minus Lucas' Dad and now Leo's.

"No, mamá, no tengo novio." Hailey answered another pestering question about her love life. Her family was determined to have her set up, but she refused them every time. "Sí, yo veo que Olive tiene un novio muy guapo."

Translation: "Yes, I see that Olive has a handsome boyfriend." I'm definitely learning more Spanish thanks to Hailey and her family these past few years. I tried to save her a few times, but it was a lost effort as someone always brought the conversations back to the dreaded topic. By the end of it, Hailey looked ready to strangle the next person to mention the words love, boyfriend, or relationship.

"How was the visit home?" Hailey asked me as I helped her wash the dishes. Lucas helped too, being the wonderful man he is.

"It was interesting, crazy even." I began to tell her about Ian, Dad, his girlfriend, how Joe helped Mom, all of it. She gasped, she cried, and she yelled.

"Good job, sir." She patted Lucas on the back when I told her he had punched dad right in the face.

"There's something else I want to tell you, but you can't tell anyone." I pointed my finger at her.

"You know your secret is safe with me." She nodded, reminding me of how well she was at keeping secrets.

"I'm pregnant."

She yelled so loudly some of her family came rushing in to check on her. She came up with some sorry excuse, but her family believed it. They know she's always been very enthusiastic and energetic.

"What great news, Liv. I am so happy for you guys! Are you still going to be able to graduate?" She asked me, worried as she thought about what it means for my future.

"Yes. It won't be due till around July, if I'm calculating it right. I'll be graduating looking like Shamu. The people in the front row better watch out." I joked, making Haily and me giggle.

"I better be the baby's godmother. Ian needs to realize I'm the best friend now. You need to have him come visit here. I want to meet Ian," Hailey demanded with a nod before continuing with the dishes.

"Okay, I'll ask him if he can come. I am not sure what he does for a living, but I am sure he'll be free to hang sometime soon."

"Great, he and I need to have a talk about who your best friend is." Hailey laughed, making me smile. She had a fun laugh to listen to.

"Don't be too harsh when you meet him."

"I won't," she promised.

In a blink of an eye, our festivities at Hailey's place ended, and we headed towards Leo's house. I'd never been before and I dare not venture to call it a house any longer. The place was massive! It smelled wonderful, with all kinds of traditional Thanksgiving food sprawled on an enormous table. We all took our seats and began to dig in as we talked.

"Lucas, are you going to tell me what the big emergency was that made you leave early?" She asked, eyeing him suspiciously and then me.

"I will later. Don't worry, Mom, it's handled." Lucas didn't bat an eye as he answered her calmly. He gave her an innocent smile which melted even *my* heart.

"I'll be waiting," she said with a nod.

Thankfully, she didn't press the matter any further. I am surprised Lucas didn't tell her. I had already told three people, and he has yet to tell one. Has he changed his mind? Does he not want this child anymore? The idea of it made my stomach turn. I quickly lost my appetite. All I could do was play with my food.

"What's wrong, Rose?" He leaned in, whispering the

question in my ear.

"Do you still want this baby?" I whispered back so lowly, even he could barely hear me.

"What? Of course I do!" He looked at me like I had asked the craziest question on the planet. Still, he hasn't said anything to anyone. Dinner continued with small banter here and there until everyone was finished eating. Leo, Lisa, Lucas and I went outside to enjoy the evening sky, while Sarah and Leo's mother chatted about trivial things inside.

"I have something to tell you guys, but you can't tell Mom yet," Lucas told them with a stern face.

"Mum's the word," Leo said.

"You know I won't tell her if you don't want me to," Lisa assured him.

"Rose and I are having a baby." Lucas smiled brightly, washing away any doubt I had created over dinner about him wanting our child. He is happy. He doesn't want to tell his mom yet. I am not sure why, but I'm sure he has his reasons. I won't pressure him.

"Christ!" Leo sighed. "You guys sure are doing things at a swift pace." He shook his head almost disapprovingly. Leo's reaction kind of stung, and I think it hurt Lucas a bit, too, as his smile lost some brightness.

"That's amazing! Oh! I can't wait to be an auntie!" Lisa smiled excitedly, bouncing in her seat and leaning towards me. "Your kid is going to be so adorable!"

"You don't think it's too soon?" Lucas asked, a bit surprised. I guess he knew they would have a similar reaction.

"I mean, yeah, but it's happened and there's no changing it, so I'll be excited for you and skip the lecture." She smiled at Lucas, grabbing his hand and squeezing it tight. She stared intently at his eyes as she spoke. "You are nothing like Dad. You are going to be the most amazing father. I know you will be. I am not worried, Lucas, and neither should you." Lucas smiled back at her, giving her nod without responding. I could tell he was feeling emotional at Lisa's words. She told him something he needed to hear.

"Now I feel like an ass. Thanks, Lisa." Leo sighed. "I worry for you guys, but of course, I'm excited to see your little baby and be a cool friend who gets to be called uncle."

"I don't know about the cool uncle part." Lucas teased Leo as always, letting me know they were okay. Lucas smiled back at Leo. "Thanks, Leo."

We spoke about all things baby for the next half hour until Sarah stepped out. We got quiet a little too quickly, causing her suspicion to rise. I realize we are not the sneakiest of couples. *It's okay. She will know soon enough.*

Chapter 46

Olive's P.O.V.

Song Suggestion: "Turning Page" by Sleeping At Last

"Merry Christmas, Rose." Lucas woke me up with a small present. He sat on the edge of the bed with an excited smile. "Open it."

I rubbed my eyes, sitting up and grabbing the box. It was small, but had a beautiful red ribbon with printed roses. I untied the ribbon, slowly opening the box to reveal another smaller black velvet box. I furrowed my brow as I opened it. Inside was a beautiful rose ring with a large stone in the center of the rose. The ring's band had delicate and dainty leaf and twig-style motifs. It was stunningly beautiful, but it looked like an engagement ring. I went to look at him to ask if he realized what he had gotten, but when I looked up, I found him on one knee beside the bed. My eyes widened and my heart began to race. I couldn't believe what I was seeing, but God, I was ready for him to ask.

"Olive Brewer, you are the light of my life. The sun that I revolve around. You are everything good and pure in my life. You are the love of my life. The one I've been waiting for, my everything, and I will never let you go. I never imagined I could be this happy again, finding someone like you. Someone who has shown me what true love is. I will never take you for granted, Olive. I love you more than words can say. You are giving me the greatest gift of life, our child, but will you grace me with one more? Will you be my wife and be mine forever?"

I could feel the tears pouring from my eyes as I nodded my head wildly.

"Yes, a thousand times, yes!" I choked out, reaching for him. We happily hugged and kissed as he placed the ring on my finger. The ring fit like he had it made perfectly, just for me. He kissed my forehead and then my nose and my cheeks. He kissed my neck and then my collar bone. I felt such happiness envelope me, seeping deep into my heart. It was a moment unlike any other. It was perfect.

"I love you, Lucas," I whispered, cupping his face with my hands. I stared into those deep brown eyes before I kissed him like never before. I let every ounce of love I have for him pour out of me like a faucet. Our kiss deepened with our tongues dancing around one another. Our hands explored one another, familiarizing themselves with each other again.

Lucas' fingers grazed the skin of my stomach as he lifted my shirt over my head. His eyes admired me with such intensity, I almost shied away. Instead, I stared back in the same manner, reciprocating his love. I took his shirt off next, not breaking eye contact until it went over his head. Our lips met again with a furious hunger and deep passion.

His hands trailed down my thighs as he pulled my sweatpants off along with my underwear until I laid bare for him. He gently kissed me once more before standing to take off his own pants. I watched him, admiring his god-like physique. He propped himself over me, kissing my nose and smiling. His nose nuzzled into my neck as his lips gave me soft kisses. My skin tingled with goosebumps at his touch.

My fingers ran through his thick, soft hair, playing with it lovingly. I felt his dick graze over my wet folds lightly, making me scoot down to let him know I wanted him in me. He happily complied as he aligned himself with my entrance, slowly gliding into me as he stared deep into my eyes. I looked right back into them, the most beautiful eyes you could look into.

I moaned as he hit my special spot. The one I swear

is made just for him. His moves were delicate and sensual, moving me to a slow rhythm, driving my body mad. I felt ready to burst in a matter of minutes. Lucas has a way of making everything feel so explosive and intense. He sucked at the hardened buds of my nipples, causing me to moan loudly. My hips swayed involuntarily against him, feeling his muscles against the sensitive bundle of nerves between my legs.

He continued to cause me pleasure until I reached one of the most intense orgasms. I milked Lucas for all he's worth as his seed squirted deep inside me-no point in pulling out now. We're already pregnant. We stayed in one another's arms, lightly kissing each other. Our hands caressed one another mindlessly.

"Thank you, Rose." Lucas broke the silence first.

"For what?"

"For saying yes." I kissed him once more, pecking his lips.

"Thank you for asking."

The rest of the morning went well. I somehow managed to hold my breakfast down. We cuddled on the couch, watching Hallmark Christmas movies together, sipping on hot cocoa. Around two o'clock, somebody took our alone time away. We had decided today would be the day we tell Davis and Carter. I had come up with some excuse to drop out of the championship, and Davis was pretty disappointed. We had a small argument about commitment before he sighed and let me withdraw. I opened the door to find a serious Davis and an ever-smiling Carter.

"Merry Christmas, Twinkle Toes," Carter greeted me when Davis said nothing.

"Merry Christmas, Carter."

"Don't call her that. She obviously doesn't care about her title." Davis crossed his arms, upset as he entered.

"It's Christmas, Davis, have some cheer." Carter elbowed him in the side, earning him a scowl from Davis.

"What did you want to talk about?" Davis asked, ready

to leave. I sighed, feeling extremely nervous about telling him.

"Sit down, this is serious." I gestured for them to take a seat on the couch. Davis' demeanor changed instantly upon hearing the phrase. I sat beside Lucas, needing his support to spill the news. Carter sat on the recliner to the right and Davis on the one to the left. I looked at Davis knowing this news was intended for him to hear. He was the father I wish I had. The person I respect the most and I need him to approve.

"What is, Liv? You're worrying me." Davis clasped his hands in front of him, having his thumbs poke at his lip.

"The reason I couldn't fight isn't because I didn't want to or because I was sick. It's because..." I bit my lip, feeling so scared to say the words.

"Because I got her pregnant," Lucas said it for me, wording it so all the blame was on him.

"It's not just his fault, obviously. I wasn't being careful either. We have a plan, and I know we're young, but-" I stopped talking as Davis got up. His face was unreadable as he stalked toward us. I was so scared he was going to punch Lucas, but instead, he lifted me off the couch and into a giant hug. He held me close to him for a long while. In all our years together, Davis has never once held me so tightly, except maybe after I spilled my life story.

"Congratulations, Liv. You deserve all the happiness in the world, and if this is something you want, then I fully support it. We're here for you always, no matter what. You know that, right?" He said, pulling out of our hug, placing his hand on my shoulder as he stared into my eyes. I felt them mist over again, feeling overly sentimental. I nodded, unable to speak through the thick emotions in my throat.

"I hope it gets your fighting spirit," Carter chimed in, boxing the air as if to show my fighting spirit. I snickered at him.

"Thank you, guys."

"You better marry this woman and care for her and your child, right, or I'm coming for you!" Davis pointed his finger at

Lucas with the most intimidating face he could muster.

"Already asked her to marry me this morning, Mr. Viking, sir." Lucas smiled, being his playful self. Davis narrowed his eyes at the nickname, but ultimately let it go.

"Good." He nodded.

Carter and Davis decided to stay for dinner. They helped us cook as we all talked and joked. I loved seeing Lucas bond with the essential people in my life. A knock at the door pulled my attention from this beautiful moment. I guess the next guest has arrived. Hailey came next, but we all banned her from the kitchen after she somehow burned butter. She was designated to work on decorations and music. Ian showed up after, surprised by the two large men in my kitchen. I forgot Ian has no idea I fought competitively.

"So happy you could make it. Come meet my important people." I greeted him, pulling him by the wrist towards the kitchen. "Meet Davis and Carter. They run an underground fighting ring I participate in from time to time."

"She's phenomenal," Lucas said, wrapping his arm around my lower back, pulling me to his side so he could kiss my temple.

"She was a title champion for a year before she met some asshole boyfriend named Julius." Carter made a face as if to say Julius was the nastiest thing ever. I laughed at his expression.

"Shit, Red. I left and you became strong. Was I holding you back?" Ian asked, looking at me differently. Impressed, maybe?

"No, you were saving me and bringing light into my life at the darkest time. You never held me back, Ian." I shook my head. I grabbed his wrist again, pulling him towards Hailey next.

"Ian, this is my best friend, Hailey." I introduced her. She turned with her beautiful wavy black hair swinging over her shoulder. She smiled her bright smile as she placed her arm over my shoulder.

"Nice to meet you," she said. "Although, I'm the number one best friend now. I'll fight you for it." Hailey joked, making Ian blush lightly.

"I've known her longer." He pointed out, making Hailey laugh.

"I know her best. Longer doesn't always mean better." Hailey winked at him, stepping towards him. She linked her arm with his, pulling him towards the table she was setting up. "Come help me, let's talk about all things Liv." She didn't take no for an answer as she whisked him away. I smiled after them, happy to see my best friends getting along. Leo came next, with Rachel at his side. I was determined to get these two together today. They would be so perfect for one another.

Lisa was the last to arrive. She stepped in, looking magnificent in a beautiful, floor-length red dress which hugged her figure in all the right places. She had a white fur shawl wrapped around her arms with white, long gloves. Her black hair was pinned into a beautifully curled bun. She was definitely overdressed for the occasion, but man did she look good.

"Sorry I'm late. I had to sneak out of the business Christmas party. Dad's pretty pissed you missed it," Lisa told Lucas.

"Let him be. I don't give a fuck anymore." He shook his head.

"Be careful, Lucas. You know how he can be." Her warning scared me a bit. I didn't know Lucas had a party he was supposed to attend, but it explained Lisa's attire. I began to worry about what Lucas' father was capable of as an abusive billionaire.

"I know." He sighed, stopping his task as he calmed himself.

"Merry Christmas, Lisa," I finally greeted her.

I introduced everyone to Davis and Carter, which earned me both perplexed and impressed looks at the news I fight in an underground ring. Rachel, Leo and Lisa had no idea, but Hailey told all of them how amazing I was, and Lucas chimed in as well. I'm not going to lie; this is by far the most incredible Christmas of my life. I couldn't believe how warm and amazing my life had gotten since Lucas entered it. I've never felt so loved, having a room full of people to spend this holiday with. A room of people I could call family. It was everything to me. I watched everyone like they were my favorite Christmas movie. I smiled as my heart filled with joy for this beautiful and rare moment in front of me. Everything felt perfect.

We all ate together and exchanged gifts, except for Carter and Davis who didn't know we were doing this. Everyone looked at Lucas, waiting to see what he got me after I gave him his gift. I had engineered a device for him to help with his car so he would feel less nervous when he drove.

"Tell me you did not forget to get her a gift!" Lisa scolded Lucas, slapping him on the arm hard.

"He didn't." I quickly defended him, feeling my cheeks tinge pink.

"Oh?" Lisa arched her brow with a mischievous grin. "Was it a sex thing? Kinky." She laughed.

"Oh my gosh, no!" I shook my hands out in front of me, shaking my head vigorously. Lisa laughed at my embarrassment. She likes to tease just like her brother, but in a more wicked way.

"So what was it then?" Rachel asked, curious to know too.

"I asked her to marry me," Lucas answered, staring right at me.

"And I said yes." Looking right back at him, I smiled as I held my hand up to show the ring.

Everyone was surprised, but it was Hailey who broke the silence. She squealed excitedly, like she usually does, starting the line of questioning from everyone. Rachel asked how he did it. Lisa asked if we had a date in mind. The only person to stay silent was Ian. I could see him wiping his hands on his thighs, a sign something is bothering him. After answering everyone's questions, I got up and grabbed Ian.

"Come with me. Your gift is upstairs."

I had already told Lucas I'd be disappearing with Ian for a short while to show him his gift. I'll take this chance to ask him what's wrong. I grabbed his wrist and guided him up the stairs to the rooftop. He looked around, admiring the plants and the night sky.

"I got you a star for being a bright light in my life when I needed it the most." I told him, taking him to the telescope I had set up yesterday, keeping it pointed at his star. "Go ahead, look at it." He leaned down, eyeing the star through the telescope. When he stood back up, I handed him the little certificate.

"I know it's cheesy, but I wanted to get you something amazing. I liked the idea of giving you a star. I hope it's okay."

"It's more than okay. Thank you, Red."

"Great, so tell me what's wrong?"

"Nothing." He shook his head, plastering an all too fake smile.

"Ian," I used a stern, warning voice, calling bullshit.

"I had always imagined finding you and reconnecting. I imagined winning your heart over and being the one to ask you to marry me. I found you a few months too late. I've always loved you, Red, as more than just your best friend. I still do." His confession was more than I was expecting, and it tore my heart right down the middle. He loved me in high school, too. I felt stupid for having held back my feelings, but I am glad I did. I wouldn't be where I am right now if I hadn't. Lucas is everything to me, and I would gladly repeat all the horrible things in my life if it's how I get to Lucas.

"I'm sorry, Ian. I had no idea you felt this way." I sighed, looking up at the stars with him. "I loved you very much in high school—as more than just friends. I never thought you would feel the same way about me. You were the only friend I had, and I didn't want to lose you, so I never told you how I felt. I am sorry my dad kept us apart. Things would have been different if he hadn't, I'm sure. I understand if you want to distance yourself from me again." It would hurt, but I would understand it.

"No, Red, I never want to lose you again. I'm still your best friend. I have to get over this heartbreak and the fantasy I had in my head of you and I. I am happy for you, I mean it. You deserve all the happiness in the world, Red. You've been through so much shit."

"Thank you, Ian." I felt a wave of relief, knowing he didn't want to leave me again. I had missed him greatly and it would have hurt to lose him again. Our friendship has always meant so much to me. I am glad he feels the same way.

Goodbye to a future that could have been.

Chapter 47

Olive's P.O.V.

"Are you okay, my Rose?" Lucas asked as we finished cleaning up the place. Everyone was long gone now, but the evening was spectacular.

"Yeah, I'm fine, just thinking," I answered, grabbing a cup off the coffee table which had only been half drunk. The marshmallows had disappeared in the heat of the coco, leaving this sort of foam at the top.

"What about?" He asked, taking the cup from my hands and washing it.

"I think I need to read Ian's letters," I admitted, biting at my cheek. "I need to know what he said." Lucas went silent, which only made me nervous. He turned the sink off, facing me. He dried his hands as he held my gaze. When he approached me, his eyes softened, feeling sympathy for me. Lucas pulled me into a tight hug, kissing my forehead.

"I'll go see my mom for a little while. I am sure she's still awake. Text me when you're done," he said, letting me go.

"You don't have to leave." He shook his head no at me before speaking.

"You should read them alone, Rose. I don't want you feeling the need to hold back on your emotions because you're worried about what I'll think. I love you, my Rose. You do what you need to, and call me when you're done. I'll come running," he promised.

"Thank you," I whispered.

Lucas left me shortly after, grabbing the gift he still

hadn't given his mother. It was late, around 10 o'clock now, but his mother was still awake and expecting him. I knew he would be fine, and I appreciated him giving me privacy for this, even if I didn't want him to go. He's right, I would hold back if he were around.

Taking a deep breath, I dug around for the box full of red envelopes Ian had given me last month. I had stuffed it deep in my closet, too scared to read them. Now it's time, we've said our goodbyes, and admitted our past feelings. It's time to get this over with and move on. There's a need deep inside me to close this chapter of my life, to know exactly what he said to me in those letters. What could have been if I would have gotten them. I know it will hurt, it will tear me apart to think about, but I need to know. I need to know how he felt all those years.

Song Suggestion: "Closure" by Hayd

I grabbed the first letter I saw, not caring about reading them in order. I opened it slowly, feeling the sadness starting to well inside me already. As usual, Ian's penmanship was impeccably beautiful. I was always surprised by how neatly he wrote. His hand writing was always better than mine.

Dearest Red,

I can't believe it's been two months since I moved away now. It feels like yesterday we were laughing and talking for hours on end. I miss you so much!

I miss your smile, your laugh, and your sense of humor. I miss our inside jokes and our late-night conversations on my roof, and our favorite hang-out spot.

I also miss our adventures together. We've been through so much together, and I'm so grateful to have you in my life. I hope you have found someone to help you through the bad times. I worry about you being alone, Red.

I know I'm not the only one who misses you. My mom and dad miss you, too. I know you miss them, too. Having you in our house only made it so much better. Life feels so different without you by my side.

I hope to get a letter from you soon. I plan to return one day, so don't forget about me, Red. Until then, know I'm thinking of you always.

Love,
Your best friend, Ian

My chest felt tight, and for a moment I wasn't sure I could do this. I took another deep breath, trying to calm myself. I grabbed the next letter, feeling like my heart was breaking into a million pieces.

Dear Red,

I've been thinking about the time we met. It feels like yesterday we were two awkward freshmen, bumping into each other in science class. I knew from the moment I saw you that you were someone special. There was something about you that drew me in, something that made me want to get to know you better.

And I'm so glad I did. Over the past couple of years, you've become my best friend. You know me better than anyone else in the world, and you stayed my friend, anyway. I can't imagine what life without you would be like, although I'm getting a glimpse of it now. It's miserable here without you.

I miss the way you make me laugh. I miss the way you challenge me to be a better person. No one is able to encourage me the way you do. You are the most amazing girl I have ever met, and I am so lucky to have you in my life. School sucks without your sweet self by my side. I wish I could have packed you in my suitcase and brought you here, too.

I hope you're doing well. I am still waiting on the letter you promised me. I hope you haven't forgotten about me already.

Your best friend forever, (Despite the long distance)
Ian.

I could feel the tears start to stream down my face, falling over the letters in the box. I continued anyway, needing to read every letter, even if I became dehydrated from all the crying.

Dearest Red,

I'm writing this letter with a heavy heart. I feel like I've lost my best friend, and I don't know what to do.

 I know my moving away has made things hard, reducing us to writing letters to keep in touch. I understand things are different now, but I feel like you've forgotten about me. We used to talk all the time, and now we don't talk at all. I have not gotten a letter from you, instead I receive the letters I sent you in return. Maybe you've decided to no longer be my friend, or perhaps you met someone new to take my place, and are too busy to write.

 I miss our conversations. I miss being around you. I know you're busy with your new life, but I wish you would make some time for me. I'm here for you, no matter what. I hope you'll reach out soon. I miss you.

 Love always,
 Ian

 My heart was breaking, reading Ian's letters. He was hurt, thinking I didn't want him anymore. I hated that he had felt this way, that he thought these things. I wished he could have known how desperately I needed him back then, how much I missed him.

 Dear Red,

 I know you're not reading these, so I decided to pour my feelings out, to admit to you what I couldn't in person. One day I'll see you again and I'll show you all these letters. I will win you over, and maybe one day convince you to marry me.

 I love you, Red, as much more than just a friend. You light my world on fire in the best way. Your smile is brighter than the stars in the sky. Those eyes of yours hold a fire behind the ice, one that keeps you going even when your life is thrown to hell.

 I love your voice, but your laugh, God, your laugh is like magic. It sends a happiness coursing through me that makes it impossible not to smile. Your hair is the most beautiful red I've ever seen. It fits you perfectly, making you stand out as you should. You don't need to be pushed into the background, all attention should be on you.

 You make my heart race and my hands sweat. I've never felt so happy yet so lost. You make me unsure of myself. It's not a *feeling I am used to. I like the way you bring out this side of me I didn't know I had. An adventurous side.*

Red, I hope you know how amazing you are. You belittle yourself because of the girls in school. You shouldn't listen to them. They're nothing but jealous bitches. Those girls don't know you the way I do. They see someone they know is a threat to their standing. You're going to do wonderful things, Red, and I plan to be at your side to see it all.

I love you with all my heart. I hope you read this one day and find me knelt before you with a ring. You're my one, Red, I am sure of it.

I love you always,
Ian

I cried for a while, feeling my heart break and mend itself again. I never knew he felt this way about me. I pictured the future that could have been with him and then let it go. I let *him* go, along with the teenage dream I had of us together.

He's still my friend, right?

Lucas' P.O.V.

Christmas was more than I could have asked for. She had said yes, and despite Dad's threats, I've been on cloud nine ever since. I need to get back to work before Dad discovers I'm trying to marry Rose. I get the feeling he'd try to stop it by any and all means necessary. He doesn't need to know until it's done and over with. I won't put Rose, or my bud, through any unnecessary stress.

"Good morning, my future wife." I kissed her forehead as I woke her. She says she's not a sleepyhead, but she most definitely is. "Today's the day."

Sleep evaded me last night, even with Rose in my arms. I was too excited for today. It's our first doctor's appointment for our bud. We'll get to see our growing baby on an ultrasound today and be sure of Rose's due date. I've been giddy all night.

"Today's the day." She smiled as her eyes opened. It was the fastest she'd ever woken up, aside from the time she had to bolt to the bathroom to throw up. She is excited too. I can only imagine how she must feel, as she's the one carrying our child.

"Let's get ready," I said, making us both jump out of bed. We got dressed and ate a quick breakfast. I made Rose a fruit salad this morning since she had been craving fruits more here lately. She says they don't make her as nauseous as most breakfast foods.

I had to keep myself from speeding my way to the doctor's office, which was pretty hard to do. I was ready to see my bud, and growing inpatient with every minute. It didn't help that we had to wait an hour after we checked in for them to call Rose's name. We followed them to a back room where she was instructed to lift her shirt. A few seconds later she was squirted with warm gel. The ultrasound wand found her stomach as the technician began to move it around.

Song Suggestion: "Light" by Sleeping At Last

I watched the tv waiting for the image of my bud. Within moments my little rosebud came into view. Our baby looked like a little kidney bean, curved with two rounded ends. I tried to engrave the image in my brain as I watched the little bean jump around as if it knew we were watching. My eyes started to mist as I continued to watch. I grabbed Rose's hand, kissing it tenderly, thanking her for this gift she was blessing me with. When I turned to look at her, I found tears streaking her face. She was overwhelmed by the sight of our child, just as I was.

We listened to our baby's strong, thundering heartbeat with joy. I recorded the sound on my phone so I will never forget it. The technician printed a couple of pictures for us and confirmed the due date was July 27th-a sweet summer baby. I squeezed Rose's hand, kissing it again as we stared at the pictures.

"You can use this towel to clean off, and I'll take you to your room to see the doctor," the technician said, handing Rose a small towel to wipe herself off with. We waited another 30 minutes in the room for the doctor. I hate how long it takes to see the doctor. I'll go with Rose to every visit if only to keep her company. These things could be boring by yourself, I am sure.

"Can you believe it?" Rose broke our comfortable silence first. "We created this."

She had been staring at the ultrasound pictures, mesmerized by our growing fetus. Her eyes glimmered with love, which only made me fall deeper in love with her. I think seeing her become a mother will only strengthen my love for her. She's perfect, and she's mine.

"I am one lucky man." I smiled at her, placing my hand over her stomach. I can't wait to feel our baby kick.

"I am one lucky woman," she countered. "Me either." I smiled at her, leaning in to kiss her temple. Her sweet vanilla scented shampoo wafted into my nose. I loved everything about her, down to her toes.

"Hello, Olive. I am Dr. Fitz. It's so nice to meet you." The doctor smiled at her, extending her hand for a small shake. "Is this your first pregnancy?"

"It is," Rose answered.

The doctor went on to describe what would be happening to Rose's body throughout her pregnancy. We discussed how her BRACA gene would affect it. Rose will need to keep her screening appointments and if they ever found anything we would talk about it then. It scares me to think about, and I pray it never happens. I can't lose my Rose, not ever.

"I know I'm dumping a lot of information on you, but I like to keep you informed. Think about everything we've spoken about and decide what you would like to do birthing wise. Any questions?" We both shook our heads no, ending our visit. We stopped by the front counter to set her next appointment up and then raced home. I knew she could use a nap. She stayed up late with Ian's letters last night. When I returned home, her eyes were puffy and pink from all the crying she'd done. It broke my heart to see her this way.

It may be wrong of me to say, but if there's one thing I'm grateful for, it's the fact her dad kept those letters. I get the feeling I would have never had a chance with her if she and Ian had stayed in touch. They'd probably be the ones getting married now. Still, the hurt it caused her was too much. It was definitely something she should have never gone through.

"Sleep, my Rose." I rubbed her back lightly as she laid beside me.

I sat up, resting my back on the headboard. I had finished her junior year and was almost through her senior year. Apparently, Francesca had gone to her school and tormented her as well. I was happy to hear she wasn't accepted into the IT crowd at this school. They had expelled her, which is what made her end up in school with Leo. She and Leo were in the same grade, but she didn't start her torment on us until their senior year. I was glad she couldn't continue to hurt my Rose, even if it put her in my path.

Dear Future Me,

We fucking did it! We survived 4 years of utter hell and came out on top. Valedictorian, baby!! Woo! Eat my shit, Jessica! Do you think they can keep me from graduating if I flip everyone off as my speech? A full minute of telling everyone fuck you.

I won't ruin graduation like that. I'll give them what they want and get what I need from them. Can't burn these important bridges, especially if I'm trying to work for NASA. I don't think they'd like reading that article. 'Valedictorian flips off the whole graduation class for a full minute.' They would not hire me.

I can't wait to be away from here. I can't wait to go to Columbia and dorm with new people. They can't be as bad as the kids here, at least I hope not. I got a full ride with dorm paid, letting me use the money I saved from working with Joe to get my first phone, laptop and small furnishings for my dorm. I am excited to finally have these things.

Dad still doesn't know I'm planning to live on campus. I don't plan on telling him until I'm pulling out of the driveway. Joe said he'd drive me there, since he has business in New York city. A little out of the way, but close enough he'd take me.

This is it. I will be free of him, of these kids, of this prison and this hurt. I can't wait to start my life anew.

A very boisterous, Past You

The entry made me smile, picturing how happy Rose felt at the time. She'd accomplished what she set out to do, reaching her goal despite the hell she'd endured every day. She's so damn strong, the strongest person I know.

Dear Future Me,

We escaped dad! We did it! I've never felt so free in my life. The feeling is new, coursing a sort of giddy feeling through me. My mind is racing with a million possibilities and my body wants to do them all. I want to see everything, experience everything. All of it.

I want to conquer this world and make it my bitch. I am going to graduate top of my class in Columbia. I am going to achieve my dream and rub it in everyone's faces. In the faces of those who doubted me or belittled me for no reason.

I am smart, determined, and caring. The world won't change me. It won't take that from me. This is my time, my time to explore, to learn, and to grow more than just academically.

Time to unpack and start a new journal as my freshman year of college begins.

I closed her senior year, feeling so close to my Rose. I know all about her high school years. The knowledge of her torments, depression, bullying, and small happy moments will forever reside in me. Everything that's happened to her has shaped her into this fierce, fiery woman before me. She didn't let it defeat her. She climbed to the top with a set goal, and she took what she deserved. She's a champion already.

Keep fighting my Rose.

Chapter 48

Olive's P.O.V.

The morning sickness has been easing as time passes. I wake every morning and stare at the now outdated ultrasound pictures. Today we are going to a gender reveal ultrasound place. We'll get to see our little bean again. *I wonder what it'll be? Boy or girl?*

"I can't wait to see my little bud again." Lucas smiled at me. I nodded, leaning against him, feeling the same excitement.

"What do you think, boy or girl?" I asked him.

"Girl. She'll be my little Rosebud." He nodded looking only at the ultrasound picture held onto the fridge by an old floral magnet.

"I say boy. He'd be my little Knight," I countered with a smile.

We walked hand in hand towards the front door, seeing our reflection in the tinted glass. The place felt like an overly decorated doctor's office with pink and gold frills. They want to freeze their clients stiff as I froze my ass off, waiting to be called. Lucas held me close, providing me with some warmth. About 15 minutes later, we were called to follow the technician. She led us to a side room with a door that wouldn't close all the way. Goosebumps erupted all over my arms as the chill air hit me. It was colder here than in the lobby.

I lay on the frozen vinyl examination table, lifting my shirt as the technician instructed. The cold air was uncomfortable, but the moment my eyes landed on the growing baby inside me, it didn't matter anymore. My eyes misted over again. I guess they will have the same response anytime I see my child. I felt Lucas' large hand on my own as he squeezed it. We watched as the technician maneuvered the wand over me.

She's a girl!

"Congratulations, guys. You're having a girl!" The technician announced as she snapped a picture between our child's legs with the words, *it's a girl,* over it.

We spent a few minutes watching and seeing our baby look more like a baby. She was beautiful, but still so small. I couldn't help the tears streaming down my face from the pure joy and love I felt. Lucas wiped them away, but his eyes were pink and misted, too. I was happy to see he was willing to cry over our child. He loved his little Rosebud as much as I.

"What do you think?" Lucas asked as he spun around the center of the room. It was gorgeous with its glass walls and ceiling. This place was beautiful inside and out, absolutely perfect for our wedding.

"I love it!" I exclaimed with a smile.

The Brooklyn Botanic Garden was like this little oasis tucked away in one of the largest cities in the world. There were a plethora of trees, flower borders, and pastoral lawns. There were shrub roses, tall bearded irises, grandiflora roses, and so many more beautiful flowers planted here. It made this place look so beautiful. The colors were vibrant and laid out perfectly.

A beautiful lily pool sat outside the glasshouse, and the view left an indelible impression on me. Perennial and annual flowers bordered two large rectangular pools. There were water lilies and lotus scattered throughout. Tulips surrounded the west side of the pool, along with alliums and other spring bloomers. Since we'll be having our wedding in the fall after our baby girl is born, they probably won't be in bloom anymore. Still, this place was magically beautiful and felt absolutely perfect for tying my life together with Lucas'.

"I like it too." Lucas beamed his beautiful smile at me.

We walked around more before we found our tour person again and decided to book our day—September 28th, before it gets too cold, but not until after the summer heat. We had thought about our date for a few months. My mind barely had room for school between wedding and baby planning.

Thankfully, my grades have not slipped in the slightest, but I do get a lot of looks when I enter my class with my rounded stomach. I often feel their stares and judging gazes on me, but I ignore them. They mean little to nothing; the only opinion that matters is that of mine and Lucas, and we are currently over the moon.

Lucas paid to have me get an ultrasound every month so we could see our baby. This is the one time I'm happy he's rich. It's a lot less stressful to plan a wedding when you don't have to worry about a budget, or where the money will come from. After this, I'm going wedding dress shopping with Lisa, Hailey, and Sarah. Lucas pouted that he couldn't come too. It was adorable, as I rarely see him act so cute. Lisa teased him about it for a few hours until he got annoyed. They were an interesting pair of siblings, constantly annoying one another yet caring for each other deeply. I know they are so close despite their clashing personalities because of their shared trauma.

We left the garden reluctantly. It was such a beautiful place and quite large, too, offering a variety of greens and venues alike. The smells were enchanting, unlike those of the city. I was happy we found this little piece of heaven. We'll have to come here more often, even after our wedding, to enjoy nature. Lucas was driving me to meet Hailey, who would take me to a dress shop she knew in town.

"Have fun." Lucas kissed my forehead as he dropped me off with Hailey. "I'll miss you."

"I'll miss you, too."

Lucas and I have not spent a moment away from each other since he returned from his trip with his mom and Lisa. He works while I'm in class or while I nap or sleep at night. I find myself resting a lot more now. Growing a baby is exhausting.

"Let's go, chica. We have a lot to see and many dresses to try on." Hailey smiled, linking her arm with mine the way she always does.

I will not lie; I'm more than excited about this part. The little girl in me is singing and jumping for joy. I've always wanted this moment and pictured it with my mother. I am sad I can't share this with her, but I am glad Sarah is here to experience this. She and I got closer after we announced our pregnancy. She's been giving me care packages every weekend and checking in on me daily through texts or calls. Sarah is a wonderful, sweet, and protective woman. She's so excited to have a grandchild.

We haven't told Lucas' dad about the baby or the wedding. Lucas says it's best to wait until after the fact for both. He's worried his dad will try to do something. I haven't spoken to my father since Lucas punched him in the jaw. Joe hasn't reported anything with Daisy either, so things are going as well as they can. We entered the dress shop, and a salesperson greeted us immediately. The many white dresses lining the walls and mannequins with the comfortable couches placed throughout the store gave it a fancier feel. I couldn't believe the sheer number of gowns. It felt like there were a million and one different styles and kinds of dresses. All I knew was I wanted to try on as many as possible.

"Of course, the size will differ once you have the baby. This is more so we can find the right dress and then come after the baby is born to get the right size." Sarah explained as the attendant seemed unsure what size gowns to get for me.

"We'll want a dress that doesn't press against your stomach as you'll have had a baby. As young and beautiful as you are, your body is still going to need more than a few months to return to its pre-pregnancy stage." Sarah added as she looked through dresses. She had taken charge of the situation already. Lisa grabbed her mom by the shoulders and sat her on the couch with a look of warning.

"Calm down, mom. Let her enjoy the moment, hmm?"

"Right. I'm so sorry, Olive. I get ahead of myself sometimes."

"No, it's completely fine. I appreciate the advice and guidance," I said with a small smile. I hadn't thought of most of what she had said.

I tried on what felt like a trillion dresses. We determined I was not one for Cinderella-like gowns. The puffy bottoms were too itchy for me and too much to handle. The mermaid gowns were out of the question with how tightly they hugged my figure. Finally, I decided my wedding dress needed to have an A-line figure, lace designs, and be floor length. Those were my three main points. After a few hours, we were all starting to grow tired, but that's when we found it.

The dress checked my three criteria. It was floor length, cascading around me on the sides and back but staying at my ankles in the front so I wouldn't step on it while I walked. The bodice was made with intricate lace detailing and had a split down the middle between my breasts. The sleeves were quarter inch straps and made of lace and silky white fabric. The lace extended over the bottom of the dress. It didn't cover the entire base, with lace stripes down the front and sides. It was perfect. *This is my dress.*

***

Olive: You're coming to my graduation, right?
#1 Best Friend: I wouldn't miss it for the world.

Ian's reply made me feel better. He and I hadn't spoken much since Christmas. I know he meant it when he said we were still friends, but he needed time to get over me. We still text, but it wasn't daily like it had been before Christmas. It made me a bit sad, but I know it's for the best. Hailey, on the other hand, texts and calls multiple times a day and drops by every other day with something new. Yesterday, it was a little red bracelet made of yarn. I'm meant to put this on our child when she's born. Hailey made me swear I would, so I did.

"I've been thinking a lot about what we should name our little Rosebud," Lucas said as he rubbed his hands over my growing baby bump. He'd been reading my college junior year journal. He's a couple of journals away from the one he's been desperately wanting to read...*his journal*.

"Okay, what have you come up with?" We'd been thinking of names for a couple of months now, but nothing has felt right.

"Abi," he said, and my eyes instantly watered. My pregnancy hormones have been wild, causing the craziest mood swings. I cry so quickly now over everything and anything. Yesterday, I bawled because I forgot I had eaten the last peach and had to have another one. Lucas ran to the store and got me five more right away. He's been so patient and understanding with me. I swear he's the perfect man.

"Are you sure?" I asked, feeling like maybe we should honor his mother in some way too.

"Yes, I'm sure. Abi Rose Porter. What do you think?"

"It's perfect." I nodded my head, shedding overly emotional tears. Lucas held me close as he rubbed my arms. He placed his hand over my baby bump and began to talk to our baby girl...to our Abi.

"You hear that? You've got a name, Abi. Do you like it? Kick once for yes and twice for no." I smiled at his antics, loving it when he spoke to her. She kicked at his hand once, making us both smile widely.

"She's a genius already," Lucas said with the biggest smile yet.

"She is your daughter."

"Our daughter. Rose, you're so damn intelligent. You're

about to graduate top of your class from Colombia with a hard ass degree, Miss Aerospace Engineer. If Abi gets her intelligence from anyone, it would be you." Lucas always lifts me up, and refuses to let me be modest. He says I need to acknowledge my worth.

We spent the afternoon cuddling while we finished making our wedding plans. We had our cake, our colors, our catering menu and our venue. I have the dress I want already picked out. I need to get the right size after I have Abi. All we have left to do is ask our best friends an important question. Hailey will be my maid of honor and Leo will be Lucas' best man. We need to find a cute way of asking each of them.

"I can't wait to marry you, Rose. You're doing so amazing with everything. I don't know how you manage it all. Three more weeks until you graduate, two and a half months until Abi's here and four and a half months until you become my wife." He kissed my nose, my cheeks and my forehead as he spoke, leaving my lips for last.

I found myself hornier than usual with these pregnancy hormones, but it's also super uncomfortable to have Lucas inside me. He's been so patient and kind with sex. I can get so uncomfortable when he's inside of me, so instead; he's pleased me with his tongue or his fingers multiple times. I always feel guilty after, but he tells me not to, and he means it, too. He doesn't care about his sexual needs being met right now. He promises to ravish me on our wedding night. *I can't wait.*

The warm May air and blistering sun, mixed with the black cap and gown, was not a fun way to spend a few hours. At least the seats were cushioned and comfy as we listened to the dean give his speech. I was graduating, and I couldn't be more excited. I had worked hard for four years, keeping my grades up and my GPA at 4.0. The college has taught me so much.

These last four years have been an experience of a

lifetime, not just on campus or in class. I learned how to live, how to pop out of my shell. Hailey met me first, followed by Davis and Carter. I made the mistake of dating Julius, but that led me to Lucas. Because of it, I met Leo on campus and got to see Lucas again. I reunited with Mom, suffered her loss, stood up to Dad, and discovered what actually happened with Ian. Now I sit here waiting to be called ceremoniously to show I have done what I set out to do. The accomplishment I felt was beyond the moon.

    I stood to the side of the stage until my name was called with my many accomplishments. The cheers from the crowd were loud and distinctive to the people I most loved. I could see Lucas standing alongside Ian amidst our group of friends who clapped like normal people. I blushed, but I loved the way they cheered for me. Having my flimsy paper in hand I made my way off the stage and back to my seat until the whole thing was over.

    "Liv!' Hailey waved me down as she pushed past the crowd that had now formed on the lawn. It was a prong of people maneuvering around one another in an effort to find their people. Thankfully, because of my pregnant state, people parted for me without much effort. I walked hurriedly towards Hailey, who took me to the rest of the group.

    "Congratulations!" Sarah said as she handed me a bouquet of large flowers. She seemed like a proud mother, making me almost cry again.

    "Thank you." I smiled at her.

    "You did it, Red! I knew you would." Ian hugged me tightly with his wide tooth grin. He held me for a moment until Abi kicked against him. He let me go with wide eyes as he looked down at my swollen stomach.

    "She likes to kick when she feels something pressed against my bump," I explained with a loving smile as I rubbed my belly.

    "She's going to be a fighter, like you." Ian's words hit me hard. I hope she never has to fight.

"I'm so proud of you, Rose." Lucas was next to congratulate me. He pulled me into his tight embrace as he kissed my lips passionately. He was full of love and radiating such joy. I think we both were. Hailey was surrounded by her own family as they congratulated her. She smiled at me as she noticed me watching, then she and her whole family walked over to us.

"Can you believe it? We're all done. No more lunch at the commons, or coffee at the little cafe. No more late night studying, or early morning classes to race to. We've done it, Liv." Hailey seemed so emotional as she spoke. She was right. I hadn't thought about how graduating meant we wouldn't be seeing this place much. I'd grown quite accustomed to the campus, and life inside it. Now it's time to venture out into my career field and put this degree to use. But somehow I think I will miss this place.

"We'll still meet up for lunch every Sunday and catch up on life, right?" I asked, not wanting to lose touch with her now, knowing we won't see each other every day on campus.

"Of course, Liv! I wouldn't miss our dates for the world." She smiled her bright smile. We hugged each other for a while, feeling an overwhelming bittersweet feeling. Why are graduations actually kind of sad?

Chapter 49

Lucas' P.O.V.

I finally finished her journals from her junior year of college. This was it. I was finally getting to her journals about me. At the beginning of all this, I wanted only to read the journals about me, but I'm glad Rose made me work for it. I understand her better now that I've read her innermost thoughts about her past. She was a cherry tomato red as she handed me these journals this morning. She asked me not to read them while she was awake. Her embarrassment was adorable, but completely unnecessary.

She was asleep beside me, lightly snoring with her peacefully beautiful face. Rose is tired of interviewing around town, trying to find an engineering job for experience until the place she wants is hiring again. I tried to use my connections to help her, but she told me she'd be mad at me if I did. My Rose wants to get her job from all her hard work. I find it very noble, but I wish she'd let me help. I placed my hand over our Abi as I began to read. One more month until she's born.

Dear Future Me,

Choose your boyfriends more wisely. Julius was a fucking waste of our time. I mean, Clover? Really? Oh yeah, choose better roommates too. The pair of them can rot in hell. My heart hurts, but I'm focusing on my anger tonight. Hailey is taking me out, and I'm determined to prove a point.

Julius isn't the only guy I can get. Despite what he said during our relationship, I am sure other guys have noticed me. I am doing it! I'm having a one-night stand, as Hailey suggested. It's an experience I need, anyway. Since I'm no longer a virgin, it's not that big of a deal anymore. Fuck anyone who calls me a slut for doing it.

Now I need to find a hot-looking guy tonight and flirt my way to his bed. I'm not sure how I'll do it, but I'm sure a little alcohol will be involved. Hurray for being 21 already! Time to get drunk and get laid.

A vengeful, Past You

I smirked, knowing this was the night she and I met. I did not know she felt this way when we met. This was her goal, her intention for the night. Damn, if I wasn't lucky enough to be the one she chose. I remember that fateful night all too well. I flipped the page, wondering what she wrote about me the next day.

Dear Future Me,

Holy fucking shit! Last night was the best sex of my life. Julius is shit in bed compared to the guy I chose last night. Lucas is his name, and Lord help me, if I didn't scream it multiple times throughout the night. The man is a fucking sex god. Hot as hell, too. How the hell I managed to pull him off is beyond me.

I am glad New York is so big. The chances of seeing him again are slim, which is great because I could see myself becoming addicted to a guy like him. I already can't get him out of my head. The way his body moved against mine was like a perfect puzzle piece I didn't know I was missing. His lips were on fire, his touches only made me hunger for more. His dick is like a gift from the heavens, made especially to please a woman.

The man knows what he's doing and I feel perhaps he's ruined me for any other guy. I am not sure if Julius was complete shit in bed or if sex should be the way it was with Lucas. Or maybe sex like that is only particular to Lucas. I know nothing about him, but I know he must have a lot of experience. His moves were swift, intentional, and all around sexy.

Also, a mental note for the future. Don't stare at your phone in front of a door. My tongue is killing me and I couldn't even speak my mind to Julius when he came and bothered me. Typing *my responses was not nearly as satisfying as yelling them in his face would have been. At least I made a new friend.*

I won't be keeping the phone he gave me for long. I'm still not an iPhone person. There's no way, but he's sweet and he's invited Hailey and I out. She won't let me say no either, so I guess we're going this weekend.

A pained and still horny, Past You

I'm not going to lie, reading this entry made me feel extremely arrogant. I had no idea she felt this way about me from our first encounter. She felt so inexperienced compared to me. I wonder if that's why she was quick to leave me that night. I had never had a girl rush out of my apartment as quickly as she had. It had left me even more intrigued by her.

Dear future me,

New York is not as big as we imagined. Our sex-god showed up, apparently knowing Leo very well. He knew what I liked to drink, and even rescued me from security at the club. I am not sure how, but he managed to make sex even better than the last time. My body is still sore all over from our encounter, but I don't regret it one bit. The only regret I have is that Leo saw me naked. Why the hell did he come into Lucas' room without knocking? Do they live together? How'd he get into the apartment?

I need to pretend like none of this ever happened. He's so out of my league, and I don't need anything complicating my life right now. Lucas is dangerous for me. I could easily lose myself in him. As much fun as he is, it would be best if I kept my distance. Yet my stupid mouth betrayed me and said yes to going out tonight. Hailey is currently working on my hair as I write. She's ecstatic for me, but all I am is nervous. Is this a date?

God help me. I don't know what I'm doing. He's going to have his way with me tonight and I won't be able to resist him. I'll let you know how it goes.

A very stupid and nervous, Past You

I remembered this afternoon all too well. I was surprised she had said yes, but I was so grateful. I had gotten her number on this day and somehow convinced her to go to dinner with me. Having her at Dad's for dinner made it so much better, even if it ended with me fighting with Dad. This night didn't end well as a whole. It was the night she pulled away emotionally from me. Fucking Janessa. It still makes me mad thinking about it.

Dear Future Me,

I fucking knew it! Lucas is not the guy for me. I fooled myself into thinking he was by the way he had accepted me after the fight. He was so happy and amazed by me. It made me feel so great. I wanted to allow him in, but when we got to his apartment, a woman was already there waiting for him.

I'm sure she was naked under her trench coat. I'm such an idiot for thinking this could be more. He's got a lot of options and I'm only one of them. He may have kicked her out, but that could be because he started the evening out with me. At least he doesn't switch girls through the night. He didn't chase after me or ask me to stay, so he must not care as much for me as I do him.

Thankfully, I ran into Leo, but he only confused me more. I can't let myself fall for Lucas, so for now on, Mom will be my priority. Dad called and told me she's sick. She's dying, and she's here in New York. I haven't seen her for 10 years and now she's here dying. What the hell am I supposed to do with that news? I have so many questions for her, so much I want to say. She owes me an explanation, so I'm going tomorrow to get her to give me one.

I won't let Lucas distract me. My focus will be school and seeing mom again. I could use some closure as to why she abandoned me. I hope she's willing and ready to answer my questions, because otherwise I'll leave without another word. If she can't answer me, then I'm not worth her time. She doesn't get to hear I love you or I forgive you until she explains herself.

What kind of mother leaves her child behind with a man who abused her? Did she not think Dad could have turned his anger to me instead?

I need answers, and I'll get them tomorrow.

A very confused and anxious, Past You

I had no idea she wanted me to chase after her. I

thought she needed space, and I don't like to push. I respect people's wishes, more so since the incident with Francesca. If someone says no or to stop, I do, no matter what it pertains to. I continued reading about how things went with her mother. She spoke about Leo and his loss. Apparently, she regretted her decision to tell us her life story, but she was happy to help Leo.

She spoke about our sexcapades and how she was going to keep it strictly sex between us. I realized how stupid I was in not showing her how much I wanted to be serious with her. She wanted me, but she was scared of getting hurt and I could see why. I was reaching the day after her surgery now, after I'd opened up to her about what happened to me. I turned to find a page missing. It had been torn out, leaving behind a small bit of paper, sticking out like a sore thumb. *Why'd she tear it out? Was it a mistake entry?* I'll have to ask her about it later. For now, I'll enjoy all the other entries about me and how much she loves me.

Olive's P.O.V.

4"You need to sit, Rose. The doctor said to sit and elevate your feet. You're starting to swell around your ankles again," Lucas reminded me as I waddled around the flat, trying to get last-minute things together.

The bassinet was put together and sat beside the bed. The bottles were sanitized and put away already. All the clothes were washed, folded, and organized. My hospital bag was ready to go, along with Abi's. I packed her the cutest-take home outfit. I love all the frills, laces, and colors on little girl clothes. Of course, I bought a shit ton of bows that are way too large for her head, too. I have those neatly organized as well. I still feel like I'm forgetting or missing something, but I'm unsure what.

Daisy had my baby brother a few months ago, and according to Joe, everything is still going well. It made me wonder if Dad had changed, but then I remembered he's Dad, and it's only a matter of time until his ugliness resurfaces. I hope Daisy is smart enough to get away when it does. Joe gave her my number again for me. Maybe this time, she'll save it and use it.

I felt another cramp coming, causing me to stop and lean against the closest thing around me. I gripped the edge of the table as I let it pass. If these Braxton Hicks contractions were any indication of how painful labor would be, I'll die. *Definitely getting an epidural.* I mean, it's got to be painful if any woman is willing to stick a giant needle in their back to stop feeling labor pains.

"Are you okay?" Lucas asked, placing his hands on my sides to steady me. "Have you been timing it?" Lucas has been reading every, and any, labor book he could find. At this point I think he knows more about it than I do. His eyes held mine with both concern and excitement. I know he can't wait for Abi to be born and we're only a few days away now.

"No, I'm sure it's Braxton Hicks again."

"You never know, Rose. You should always time them." I think he wanted it to be labor already.

"Okay, I will." I smiled at him, nodding my head, stepping away from the table since the pain had passed.

I let him guide me to the couch and sit me down. He lifted my feet, placing pillows under them to keep them elevated. All throughout this pregnancy, he has been taking great care of me. He's gone to every doctor's appointment, reminded me of my prenatal vitamins, bought all the food I crave, no matter how crazy or how late in the night it was. If I craved it, he'd make it appear before me. He refuses to let me squat down or reach for something too high. *He's my perfect man.*

As I watched TV, another wave of pain rolled over me, causing me to clutch the edge of the couch cushion. Lucas was by my side in an instant again, taking my hand and eyeing me with worry. Once it passed, I saw him log the time on his phone. Our routine continued until; eventually, I knew it wasn't Braxton Hicks anymore. The pain was actual labor! *Our Abi is coming today!* I've never felt so nervous and so excited at once. Knowing our Abi would be in our arms in the next 24 hours was unbelievable. We'll finally see her face, feel her skin, touch her hand. I'm excited to see what her hair will look like, what shade her skin will be, and what I can't see on an ultrasound.

"Come on, Rose. It's time to go to the hospital."

Lucas helped me up, grabbing everything we needed. He rushed around the room like a maniac. He was excited, but worried for me. He hates to see me in pain, and *fuck me* are contractions painful. It feels like someone has their hands around my uterus and is squeezing it with all their might. I grunted as I tried not to yell when another stronger contraction hit.

Lucas drove carefully, as always, but he did so quickly. He had a wheelchair brought out to meet us, so I wouldn't have to walk in. The contractions were only three minutes apart now and felt like they lasted an eternity. I gripped onto the arms of the wheelchair as I bit my tongue, trying not to make a sound.

"You're doing so well, Rose. Remember to breathe," Lucas encouraged me, making me realize I was actually holding my breath. I closed my eyes and focused on taking deep, clear breaths. It helped a bit, giving me something to focus on aside from the pain. The nurse set an IV drip once we got to a room. She asked if I'd like an epidural and I immediately yelled yes. Lucas tried not to laugh, but he couldn't help the smirk.

"I'm so sorry, Rose. I don't mean to laugh at your pain. You scared the nurse with your tone," he chuckled. I knew he wasn't laughing at me.

He kept me distracted by talking about things that would excite me. We talked about our wedding, our honeymoon, and my job prospects. I'd been offered a job at a few of the places I'd interviewed. My worries about not being hired because I'll be a mom were unfounded. They didn't care. They only cared about my work ethic, my ability, and my degree. I checked those boxes for a lot of places.

We were weighing my options when I felt a trickle of water between my legs. It was like a leaky faucet had opened up between my legs. The nurse came in and checked me and I was at six centimeters now. Four more until it's time to push. My contractions only intensified after my water broke. They'd placed a towel between my legs to keep me from getting too wet as my water continued to leak out of me. It definitely wasn't like the movies, where it looks like a large water bottle popped. It was slow and constant, and frankly, a bit annoying.

I held onto Lucas' hand for dear life as I reached eight centimeters. The pressure I felt below was insane. I thought my tailbone would snap from it. I could feel my body wanting to push, but I held back as it wasn't time yet. The nurse started to wheel things in and I tried to focus on what she was bringing. She brought in a little warmer, which she went ahead and turned on. There was a scale and a rolled-in instrument tray. I tried not to look at those, worried I'd see some sort of scary looking instrument they'd use on me.

The doctor came in next, and before I knew it, it was time to push. I'd never been so grateful. I was ready to release the pressure I was feeling. My legs were placed in the stirrups as my ass almost hung off the bed. My OB was covered in a blue disposable gown, cap, and booties. This was apparently a very messy ordeal.

"Okay, Olive, it's time to push. On the next contraction I want you to grab the back of your knees and push until I count to 10 as hard as you can," the doctor instructed me. I nodded and did it on the next contraction. Lucas helped by pushing my back up and my legs close, almost like he was folding me in half. It helped more than I thought it would. I felt a strong burning for a second and wondered if I had torn down there.

"There's the head, mama. You're doing great," the doctor called out, giving me more motivation to push harder. The shoulders were next, and then she slid out with the next push. I laid back, utterly exhausted, when I heard her beautiful little cry. She was placed on my chest as Lucas cut her umbilical cord. We both cried as we stared down at the life we created. She was so small and absolutely perfect. Lucas kissed my sweaty forehead without a care.

The overwhelming feeling of pure love had me in tears for a while. Abi was everything to me. My number one priority. Lucas and I will give her the childhood neither of us were able to have. She'll grow up in a home like Ian's. A warm and loving home, and welcoming to all.

Welcome to the world, my Abi Rose.

"She's beautiful, Twinkle Toes," Davis cooed as he peered at her in my arms. He refused to hold her, worried he would somehow hurt her. "She's so tiny. I remember when my daughter was this small. Now she's grown and wants nothing to do with me half the time." He shook his head lightly as he spoke.

"Don't tell me that," I scolded. "I don't want to picture her grown up already. I just had her." Davis chuckled his hearty laugh. "Sorry, kid. I guess I should stop calling you kid, too. Can't call you kid when you have a kid."

"Mhm," I hummed. There was something I have been meaning to ask Davis for months now, but haven't had the nerve. Even though I am still exhausted, I feel like now is the time, or I'll never do it. "Davis, can I ask you something?"

"You already did," he joked, earning him a shove from me. "Alright, what's up? If it's about babysitting, the answer is yes, but only on Sundays, Tuesdays and Fridays. Those are my free days." He smiled widely, surprising me with the offer.

"It wasn't about babysitting, but I'll definitely keep those days in mind." I smirked.

"Okay, what's up then?"

"You know I'm getting married in September," I started.

"Yes, of course. I got the invite, thank you." He was all jokes today, letting me know he was in a great mood.

"Normally, the bride has her father walk her down the aisle." Davis stiffened beside me as I continued. "Obviously, I'm not having my dad at my wedding. Hell, he doesn't even know I'm getting married, or that I had Abi, let alone that I was pregnant."

"Rightfully so, that asshole," Davis interrupted again.

"Yes, that asshole," I agreed, nodding my head. Abi began to fuss in my arms, but Lucas took her so I could focus on my conversation with Davis. Lucas was already so great with Abi, calming her instantly. "I was wondering if maybe, I mean, if you're okay with it. I know you have a daughter of your own but-" I started my sentence about three different times but never once got to the point.

"Spit it out already, twinkle toes. Quit dancing around, this ain't the ring."

"Will you walk me down the aisle?" I quickly blurted, blushing hard. I'd never seen Davis look at me the way he was now. He was taken aback by the question. His eyes clouded for a moment before he rubbed them. I guess he never realized how close I felt to him before.

"I'd be honored, kid." He smiled, a whole-hearted smile I'd never seen before.

"Thank you, Davis."

Chapter 50

Lucas' P.O.V.

Song Suggestion: "Only You" by Julia Westlin

I felt incredibly antsy as I waited for my Rose at the end of the aisle. Everything looked spectacular. The flowers in the garden were vibrant and beautiful. The cool September breeze carried in their floral scent. Mom held Abi in her arms, sitting in the front row before me. Abi's strawberry blonde hair was almost hidden behind the large white bow she sported. The white dress almost swallowed her whole, but she looked so adorable.

My Rosebud has stolen my heart completely. She and I have late-night talks as I work and rock her back to sleep. She and her mother are everything to me. They are the sun I revolve around, the lights of my life. I am the luckiest man on the planet. I know this, and now I'm the luckiest man, waiting for his beautiful bride to emerge.

The music began to play, and everyone stood as Rose came into view. My heart stilled and raced all at the same time. My eyes misted as the moment took over me. She looked breathtaking; in fact, she took my breath away. Her hair was tucked into a beautiful low bun with a veil. Her dress was glorious and made just for her. She was a picture of perfection, and she was all mine. *My wife.*

She clutched onto Davis' arm, trying to ease her steps. She was ready to run to me and it made me smile further, causing a tear to escape my misted eyes. I love this woman so much. I love her more than I ever knew could be possible. She's changed me, my life, my world. I am forever grateful to her.

My heart swelled further with every step she took. I saw her dazzling smile as I stepped forward to take her hand from Davis. When asked who was giving her away, Davis replied he was. Rose stood before me, ready to tie our lives together for eternity in front of our friends and my family. Hailey took the bouquet from Rose with a significant smile. She winked at me, making me smirk. I liked Hailey, and I was glad Rose had her.

"Dearly beloved, we are gathered here today to witness the union of Olive and Lucas Porter. Their love is new, but has grown and flourished through the year, as witnessed by their child. Marriage is a venerated institution, and one deserving of deep reverence. Today we observe the union of Lucas and Olive in holy matrimony, a commitment they have chosen to undertake with all the sincerity it warrants." Our officiant started, but my eyes never left my Rose. She held my hands tightly between us as we faced one another.

"While marriage is a sacred and serious tradition, it is also cause for tremendous joy. Married life is full of surprises, adventures, and memory-making–all made possible by the enduring power of love. When Lucas and Olive complete this union, they will begin a new life of partnership, one defined by shared hopes, dreams, and successes." I could feel the officiant's eyes turn away from the crowd to us now.

"Lucas and Olive, as you learn to live as one; you will encounter many challenges that can help you grow. Do the things that make life precious–cooperate with each other, always make time to laugh together, and never lose appreciation for the love you share. Remember, too, to adhere to the vows you will make today. Seek strength from each other, give hope to each other, and let your trials help you grow together. They say love can build bridges and climb mountains — and they're right. You find that as it grows and matures over time, your love for one another will prove both fulfilling and empowering." I took his words to heart, fully ready to do whatever it took to keep our love and marriage strong.

"Yes, there will be challenges in life, but the strength of your bond will offer you protection against life's storms. Always make your relationship a priority and continue to nurture each other. Through a commitment to love, and with the power of faith, together you will navigate any obstacles that come your way."

"Lucas and Olive, I invite you to express your sacred vows to one another. Please face each other as you declare these vows before the presence of your family and friends. Lucas, you may start." I was suddenly nervous as hell, but ready to spill these words to her.

"My Rose, my Olive. You are the light of my life, my savior from the dark. You've changed my life for the better in a single year. There is no one I love more than you and the daughter you have gifted me. I cannot tell you how much I love you because there is no way to measure it, no words to express it. It's an overwhelming feeling that takes me over whenever I look at you—only shown by my affection, actions, and care. I promise to cherish you all the days of my life. I promise to help raise our daughter with you and take over when you feel overwhelmed. Abi and I will be by your side always. I promise to encourage and push you when needed. You will do great things in your career and as a mom. I promise to make you and Abi my priorities *always*. To care for you when you're sick, to enjoy the good and bad moments together. I promise to give you all the happiness I can give you. I love you, Olive, more than words can express." My voice cracked as my love manifested in a few tears. The emotion was thick and raw in my throat.

Her eyes shimmered as she tried not to cry along with me. She squeezed my hand before letting it go. She turned to Hailey, who handed her a piece of paper. I furrowed my brow in the slightest as she opened it. It was torn on the side, as if she had ripped it out of a book. It was the missing page of the journal she denied knowing about. I almost laughed, but contained it, ready to hear what she had written on it.

CHAPTER 50

"Dear future me, he's the one. There's no denying Lucas Porter is the love of my life. He's more than I could have ever thought. My rescuer who's saved me countless times and lifted me up when I'm down. He's kind, protective, playful and all around fun. There's no denying he knows me well, even in such a short amount of time. This feeling is overwhelming and all-consuming. I know it's love. It's love for him. So I will choose *him*. I will fight for *him*, keeping him in my life for as long as he'll have me. He is my addiction, my air, my life. I can't imagine not having him by my side. I hope he feels the same way. A hopeful Past You." She looked up at me, her voice small and cracking with tears. "It's always been you. Since the day you opened up to me. Since the day I laid eyes on you. I love you, Lucas. I promise to stay by your side for as long as you will have me. To fight for us, for you, for Abi. I will claw my way up in this world and give you both everything I can. You're my life, and seeing how you care for Abi has only further cemented my love for you. You're a wonderful father, and I know you will be the best husband. I promise to fight off your darkness, and stay by your side always."

Her vows were everything I wanted to hear and more. Her journal entry was perfect, and the fact she took it for this moment made me smile. I loved her antics, her spirit, and her love. This moment couldn't be any better. I turned to Leo, grabbing my ring and placing it on her delicate fingers. Her hands shook before me, but I steadied them for her. She placed my ring on my finger and I swore I would never take this ring off for anything.

"By the power vested in me, by the state of New York, I pronounce you, as husband and wife, lawfully wedded before your family and friends. You may now kiss the Bride." I didn't hesitate to lean forward and kiss Rose with everything in me. I held her face in my hands and kissed her tenderly, pouring my love into her.

"Ladies and gentlemen, it is with great honor I officially present to you Mr. and Mrs. Porter!"

Mrs. Porter, my wife.

The festivities continued as we took our pictures. Abi, of course, was included in most of them. She was the center of attention, and Rose didn't mind at all. Abi was a wonderful baby. She barely fussed, and she slept well during the night. We were extremely blessed with her.

"Ian!" Rose waved him down. "It's best friend pictures. Come on!" She gestured for him to come over with her arms.

"Sí, come on Ian, unless you're ready to relinquish the title to its rightful owner," Hailey laughed.

Ian jogged over quickly, wrapping his arms around the two, smiling widely at the camera. I loved seeing her smile and being happy with her friends. It was a picture-perfect moment. One I'll cherish forever. We entered the reception, greeted by the cheers of our friends and family as they presented us. Rachel whistled the loudest, pinching her lower lip. We headed to the dance floor for our first song. "The Story" by Davis Naish began to play as I swayed us around the dance floor.

"You look so beautiful, my Rose. My wife." I smiled down at her before kissing her forehead. She leaned in, pressing my lips further into hers.

"You look dashing yourself."

"Thank you for today. I'm happy you hid the journal entry from me, you sneaky little devil," I laughed as she blushed.

"I am glad you liked it. Now I have to figure out how to get it back in the journal. I'm not sure glue will work." We both laughed as we continued to dance.

"You're my world, Rose. You and Abi both."

"I know, you're ours too." When the song ended, I kissed her lips tenderly again, earning oo's from everyone.

"Ow, get a room, you two!" someone yelled from the crowd, making Rose turn that beautiful shade of crimson.

"Thank you for my happy ending, Rose."

Olive's P.O.V.

Song Suggestion: "To Build A Home" by Holly Henry

"Can I open my eyes yet?" I asked Lucas, feeling so impatient. I wanted to know what this surprise was.

When we arrived home from our honeymoon, he said we had one stop before we would get Abi. I was ready to see my daughter, but he said this couldn't wait. He tied a tie over my eyes. I'm sure it was the tie he wore at the end of the aisle as he waited for me. I will forever remember the moment when our eyes met, and the rest of the world faded away. *My husband.*

"Almost," he said with his hands on my hips as he guided me. I could see cobble stone steps through the small slit left between my cheeks and the tie. *Where are we?* He finally stopped pushing me forward. I could feel him step around me and stand before me as he slid the tie off my face. My eyes squinted as they got reacquainted with the light.

"I had this made for us when I found out you were pregnant. I used what I knew from your journals, and from the Daniels' house as a sort of guide."

Lucas was so excited as he spoke, flashing his beautiful smile at me. Those intense brown eyes held my gaze lovingly for a moment before he stepped out of the way, allowing me to see the most spectacular view. Amongst a planted garden, with a lot of the same flowers from the botanic garden we were married in, stood a tall stone house. Weathered stone covered the exterior of the house, along with various large windows. Elegant white shutters framed each window, which added a touch of sophistication to the overall design.

The beautiful garden surrounding the house is an oasis of colorful flowers, verdant trees, and well-manicured bushes. A winding cobblestone path led up to the house through a white archway covered in vines. It connects to a small wooden fence which encircles the entire property, constructed from rich, aged wood. They adorned the fence with intricate carvings and patterns, making it even more beautiful. It was absolutely perfect and all I could do was tear up as I stared at its marvelous beauty.

"Is this really ours?" I asked in utter disbelief.

"It is, do you like it?" He asked, wrapping his arms around my waist from behind and resting his chin on my shoulder the way he loves to.

"I love it!" I cried. My joy flowed out of me through the tears slipping down my cheek.

"Let's go get our Abi and bring her home. I've had all things moved in already, so you don't have to worry about packing or unpacking. That's the beauty of having too much money."

"For once, I don't mind this." I laughed. We headed out to Sarah's house to collect our beautiful baby girl. My world lit up again when I looked at her round face. A week without her felt like an eternity. Her head looked even smaller with the large flower on her headband. Sarah had dressed in an adorable white dress with pink flowers which swallowed her whole.

"My baby!" I cooed as I picked her up and nuzzled my head against hers. I sniffed the beautiful baby smell I had missed so much.

"Did you show her yet?" Sarah asked Lucas with an excited smile. She knew of the house.

"Yeah, I did."

"I love it," I added.

We spoke about the honeymoon and Sarah filled us in on what she and Abi had been up to while we were gone. I was happy to have Sarah in her life. She will teach Abi things I cannot, things you learn to grow up with money. I want her to be successful in any situation she may be put in. We left her house with our baby in tow and smiles all around.

"Ready to see the inside?" Lucas asked as he opened the red front door.

What he had accomplished was my lifelong dream. He had given me a house which gave me a warm and inviting feel. He adorned the cream-colored walls with various pictures ranging from our wedding to Abi's newborn pictures. It felt surreal to see myself in these loving pictures, to be surrounded by a family. The hardwood floors were dressed with plush area rugs, each adding a layer of comfort to the space. To the left was the living room with a plush sofa and several armchairs ranged around a fireplace. There was a built-in bookshelf filled with books, more family photos, and various mementos, including the framed journal entry I read at our wedding.

To the right was the dining room, which beckoned to be used for large family dinners. There was a large wooden table surrounded by comfortable chairs. A sparkling chandelier hung above, adding a touch of elegance to the room. The kitchen, which was beyond the dining room, was large, begging to be used to make enormous meals. It was spacious, with granite countertops and stainless steel appliances, plus plenty of storage space.

Once I felt satisfied exploring the first floor, we all headed up the stairs to discover the second floor of our new home. The first room I ventured into was Abi's. Lucas had her walls painted a soft shade of pink with shelves hung against them. Stuffed animals share space on the shelves with books and toys. A comfortable rocking chair sat near the crib, perfect for late-night feedings and quiet moments with my Abi girl.

Our room was down the hall from Abi's, but unlike hers, we had double doors opening to our room. In the center sat our sizable king-sized bed, as if on center stage, illuminated by the sunlight casting in from the large window. The window took up nearly an entire wall to the left. The sunlight bounced off the light-colored walls, giving it a warm and inviting feel.

To the left were two separate walk-in closets, one for him and one for me. Although mine held more clothes than I owned before we left for our honeymoon. Between the walk-in closets was the door to the en-suite bathroom, which split into two sections. One side featured a large soaking tub for two and the other a spacious glass-walled shower. The vanity has two sinks, providing ample space for us both to have our own area.

This room, Abi's nursery, the whole first floor, the entire house, was absolutely perfect. Lucas had made us a house in which we could build a home in. The thing I most longed for, he had given to me without me having to say a word. He built my dream house from my journal entries and visiting the house I most envied.

"Thank you, my husband. Thank you so much." I cried as he kissed my forehead tenderly.

Epilogue

Olive's P.O.V.

"We have to wait until he leaves, and then we can go in through the back. There's a window that never locked and I'm pretty sure he never fixed it," I instructed Daisy and Lucas.

Little David sat in Abi's car seat in the back, peacefully sleeping while we adults felt like we'd received adrenaline shots. Joe had called me yesterday to tell me Daisy had showed up at his door. She'd lost my number but remembered where he worked. She had David in one arm with the other cradled to her chest, broken. According to Joe, and now I see for myself, she had a black eye and a cut on her eyebrow.

I know dad is going insane searching for Daisy and David right now. I was glad she didn't leave David behind the way mom left me. Of course, David is only a baby, which may be why she couldn't leave him. I know it will complicate things, but since Joe took her to the police station to press charges, it will make things easier for her to get sole custody. Lucas is hiring one of the best family lawyers to make sure Dad is never allowed time to live with David. Dad will never change, no matter who the woman is. He needs help, more than any of us can give him.

"We'll grab your things and then you can stay in the flat my mother left me. There are women there who have gone through the same thing as you and will help you with David. I called Penny already, and she's having clothes donated for you and David, so you don't have to worry about those things. We need to get your important documents and anything you absolutely can't live without. Do not worry about anything else. Got it?" I reiterated, needing her to understand we were not packing all of her things, but grabbing the few things she absolutely needs.

She nodded her head, still not speaking. I am guessing she feels shame, or perhaps embarrassment for needing help from the people she assumed were liars and insane. I was happy she sought help the moment dad hit her.

I watched as Dad slammed the front door open, cursing beneath his breath as he got into his beat-up pickup truck. His engine sputtered to life and, with a peel of his tires, he reversed out of his driveway and onto the road. Daisy and I quickly got down, making our way around the back of the broken window in my old room. I pulled on it, holding my breath, until it began to crack. *For once, I was glad this window was still broken.*

I climbed in, scraping my arm on the broken window sill. I winced, but pushed past the sting and raced to the back door to open it for Daisy. She can't climb with a broken arm. The familiar smell of alcohol and cigarettes permeated the air, bringing me right back to my dark teenage years. I kept looking over my shoulder as if at any moment dad would come marching down the hall demanding we spar. The adrenaline was coursing through my veins as we rushed through the house, collecting anything Daisy told me to grab.

My Knight: He's back, get out, or hide.

I read Lucas' text a little too late, as the front door knob jiggled with Dad's attempt to unlock the door.

"Hide," I whispered to Daisy, who stared at me petrified. Her mind did not choose flight or fight, it chose freeze since she was not used to high-stress situations, shocking her in place. *Fuck!* The front door swung open, hitting the wall behind it hard enough to make a hole where the doorknob hit. Dad's eyes scanned the house, realizing what was happening. His eyes locked on mine with a deadly fury, and I knew I was about to fight for my life.

"Daisy, run." I told her as calmly as I could. She snapped

out of it, grabbing her things and racing to the back door. Dad gave chase to her, but I stood in his way, preventing him from getting to her. He swung his fist back, ready to punch me, but I dodged it with surprising ease.

"What the hell are you doing, Olive? Get out of my house!" He fumed, bringing his fist back again.

"No!" I yelled back, dodging his fist and hitting his side with my own. "I warned you if you hurt her, I would help her escape you. I wasn't kidding, Dad. You fucked up again, and this time you won't break her the way you broke mom. I won't let her stay with you a minute longer, nor will I allow you to instill fear in her and David."

I could feel the fear leaving me with every word I spoke. I felt strong as I stood up to him. His punches were not connecting as I danced around him the way I do in the ring. Dad had gotten rusty without me around to spar. I am guessing he stopped fighting in the ring, too. He extended his leg out, catching me off guard, as dad was never one to kick but only punch. His foot hit me right in the stomach, knocking my breath out. The following punch was harder to dodge as it grazed my side. I pushed past the pain, kicking him in the side, putting myself in a precarious situation as he grabbed my leg with his underarm and held it in place. I hopped awkwardly, trying not to fall as he pulled me around.

"You need to get help, Dad."

It shattered my heart to see him like this, and I don't know why. All I could see when I looked at him was his brokenness, although his sadness should have elicited fury in me. I couldn't understand what had caused Dad to be this way, and I didn't know if I ever would, but I felt a deep sadness for him.

His response was to elbow my knee, bending it back as he tried to break it. My other leg jumped up, using it to push off dad and try to release myself from his grip. I freed myself, but landed with a hard thud on my back, rolling away as he tried to stomp on me as if I were a roach. I jumped up, punching him in the stomach a few times. His abs were like a hard muscled shield, causing little to no pain from my small punches.

I was too close to this, not thinking clearly because of who the man before me was. My lungs filled as I took a deep breath, calming the disarray in my mind. I reminded myself this was like any other fight. I need to stop thinking about him as my dad and more than an opponent in the ring. My eyes observed him, looking for any slight movement of his muscles.

I let myself enjoy the moment the way I do in the ring. I danced around him again, twirling and avoiding his every punch and kick. He grew more furious with every move I dodged. He was losing himself to his frustrations, and I knew this was when I had him. As his movements became fatigued, his punches lost their power and speed. I dropped, sweeping my leg from behind him, and knocking him down on the floor. I jumped on him and punched him right in the throat, causing him to cough. My fists punched his side multiple times, but with each punch, a tear would drop from my eyes.

"You're a terrible father. I needed more from you. I needed so much more, but you gave me so little. The little you gave me came with your punches and small car rides to school. I needed a father, especially when my mother left me, but I got an alcoholic instead." I spilled my heart out as I continued to punch him beneath him. He stilled as I spoke, taking every punch without a fight anymore. "You broke me, you and the hell at school pushed me to slit my wrists. Even after that, you didn't change. It took you less than a month to go back to your usual self. All I ever wanted was to feel loved, appreciated, wanted, but all I got was neglect. You're not a dad, and I honestly hoped you would change. I hoped maybe David could have you as a father even if I couldn't, but you proved me wrong again. You don't change Dad. Please, get help. Use this day as motivation, and get help." My voice faded as I went, growing smaller with each punch.

I got off him, looking down at the broken man before me. The one I could never beat while I lived here, but easily defeated tonight. I felt so many emotions it was hard to tell which was more prevalent: hate or love, or perhaps a brokenness inside me. I let a few more tears escape me before wiping them away and walking out the front door.

I ran towards the car, jumping into the passenger seat. Lucas didn't waste time racing off into the night. He noticed my bloody and bruised knuckles, grabbing my thigh instead, squeezing it comfortingly. The car ride was silent, along with the tears that escaped me. I may be bloody and bruised, but somehow I felt healed. I needed this night to win a fight, to spill my guts out to him. Maybe one day he will get help and change himself.

Get better, Dad.

Author's Note

Thank you guys so much for reading my book! I sincerely hope you enjoyed it. Please follow me on Instagram @rae.knight.author or join the reading group The Knightly Page Turners on Facebook. There are a total of 4 books planned for this series, this one being the first. I hope to hear from you all. Feel free to contact me with any questions you have about the book.

https://www.instagram.com/rae.knight.author/

Made in the USA
Middletown, DE
20 March 2024